Michael A. Riegler

A DRAGON IN THE CHURCH

Published through Lulu.com

Raleigh, North Carolina

Copyright 2015

by

Michael A. Riegler

All Rights Reserved

ISBN—978-1-329-80258-2

Printed in the United States of America

Published by lulu.com

Raleigh, North Carolina

I dedicate this book to my wife, Anne,
the love of my life, my biggest
supporter and a fine pastor
in her own right.

Preface

The characters and the events portrayed in this book are fictional. The people are largely based on composites of several different parishioners in the churches that I have served, or from stories I have read or heard. After that, the imagination takes over and embellishes for dramatic effect. *A Dragon in the Church* is not an autobiography. The main character is not me. His wife is not my wife.

That is not to say that the book does not contain truth. It does. I love God's Church, the gathering of all Christian believers. I love and support the United Methodist Church. I love the people I have served as pastor, and the people I am serving right now. And, most of all, I love God—the Father, the Son and the Holy Spirit. So, if in the reading of *A Dragon in the Church*, we are led to question our own attitudes and practices—if we are at any moment uncomfortable—then good. In the spirit of a challenging sermon and a good *call to action*, let us seek to better be God's Church.

Chapter 1

I woke slowly and unevenly, my body sluggish and heavy, my mind trying to stay turned-off, fighting off consciousness but losing the battle. Acrid slime in my mouth, dryness in my throat, and an un-ignorable pressure from my bladder made the painful fact clear; the day could be delayed no longer. As I shuffled from the bedroom, I snuck a peek at my wife. She was still asleep. I tried not to wake her. Who wants to be cheated out of a little more sleep? I went in the bathroom to take care of business. Afterwards, I washed my hands and considered brushing my teeth. It seemed like too much effort, much too soon. I turned and looked at the scale, or rather, the *Health-O-Meter*, as the label boldly proclaimed. I had promised myself that I would get on it every morning, no matter how poorly I had controlled my diet the day before. I didn't want another ten pounds to sneak up on me when I wasn't looking. I sighed and walked past it. Maybe tomorrow.

Breakfast promised no pleasure, but at least required little thought. Small sauté pan, sprayed with some non-stick stuff, crack in five eggs (to keep my sugar down), stick the lid on and cook for three minutes. Every morning. Yum. I sat at a TV tray in front of Sports Center, drinking Diet Coke and eating my round egg-thing. The good life. I checked my e-mail and Facebook, which left me annoyed, no surprise. Election season had barely begun, and already the supply of angry drivel seemed endless. I should have known better, but then annoyance was feeling more and more natural to me, so how much difference did it make, really?

As I packed myself into a pair of kaki's that were still on my fit-into list and paired it with one of my dozens of golf shirts, I heard Jenn moving about and laughing. Must be on the phone already. I finished dressing and grooming and put on my best happy face.

"Morning, baby! I love you! Have a good night?"

"Fine," she said, with a welcoming smile. "How about you?"

"Fine," I said. "Sleep good?"

"Yeah. You?"

"Slept good, woke up a couple times, but I got right back to sleep."

"Good. Sleep is good. I love you, sweetheart. You out of here already?"

"Yeah, I have a full day ahead."

I went to work. It was only a mile away, but I drove about three miles past the parking lot, cut across on another country road and worked my way back to the entrance where I had already once been. The extra ten minutes of the blasting air conditioner got me cooled down and dried out. I would likely be all sweated out soon, anyway, but at least my entrance would be crisp-looking. A few minutes of quiet time also allowed me to work up the enthusiastic, highly motivated persona that was expected of me at all times. I parked on the far side of the lot and walked slowly to the door. After a slight hesitation, a couple of sighs and a burst of determination, I charged through the door shouting, "Good morning, people of God!"

The day was Tuesday, so my greeting was returned by the Crafty Ladies Quilters Group. "Morning Pastor!"

Chapter 2

"Pastor, come see our latest creation," commanded Berta Lou Gallagher, the unofficial leader of the group. Everybody in the church knew that disagreeing with Berta Lou would not turn out well. Everybody included me.

"A work of art, ladies. Each quilt is more magnificent than the last. I don't know how you can possibly keep it up, but you do."

"Thank you, Pastor," several elderly voices murmured, not a one of them looking up. The work demanded full attention, each stitch as important as the last. This was one of the best ministries of the East Fork First United Methodist Church. The quilts were produced in a continuous stream, and sold at various church functions and in a local arts and crafts store. The proceeds provided the main source of funding for the Welcome Home Soup Kitchen. To date, over a thousand quilts had been sold, supplying food and supplies to the tune of sixty thousand dollars over twelve years. The soup kitchen, run in the Fellowship Hall of the church, served free meals to all comers, on Tuesdays and Saturdays. Be they poor, hungry or just lonely, all received good talk and a full belly. In conjunction with the Crafty Ladies, the Welcome Homers did marvelous work in our community.

The queen of the Welcome Homers was Berta Lou's sister, Virginia Louise Dekker. The other church ladies called her Virgy Lou. As the eldest of the sisters, I always addressed her as Mrs. Dekker, supposedly out of respect. Truth is, I couldn't say

Virgy Lou without smirking. The important thing was to tread very carefully in the scant neutral zone between the two kingdoms. The Crafty Ladies and the Welcome Homers functioned smoothly only so long as the two *Lous* each thought themselves dominant. My job, not by choice but by necessity, was to stand between them and suffer the slings and arrows of both, so that neither of them felt the need to retaliate or escalate.

"Pastor, we need to have a talk," announced Berta Lou, just loud enough to seem like normal conversation while ensuring that all of her followers could hear. Whatever travesty had occurred, I knew immediately that 'we need to have a talk' really meant *don't worry, girls, I'll straighten out the pastor . . . again.*

"I'm always happy to chat with you, Berta Lou (one must never say just *Berta*). Give me a few minutes to settle into my office, and I'll come down and get you."

"Very well," she replied, "but I'm not going to be available much longer."

It was 9:00 a.m. and not once had I ever known her to leave the Wednesday work bee until it ended at noon. In church talk, she had just proclaimed for me and her audience, *I am important and it would not be wise to keep me waiting.*

"I won't be long," I threw over my shoulder as I headed toward my office. As soon as I was safely turned around, my ever-present grin collapsed. I reignited my smile to half-mast, enough to satisfy Janice, the church secretary (I introduced her as the *administrative assistant* one time and she burst out laughing). Janice would be busy with whatever her present task was, and would not be particularly preoccupied by my arrival.

"Good morning, Janice!"

"Good morning, Pastor," she replied.

"Any news, calls, messages or disasters yet, this morning?" I asked. Janice opened the office every weekday, without fail, a good hour before I ever showed up.

"No, quiet so far," she said. As I walked past her and toward my office, she added, "Berta Lou is looking for you." The last thing I heard as my door closed was Janice giggling.

I sat and put my head down. It really wasn't that far of a drop, as my desk was uniformly covered by about a foot of papers, books, hymnals, envelopes and sermon props. I believe in doing things completely, wholeheartedly and well. As I don't have it in me to keep a perfectly organized office, I have settled for creating the perfect mess. When visitors comment on the conditions, as Beta Lou would be doing shortly, I shout out, *That's me all right—I'm a bad man!* No one has any idea what that means, including me. But, people laugh and move on, so I keep doing it.

I didn't seem to be soaking up any usable energy from the pile of religious material, so I resorted to prayer. "Dear God," I prayed, "please give me the energy and the patience to once more satisfy Berta Lou that, as close as the church has come to total ruin, she has saved it once again by setting me on the straight and narrow in the nick of time. And, if it isn't too much to ask, O God, equip me with fake sincerity equal to the task. Amen."

With a heavy sigh, I took the step that would commit me to seeing this daunting encounter through, whether I liked it or not. I opened my door and said, "Janice, tell Berta Lou that I am ready to see her."

Janice smiled and made the sign of the cross, which Methodists think is funny, but should never be told to Roman Catholics. I sat at my desk and awaited my fate. As Berta Lou stepped into my space, ready to speak before even reaching her chair, I beat her to the punch.

"Berta Lou, how good to see you again today. I've been praying about you!"

After reassuring Berta Lou that I would make a priority out of discovering "who" or "what group" had "given themselves permission" to "improperly remove" quilting supplies from the yellow, multi-level, wheeled storage rack "properly designated" to the "sole use and control" of the Crafty Ladies Quilters Group, and replace said supplies with "inappropriate in any case" Styrofoam food storage containers (the use of Styrofoam being strongly discouraged by the United Methodist Book of Resolutions) and, having then discovered the guilty party or parties, to reiterate and reemphasize the "proper use" of the aforementioned wheeled rack and the "sole organization" to whom "such use is designated" and, having escorted Berta Lou back to the work room as evidence of her successful meeting with the pastor, I returned to my office, closed the door and tried not to cry.

I pulled myself together. Mostly this means no more than I forced myself to get started on the work of the day. I opened my magic date book and ran down the day's schedule. Listed, I found *10 a.m., Premarital counseling-Frank and Sylvie.* Frank was long divorced and Sylvie had been a widow for six years. They had been together for over a year, but still lived separately. This is unusual enough, these days, but earlier I had also discovered that they were committed to waiting until marriage to consummate their relationship. They wanted very much to structure their marriage in a positive and Godly way. My mood picked up immediately.

Next on the calendar was a noon meeting of the East Fork Area Ministerial Association. Besides me, there were only three men and one woman who regularly showed up for this twice a month get-together. Stan from the Church of God, the Most High Reverend Catherine Thorne of the Episcopal Church, the Roman Catholic Father Fred, and I had met for a long time. The only other active attendee was a man who had appeared on the scene a few months previous. He simply showed up at a meeting and introduced himself as 'a sinner saved by Jesus Christ who is answering God's call to serve.' We eventually learned that his name was Carl, and he was the pastor of a small, previously abandoned church on a four-corners ten miles outside of town. While the group rarely accomplished anything, I decided to suffer through another meeting, so I could find out a little more about Pastor Carl.

I also had a Finance Committee meeting scheduled for 3:00 p.m. The regular meeting time worked so long as the committee was populated with only older, retired folk. For many years, way before my time at East Fork First UMC, the Finance Committee had, indeed, consisted solely of retirees. No wonder why. Soon after my arrival, I had suggested that the meeting times of key committees be changed to evenings, so that some of the growing number of younger adults attending the church could serve. All I got was the look a dog gives when you hide its biscuit under a box. The dog simply cannot conceive of a world in which he cannot see his biscuit. So, the dog will sit and wait for his biscuit to return. The good people who had been running the church for decades simply could not conceive of meetings held after dark. Nor could they conceive of young people or new people being given the power to control money or anything else that *mattered*. In my first couple of years at the church, I had worked hard to clear this logjam of leadership.

The final entry on my day planner instantly caused me considerable dread. For 7:00 p.m. I had inked in the name *Bob Williams*. The two words spelled out a name only, but connoted far more. Bob was a polite enough man, seemingly gregarious and jovial. He could shake hands and slap backs with the best of them. Personal networking was to Bob a necessary skill. Bob was able in many ways. It was no mistake or stroke of luck that the citizens of East Fork and miles beyond bought their cars, hardware, groceries and financial services largely from places with *Williams* in the name. To be fair, they also picnicked at Robert Williams Memorial Park, named after Bob's late father and the main architect of the Williams fortune, watched their children play at the extravagant Martha Williams Playland, named in honor of Bob's mother, who was still active in the community and the church, and scheduled their wedding receptions at the Williams Community Center, all generous gifts to the public. Bob was also most generous to the East Fork First United Methodist Church. And, Bob had a strong sense of ownership in everything in which he invested. *Bob Williams* written on a little line carried far more meaning than one might first assume.

Once again, my head met the mess on my desk.

"It's 10 o'clock," Janice called through the doorway. "Frank and Sylvie are here."

"Thank you. Send them in."

I picked my head up from the desk and put my best smile on my face and in my voice. "Good morning! How are the two lovebirds today?"

Meeting Sylvie, you might be tempted to dismiss her as very ordinary. She was short and squat. She paid little attention to fashion. In an uncharitable moment, one might even think *dumpy*. Her hair was done up in tight, decidedly old fashioned curls. Going out in the weather, she would actually tie a cheap, see-through plastic bonnet under her chin. She was only fiftyish, but someone had once described her as *living older*. This image had become especially pronounced since her husband died suddenly six years earlier. Now, she looked pretty much the same, but her personality seemed newly-fueled by an extra thousand watts of pure energy.

"Good morning, Pastor!" she replied. Her voice carried a lilt bordering on a giggle. "I am loving this man almost as much as I love the Lord . . . I'm near drowning in the stuff!"

"Now, calm yourself, Sylvie," Frank said, patting her on the shoulder. "You'll scare the poor pastor!" Frank's smile about split his rugged face. Frank was older than Sylvie. From the neck down, he looked every one of his sixty years. He had been six feet tall, but years of hard work had left him bent over. His gait belied a perpetually sore back. His hands were large and gnarled. His left pinky finger had disappeared decades before.

Frank had been married for a while in his twenties. He was a third-generation truck farmer; his family had a pretty good sized operation. He had been a quiet man in those days, so I've been told. He was honest and hard-working. Perhaps too hard-working. One day, when his daughter was five and his son three, his wife just ran off with a previously unheard-about boyfriend. After leaving the kids with Frank's mother, she just never came back. To hear Frank tell it, he never pursued her either. 'If she don't want us, we don't want her' was his only comment on the matter. Frank and his family raised the children. 'There was no choice to be made,' Frank would say, 'a man does right by his children, no matter what anyone else does.' So, for years, Frank did what was right. He also suffered in the process. He became bitter and untrusting and grew, as country folk are wont to understate, a bit odd.

You'd never know it now. His year with Sylvie had opened up and revealed a Frank no one had ever seen. From the neck up he appeared as an excited forty-year-old, his face inhabited by a constant grin, always looking as if he was about to laugh.

"Don't scare the poor man," he repeated. "Besides, everyone in six counties knows that you don't love me half as much as I love you."

Sylvie beamed and punched him in the arm.

"Let me start out with admitting that I have nothing whatsoever to teach you two," I said. "You are an inspiration to everyone around you, and that includes me. I am just very happy for you, and want to give you a wonderful wedding."

"I'm thinking we might need to move the date up a ways," Frank said through a grin. "Weddings are fine and all, even if you do have to get crammed into a suit somebody else wore the week before..."

"You stop it, you silly man," Sylvie chirped, pretending to be angry. "I told you that you didn't have to wear a tux if you really didn't want to. Why do you say such things?"

"Number one, you want me to wear it and you know it. You want nice pictures and that's fine. Number two, I want to give you everything that might make you happy, and then some."

Her face softening, Sylvie asked, "Then why do you go on about it, so?"

"Why, "Frank said, struggling not to laugh before he could get the words out, "It is worth a lot more if you fully understand what a terrible sacrifice I'm making!"

"So, why do you want to move up the date?" I asked.

Frank looked at Sylvie, raised his eyebrows several times and pretended to twirl his nonexistent mustache.

"Frank!" Sylvie all-out squealed, her face going rapidly red. "Not in front of the pastor! What is he going to think of us!"

Frank looked at me as if he had just stepped in it big time.

"What I think of you two," I said, "is that everyone in seven counties is going to be jealous and wish they could be as happy as you."

I silently resolved to go home as soon as I could and treat my wife better than I had, lately.

Chapter 3

I arrived right on time at the regularly scheduled meeting of the ministerial association. We said grace and filled our paper plates with sandwiches and healthy vegetables (I have always wondered how vegetables that had been killed, cut up and put on a plate could be *healthy*, being dead and all, but no one else ever seems to care). The meeting convened. First, we made it though the reading of the minutes and the financial report, which only proved that we did almost nothing and had almost nothing. Then we started the traditional sharing time.

"I really wish that I could get some of you guys to attend my Thursday night class on *Surviving the Tribulation: 7 Years of Hell on Earth*," Pastor Stan said. "It has been a powerful time of God's Word, properly explained. Last week I had two people leave in tears! You shouldn't be missing this. And, we have just hooked up with a new supplier for foods that will last in storage for decades. You guys don't want to be caught unprepared, do you?"

"I think we all prepare in our own ways, Stan," the Most High Reverend Catherine Thorne responded. "Besides, don't you think it is more important to live properly in the here and now, instead of obsessing about some future, far-off heaven?"

"No!" Stan nearly shouted. "Today is about getting ready for what is next! That's the whole point. We are not residents of this world! We are only passing through and all I care about is whether my permanent residence is in Heaven or Hell!"

Stan was flushed in the face and beginning to accumulate spittle at the corners of his mouth. Just another time of sharing.

"We know, Pastor Stan," said Father Fred. "We understand..."

"Hell is forever, too, you know!" Stan spat out.

"As I was saying, we understand all that you are saying. To fail to agree with that postulated by another does not stand as proof that one does not understand what has been offered. I assure you, I understand your belief system. I can quote you the history of its origin, if you wish. But, I do not accept or agree with it." Father Fred was beginning to roll. "I believe what we really should be discussing is the matter of authority. The question should be, *From what source do we receive answers that can be unconditionally accepted, embraced and lived out?* Now, with all due respect to later traditions, it takes only a cursory look at the history and development of the Church from the first days right up to this very moment to see that the gifts of holy knowledge and authority have only one unbroken chain."

"We know, Father," the Most High Reverend Catherine Thorne broke in again. "We Protestants are Christians, probably saved by Jesus, but only nominally and tangentially a part of the Church, until we see how separate we have made ourselves and return to the Roman Catholic Church. As you just said, to disagree does not imply a lack of understanding."

"Both God's love and the purview of the Church are boundless," Father Fred answered, with a tired smile.

She saw her opening. "It is hard to acknowledge the authority of a church that cannot even model Christ in the world in this very time and place. The Roman Catholic Church, and to some degree every church represented here, has contributed to the true tragedy of today's Church, our abuse and exclusion of the Lesbian/Gay/Bisexual/Transgendered/Questioning community. This is not something that our precious Lord Jesus would tolerate, much less practice. He taught love and acceptance of all manner of people, no matter what the social mores of the day. While you prattle on about who's church is the real Church or what is going to happen in some far-off time when Jesus finally returns, we are perpetuating a practice that will one day embarrass us and leave us as mystified by our own nation's behavior as when we attempt to comprehend how slavery could have once been a legal and common practice."

"I'm sorry if I somehow offended you, Pastor Thorne." Father Fred spoke in a soft, gentle, practiced sort of way. "I was only saying that all of what we face as Christians today might be better approached by the one Body of Christ, through the many great gifts that God gave us through the one true Church."

"I appreciate your apology, Father Fred, but still you change the subject away from what I have proposed," Reverend Catherine Thorne replied.

"To be accurate," Pastor Stan broke in, "you changed the subject, rather abruptly, away from what the Father was talking about, and he is just trying to get it back. Nor did we allow much discussion of how close the time is coming when Christ will set in motion things that will make us all forget everything else that has been going on."

"I see," the Reverend Thorne replied. The look of a teacher thoroughly exasperated with a group of unruly second-graders, but unwilling to give up on them, covered her face. Then, she said, "Once again, it seems as if some opinions are to be given more credence in this group. Perhaps if I were a man, we could focus a little longer and explore a little deeper a subject that we all know is the greatest challenge facing the American Christian Church today."

Silence settled into the room. This impasse had been reached many times before. Everyone in the room was a devoted Christian and leader in their respective traditions. None desired conflict or hurt feelings, but neither could they help themselves from creating them.

I looked over at Pastor Carl and said, "Do you think the Tigers have a chance to win the series this year?"

Carl let out a quick and short little laugh. None of the others thought I was funny. None of the others wanted to laugh. But each one did, as forced and insincere as it was. Another altercation averted. Another working relationship retained, at least for the time being.

After a closing prayer for a unified community, and amid mumbled goodbyes and well-wishes, we adjourned and made our ways home. *I'll have to find some time to get to know Pastor Carl,* I thought on my way out.

Chapter 4

As I arrived a couple of minutes early for the Finance Committee meeting, the members were already in their customary places around the table. To my right was Janice, who served not only as church secretary, but as the treasurer.

Annabel Ustiss was right of her. Annabel had served on Finance for over thirty years, having replaced her father who had served for thirty-five. Her main position on all matters was to support programs of the church that represented *the way we've always done it* and to fight programs that *we've never done that way before*. In my early years as East Fork First UMC's pastor, I had a difficult time believing that her opinions could actually be totally based on that line of reasoning—or perhaps it was more a way of feeling—but in the long term I became convinced.

On my left was Sid Colms. Sid was against spending money. Period. The power bills were too high, the pastor's salary exorbitant, hospital visits (which generated mileage expenses) frivolous and anything new, unnecessary.

Janice, as an employee, does not have a Finance Committee vote. With Annabel and Sid guaranteed to oppose anything new, the hope of accomplishing anything fell on me, Dosie Wainright and Jeremy Clark.

Dosie was in her mid thirties, the stay-at-home mother of three school-aged children and a member of the church for only ten years. Thus, she was considered okay to watch the children, sing in the choir or contribute pies to the occasional bake sale, but far too new to be trusted with the church's money. But, as pastor,

I am the chair of the Committee on Nominations and Leadership Development and I had managed to get Dosie elected at the annual church vote.

Jeremy was the newest member of the Finance Committee, dedicated, dependable and smart as a whip. He was also a home-schooled sixteen-year-old. I had to invoke a clause in the *United Methodist Book of Discipline* (rule book), strongly encouraging the inclusion of a *full voting rights* youth member on major committees. After answering a swarm of questions from the older membership, convincing them that, yes, this is not only legal, but proper, the balance of power began to shift. For some, this was nothing short of cataclysmic. However, for most of the folks sitting in the pews on Sunday mornings, it was really no big deal. They had never known how things were done in the first place and didn't care to know now.

Annabel, naturally the Chair, called the meeting to order. After an opening prayer (always performed by me, the paid clergy person in charge of all corporate prayer) and the approval of the old minutes, we started the discussion of the previous month's financial report. First, Janice read the key figures, ending with her long-practiced *thumbnail view*. I have never figured out what a thumbnail view is, but I suspect it sprung from some mixture of metaphors.

"In short," Janice concluded, "for the first eight months of the year, attendance is up nine percent (the table offered mild applause, two *oohs* and one *ah*) while giving is up four percent . . ." Janice paused and looked to Sid, allowing for his interruption.

Sid interrupted with "The new people don't give hardly anything, you know. That's how you end up with more people without them doing the church much good."

"Noted." Annabel said, looking completely disinterested in Sid's opinion. "Go on, Janice."

"The expenses for the church, including pastor expenses, payroll, one month's apportionment paid to the conference and all regular bills, were seventy-four thousand, three hundred and sixty dollars . . ."

"If you hadda told me twenty years ago it would cost us seventy-four grand a month to run this place Ida said you were crazy," Sid stage-mumbled.

". . . income was seventy-four thousand, eight hundred and ten dollars..."

"Almost managed to spend it all."

". . . a net gain of four hundred and fifty dollars."

"Coulda banked a whole lot more than that."

"Let's go around the table and give everyone a chance," Annabel said while shooting the evil-eye at Sid. "Dosie?"

Dosie studied the report for a few moments, before offering, "I am concerned that the line for paid Sunday morning child-care and nursery school workers is only half the usual amount."

"Paying babysitters . . ." Sid started sarcastically.

Annabel bristled. "You'll wait your turn Sid. When I'm dead and gone, maybe they'll let you run this meeting, but I am still upright. Dosie?"

"As I was saying, the pay is down because we lost one of the workers, and the mothers have been watching their own children for almost a month."

Everyone paused and looked at Sid, but he managed to hold his tongue.

Dosie continued, "I really think that the Staff Parish Relations Committee needs to make this a priority."

"No need to vote, I'll see to it myself," Annabel answered with satisfaction. Finding something real solid to complain about was always a nice nugget to mine from a meeting. "Jeremy?"

Despite her best efforts to be polite, Annabel had a hard time saying the teenager's name without adding an *I still can't believe they've let you in here* inflection.

"Looks good to me," Jeremy started. All except Dosie nodded approvingly. He continued, "However, only twelve percent of the churches in our denomination are experiencing any growth in attendance, so up nine percent is great. Even fewer are exceeding year-ago giving, so the correlation of increased attendance to total giving is actually a lot more positive than it first appears. We're not just treading water, we're actually making headway. I still would like to see less spending on traditional media, like phone books, newspaper ads, and even bulletins. If we moved that money to electronic and social outlets, our outreach with young . . . less ol . . . um, let's say age groups we're not reaching real well right now, would be increased. Other than that, this looks like a good month."

As the rest of the group sat and stared at Jeremy, I laughed (on the inside). Finally, I spoke. "Sounds like you've been surfing the national website, again, huh Jeremy?"

"Well, browsing, but yeah. It's really pretty good."

"Let's get back to the business at hand." Annabel got nervous when talk of anything digital came up. "Pastor?"

"I want to thank everyone for their continued good work. I meet with a lot of pastors who would love to have this kind of report. An awful lot of them are having serious trouble. I am drawn to the year-to-date numbers on missions: over eight thousand local, four thousand regional, and almost twelve thousand international."

"It's backwards. We should take care of our own, first," Sid snarled.

Annabel responded, "We have always supported Methodist missionaries around the world, and I would appreciate it, Sid, if you would remember that. It shan't be on my watch that the missionaries to the less fortunate and less developed of the world shall cease to spread the Good News and keys to decent living to those who need it most."

"At any rate," I interrupted, "I commend the church for remembering that to love our neighbors is to share from our bounty (when not wearing my pastor hat, I cannot imagine saying something like *bounty*). Well done."

We got through the rest of the meeting without bloodshed. Sid reminded everyone that the parsonage (the church house whereby all living expenses are provided to the pastor) had both cable TV and an automatic dishwasher, neither of which he and his wife had and they worked hard for their money. We'd all heard it before, so I just sat there and waited for it to be over. A few minor details were handled and we wrapped it up, at only 4:15.

T-minus two hours and forty-five minutes to the *Williams* confrontation. Finally, a little time to see my wife.

"Honey, I'm home!" After 21 years, I still found the classic announcement of one's arrival to be mildly amusing.

"I'm almost finished with my bulletin for Sunday," she said. "I'm teaching tomorrow, so it's got to get in tonight."

When I met Jenn, I was nearly thirty-six. I had been through a bad first marriage, made a change in careers and, after that, an even bigger change. I felt called to be a pastor. I chucked everything (I had no children, which made wholesale change considerably easier) and enrolled in the Methodist Theological School of Ohio. I had finished my first year, when I ran into this unconventionally beautiful, sassy little blonde woman, with a big, powerful personality. She was thirty-four and had a sixteen year-old daughter, Lisa. She had never married, but had kept herself together, held a job, raised Lisa and become a teacher. She did it all without a whole lot of support from anyone else, but maintained a positive outlook on life that put everyone else I knew to shame, especially me. I met her at church. I loved her right away and, after a while, she decided it was safe to love me.

She taught. I pursued my Master of Divinity degree. We were married a month after Lisa graduated from high school. The following December, I graduated from seminary.

In the United Methodist Church, pastors are appointed by the bishop, a *higher authority*. The pastor does not choose a church to serve. The church does not choose its own pastor. When the bishop says so, we are *sent*. When the old pastor in one church is sent elsewhere, the vacancy is immediately filled by the new pastor who has been sent. The church then has little choice but to *receive* their new pastor. It is pretty much an arranged marriage.

When I graduated, we returned to my home conference in Lower Michigan. Very soon, we were sent to a group of three small churches in three tightly clustered little towns. We United Methodists call it a *three-point charge*. One will notice in the telling of *my* story, that the new wife and the new step-daughter have little say in the proceedings. Similar to being a military family, to be a United Methodist clergy family comes with the expectation that everyone involved is prepared to move anywhere and anytime.

When the call came, my wonderful wife simply said, *Okay, where are we headed?*

Lisa went to college. We were off to Podunk, East Podunk and Lower Podunk, Michigan, in the extreme northern part of the lower peninsula, to serve God's Church and be the hands and feet of Jesus in the world. In all sincerity, that's exactly what we did, filled with excitement and fervor. Jenn quickly found a teaching job in the local, consolidated school system, we moved into a simple, well-kept parsonage and our professional ministry was off to the races.

Four years later we were moved to Stanwick UMC, roughly eighty miles to the south of the Podunks. It was one, larger church (a single-point charge) widely understood to be a promotion for helping three little churches grow and prosper.

A Dragon in the Church   21

Jenn smiled her magnificent smile and said, *Goodie! Let's go check out the schools.* It took a year, but a teaching job did come available and the administration was smart enough to see a good thing right in front of them. Jenn got in. The town and the church became our home. The church prospered. Life-long relationships were formed. We stayed nine years. Then, the bishop instructed the district superintendent to make the call. Evidently, I was now exactly the right pastor for the East Fork First United Methodist Church, in a prosperous bedroom community to the city of Grand Rapids. And, the East Fork First United Methodist Church was exactly the right church for me. So sayeth the bishop.

Jenn smiled her magnificent smile, only this time it had a few brittle cracks in it, and the corners of her mouth quivered a bit when she said, *Goodie. Let's go check out the schools.*

That was four years ago. Good years, mostly. Jenn eventually decided to take a break from fulltime teaching. She became a substitute teacher. The other teachers all asked for her, and she could work as many or as few days as she pleased. She also took a part-time hourly position at the West Fork First Congregational Church, as church secretary. The office was only open two days a week and she did clerical things at home. Thus (pastors say *thus* a lot) when she said she had to finish *my* bulletin, she most assuredly did not mean *my* bulletin.

Now she asked, "Have a good meeting?"

Jenn was sitting at her desk, working. That meant it would be best to greet her, kiss her on the cheek and move on. She liked to finish a task once she got it started. She knew that I know that, but she also knew that it would be best of her to open the door just a crack, in case I had something bothering me enough to interrupt her work. It was just one of the many little marriage dances that couples do.

"Whatcha' working on?" I asked.

She set down her pencil, made a few strokes of her keyboard to save her work, and turned toward me. I had gone a step beyond *I'll let you finish your project* and a step into *I would really like to talk.*

Jenn asked, "Did anything unusual happen at your meetings today?"

"Well," I replied, "I woke up tired, Berta Lou publicly guided me to a series of appropriate actions, which will guarantee an urgent meeting with Virgy Lou, my office is a mess, Janice laughed at me twice, Frank and Sylvie restored my hope and made me a little horny, I don't want to go to ministerial association meetings ever again, I prayed to open a meeting, the *thumbnail* view for the month was pretty good, you and I should have our dishwasher and cable TV removed, Annabel scolded Sid, Dosie remains enthused and the smartest person in the whole room is a sixteen-year-old kid. Plus, in just under two hours, I get to sit down with the Double Diamond PooBaa of the church, Mr. Williams himself."

"So, what I'm hearing you say is," Jenn said through knowing laughter, "Blah, Blah, Blah . . . same-old, same-old . . . I'm scared of Bob Williams, and I got a little horny. Am I understanding what it is that you intended to communicate?"

"Yeah, that's about it," I replied lamely.

Jenn got up and walked out of her study, slapping me on the fanny as she passed.

"Where you going?" I asked.

"Well, Big Fella, there's only one thing on the table that I can fix." She disappeared into the bedroom as she said, "Come on. I've got work to do, chop-chop!"

Life is still good.

Chapter 5

My wife is a genius. She knows me well enough to know that being with her for what we call *marital activities* has a powerful effect on me. Sure, one would expect that man and wife would enjoy each other, love each other and even just be physically relaxed. But, for me, intimacy with Jenn has also been a consistent source of strength and serenity and confidence and power, sort of a refueling of body, mind and soul. Filling up the ole love tank, as some would say. At any rate, I felt a lot more prepared heading to my meeting with Bob Williams. Dread had been replaced by acceptance that, whatever happened, things would work out okay.

I actually had an hour to spare—Jenn really did want to get back to work—so I found myself swinging by Pastor Carl's little church at the crossroads. For reasons I could not begin to understand, he had gotten into my head. I told myself to quit expecting that I was going to have some big, meaningful experience by simply getting to know the man. Maybe he was just the simple, quiet man that he appeared to be, with nothing but more simplicity and more quiet beneath the surface. Still, as I tooled slowly past and saw his old pickup parked at the side door, I felt of jolt of anticipation, even though I was out of time and couldn't stop. But, I did get a look at Carl's building. It was cute, or had been at one time. It was almost square, maybe forty feet wide by fifty feet deep. The side walls each contained three tall, narrow windows, peaked at the top. There were small sections of stained glass remaining, but the bulk of the window space was filled with buckling plywood. The white but peeling front door was three feet off the ground and was made of heavy wood. At eye-level the door had six tiny windows, arranged in a perfect cross. The glass was new, the caulking fresh and bright white. Four crumbling concrete steps led directly up to the door. There was no semblance of a porch. To mount the steps was to enter the building. Along the ground-line, broken and boarded up windows ran all around the little church, suggesting a basement not entirely underground. Above the front door was a classic, if somewhat squat, bell tower. It looked to be newly refurbished, most of the wood new, unfinished and ready for paint. Hanging in the tower was a beautiful old bell, a bit dented here and there, but highly polished and gleaming in the sun.

Most of the church looks as if it hasn't felt a human hand in decades, I thought, *but the reclamation project has begun with the bell and an obscure cross of windows. What an odd way to start. Surely it makes more sense to stabilize the foundation and the roof first.* I had no idea at that moment, a tiny mustard seed of a moment, that a whole new way of thinking had taken root in my mind. Feeling a strange mixture of determined and foolish, I resolved to clear my schedule for the next evening and drop in on Pastor Carl and…and whatever he called his church. For the first time it dawned on me that I had never heard the church called by name, nor did it have any kind of identifying signage. It also dawned on me that I had just enough time to return to my own church for the suddenly less-interesting Williams meeting.

"Hi, Bob. Come on in. Coffee?"

"Good evening, Pastor. No, thank you. I don't think this has to take very long."

"Fine, have seat. What can I do for you, Bob?"

"I want to make sure that we are on the same page."

"All right. I'm in favor of good communication. Please begin wherever you'd like."

"Well, Pastor, as you know by now . . . How long have you been with us?"

"Just over four years."

"Yes, as you have learned in the past four years, I and my family have varied interests in and around the greater East Fork area. It is not hard to find the Williams name on one building or another."

"I'd say that's an understatement, if anything, Bob."

"Yes, and to keep track of those various enterprises I like to handle things in a certain way, as you would imagine."

"Yes, I would imagine so."

"Well-defined goals, a workable plan using the best business practices available and careful attention to communication and follow through are at the core of my method."

"I see."

"Well, I'm getting a bit ahead of myself here, but that comment kind of hits the nail on the head. I am not sure that you do *see*, Pastor."

"I'm afraid you'll have to elaborate on that."

"While certain facts and information might seem, on the surface, to indicate that the church's performance, during your time as pastor, has been successful, I believe a more careful analysis shows otherwise."

My temper flashed and my stomach felt suddenly queasy. My mind filled with angry retorts and facts and proofs and counterarguments. But, I kept my face as blank as I could, and said nothing.

"Anyway," Williams continued after an awkward pause, "I acknowledge that attendance is up and there have been a few new members received. However, the slight increase in people has not resulted in a similar increase in giving."

"Meaning?" I asked.

"Meaning, and I think this is borne out by my biggest objections, that while there are a few more people coming through the doors, that they are not of the quality that would contribute to the long-term success and stature of the church."

"And?"

"I think this is a direct result of your unwillingness to respect and consider the history of our church and the methods by which it was built to be what it is today."

"Which is?"

"I am bothered that you have to ask that question. We are and have long been the preeminent church in this entire county. Our members represent the backbone of our community: leaders, doctors, teachers, nurses, successful business owners, the people who make a town thrive. We have the best and most professional music program, hands down. Our contributions to local, regional and international missions exceed those of any other three local churches you can put together."

Williams was getting overly worked up, his voice rising. He caught himself, and visibly willed himself to slow down and lower his volume.

"I am sorry, Pastor. It's just that I care very much for this church. I was caring for this church long before you were sent here, and I suspect that I will still be caring for it long after you have been sent away."

"I see. What is it you believe I have done?"

"You have cheapened us," Williams proclaimed, his face screwing up in a look filled with disdain. "Music with drums. People who clearly do not fit in or contribute. Teenagers making important decisions. Sermons that leave many of our members uncomfortable."

"I see."

"Please quit saying 'I see.' Clearly you do not see. We are a successful church. We are an important church. We help a lot of unfortunate people, and we serve our own membership well. We do not want to be something else!"

Williams leaned forward, getting too close to my face and causing me a seed of rage.

I mentally took a deep breath and leaned back. "I...understand."

"I don't think you do. I am trying to be helpful to you. I am trying to be proactive and constructive. At present, much of the membership is still rather unaffected. They may be uncomfortable with some things, but they have not become dissatisfied enough to take action, as yet. If you would just be open to constructive criticism and re-directive instruction . . ."

I said nothing, but I could feel my own eyebrows arch and my eyes go wide.

Bob paused. When he again spoke, his voice had gone low and slow. "In my business career, I work hard to have a creative relationship with my management team. They are given clear expectations and goals, with a certain amount of freedom to succeed in meeting them. When they get off target, I expect them to accept re-direction. Some of my very best people have come through this process with flying colors, and ended up stronger for it. This is what I am offering to you. You would do well to see this as a favor."

"I see."

"I hope so, but I am not confident. I have written out a few things that, if they are tweaked in time, should avoid any public trouble. I advise you to take them seriously."

I said nothing.

"Is there nothing you want to say, Pastor? Some response? A question, even?"

"No response, right now. One question, perhaps."

"Which is?"

"Am I to understand that I am a part of your *management team*?"

"No. I used that as a helpful example. I am aware that you are not my employee, at least not directly. But you do work for this church, where I wield influence. The tide is building and I am the one being honest enough to offer you help. You would do well to listen."

"Oh, I assure you, Bob, that I am an excellent listener. There is nothing being said here that I do not understand. Will there be anything else?"

"Whatever else there is remains to be seen, Pastor. I've said all that is necessary at this point. However, I will be watching."

"Thank you for your time, Bob. Good night."

"Goodnight," Bob mumbled as he exited the office and then the building.

The whole thing had taken twenty-two minutes. An hour later I was still sitting at my desk. My mind raced with an unsortable avalanche of responses. I was not without power. I was not without influence. I was considered an effective pastor—no—beyond effective. Any list of the top pastors in the district would have my name on it. There were things that I could do that would have Bob Williams wondering just what Pandora's Box he had opened. Maybe he thought he was holding all the cards, but his many businesses needed customers and customers can be swayed. I had supporters in the church. Lots of them. Mr. Williams would wish he had never stepped into this mess. My only decision would be whether to let him recover, or just break him and kick him to the curb. He might have thought I worked for him, but he would soon be reminded that the same church that did not hire me could not fire me. I would get to the bishop first and make it clear that I would need firm backing in my quest to straighten out a rogue church. It would get bloody and false claims would be made, but perseverance and time would see me come out the victor . . . the victor . . . the victor.

A Dragon in the Church   29

My hurt and disappointment subsided. This was one of the things that I hated most about church, the battles for power and rightness and turf, and victory. It is sad, and I had to remind myself that I wanted no part of it. The Holy Spirit called me to salvation. Jesus Christ provided it to me. God the Father called me to serve his Church and his people. He did not call me to do battle in pursuit of personal victories. As the energy of rage ran out of me, I slumped in my chair and found my breath coming only with effort. I don't know how fast depression can develop, but it sure felt like it was enveloping me quickly. I thought of how energized and ready to take on the world I had been after my interlude with Jenn. I remembered that I had felt that way, but I could not get the feeling back.

I knew that I would regroup and pull myself together. Programs could be tweaked, communication improved, people cajoled and influenced and convinced. It might take longer than I had hoped, and come with more effort and pain than what seemed necessary, but I would get everyone back on board. It's what I do.

I looked at the thin folder that Williams had given me. Evidently it contained some sort of plan or to-do list that would have to be implemented to re-acquire the support of the most influential person, with the deepest pockets, in the East Fork First UMC. I had not the strength nor the coping power to immediately handle another criticism or disappointment. I filed the folder at the back of my *active project* drawer. I would deal with it on another day.

I thought about my earlier anticipation at meeting with Pastor Carl. I decided to gloss over the Williams meeting when I returned home. I usually shared everything with Jenn, but her growing dissatisfaction with the church, and my place in it, would not benefit from another major upset. It would be better to somehow smooth off the rough edges before letting her in on what had just happened. I would sit on the whole thing until I had a meeting with Carl. For right now, I would behave as if this had never happened.

I checked the time and realized that it wasn't really that late. Meetings often run later than the 9:00 p.m. that was now approaching. I would think up some vague program plans and short-term goals that had been brought forward by Williams, all routine stuff, to placate Jenn's desire to stay in the loop. It wouldn't take long to get off the subject and on to getting to bed early, having been *worn out* in the afternoon. She would buy it.

Pastor Carl had said to drop in at his church anytime between 5:30 and 9:30 in the evenings, I thought. I made a mental note—*Tomorrow: Pastor Carl @ 5:35.*

Chapter 6

By the time the little white church came into view, I could hardly breathe. The church had a small, overgrown gravel parking lot on either side. It was the only structure on the intersection of Compton Road and, wouldn't you know it, Williams Road. The other three corners were fields, one filled with mature corn, and the other two fallow. I slowed and looked closely. On the outside, it looked exactly as it had the last time. For a moment I feared that maybe Pastor Carl was no longer working on the place, but as I pulled around to the far side, I saw his truck. I let out the breath I had not realized I was holding and pulled in next to the pickup.

I saw no activity, so I walked around to the front. I really enjoy checking out churches, especially sanctuaries. I prefer to enter the way Sunday morning church-goers would, and try to get into character as a first-time visitor. I admit it; I am a church geek. I stood on the cracking walkway and faced the door. I pulled back my shoulders, offered my elbow as if my wife was there to take it, and whispered aloud, "This looks like a quaint country church, let's give it a try." I didn't even feel stupid, which goes to show how deeply runs my inner geekdom. I ascended the stairs, found the door unlocked, opened it and stepped inside. There was no lobby, no vestibule, no narthex, just outside and then sanctuary. The first impression evoked a mixture of elation and sadness. It was like seeing a Rembrandt or a Da Vinci for the first time, only it was so rotted away that you could barely recognize it.

At one time this had been a masterpiece of woodworking, all oak, if my wood-identifying skills were accurate. The floor was solid, but dull and scuffed and gouged. The unpadded pews were just as substantial, but of a slightly lighter hue. Some were cracked at the legs and the end pieces, but they still appeared as if they would last forever. The walls were of a beautiful crisscross pattern that had to have been carefully pieced together by hand. However, some boards were missing entirely and around the windows were water stains and deteriorated sills. As I had noted from the outside, much of the window glass was gone, thankfully replaced a long time ago by plywood. What remained was gorgeous stained glass. My mind automatically filled in the enormous gaps. I could see that once they had been glorious scenes from the birth, life, death and resurrection of Christ. The plaster ceiling was now mostly on the floor. Much of it had obviously been hauled out, but there was still plenty of mess to go around. The small chancel held a rustic pulpit, very heavy and looking to be in reasonably good condition. The platform was the only area that had been carpeted, but it was rotted and smelled like it.

Then my eyes riveted on the sturdy, solid oak, hand-hewn cross hanging in the very front of the church, taking up most of the vertical space from maybe two feet off the floor and up to a foot or so from what I guessed to be a sixteen-foot ceiling. The wood was stained much darker than the rest of the room and stood out strong and proud in the middle of decrepitude and frailty. I was already composing a sermon in my head, depicting the bulk of the run-down church—the battered floors, the broken windows, the rotting wood and the fallen plaster—as *use-ta-bees*. Use-ta-bees are sorry remnants of a time when things were better, at their peak, vibrant and vital and alive and filled with hope. Today, many Christian churches and denominations exist largely in a use-ta-bee status. In contrast to the rest of the sanctuary, however, the cross seemed to be making a *been here-still here-will always be here* statement.

"Well, hello, Pastor. I'm glad you could stop by."

I started, even though he spoke quietly. I hoped my flinching wasn't too noticeable.

"Good evening, Pastor Carl. I hope I'm not here at a bad time."

"Never a bad time to be together in church, Pastor. Sorry for the mess, but at this stage you kind of have to use your imagination."

"I was just doing exactly that. I am pleasantly surprised at some of what was . . . is . . . here. Some of this woodwork and stained glass is beyond what one usually finds in a country church of this era. The glasswork and the craftsmanship on the walls are stunning. And the cross! I was having a hard time looking away from it. Do you know…"

I suddenly became highly aware that I was giving a lecture to the man who was dedicating his time and talent and hard work to the very features that I was blathering on about. "Sorry," I said. "I get a bit carried away. I really like churches."

"Hey, that's fine," he responded. "I'm glad you find it interesting. Churches seem like a good hobby for a pastor."

"Yes. Thank you. Am I interrupting?"

"Not as long as you don't mind if I work while we talk. I have a long ways to go."

"Sure, go ahead."

I had come to one of those moments when you realize that you don't know what the heck you are doing. I had come out here all wound up about a hundred different things that I somehow had convinced myself Pastor Carl could shed some light upon. Now, I was at a complete loss for anything to say. As I stood there staring, he resumed working. He walked deliberately to the left rear corner of the sanctuary. He picked up a piece of two-by-four approximately eight inches long and wrapped in sandpaper. Standing to the right of the entry door, he reached up to head-height and started sanding. For a minute or two, I stood and watched as he stood and sanded. I said nothing. He said nothing. He did not turn around and look at me. He appeared unhurried and unconcerned. I noticed that the entire area above the doorway and to the left, all the way to the other corner, was already sanded smooth. Each of the intricately placed individual boards appeared fresh and unblemished. Three boards were obviously brand new, pieced expertly into the pattern. With all the years of finish and wear removed, the old wood quite nearly matched the new. The renewed area represented perhaps a tenth of the total wall space.

"That is truly beautiful wood," I said, quietly. "You really brought it back to life."

"Thank you. I love the smell of warm sawdust, don't you?"

"Yes, actually, I do."

Carl went back to sanding, up and down, removing old finish and stain and rough spots. I noted that there were two more new boards on the section he was now working. Looking around the rest of the room I saw a good twenty-five or more in need of replacement. Obviously his plan was to deal with one section at a time.

"I like to work each section until it is done, before I move on," Carl said, without turning around. "That way, I don't have to do any one job for too long."

"I see," I said.

"I'll do the staining all at once, though, so it will be even."

I was thinking that it would save considerable time to stick with one task all the way around the room, before switching to the next. It would save the switching of tools and equipment, not to mention having to shift gears and focus all the time. I was imagining the best model of electric sander to zip through this job when Carl spoke again.

"There are faster ways to do this, of course. But, nothing beats the feel of the wood and the uncovering of each beautiful detail."

"Yeah, I guess."

"Besides, since I started working out here, I've had ten times more prayer time."

As I stood and watched the other man work, my mind grew cluttered with unexpected thoughts and emotions. I was embarrassed that I had caused this odd situation by creating a whole scenario that existed only in my head. My need to find help had run away with my usually rational thoughts. I was also peeved with Pastor Carl. He just stood facing the wall, sanding woodwork as if he were all alone in the world. He didn't speak unless I did first. He didn't ask me about me. He didn't offer me a cup of coffee. *Obviously, Carl is socially retarded*, I thought. I felt wholly awkward and started thinking up an exit strategy.

"Feel free to look around," Carl said. "The basement has some interesting features." Still, he engaged the wood.

"Thank you, I will," I said. *Good! A way out.* The front door would take me right back outside, so I moved the other way. My attention had been so focused on the cross that I had failed to notice a narrow doorway in the corner. I pulled the pitted door open and stepped through. I was in a small room, the only space on the main floor besides the sanctuary, directly behind the wall holding the cross. To the right was the bulk of the room, filled with tools and sawhorses and lumber. To the left was a stairway of only three steps. I stepped down and found myself on a tiny platform, maybe four feet square. Turning left would take one down a dark, narrow, steep, concrete stairway—cracked but solid. Turning right, one would enter a very small bathroom, no bigger than a broom closet. My experience told me that it had indeed been a closet, until the pastor or the governing board of the congregation had decided many years ago that, despite inevitable resistance from some of the oldest and longest term members, the outhouse had to go. Turning neither right nor left would take one directly outside, through the only other exterior door. I turned left and went down. The steps were uneven in height, each one descending a random distance. I estimated the first to be an eight-inch drop, the second six, then nine, seven, five, another seven, another eight, a nasty ten and a surprise four at the finish. I chuckled out loud as I thought, *no labor expense for this project. Each member of the committee designed his own stair.*

I stepped off the bottom step and found myself in the kitchen. The appliances were all missing, as was the sink and faucet. Probably all salvaged when it was assumed that the church was closed for good. But, the cupboards and cabinets were still in place and looked pretty good. Turning right, I entered the rest of the basement. It was a single room, mostly empty, with a few remnants of broken furniture and odd parts of things lying about. The basement was actually only sunk into the ground about four and a half feet, yet the still-decent drop ceiling was almost seven feet high. The effect was that an average height adult could look straight out the windows, just above grass level. It was a clever design, really, and explained the four steps at the front entrance to the sanctuary. The main floor of the church was three feet above the ground. The basement floor was also wood, probably over concrete. I smiled as I walked about. At either end of the room, running long ways from front to back, I could still see the faint outlines of what had once been the triangle targets of a shuffleboard court. *Wednesday night youth group,* I thought. *How cool is that?* I started to cry. No reason. No warning. Just tears.

I stayed in the basement for a good half hour. At this point I wanted nothing more than to escape this place with my dignity intact. I struggled to lose my cry-baby look. I finally went back upstairs. Pastor Carl was still sanding away, but had moved over a foot or two. I kicked a couple of things to announce my arrival.

Carl turned and looked at me briefly. Then he returned to his task. After a short pause, he said, "Brings back a whole other time and place, doesn't it?"

"Yes, it surely does," I replied. My face still felt full and swollen, so I schemed how to exit without having to engage face to face. "This is quite a project you've got going here."

"Lots to do," he said.

"There are some really nice features, though," I continued. "The layout is quite common, but the woodwork and the stained glass are exceptional."

"Yes, someone loved this place, once."

Pastor Carl stopped working and turned around. His gaze drifted slowly and calmly around the entire space, taking in all its features. When he spoke next, his voice was low and husky and quavered just a little.

"Sometimes, people decide that God is done with something before he really is. God has plans for this space."

When Carl's eyes landed on me, in my all red and puffy splendor, his own eyes were tearing up. Unlike me, he made no effort to hide it. Neither of us spoke for a long, lingering moment. Oddly, the awkwardness and self-consciousness I had been feeling were gone.

"Aren't we a pair," he said.

"Yes, it appears we are," I replied, "but a pair of what, I wonder?"

Pastor Carl smiled. "I think,' he said, "The bigger question is, a pair *for* what?"

"What do you mean?"

With a grin of recognition, he shook his head, chuckled, and said, "I have no idea."

As I started to speak, he interrupted with, "We need to be apart now." I must have looked startled, because he hurried to add, "When can you come back? I'm here every weeknight."

"I'll come tomorrow," I blurted too quickly. I recognized the urgency as the same feeling I had when I asked Jenn out for the first time and I couldn't believe she said *yes*.

"Are you sure that you shouldn't check your schedule?" Carl asked.

"I don't care what's on the books, I'll be here."

I drove home slowly, my mind processing and reprocessing everything that had just happened. I realized that I had no idea what that was. Still, what I had too-quickly written off as a pointless, wasted trip had in some way turned into anything but.

Chapter 7

"How was your visit with your new little friend?"

I could always count on Jenn for a little humility-nurturing. On the ride home, I had done my best to come up with an answer to just such a basic question. I knew Jenn would ask; she had never ceased having interest in my work or in me. It was general church and congregational stuff that she had lost her tolerance for.

"I really don't know," I finally answered.

"What don't you know?" she pressed. "Either you enjoyed it or you didn't. It was worth the time or it wasn't."

"I think I enjoyed some of the time that I spent with Pastor Carl. Some not so much. I am pretty sure that most of the time was wasted, but I am really anxious to go back and do some real talking. I don't know why. How's that?"

"Keep talking. Usually you start making sense along the way."

"Carl is a mystery. He turned up at a ministerial association meeting one day. Nobody ever just turns up. We beg other area pastors to join, but they never do. None of us had heard of Carl or his church. In fact, I am not sure how a guy like Carl would have even known we existed, much less when and where we meet."

"What's he like? You seem awfully interested in him."

"Pastor Carl is a hard read. I normally pick up pretty quick on people and where they're coming from. Right?"

"Best I've ever seen."

"Thank you. I'm frustrated, because I am not understanding much about Carl."

"Describe him for me."

"Okay. About five-ten, guessing maybe fifty or fifty-five. Average weight. Nondescript face, an everyman sort of look. Clothes clean and neat, but real plain. He has sort of an always-ready-to-get-to-work look about him. He's slow and quiet. Very quiet, most of the time. Calm. I'd call him calm."

"How so?"

"At the meetings, when we get rolling debating and arguing about theology, doctrine—even gun control or abortion or homosexual rights in the church—he never seems to rise to the bait like everybody else. You know?"

"Oh, I know. I've been in this church business almost as long as you have."

"Yeah, you sure have. Anyway, he sits and listens closely, but he simply smiles and lets it go on around him."

Jenn nodded her head and replied, "Maybe he's just stupid."

I laughed so suddenly I snorted. One of the reasons I love Jenn is that she thinks a lot like me and we find the same things funny.

"I wondered that, too," I said, while checking to see if anything had come out of my nose. "But, he does speak up once in a while, and when he does everything and everyone else stops. The rest of us can be going a hundred miles a minute, each one of us defending or explaining the same issues that we defended last time, and Carl will say one sentence and it all stops. I've never seen anything like it."

"What does he say?"

"I'm not entirely sure. If I really try to remember, it is usually something that would seem overly simple."

"Like?"

"Well, one time we were really roaring on about some hot topic—I don't even remember which one right now—and he said, 'If we were to figure this out, where would it take us?'

Now Jenn snorted. "I'll bet that did stop the house," she said.

"It did. You should have seen the others trying to regroup and get their argument going again. They couldn't do it."

"The others?"

"Of course, the others. I am much too evolved to get caught up in such nonsense," I said with an exaggerated smirk.

Jenn just slid her chair a few inches away from me, avoiding the inevitable lightning bolt.

"I know, I know, funny lady. But that's the point. I am trying to communicate to you what Carl is like."

"And you are doing a very good job, Lamb Chop. You are the best of all the communicators!"

"Moving along," I said, "I got more of the same this evening. Quiet. Detached. Rude, almost. Weird. Then all of the sudden he was insightful and powerful in a way that felt insightful and powerful more than it could be explained as insightful and powerful."

"That's quite a sentence."

"Does it make sense to you?"

"In a way, yes. It isn't unheard of for a person to have an inexplicably profound effect on other people. It happens."

"Well, it's happening here."

"If you dig, you'll find out what it is. There is usually something there that is just harder to grasp. I'll bet that you will eventually discover an intelligence or wisdom or body language or technique of some sort that will explain the effect he is having on you."

"Think so?"

"I do. Meanwhile, go with it and see what happens." She moved closer to me, again. With a compassionate but no-nonsense look, she said, "You've been struggling for a while. It's time you faced it."

"You've noticed?"

"To me, you are the proverbial open book, my love. You are still strong in God. Thank heavens—and I mean that literally—you are still strong with me and Lisa. But, you are battling with almost everything else, including your call to ministry. I'm not sure exactly what it is, but you need to come to grips with yourself."

I just sat there, stunned at her blunt insight.

"You also need to come to grips with that butthead, Williams. Please him, appease him or shut him down. But, none of a half a dozen pastors before you has fixed the problem and so it falls on you."

"You know about that, too, huh?"

"I know everything, sweetheart. Your life will go so much easier when you finally come to accept that."

"I yield, my love, I yield."

"Now, you are the smartest and most perceptive man that I have ever met, and you have some feeling that Pastor Carl may help you. I suggest you trek on and see what you can see."

Chapter 8

I think it was a good thing that Pastor Carl was not available until 5:30 each evening. My thoughts had become so preoccupied with him that I had to force myself to get on with my typical daily work.

"Good morning, Janice," I said. "Please notify Phyllis I will not be attending the Memorial Committee meeting this evening. It shouldn't be a big deal. I don't go to all of their meetings anyway."

"Phyllis said they've got some big decisions to make tonight. The Morgan funeral generated almost eighteen hundred dollars in memorial money. The committee is caught between new candlesticks for the altar or a fountain in the Meditation Garden. It could get ugly," Janice concluded, trying to bury a wicked grin behind her computer screen.

"They will get through round two without me. It won't get settled until at least round four, anyway."

"I'll call her. She doesn't have email, yet. 'Never will,' she says. You off somewhere tonight?"

"Just another meeting. No big deal, but I do want to take a look at the schedule for the next week and free up as much evening time as I can. Could you work on that, please? See which meetings can do without me, move a couple of counseling appointments to before supper time, move two meetings to the same night . . . that sort of thing."

"You're making me curious, but I'll see what I can do."

"If there is anything to be curious about, Janice, I'll be sure to let you know. Right now, I'm just meeting with a guy

43

who I think can help me figure out how to best handle certain situations."

Truth is, Janice had always been a source of support for me. She will play around and tell a few jokes and stories. But I could always count on her.

"Janice, I need you to give me a hand on this. There are some things on the burner that I have to handle just right, or the church will slide back into conflict. And I have to keep it on the Q.T. until it's time. Can you help me?"

"There you go. Speak clearly and I know what to do. I'll keep a lid on things as much as I can and you keep me up to date. Deal?"

"Deal."

So, I visited a couple of folks on the shut-in list and returned to my office to send a thank you note to the Kiwanis Club for yet another generous gift to the East Fork Ministerial Association Food Bank. The food bank was started many years ago by several churches in the area. Now, its operation fell mostly on my church, although many individuals and organizations kept up a steady stream of financial support. In the previous year we had fed nearly three hundred families.

This was part of my struggle. My church was filled with unfortunate and ever increasing politics and turf wars and personal agendas and social wars. But, we still managed to provide a great deal of help to those in need. The soup kitchen and the food bank and the baby pantry provided safety-net services to hundreds of locals. I had a ten-thousand dollar Pastor's Discretionary Fund at my disposal, to use as I decided to help those having trouble with heat, or rent or gas or medical bills, and each year I spent every bit of it. Adding in what was spent on regional and foreign gifts and mission trips, the East Fork First United Methodist Church contributed at least eighty-thousand dollars a year in aid to the *least of God's children*, plus hundreds of hours of volunteer time.

Is it not enough? I thought to myself. *Shouldn't I be satisfied that, no matter how frustrated I get with some of the people in the church and the bureaucracy of the whole thing, that we are still doing good works?*

I had given myself this argument many times, whenever I started to question whether my work as a pastor was really fulfilling God's call. It usually worked to smooth over my discontent and get me back on track.

But what does it mean for me to be "on track?" I wondered.

Unlike many of the soul-searching questions that I had been asking myself, I actually knew the answer to this one. To be on track was to get on with being a *highly effective pastor* leading a *vital congregation* of the United Methodist Church. It meant to maintain the programs of the church, keep membership and attendance numbers up, make sure the apportionments (contributions to the hierarchy of the denomination) were paid in full and on time, get all the paperwork in and avoid conflict in the church. To be on track meant to have the formal power of the Staff Parish Relations Committee, and the informal, much greater power of influential members, report that *we like our pastor* instead of, *we want a new pastor.*

I closed my eyes and purposefully thought good thoughts: successful stewardship campaigns, baptisms, weddings, funerals (most people don't believe it, but pastors will tell you that they prefer funerals over weddings), new members, a pat on the back from the bishop. This exercise had always made me feel better.

It isn't working.

As I sat there feeling sorry for myself and failing to cheer myself up, my e-mail beeped. I sighed as I looked at the I.D.— Condi Cloverton. Condi was the Music Director of the church. When I arrived four years earlier, I was surprised to learn that her salary was exactly one dollar less than that of the Senior Pastor. Me. And, any time the pastor's salary was increased, Condi would receive a corresponding increase to keep her within exactly one dollar. Now, I honestly was not worried about who made how much money. Besides, the position or rank of the Senior Pastor had been at least nominally protected by the extra dollar. However, in church-world, to spend so exorbitantly on a music person was a clear indication of two things: emphasis and power.

Just seeing Condi's name put me to thinking about my arrival in East Fork. When a bishop matches a new pastor with a new church, a first meeting has to take place. This is done at a meeting at which the district superintendent (a pastor in charge of about sixty other pastors) brings the new pastor to the Staff Parish Relations Committee for introductions and a discussion of the new arrangement. It is usually called an interview, but *interview* implies that information is being gathered to use in making a decision. Some call it the *Put-In* meeting. I like that better.

Anyway, four years ago The Reverend Kathy Lehman brought me to the East Fork First United Methodist Church for my Put-In. As the kind of church that it was, a well-off, downtown, upscale, powerful church, the committee held certain expectations of being graced with a *leading* pastor. That means someone with sufficient education, experience and reputation to continue their church's glorious history. They were not disappointed. I am that pastor. We did the obligatory introductions and started in on the *tell us about yourself* segment of the show. I gave some general history about my personal life, family, hobbies and such (it didn't seem like a big deal at the time, but I did notice a grimace or two at the term *stepdaughter*). I smoothly moved into my education and history with other churches. As humbly as possible I included some of my successes and statistical evidence of growth and prosperity achieved in those places. It's what one does when trying to get off to a good start and give the committee members some specific, positive things to report to the rest of the congregation, who would be anxiously awaiting the scoop on the new pastor.

When I had wrapped up my nicely polished fifteen-minute presentation, the DS asked the SPRC Chair what the committee would like their new pastor to know about East Fork UMC.

Daisy Watkins, a surprisingly mousy and reserved-looking woman to be serving in this capacity, immediately said two things.

First, Daisy said, "We wish to welcome you to our church. We have had many fine pastors over the years—and some others—and we are confident that we will have many fruitful years with you. We hope that before suggesting (there was a subtle yet distinct emphasis on the word *suggesting*) a bunch of changes, that you will take the time to carefully observe. We think that you will find that there are good, carefully-considered reasons for what we do. This has been a leading church for a long time. We must be doing something right."

This description—perhaps it was even a plea—is common. Some version of this speech is given at most Put-In meetings. Churches are naturally stable institutions that are resistant to change. The membership of a United Methodist church is often especially sensitive to pastors—whom they have not vetted or selected themselves—who want to change *their* church by coming in with a new agenda already in mind. And, the truth is, many churches are years behind the times and stuck in old, ineffective ways. Most would benefit from new approaches. This tension between the need for change and the desire to stay the same is almost universal, especially when a brand new pastor/congregation relationship is about to start. So, I was fine with this. I am an expert in working through resistant attitudes.

Daisy's second speech was considerably less common.

"Also," Daisy said, "We have decided to address right up front an issue that has been a source of conflict for several years and several pastors. An issue that we have traditionally left alone until it came up."

This spiked my attention, a lot. If my presentation was polished, Daisy's was downright rehearsed.

"We here at East Fork First United Methodist Church have long offered the very finest in sacred music. All around the region, if you ask a knowledgeable church person who has the finest Christian music, there will be only one answer—East Fork First UMC. When Frederick Barnhausen passed away—that wonderful man is in a special place in heaven, I am sure—after thirty-seven years of providing our community, our congregation and our God with indescribably beautiful, sacred, reverent music, we were all highly concerned about how we could ever keep up such a high standard of performance and worship."

I was beginning to get a handle on where this was headed.

"Then, soon to be twenty-five years ago, God blessed us with Condi Cloverton. We had advertised for a music director at a salary 'negotiable based on experience.' We had hoped to at least find a decent organist—Frederick was spectacular—who could lead the choir and organize annual music events, holidays and cantatas and such. We had resigned ourselves to a step down. Then in walked Condi. Only thirty-five at the time. Julliard. Performance Organ at Duke Divinity. Carnegie Hall, twice. Even in the first interview, her grasp of music and its language and her heart for the time-tested classics was evident. We hoped that her playing would be half as impressive, and yet it was more so. Glorious. Only marriage and a commitment to family kept her from a world-wide career."

Daisy stopped talking. She had yet to say anything that I could respond to, so I waited. I snuck a peak at the DS, and caught her eye. Reverend Lehman asked, "And?"

Here Daisy's polish left her. "And, Pastor Kathy, we are sick and tired of every new pastor coming in here and trying to take over the music. I don't know why they can't just see how qualified and talented Condi is and accept it as a blessing! But no! Every one of them wants to pick their own hymns and

A Dragon in the Church 49

change the order of service and try to tell Condi what to do! Worse, yet, the next thing we start to hear about is *diversity* and *contemporary* and *what about the young people?* Well, maybe the young people would benefit by learning what truly fine music is really like! So the fighting starts, and we have to take action to protect Condi and our music program from the latest pastor. Why can't anyone see that this is our best thing!?"

Mary Evans, a grand old lady of the church who had been on every committee at least three times in fifty years, reached over and patted Daisy's left knee, twice. Daisy gulped and tried to compose herself. Mary took over.

In a very gentle, barely audible voice, wizened by many years and in perfect serenity, Mary said, "Pastor, we limit Condi's salary out of respect for your position in our church. We are hopeful that you will see the wisdom of returning that respect. Now, I think we would all do well to move on to something else. After all, this is the first day of a new season here at East Fork First. Everyone in this room hopes for it to be a wonderful time."

My e-mail beeped again, dragging me back to today. This one was for Viagra at just $2.00 a pill. I deleted that and paused over the button to open the message from Condi. My relationship with her had been both rocky and yet another example of my excellent mediation and conflict resolution skills. From the beginning it was clear that orders or demands were not going to get me anywhere regarding music. So, I collaborated with her, very slowly at first. It helps that I love classical music and can speak the language a little bit. Over four years we had learned to discuss and jointly decide on music selections. We had made an even bigger deal of the *Wonders of the Season Classical Music Celebration* at Christmas time.

The big win was when I finally got her to stop trying to block the creation of a praise band, complete with guitars and drums, to play at a new, totally separate, contemporary worship service. I actually prefer a service that blends styles of music and can hopefully unify all of the different age-groups and cliques in the church, but it was clear that that was a mountain too high to climb. In fact, to get the use of the praise band approved, I had to promise the Church Council that all of the modern, offensive instruments would be completely removed from the sanctuary after each contemporary service, so that the people in the *regular* service wouldn't have to look at them. At any rate, Condi and I had formed a workable relationship. In fact, just a few months ago, Condi had mentioned in one of our meetings that she had heard that "the praise and worship band was considered excellent by those who enjoy such things." That felt like a huge compliment!

Still, given what was percolating with Bob Williams, I expected that Condi's message meant more trouble. I pushed the fateful button and the message popped up.

Good morning, Pastor, it read. *I thought I should notify you ahead of our planning session tomorrow morning that something has come up. It seems that some people in the church, represented, it seems, by Mr. Williams, have begun to blame me for—and I quote—"the music problems in the church." I may have simply read too much into it, but there seemed to be a clear indication that I am paid too high a salary to not have the music department fully under my control. I tried to explain to Mr. Williams that my position on the use of less-than-sacred music in the church was not one of support or participation, but rather a position of cooperation and collaboration with our pastor. He said some things about duties, job descriptions and responsibility before eventually moving on. I bring this to you now so that you can think about it before we meet. I am quite upset, but not sure about exactly what. Am I in trouble? I have tried to be helpful; am I supposed to fight, instead? Please advise me, as I feel as if I have become the rope in someone else's tug-of-war. Sincerely, Condi Cloverton.*

Chapter 9

By 4:30 I couldn't take it anymore. I went home to an empty house. Jenn was subbing that day and wouldn't be back for a while. She knew that I would be running off to see Pastor Carl. I changed into jeans and an old Detroit Tigers T-shirt that I had almost completely worn out. As I pulled on my rattiest pair of tennis shoes, I figured that I would get around Carl's unbreakable attention to *sanding the wood* by joining him. It would give me a comfortable way to stand next to him during the long, contemplative delays that seemed to precede whatever he was going to say. Besides, I was getting an urge to do some tangible work that I could see and touch and smell and measure. Some fix-up time might be just the ticket.

I arrived at the little church about thirty seconds before Carl pulled in. *Why couldn't I have waited just a couple more minutes?*

"Evening, Carl," I said. "I thought I might give you a hand tonight, if that's okay."

"Glad for the help," he answered, "especially from someone who loves the meaning in an old place like this as much as I do."

"It will be fun," I replied. "And, we'll get that much more done."

"Oh, it will get done when God is ready for it to be done."

"Yeah . . . of course . . . all in God's time."

With that, Carl moved purposely, but seemingly without hurry or worry. He entered the church, set a small cooler down in the back pew and picked up his sanding board. He had finished the back wall, and was ready to proceed up the left.

"I have no plan beyond the next job," Carl said. "You can work with me or choose your own poison." He started sanding.

If I started right next to him, it would take only a little while to run into the first damaged board. Looking along the length of the wall, it was obvious that there would be a stop every few feet, as there were at least a half a dozen replacements needed.

"I fancy myself a bit of a woodworker. How about I tackle these bad spots and try to keep good wood ahead of you?"

"Excellent idea," Carl replied, and kept on sanding.

In the tiny back room I found a crowbar, tape measure, square, and a circular saw. Soon I was intently removing old wood, measuring and cutting new, fixing it in place with finishing nails, setting them and filling in the holes with Plastic Wood.

A couple of times I sought approval from Carl, but without even looking he simply replied, "You've got the feel of it. It'll be fine."

I was really enjoying myself. The third replacement board went in okay, but was not an exact match to the one next to it. The gap between them was minutely narrower on one end than the other. No one would ever notice it, unless they were staring right at it. So, I moved on and did a couple more. Carl kept on sanding, and when he reached the first of my new boards, he said "very nice" and continued on. I was embarrassed at how excited that made me feel, so I kept my man-face on and kept working.

I wrestled with the board that was fine, but not perfect. I told myself over and over to just let it go, but then I caved in. In prying it away from the wall, I split the board and ruined it. I wanted to swear (Yeah, I still swear sometimes. Never the "God" ones, but there are some good ole Anglo-Saxon four-letter dandies that seem just right once in a while, but never in front of anyone but Jenn) but this seemed like a time and place for restraint. So, I moved to the backroom, cut another board, made a small adjustment and nailed it down. Perfect.

Carl glanced over and smiled. "How about a break?" he said.

I had settled into the work so completely that his voice startled me.

"Let's sit," he added.

Carl sat in the rear pew and picked up his cooler. I sat down a carefully considered three and a half feet from him, enough to stay a manly distance apart without seeming rude.

"I didn't know what you like. I hope mayo is all right."

He handed me a white bread sandwich wrapped in waxed paper. It was cut on the diagonal, revealing a thin layer of lettuce, a slice of American cheese, a slice of bologna and the white of the mayo lining both slices of bread. I couldn't remember the last time that anyone had served me something so simple.

"Doritos or Fritos?" he asked. "I'm good with either."

"I haven't had Fritos in forever," I replied. "Used to be my favorite."

"Then have a trip down memory lane. I was secretly hoping you'd leave the Doritos, anyway." He looked at me with a kind of forced smile.

I realized that Pastor Carl had made a joke! I realized two more things. Pastor Carl was not funny. And, he had just let me know that he would like to be friends.

"Then everybody is happy!" I replied more boisterously than needed.

"I do my own food," Carl said. "So, it isn't much."

"It's just right, Carl. Thank you for thinking of me."

And it was just right. It was the best sandwich that I had eaten in a very long time.

We ate quietly until we were nearly finished. I didn't want to let the opportunity get away, so I probed a little. "You said you do your own food. Do you live alone?"

"Yes. I was married once, but that was long ago. Cancer. No kids."

"I'm sorry. Maybe that wasn't the right place to start."

"Not to worry. It is part of my life."

"Are you from around here? I don't guess I had heard of you before you showed up at that first meeting."

"No, I don't even know where I'm from anymore. I've moved around so much that I don't know what to call home. I've only been in these parts for a while. How about you?"

"I was born near Detroit, moved to Traverse City when I was in elementary school, college at Western Michigan, seminary at Methesco, in Ohio. Now, being Methodist, you know, I go where the bishop tells me."

"Is that hard, being sent like that?"

"Yes and no. I don't mind it myself. I like it, actually. It settles a lot of things that can be hard to settle on your own. But, it is tough on the family, and I don't like that."

"Family?" he asked.

"I have a wife and a stepdaughter. Jenn is my wife. She's a teacher, although she only subs since this last move. She's great and more devout than I am. My stepdaughter Lisa is a sweetheart. She's a dental hygienist."

"They sound nice."

"Yes sir. Whenever I get to questioning things, I never question how important my family is to me."

"That's good. A man's got to be a hero for his family."

That last comment hit me kind of hard. I didn't even know why. While I tried to figure it out, I finished my Fritos.

"There is much to do here," Carl said, his eyes moving slowly around the sanctuary. I think he was changing the subject on purpose. "But, it is going to be worth it," he continued. "This is a special place."

"I think so, too," I replied. "Do you have a timetable or anything?"

"Oh, no. I'm just trying to honor whatever God has in mind."

"I have wondered something, if you don't mind me asking."

"Sure, go ahead."

"Why don't you have some help from your congregation? It seems like the perfect kind of project for some good old-fashioned work bees."

"Oh, there is no congregation. Not yet."

"I'm sorry. I know I shouldn't make assumptions. It's just that, usually, there is a group of people who decide to form a church and . . . well, you know . . ."

"It's quite all right, Pastor. I came to the ministerial association meeting and said I had a church. This is my church. So far God has placed this building in my hands and instructed me to bring it back to its useful state. We have all preached the sermon about how the church is not a building, but is rather the gathering of God's people. Still, for now God has given me just this much to do. The congregation will come later. I have no idea what order he wants things, only that I should do my best to carry out whatever is next. I am very happy with that arrangement."

I thought a moment and replied, "I must say that I am impressed. There was a time that I could talk like that and mean it. Not so much lately. So, thank you for your example."

"You're welcome, Pastor, for what little I have done. It's God who gives us meaningful work to do. So, as it is obvious that other helpers are not on the way, are you up for a bit more working of the wood?"

"Yes, I sure am."

We kept working. There was not much more talk. Engrossed in the work and in my thoughts, I was surprised when, at precisely 9:30, Carl set his tools down right where he was standing and said, "Time to stop."

"I've only got one last board to finish this wall. Only take me another ten minutes."

"Suit yourself," he said, matter-of-factly. "See you next time."

"I'll be here tomorrow evening at 5:30."

"I'll look forward to it," he said, and started to leave.

"Should I lock up?" I shouted.

"Can if you want, but you'll have to install locks first."

I think he was laughing again, but with Carl it was hard to tell. I finished up the last board. I had set a goal for myself to make all the necessary replacements on the left wall, before going home for the night. Once I set a goal I like to meet it and measure it as completed.

I was ready to leave and anxious to get home and debrief a bit with Jenn. Still, I felt the need to sit down in the front pew, near the big cross. For the first time in longer than I would ever want to admit, I prayed in solitude. "Thank you, God," I whispered. "Help me."

Then, I went home.

Chapter 10

A new pattern developed. I went to the church each day, as I always had. I did my work and made the necessary visitations. Each week I prepared a well-crafted and entertaining sermon, complete with an appropriate passage of scripture, an opening joke, two or three well-supported points, a humorous but meaningful real life sermon illustration and a clear, but not too challenging, call to action. I am a master of the well-received sermon. I got my paperwork in on time and made it to all of the absolutely required meetings. I was doing my job. However, I was not around as much as had become expected. People were beginning to notice.

Each day I tried to manufacture some alone time with Jenn. In recent years, I had not been as attentive to this as I should have been, always assuming that she understood and appreciated my responsibilities. Which, she did. Still, she is the most important human being in my life and I love her and am strengthened by her and, truth be known, I need her. And, she is smart and insightful and discerning. At this particular season of my life, I needed all the smart/insightful/discerning I could get.

Three or four evenings a week, I managed to free up time to work with Pastor Carl. The little church with no name was coming along. The sanctuary was really shaping up. The walls were finished, and spectacular. We had made progress on the windows, when one evening Carl announced that it was time to tackle the roof.

As we worked, our conversation grew more open and fluid. We got into some theology and philosophy. We discussed scripture. Carl never talked about himself very much, but I came to know that his relationship with God was highly personal. He was not affected much by doctrine or rituals or tradition. He merely read the scriptures, lived them out, prayed and listened for God in his life. As he encouraged me to reveal more about myself, I was surprised at how far my approach to faithful living had drifted.

After things had gone on like this for nearly four weeks, I arrived at my church one morning at 9:00 a.m. Janice was hovering near the doorway, sorting mail into the church member's boxes. At least, she appeared to be doing that, until I saw that she didn't really have anything to sort.

"What's up?" I asked.

"Bob Williams is in your office, waiting for you." Her hands shook and her chin quivered. "He didn't ask permission; he just walked right in. I'm sorry."

"There is nothing for you to be sorry about, Janice. All is well."

"All is well? All is well!?!" she whispered so hard it came out raspy. "He doesn't look like all is well."

I smiled at Janice and said, "I meant all is well for you. I'm in deep trouble. Don't worry. I'll handle it. It's what I do."

"Dead man walking," I said, hoping to sound brave by cracking jokes at my own execution, and went in. "Good morning, Bob. I am so glad that you have stopped by this morning. Calling you and setting up a meeting is the first thing on my to-do list this morning, so this is fortuitous, indeed."

"It's been over three weeks since . . ."

"Yes it has, and that's the first thing that I wanted to get to! My sincere apology for the delay. I have taken your concerns seriously. I have analyzed the situation, taken in the new information and begun to discern an action plan. Done properly, this takes time. I have covered the situation in prayer and contemplation, seeking God's will for the immediate and long-term future of the church."

"Well, Pastor, that is all good, of course, but . . ."

"But words is words and action is action, right Bob! True enough, but there are some differences in being a business man and being a pastor, wouldn't you agree, Bob? Of course. I see this process, even though it is necessarily slow, resulting in a workable series of SMART goals. Specific. Measurable. Attainable. Realistic. Timely. I am committed and I will not get ahead of the process. This has to be done right. So, when I have completed a thorough report, and the action plan suitable to address the issues raised, then and only then will I sit down with you and reveal the results. Anything else would be shoddy work on my part, and I do not find even the notion of shoddiness acceptable in the performance of the pastor of the East Fork First United Methodist Church."

"I must say," Bob said, stammering a bit, "I expected this meeting to go a whole other direction. I applaud thoroughness, but still, I am wondering how long . . ."

"All in God's time, Bob, all in God's time. This has been an excellent meeting. Before you go, I think we should pray. Shall we pray, Bob?"

"Well, sure . . . I guess."

"Excellent. Let's bow our heads." And then I prayed, sincerely, that God would show us the error of our ways and guide the East Fork First UMC to a season of renewed vitality. "Amen. Bob, what a fantastic day this is already. I am so glad that you stopped by today. I'm sure that it is no coincidence. I am looking forward to seeing you again real soon."

Bob left.

I'll admit I sat in my office for twenty minutes, gloating. Bob had just begun to feel the pain and frustration of trying to dominate me! But, I calmed down and thought about what had actually just happened. I probably should have felt bad that I had manipulated Bob, but I didn't. Bob is a big boy and a bully. He was nowhere near done with me. No problems had been solved. Only postponed. I sighed in recognition of that reality and opened my desk drawer. In the very back, Bob's list of observations or demands or instructions or threats or whatever they were, was still exactly where I had put it weeks ago.

"I guess it's time to read this," I whispered out loud, and opened the folder. I looked away and tried to prepare myself. Obviously, what I was about to read would not make me happy. It was criticism, after all. But, perhaps by putting it off for so long I had created more fear than was called for. I assured myself that Bob was not a monster. He was, in fact, a consistently reasonable man. I looked down and read:

Observations for the Pastor
by
Bob Williams

Oddly formal, yet poorly done, I thought.
- A teenage boy has been allowed a seat and a vote on the church's Finance Committee. This is unprecedented and irresponsible.
  - By the next regularly scheduled Finance meeting this situation will be rectified by removing the boy from the committee or, at least, rescinding his right to vote.
- Under the direct influence of the pastor, the music program of the church has moved in unfortunate directions. Guitars, drums, untrained musicians and music of a less than sacred nature have been integrated into the various functions and services of the church.
  - Immediately, all control of the music program at EFFUMC shall be turned over to Music Director Condi Cloverton, including the choice of hymns to be sung during worship services.
  - Condi shall be instructed to return the church to its well-earned reputation as offering the best of sacred, traditional Christian music.

A Dragon in the Church 61

- The pastor will cooperate in any manner needed to carry out this mission.
- The directions taken by the church have been insensitive to the needs of the long-term members who have provided, and continue to provide, the great majority of the church's financial support.
  - As soon as possible, a meeting restricted to those who have been official members of the church for in excess of ten years shall be called.
  - The concerns of this group shall be duly noted and honored in every reasonable way.
- The pastor has routinely preached sermons on topics and subjects that are not desired by the majority of the membership. Topics such as, but not limited to: abortion, homosexuality, anti-patriotism and God's so-called "preference for the poor" make good examples.
  - The pastor is now advised to stick with sermons that the membership find positive and suitable to Sunday worship.
  - If the pastor fails to demonstrate improved judgment on this matter, a committee shall be formed to preview his choices ahead of time, with the power to rectify any inappropriate situations before they get a chance to occur.
- The church has been embarrassed by the fact the pastor cannot influence even his own wife to attend the church.
  - Barring medical emergencies and unusual circumstances, the pastor's spouse—who after all benefits from living in the parsonage owned and kept up by the church—shall regularly attend Sunday services.
  - It is reasonable to expect that church participation of the spouse, additional to Sunday services, would be evident.

- As a final statement in this document, let it be shown that the pastor has been reminded that he is an employee of the East Fork First United Methodist Church and should behave as such.

I was wrong. It was not better than I had feared. It was worse. I was grateful that I had not chosen to read this thing in front of Bob. I have my limits. At first I decided to keep his list of *observations* to myself. But I knew that I couldn't do that; I was past the point of handling this alone. I at least needed to vent and complain and talk through some of the outrage I was feeling, or have my head explode. So, I decided to open up to Pastor Carl first and get his advice. This might spare Jenn some of the anguish and anger that she would certainly feel. I could let her know what was going on after I had gotten a handle on the situation. She would understand.

I came to my senses and soon I sat watching Jenn shake her head in disbelief. She kept her eyes down for a bit, processing. Then she looked up. As soon as her eyes met mine, her chin started to tremble, her lips clamped shut and tears began to form.

I held her close and whispered, "Don't try to talk. Everything will be fine. He's just one guy. This will pass."

It might have seemed a brave speech by a strong, Christian man, if I hadn't started blubbering myself. My strategy worked. Jenn can't stand to see me cry. Even her own despair takes a back seat to her need to comfort me. For ten-minutes-that-seemed-like-an-hour I let her do just that. I cried and cried, until she started to feel better. I'm generous that way.

"Okay . . . Okay," she said. "Enough. What do we do now?"

"I'm not sure, yet," I admitted.

"We have to do something. This is officially over the line. I will not stand for any more of this. More to the point, I will not stand quietly by and watch my husband be treated like a hired hand. What is wrong with these people?"

"I don't know how far this goes, beyond Williams," I said. "I don't know what the situation really is."

"You are a fine pastor. Any list of the best pastors in the Gateway District is going to have your name on it. What more do they want?"

"That's what I need to figure out. I will gather some information. I have a few people I can talk to in confidence. I can develop a workable model of what's happening, minus the emotions of the moment."

I could see my wife's face go hard, her tears suddenly dry. She leaned away from me.

Gaining momentum, I pressed on. "Once I know the true dynamics of the situation, I can formulate a response. A lot of this is just misperception. I can clarify that. Maybe I have tried for too much change too quickly. A compromise here and there, not on the big stuff, but on the things that are mostly style and preference, I can bring this back together. I can save this."

Jenn stared at me in a way that I never experienced before. She started to speak three different times, but stopped herself.

Finally, she said, in a tone clipped and carefully measured, "You are my husband. I love you. I will not leave your side. But do not speak to me again about compromise."

My wife stood and left the room.

Chapter 11

Pastor Carl took an awfully long time reading what I would forever refer to as the "infamous Williams memo." I had apologized for jumping right into my problem and asked him to read the memo before we even got started on the work.

I had experienced conflict in the past. For pastors it is just part of the lifestyle. But I had never been through anything quite as upsetting as this. It took me considerable contemplation to figure out why this struck me so powerfully. It was so . . . dismissive. I had long realized that churches usually have one of two distinct attitudes toward a pastor, especially a new pastor. In fact, I had once given a talk on the subject for a continuing education event for my fellow pastors. I titled it *Leader or Lacky?*

There are churches who envision the pastor as a spiritual leader. They assume and trust that the pastor has the ability to take the church and its members on a journey toward something important. They may see that important thing as a growing relationship with Christ, or a better understanding of scripture, or more vibrant worship of God or more powerful prayer or something else. They may even see the goal as something more temporal, like the growth of the church or increased missions or a stronger service to the community. But, in whatever fashion, the pastor is the leader. When a pastor leaves and is replaced by an incoming pastor, the assumption is that the church will enter into a new season. It might be good or it might be bad, but surely the new pastor will take us somewhere we have not been before.

And then there are churches—a lot of them—who see the pastor as a hired hand. They may not use the words: *You work for us and we pay your salary, so you will do as you're told. You're job is to please us and do things the way we already do them. You will be especially careful to please the right people: the leading family or families of the church, the matriarch or patriarch and, especially, the deep pockets. If you understand your place and perform to our satisfaction, everything will go just fine. But, Mr. or Ms. New Pastor, woe to you if you don't!* But, without being quite so blunt, they have their ways to make the pastor and the pastor's family understand who is in charge. And, most especially, who is not. I had never had a church treat me as anything but a leader. Until now.

Pastor Carl shook his head. He folded the paper, hiding the words, but he did not put it down or hand it back to me. Despite our deepening relationship, I was still prone to exasperation at his methodical actions. I was about to tell him so, when I realized that he was praying.

He opened his eyes and said, "I think we both need to paint awhile. Then we'll talk." After a half an hour or so, Pastor Carl said, "You must be terribly upset."

"That's an understatement," I replied, too quickly. "I have never in my life been treated in this way. Who does Williams think he is? He's not even on the Church Council. He doesn't write my job description. The church doesn't even write most of it! That comes from the denomination. I have been successful wherever I have been appointed . . . and I'm being successful right now. The church is doing fine! New members. Baptisms. The budget's in order. The church is doing fine, and so am I. We have a lot of churches who would be happy to be in our shoes, churches who have to cut staff and programs because they can't pay the bills."

Pastor Carl let me go on until I wound down and realized that I hadn't let him speak in quite a while. Once I let him, he said, "Can't blame you for being hurt. Anyone would be. What's hurting the most right now?"

I couldn't answer right away, and painted with an angry fury. True to form, he just went back to painting and waited.

Eventually, my anger wore out, I slumped and said quietly, "I don't get what happened with Jenn. She walked away from me."

"Thought so," he said. "A stiff-neck like this Williams can hurt you plenty, but not like someone you love."

"Yeah," was my brilliant reply.

"Are you asking my help?" Carl asked.

"Yes. Definitely. Please."

"All right, then answer a few questions for me."

"Okay."

He looked at me and asked, "In fifty words or less, why did you become a pastor?"

"I am not sure how that is going to help," I said, my voice whinier than I wanted. "My problems are right now."

"I am asking you to just trust me on this," he replied.

"Okay. Okay. When I was in high school, I wanted to be a doctor or a lawyer, which just seemed to be the thing a guy like me would do . . ."

"That's twenty-eight words already," Pastor Carl interrupted, "Are you sure you want to use up so many words on what you didn't do?"

"Are you kidding me?" I said, whining morphing into anger. "Why fifty words?!"

"When you have few words to use, you have to say only what matters most. You're plenty smart. You will edit out the fluff very quickly, once you realize that I am only going to listen to a fifty-word answer to each question."

I glared at him like he was my enemy. I expected him to crack or laugh or apologize or something. He did not. He looked me in my angry eyes, and waited. After a while, I felt the hostility drain slowly away, replaced by resignation. I needed help. I knew it. I couldn't keep fighting. I couldn't say no to everything.

So, I whispered, "okay."

"Good," he said.

"Can I have my twenty-eight words back?"

"Sure, I will grant you a one-time do over." He chuckled. A good natured, natural looking, natural feeling chuckle. Pastor Carl was not much of a chuckler, but his good humor felt reassuring to me.

Very Pastor Carl-like, I relaxed and worked out my answer in my head. "Accountant. Then bank manager. Did fine, but felt there should be more. God had worked on me for years. Resisted. Ran away from it, really. The call from God finally came, too strong to say no. I changed everything and enrolled in seminary. Met wife and step-daughter—that's only one word—love them, love God."

"Close enough," Pastor Carl said with a nod. "What did you think being a pastor would be like?"

I painted for ten minutes. I knew by now that Pastor Carl wouldn't break the silence, no matter how long I took. "Time. Time to study, read scripture, pray. Preach, love to prepare sermons and preach them. God's Word and God's Way. Really enthuse people to follow Jesus, for real. Evangelism, people saved. Baptism and Communion—love it, makes me cry. Change the world, grow the kingdom. Have my family and a church family. No need to make a living doing anything else. That's too many, isn't it?"

"That's okay. Just don't take advantage of the rules. Next question. How does what you thought being a pastor would be like compare to what it really is?"

"It's different, for sure. I get some of what I expected, but there is so much politicking and conflict management and massaging of people's egos and feelings and paperwork and meetings and dealing with other people's problems, not that I mind visiting and counseling with people when they have real needs . . . this part doesn't count on my fifty, but so much of it seems trivial . . . okay back on track, and the conference and the district with all its demands and expectations . . . well, it's not too much like I thought, except when it is."

"You said once that you love being as pastor. Did you? Do you still?"

"Loved it big time at first. Small churches, smaller problems. I had time to study and preach. Loved the people. Loved doing God's work. My wife was happy. She loved the people and they loved her. But I wanted to be more successful. I am trying to still love it. Fifty."

"Excellent. This is the last fifty-word question for tonight. You said you wanted to be successful. How does the United Methodist Church decide if a pastor is successful or not?"

"Officially or real world?"

"Good question. Real world."

"Confirmed and affirmed call. Divinity Degree. Social Skills. Excellent writer. Magnetic preacher. Good administrator. Effective counselor/visitor. Strong leader. Strong Teacher. Conflict resolver. Satisfied congregation. Few complaints. Increase attendance/membership. Good missions programs. Strong finances; apportionments fully paid. Good connectional participator. Extra points for being young, minority or female—well, white men are still treated best, so strike that. Intangibles, I guess. Image."

"Okay," he said, "one last question. This time you only get twenty words."

"Oh, come on!"

"Twenty will be enough, and this time the answer is written. We'll go over it next time. And, after I give you the question, we are going to be quiet and work and then go home. Deal?"

"I guess so; negotiation isn't working anyway."

"In exactly twenty words, when you were first called to the pulpit, what kind of pastor did God want you to be?"

Chapter 12

"Things are starting to heat up," Janice reported.

"Good morning, Janice, how good to see you!" I said, with more than a little sarcasm.

"Yeah, yeah. Gooood morning. A real pleasure. Now, like I said, things are starting to heat up."

"How so?"

"People are beginning to notice your new schedule."

"You mean the fact that I have not been around all day and most evenings as has become the expectation? And, there have been several committee meetings that have missed me, even though there is no real reason for me to be there?"

"Yes." Janice sat calmly, her eyes locked on mine.

"Okay. How bad is it?"

"Not too. Not yet. So far it's mostly just a growing awareness. People are starting to ask ahead of time if you are going to attend meetings."

"Anything else?"

Janice hesitated, sighed, and then said, "Bob Williams called yesterday. He asked for a copy of your *schedule* or *activities report*. I told him that we don't actually have anything like that."

"What did he say?"

"He harrumphed and said, 'that'll change' and hung up."

Our conversation was suddenly interrupted. A force of nature, a five-feet-zero ball of righteous indignation topped with a generous dollop of white hair had entered the room.

"Pastor! I am glad you're here. It's been a little hard to find you lately. I hope there is nothing wrong. Anyway, as long as I have you now, we have a problem to work out."

"All right. What is it, Mrs. Dekker?"

"Pastor, please call me Virgy Lou. Everyone else does and, after all, you have known me for years now."

"Yes, Ma'am."

"There you go again. Anyway, the annual Community Dinner is coming up and, as I don't need to remind you, this is one of the churches biggest and longest running events."

"Yes Ma'am."

"Well, while we graciously allow the sewing group to use our yellow, multi-level, wheeled storage rack most of the year, we quite reasonably need its use for the Community Dinner. I carefully unloaded the sewing group's . . . materials . . . and piled them neatly onto their own shelves. I did it myself because I do so hate to bother others with such menial work. Anyway, as we have now loaded the cart with essentials for the dinner, there seems to be a real fracas going on. Berta Lou is fit to be tied. Every year it is the same thing! I am really too old for all this turmoil. I expect what Berta Lou needs is a talk from you, Pastor. She has a constant need to look important, you know."

"I understand, Mrs. Dekker. I will talk to Berta Lou."

"She is here now, and quite worked up."

"Very well, I will be down in a minute."

As I walked by Janice, she looked ready to make a crack of some sort. I silenced her with rolled eyes and a waggle of the finger. I closed the door on my office and sat down. Once again I found my head cradled by the stacks of papers, but not a comfortable level.

"Janice! Have you been cleaning my office, again!?"

"You should be thinking about what you're going to say to Berta Lou, don't you think?"

"Yeah, yeah. In a minute. Janice, find out if Bob Williams is in his office today, would you please?"

"He's not. Business meeting in Grand Rapids. He won't be back until tomorrow."

"Should I ask how you know that?"

"Better not to."

"Okay." I dialed Bob's office number and quickly got his secretary. "Oh, not until tomorrow? All right, can you give me his voicemail? Thanks."

After the usual pauses and beeps I got the answering machine message, *Hello! This is Bob Williams of Williams Enterprises. There is the okay way, the good way, the excellent way... and then there is the WILLIAMS WAY! Please leave a message and I will get back to you faster than the other guys!*

At the tone, I said, "Hi Bob, this is your pastor. I just wanted to let you know that I am making excellent progress on my report. Another couple of weeks and I will be ready to fully address your concerns. Sorry I missed you. God bless and have a great day."

As I was trying to decide if I had just told a real lie or not, I saw Janice standing in the doorway. She closed the door behind her and said, "The clock is ticking, Pastor. Are you going to be all right?"

"One way or another, yes. But I really don't know how that's going to look."

Janice looked at the floor, then peeked up at me, almost through her eyelids, and said, "You understand I am on your side, right? That you can trust me?"

Truthfully, until that very moment, I had not been sure where Janice would land if the cards started to fall.

"Yes. Yes, Janice thank you. I think I knew that, but I sure do appreciate hearing it."

"Truth is truth," she said.

"Good. Now, could you go tell Berta Lou that I am anxiously awaiting her presence?"

"You sure? She's really revved up this time."

"I'll handle it. People get all revved up, and I unrev 'em. That's what I do."

By the time Berta Lou left my office, both she and Virgy Lou were convinced that they had, somehow, won. Neither could explain how or what she had won, but they were sure that they had. Like I said, that's what I do.

I was free to visit Pastor Carl that evening, and Jenn assumed that I would. However, I chose not to. After office hours I circled back around and reentered my church. There were no meetings scheduled, for once. I went to the sanctuary and turned on the back-lights for the main cross. I took a seat in the front pew and tried to empty my mind. When I first arrived at East Fork First United Methodist Church, I did this quite often. It is a great atmosphere in which to pray and think and think and pray. Now, I realized that it had been months since I had arranged this kind of solitude. It was with considerable sadness that I realized that I had lately prayed very little. We pastors do so much on-duty praying, that it is easy to fool oneself into thinking that your prayer life is active, when it is not.

As I settled in, I gave it a try. My efforts were weak at first, stiff and strangely formal, but after a bit I felt the old, familiar comfort and peace that comes from being in conversation with God. I prayed for wisdom and perseverance and insight. I prayed for Jenn and Lisa and those in the church who had needs and for our community, our country and our world. It was a really good prayer. As it got to feeling over-long, I stopped myself and prayed the one question that I had been avoiding.

"God," I prayed, "What kind of pastor did you want me to be? Just how far have I fallen short?" After thinking that I was finished, I was moved to pray the actual question, "God, what kind of pastor do you want me to be now?"

Chapter 13

"Well, Carl, it took me some time, but here is the answer to my homework question."
"Very good. Thank you for sticking with me on this, Pastor. Let's see what we've got." He read out loud,
- *Spreader of the Good News.*
- *Teacher of the Word.*
- *Caretaker of the people.*
- *Reliever of suffering.*
- *God's bold, prophetic voice.*

"Excellent. I can see that you have put a lot of thought and prayer into this."
"It was harder than I wanted it to be. More disappointing, too."
"How so?" Carl asked softly.
"At the time, I understood what God was asking, maybe not the gravity of it, but mostly I understood. And, I vowed to be that guy. Out loud. But when you asked me, I didn't even have a ready answer! When did I lose that? How did I lose that? In the UMC we spend all kinds of time talking grandly about *God's call upon us to enter professional ministry.* You would think that might include remembering what God wanted in the first place!"
"Yes," Pastor Carl answered, "it is so easy to get right on with the doing of God's work, without stopping once in a while to find out what work God actually wants done."
"Okay, what now?" I asked.
"I would like to move on to something else that might be helpful."

"Move on? Aren't we going to talk about how the kind of pastor I have really been compares to the model that God wants from me?"

"Oh, heavens no! That's not my job. I would imagine you have already started down that road and, in the end, you are the only one who can do it."

"Well, it is certainly true that I have been thinking about exactly that pretty much nonstop."

"I would think so," Pastor Carl said with a nod. "How do you think we are doing with our renovation?"

It took me a moment to switch gears, but I replied, "Good, I think. The walls look great. The roof is solid again. I still don't know how you knew to postpone what we were doing to get on with the shingling. We weren't done twelve hours when it started to rain."

"Just a feeling I had. Lucky, I guess."

"I expect that there was more to it than luck. Anyway, the windows are almost done, although I feel bad that we had to put in clear glass where there used to be such beautiful stained-glass artwork."

"Someday, my friend, some day." The way Pastor Carl said it, I had no trouble believing that someday would come and the stained glass would be replaced.

I continued, "I'd vote for tearing into this floor. A few repairs, a good, deep sanding job and some new finish will have it looking great."

"Very well, the floor it is."

As I got the equipment organized—I had finally convinced Carl to allow the use of a heavy-duty floor sander—he sat in front of the cross and prayed. I had grown so accustomed to his peculiarities and unpredictable ways of behaving, that I did not think twice about it. He often stopped to pray in the middle of a conversation, sometimes interrupting his own sentence for what he liked to call his *consultation with God*. Amazingly, within five minutes or a half an hour, he would pick up mid-sentence and finish his original thought. I brought the sander to a roar and got to work. I had also learned that you could not disturb the man, even if you tried.

After forty-five minutes—a long one, even for Pastor Carl—he stood up and got out the sandwiches and chips. This was the same as setting off the whistle in a factory. Time to eat! As we sat there chewing, Carl said, "Tell me why your wife no longer attends your church."

I was immediately angry. I flushed. I started to sweat. I think I was even shaking. Pastor Carl slowly chewed his food. I held on, waited, tried to breathe and calmed myself. Carl was not just some everyday person. Nor was he at fault for anything that had occurred. Within ten minutes, I was breathing evenly again.

Pastor Carl whispered, "Seems like that's a doozey."

"And that's a doozey of an understatement." I tried to sound like I was joking, but I didn't pull it off.

"I'm sorry if it is a raw subject. But still, I would like to know."

"Yes, I think you need to know. There's no getting to the bottom of my struggles without dealing with this. Next time. Next time I can tell you, and show you. Fair?"

"Fair."

When I got to the office the next day, Janice told me, "At 11:00 most of the Finance Committee is going to be here for what Annabel called 'an emergency sit-down.'"

"What's the emergency?" I asked. "Have we got a money problem of some sort?"

"I don't think so," Janice said, "and I would almost have to know about that ahead of anybody else."

"True," I said. "So what's up? Don't tell me you don't know."

"No, I won't say that. I have been asked to be at the meeting, too. It evidently has to do with Jeremy. Pastor, I am pretty sure this starts with Bob Williams."

"Ah," I said, "now I see. Everybody has been invited, except Jeremy. Right?"

"Right," Janice answered.

"Do we expect Bob?" I asked.

"I don't think so. Annabel is trying to find out what is going on before facing him."

"Okay," I said, "I know what's happening, unless there is a new surprise. Let's pull ourselves together for the meeting. We've got a little over an hour."

At 11:00 a.m. sharp, Annabel Ustiss spoke. "I call this special meeting of the Finance Committee of the East Fork First United Methodist Church to order. I will waive the reading of the secretary's report and the treasurer's report, as I have called us together to discuss only one topic. Regular business will be held until our next scheduled meeting. Let the record show that in attendance are: Janice Pohl, the treasurer, Sid Holms, Dosie Wainright, me, Annable Ustiss, Chair, and the pastor. Absent, and not notified of this meeting, is Jeremy Clark."

"Well, good morning all," I said. "Annabel, we're being unusually formal today, I see."

"Yes, Pastor. I think we might want a presentable record for this one. That's not to say that we don't always have good records. Sorry, Janice, if it came out sounding like that."

"It's okay, Annabel. I understand," Janice said, kindly.

"All right, all right," Sid broke in, "What's the mystery? What are we doing here?"

"Let me begin by saying that this is a delicate matter, and I hope that all concerned will listen and take the time to consider carefully all of the different aspects and ramifications of this discussion."

"Spit it out, Annabel," Sid spat out.

"It's all right, Annabel," I said. "We have plenty of time to process this. Why don't you just go right ahead and say it, and then we'll work it through."

"Okay," she said. "I was contacted by Bob Williams regarding the makeup of this committee. Now, you all know how Bob can be, and you all know that Bob and his family are the biggest financial supporters of our church, and this is, after all, the Finance Committee. I think it important that we consider . . ."

"We know all about Bob," Dosie said. "Please move to the point." Dosie didn't speak often, so she was clearly heard.

"All right. I'm sorry. This is most unusual. Okay. Bob asked me if the pastor had followed through on his expectations that Jeremy would be removed from this committee. He said that his opinion and desires in this matter were made clear, and that he was frustrated by the pastor's lack of action and communication, reporting wise. I am the Chair of this committee and I had no idea what he was talking about! I was so embarrassed! When I told him that this was all new to me, Bob got very angry and indicated that he was—his words, not mine—'done messing around with come and gone pastors.' He told me that anybody could see that it makes no sense to trust adult matters to a child and that it would be like his making a twelve-year-old the manager of one of his stores, and how ridiculous would that be!? He said if no one else would protect this great and historic church of ours that he would have to do it himself. When he finally wound down, I asked him what he thought I should do. I am the Chair of the committee after all, I told him, and he just barked out, 'Nothing! Don't do anything!' Then he said, real snide-like, 'Just watch!' And then, off he went."

The rest of us sat in stunned silence and watched to see if Annabel was finished. She made no move to speak further.

Finally, Sid broke the silence and said, "All-righty then."

"Thank you, Annabel," I said. "Thank you for dealing with such an emotional situation. That must have been really hard for you."

She nodded, obviously scared to speak, for fear of unleashing tears.

"Let me see if I can clear part of this up," I continued. "Bob has recently expressed his dissatisfaction with me, regarding several issues. His concern over Jeremy being on the Finance Committee is one of those things. He made it quite clear that if his opinions on this and other matters were not acted upon, that he would bring his considerable power and influence to bear. That is why, in his mind, he feels that by now I should have done something about Jeremy. I am so sorry, Annabel, that he got to you before I had a chance to explain. I thought it would wait until our regular meeting."

Annabel looked a bit better.

"Okay, fine. So this started out bad. Let's get over it and decide what to do. What exactly is the deal about Jeremy?" Sid had a way of cutting through any extraneous feelings or facts.

"Okay," Annabel said, recovering her composure. "We have the basic facts. We know how Jeremy got on the committee. We know Jeremy. We know how Bob is and what Bob thinks and what he wants done. So, I would like each of you to take your turn to offer your concerns or opinions. Who's first?"

No one spoke.

"All right," Annabel continued, "Sid. What say you?"

"I won't pretend that I haven't been against this from the beginning. Church money is nothing to be trifled with and isn't a job for a kid. But, Jeremy is a smart boy and has been real dependable. But, he is still too quick to spend money for new programs and music and giveaways and such. But, he hasn't done anything wrong. So, I'm on the fence. But, push comes to shove, I will vote to take him off. Rule number one on handling money, I don't care if it's your family, a business, the government or the church, is that you better have more money coming in than going out. Bob puts in too much to mess with over one kid. He'll grow up and then he can do this. That's what I figure."

"Thank you, Sid," Annabel said. "Dosie, you're next."

"I will support Jeremy in any and all votes we might take. He has behaved in exemplary fashion and knows more about what is going on than most of us. He has my full support."

"Why, thank you for being so succinct and clear," Annabel said, and she seemed to mean it. "Janice, you've been scribbling away. You're the treasurer. What do you think?"

"As you know, as an employee, I have voice but no vote on matters before this body. Using my voice, I think it would be a travesty for our problems to land on Jeremy. He has done everything that has been asked of him and more. We need to settle whatever is coming down the road without allowing someone like Jeremy to get hurt. That's what I think."

Annabel said, "Thank you, Janice. We value your opinion. Now, I have had longer than the rest of you to reflect on this matter. It has been very difficult—in an out, up and down, yes and no. I have relied on past history to guide me. This church did not become the important institution it has been for over one hundred and fifty years based on wrong practices, I think we can all agree. On the one hand, we have never, to my knowledge, removed someone from a committee because someone else wanted them off. We have always followed strict voting procedures. On the other hand, we have never allowed one so young as Jeremy to have power equal to an adult, something that I have been uncomfortable with from the beginning. Perhaps we are facing this bitter pill because we strayed from tradition in the first place. East Fork First United Methodist Church is well known and respected in this community, and has long been the home of the most solid, productive and influential people in our entire region, those who can be supportive of such a church. Everyone knows that. There are other churches set up to better serve other kinds of folks. As prickly as he might be, Bob Williams has long carried a significant part of the East Fork UMC legacy on his shoulders, and his bank account. This is the Finance Committee. We must care about the well-being of all the people in our charge, certainly including Jeremy, but we have been specifically charged with minding the financial stability of the church. There are other committees that we can enlist to help Jeremy with any disappointment or hurt he might experience. I suggest that we respect Bob's wishes, and deal with Jeremy in as gentle a way as we can. He is young and strong, with many possibilities ahead of him. He'll be fine." Annabel looked around the table, seeking comment before moving on. She found none, and said, "Pastor, what do you have to say?"

"I will not be voting on this, at least not now."

"And, why is that? Your vote would seem crucial."

"Jeremy is properly on the committee. The *Book of Discipline* not only allows a youth, specifically meaning a teenager, to serve as a full member of the committee, but encourages it. Jeremy was properly nominated by the Leadership Development Committee and was elected by the entire church body at the yearly Charge Conference. He has committed no infraction to justify his removal and so he can only be removed by a vote of another Charge Conference, called and attended by our district superintendent. We would have to bring charges against Jeremy for the DS to schedule such a meeting, who, by the way, sent me a personal note congratulating me for successfully placing a *youth* on one of our major committees. I will not be voting, because no one will be voting. At least not now, and not this committee. Changes could happen at next year's Charge Conference, but certainly not until then. The United Methodist Church does not operate under duress. The one who will be okay and get over it, will have to be Bob."

"If that is true, and I do believe you pastor, you have never been wrong about this kind of thing, what am I supposed to do now?" Annabel was decidedly nervous.

"This one is easy enough," I said. "Annabel, Dosie, Sid, Janice, all questions on this matter, from Bob or anyone else, are to be referred to me. Period. This is not your fight."

Chapter 14

"I need to lay a foundation, for this to make sense," I said. Two days had passed, and Carl was every bit as patient as he had always been.

"Take all the time you need," he replied. "You know this story and I don't."

"I have always wanted to be successful. In fact, usually, I have been successful. I'm not as sure as I used to be about just what that means, but for now let's leave it at that. Even before I answered God's call, I always gave my best effort to whatever I was doing."

"Good," was all he said.

"So, when I became a pastor I was extremely motivated to be the best pastor ever, as silly as that sounds. So, I worked hard, tried to learn quickly and figure out what was going to work best and what would not. I know you are going to want to know what I mean by 'work best' but let's just stipulate that I used to think I knew and now I don't. Anyway, we go through all kinds of trainings, a lot of it geared toward measurable success. I want you to understand that the United Methodist denomination is a good thing, a wonderful thing, that I and millions of people love. But, we have been shrinking in the United States, every year for over forty-five years."

Carl was being his own inscrutable self, but at this he commented, "That's quite a streak."

"Yes. So, what I mean is, there has been a lot of attention paid to training the clergy to be effective—to build numbers, create consensus, draw new people and resolve conflict with the ones we already have. There's a desperation to it, really. And everyone wants to measure where we are. Pastors who can reverse the trend and add to the ranks are highly prized by the hierarchy. Pastors like—pardon me for saying it myself—me."

"That doesn't surprise me. You are very capable."

His praise struck me like a cattle prod. *Why do I need to be complimented so much?*

"Go on," he said.

"So, we do certain things. We create new programs, we use technology and social media, we contemporize the music and we even set SMART goals."

"Now that's a new one on me," Pastor Carl admitted. "What are smart goals?"

"It is an idea lifted straight out of the corporate world. SMART goals are Specific, Measurable, Achievable, Realistic and Timely."

"No kidding? Wow. You mean . . . ?" Pastor Carl looked puzzled. He seemed to catch himself elaborating, and stopped. "Go on," he said. "What kind of goals?"

"SMART goals are by nature tangible things, like new members, baptisms, people signed up for mission trips or Bible studies, financial goals. Stuff like that."

"All right, well, those can be good things. How does this affect what you do?"

"To be successful in this sort of an atmosphere, you have to do the things and use the skills that will get you the best result most of the time. Catchy music, powerful and entertaining sermons, advertising programs, improvements in services, all sorts of things. But, to get to your question about my wife, one of the things you absolutely need to be good at is conflict resolution. And, I am known as an expert."

"What makes you an expert?"

"Mostly a good track record. There are proven techniques. Stay calm when conflict starts. They call it the art of *being the non-anxious presence.* It helps to tone down the emotions when the leader stays cool. Listen. Listen some more. People relax when they get to have their say. As much as you can, treat everyone involved equally, don't take sides. Value all opinions. And then find a solution, especially if you can find a solution that nobody else even thought of. A collaboration is best, but often a compromise will do. That way everyone can feel like they won and nobody has to feel like they lost. It works."

"And your wife?"

"Okay, I think this will make sense now. Things were going along quite fine in the church. We had been here about two years. Jenn didn't find this group to be as warm or welcoming as our previous appointments, but she was as active as ever. She has always been a great asset to the ministry. Anyway, things were going pretty well. Attendance was up five percent and we took in ten or fifteen new members, things like that. I decided to improve communications and the sense of being a church family by using more technology. I set up a separate e-mail account and called it *Talk to the Pastor*. I encouraged the congregation to e-mail me with comments, concerns, complements, ideas, anything they would say to me if we were having a private conversation."

"Dare I ask how that went?" Pastor Carl asked with a sad smile.

"Sure, you can ask, but I'll bet you already know where we're heading. I announced this program in church at the Sunday morning services. By Sunday evening, I had a few e-mails, but I purposely waited another day to get a good cross-section. By Monday evening, the suspense was killing us, so Jenn and I sat down at the computer and took a look. We were actually kind of excited."

"And?" Pastor Carl asked.

I held out two sheets of paper. "We got this. I'm not sure why I printed it off and kept it, but here it is."

Pastor Carl sat down and started reading. I didn't have to look. I had long since memorized every last one of them. They read:

- *The pastor does a nice job of running the church. After the last pastor, I appreciate some organization.*
- *The pastor seems to be friendly enough, but his wife could stand to get her nose out of the air, as if she has anything to be proud of.*
- *The sermons go right over my head. I would appreciate language that regular people can understand.*
- *Perhaps the pastor's wife thinks that skirts that might have fit her once still do. It's indecent. Get some bigger clothes or lose some weight!"*
- *The status of our church in the community has taken a few hits over the years, and you seem to be bringing that back up. Good job.*
- *I was running the Sunday school for years before you two got here, and I will still be running it when you're gone. The pastor's comments are part of the deal, but the pastor's wife should just butt out.*
- *Your sermons make me feel like I am a bad person. There are a lot worse people around here than me. Why don't you try going after some of them?*
- *I am glad that our pastor is highly educated and well thought of, it enhances the reputation of our church.*
- *I wonder if the pastor's wife has ever repented or apologized for her ways as a young woman. I wonder if we should have someone who sets such an example teaching our children, it's not as if people don't know.*

Pastor Carl read the whole list slowly and methodically. He stared at the paper well after he had finished reading it. For the first time in my association with him, it appeared as if he simply did not know what to say. Using a trick that I had so recently learned from him, I said nothing and waited.

Finally, he said, "I'm sorry this happened. It must have been terribly upsetting for both you and your wife."

"To say the least. Without question, reading this right alongside Jenn was the most gut-wrenching and hurtful thing that has happened in my entire career."

"I would think so," Pastor Carl replied, shaking his head sadly. "People seem to be so clueless as to the destruction that comes with words. How did your wife take it?"

"Jenn is usually strong, upbeat and endlessly resilient, but this one almost tore her apart. She cried for hours. When the crying stopped, she got quiet. When the quiet stopped, she got mad. It went on for days."

"What did you do?"

"I listened. I told her over and over again how much I love her and how valuable she is to me. Then, I listened some more."

"What did you hear?"

"What did I hear? Well, hurt and anguish, I guess. She was so upset. So was I, of course. A lot of times women want mostly to be listened to, instead of looking for solutions to problems, so I concentrated on listening a lot."

"Uh-huh," was Pastor Carl's only response.

"I empathized and sympathized and did everything I could, but there was no way to un-ring the bell once she had read the e-mails."

I was getting defensive.

"I understand," Carl said. "What did you do at the church, about the situation?"

"Well, I took the e-mail site down right away, I'll tell you that. And I preached a straight-talk sermon on gossip and the danger of a loose tongue. People knew full well that I was not happy."

"And?"

"And what!?!" I nearly shouted.

"And, how did your wife come to the point of attending another church?"

"I tried to smooth over the rough edges. I pointed out all the supporters she had in the church. The messages were from just a small group. We talked about perseverance and how Christians can expect some persecution. I built her up in all the ways I could think of. But, in the end, the strain on her was too much. She said that she simply could not keep walking back into that place where people thought such things about her. When it became obvious there was not going to be a smooth solution any time soon, we agreed that putting some distance between Jenn and the problem might be best for all concerned. So, that's what we did."

"I understand . . . the best for all concerned."

As the words *best for all concerned* came out of his mouth, Carl's voice dropped and his face went blank—almost slack. His affect struck me for what it was—polite disdain.

I ran.

Later, as I pulled into the driveway, I noticed that, while I had long been comfortable referring to the parsonage as *my house*, it was beginning to feel like it belonged to someone else. Anyway, I pulled into the driveway after driving around aimlessly for over an hour. I had worked my way from *hurt* to *anger* and back down to *hurt* again. Now, I was rapidly progressing to feeling foolish. When Pastor Carl had said, 'I understand . . . the best for all concerned,' I went nuts. I felt a rush of condemnation and frustration and defensiveness and an overwhelming sense of something I couldn't face. At first I thought it was anger and half of my brain formulated excuses in a logical frenzy, while the other half prepared angry, scathing remarks to throw back at Carl for daring to question me. Me, who knows ten times what ole Carl the Rustic Wiseman will ever know, and has the diplomas to prove it. But while I was deciding which cutting blow to deal the man first, I was interrupted by my own blurred vision and that inescapable feeling of eyes pooling with hot moisture. The harder I clenched my teeth the more the quivering in my lower jaw spread to the rest of my face. Panicked, I let out some horrible retching noise. I don't even know if I was trying to say something or not. I ran from the little church, fumbled my way into my car and graveled my way out of there.

The first few miles were spent trying to gain control. My only response to my own crying has always been to make it stop, right away, no excuses. So, I stopped crying. Then I did what I do when upset strikes; I replayed it in my mind, over and over again. On the fifth time through—about thirty miles out—I was able to admit that Carl hadn't contributed much to what I was feeling. I doubt he even knew what happened. Then again, he probably did. Anyway, the whole thing just blew up from a tiny spark. Obviously, a lot of built up emotion had come bubbling out. *More like projectile vomited-out,* I thought, finally allowing a self-deprecating chuckle. Thirty-five miles into the country, I turned around and headed back. I figured I would get myself under control by the time I got home. I thought about Carl. How was I ever going to face the guy again? But, as I pictured him working away—probably taking a break and figuring it was safe to eat both of the evening's sandwiches—I was strangely confident that Carl would handle the whole thing just fine. I would go back to Carl. I had to. The next time we were together, he would probably work awhile and then pause and say, "As I was saying, 'I understand . . . the best for all concerned.'" Yeah, I'd go back. There was stuff inside of me that had to get worked out. I also knew that until I did, this particular quandary could not be shared with Jenn, until it wasn't a quandary anymore.

Driving around, I had promised myself that I would lay my upset to rest by the time I got home. Now, sitting in the driveway, I was at anything but rest. However, my raging emotions had coalesced into a particular feeling. I could not label it. I did recognize it, though. I tried not to. I was having the feeling that a man gets when he realizes that all the other dads are tougher than he is, or richer, or stronger, or whatever. Or, when he gets thrown into the middle of a dangerous situation, and only hides and wets himself. Or when he is in a locker room for the first time in a long time and, looking around, doesn't want to let go of the towel around his waist. Or when a man realizes that he can no longer do what he used to do. Or when a husband overhears his wife reminiscing with a girlfriend about some guy they used to know and she seems a little too excited. It is a feeling that only takes a few seconds to explain to another man, and no amount of explanation can help a woman to completely understand. It is part fear of inadequacy, part fear of weakness, part fear of being found incompetent, lacking, incapable, irrelevant, ordinary . . . less than ordinary. In any case, men know it as *it*—whatever it is that makes a man satisfied that he is, indeed, a man. Men know that either you've got *it,* or you don't. I have talked this through with men, during counseling and such. I have heard some of their examples and helped them to recognize what was going on, and how to fix it or get past it or work it through.

Still, it's terrible when it happens to you. I now understood that the same feeling comes when your wife, whom you love dearly and claim you would die for, needs a rescuer and a hero and a knight in shining armor, and turning to you in love and need and hope, finds instead an *expert mediator.* And that your wife knows that when help is needed and love is on the line, she can always count on you for . . . *excellent mediation.*

I was having a hell of a hard time facing the fact that my *it* was gone.

"Honey, I'm home!" I knew I looked like the big crying baby I was, but I had to go in the house. Jenn was in the living room, on the couch, reading a book. She had her feet curled up under her bottom, her knees sideways in front of her. I could never understand how she could sit comfortably that way, but I had always loved the way it looked. She seemed so *centered*, so at home, so *present*.

"Hi Honey, I'm glad you're home." Then she looked up at me. "Oh my, you look like something's caved in on you."

"Yeah, but I'm starting to get used to it."

"Do you need to talk?" She marked her book and closed it, setting it carefully on the cushion next to her. *A barrier?* Her feet came out from under her and landed squarely on the floor, ankles close together. She started to cross her arms but thought better of it and folded her hands neatly into her lap. She kept her face soft, but without notable expression. Her voice was gentle and slow and *polite*.

She said, "I'm always ready to listen, my love. How can I help?"

I could tell that she absolutely meant what she said. She loved me. She was ready to listen. She wanted to help. She was entirely sincere. She was not lying. She was not being sarcastic. But, for the first time in our entire marriage, through all the easy times and the hard, she had to *try*.

"Oh, I was going over some of the church problems, the Williams stuff and all that, trying to get a handle on it . . ."

"Yes," Jenn replied.

"Yeah, and I guess I got more upset about some of it than I intended to. Sorry, I don't mean to be so pessimistic lately."

"You are not being pessimistic. You are never pessimistic. What you are is down. Battered and hurt and down. It's a different thing." Her voice had grown just a tiny bit sharp, as did her face.

"Yes. You're right. Of course. I am just having a hard time shaking it."

Jenn's face immediately softened again, and her eyes connected with mine in a way she had been avoiding. Her nurturing self was poking through. She was used to my default position of pushing back, and I obviously had no pushback left in the tank.

"Really, Hon," she said, "sit down. Talk."

I sat. "Didn't Lisa start a new job this week, with that new dentist in Fowlerville?"

"What an odd thing to bring up."

"Did she? . . . start the new job?"

"Well, yes, she did."

"Tell me about that."

Jenn looked at me for a long moment, and then decided.

"Well, she's going to be in charge of six other hygienists. It's a big step up in pay."

"Wonderful. How is she feeling about it?"

"She's excited. A little worried about the drive in the winter. It's almost twenty miles where she was only driving three."

"She's sensible and tough. She'll handle that."

Jenn gave a tiny smile. "That's exactly what I told her."

"What about the work? She's always been responsible for just her own work. This will be different."

"Yeah, but she seems to be looking forward to the challenge. And, she will still be working on patients most of the time. I think she'll be great."

"Of course she'll be great. You two have always been great."

Jenn simply sat and looked at me. She struck me as like a confused cat.

I stood and moved to her, and gave her a kiss on her beautiful lips. She didn't resist, so I gave it just a little extra oomph.

Then I said, "Tell Lisa I love her, and set something up so we can see her pretty soon. It's been too long."

"All right. I will."

"If you don't mind," I went on, "I'm going to hit the hay. It hasn't been a good day and I have to get on top of some things."

"Get on top of some things?"

"Yes. I need to get on top of some things."

Normally, Jenn would never let me get away with opening up a huge can of worms and then slamming it back shut again. But, things were anything but normal. I don't know if she went along to give me some space, or to hold on to some for herself. Probably both.

She said, "Of course, Honey, I hope you feel stronger in the morning."

"I hope so, too. Sometimes we live on hope. Goodnight, my love."

As I turned to move toward the bedroom, she stopped me, saying, "You know that I love you, don't you?"

"Yes, I absolutely do," I said, and went to bed.

Chapter 16

I struggled to make it across the parking lot from my car to the office door. It had been a restless night. Despite successfully negotiating my way out of a long, draining conversation with Jenn, I had still found it impossible to shut off my brain. I ruminated continually until well after 3:00 in the morning, playing all the disturbing conversations and realizations through my head, which only served to recreate the same awful feelings. Still, no matter how physically exhausted, emotionally and spiritually drained I was, I had to report for office hours. Otherwise, I would have a real rebellion on my hands.

For the first time in a long while I was tempted to park right next to the door. When I had first arrived as pastor of East Fork First United Methodist Church, the very best spot was boldly labeled "Reserved for the Pastor Only." Even the church secretary had a spot further from the door than mine. One of my first unofficial actions was to remove the sign and store it behind the pole barn. I made a point of parking on the far side of the lot. As a model of the *servant leader* that our denomination likes to talk about so much, it seemed to me inappropriate to take a choice spot.

Actually, I had learned that many years ago from my father. Mom and Dad operated a supermarket, and Dad would throw a fit if any employee, ever, took a good parking place. At store meetings he would explain a bit gruffly, 'I pay you to be here. Customers only come if we convince them that we are their favorite place to shop. Parking near the doors is a fireable offense.'

I saw him do it, too. Fire someone, I mean. In fact, in later years, I had done it myself. Anyway, I had the spot relabeled "First Time Visitors Only." I am filled with humility. Of course, I especially like it when people notice how marvelous my humility is. I suppose that ruins the whole thing.

I made it to the door with growing trepidation. There were two cars in the lot that were not usually present first thing in the morning. And one of them belonged to Bob Williams.

Janice was pretending to work at the mail boxes near the door. As soon as I cracked the door open she whispered, "Bob is here and he is loaded for bear. He has demanded that Daisy Watkins be here to schedule what he's calling an 'official' meeting. Pastor, so you know, Daisy is scared to death and wants nothing to do with this."

Daisy was the Chair of the Staff Parish Relations Committee. In the United Methodist Church, this is a kind of personnel committee, charged with hiring, training, encouraging and, when necessary, the disciplining of every person on the local church payroll. Oddly, this includes the pastor, who is not hired by the SPRC and cannot be fired by the SPRC. Still, any attempts to deal with performance issues of a pastor will at least begin with this committee. Daisy was a sweet woman who mostly preferred to avoid conflict altogether. However, when Bob Williams demands a meeting, no one at East Fork UMC is going to deny him.

"It's all right, Janice. I've got this." I entered my office where Bob and Daisy were already seated. She jumped up immediately and babbled her *good mornings* and *how are yous*. Bob remained seated and did his best to lock eyes with me. It appeared that lack of respect would be one weapon of the day.

"Good morning, Daisy," I said. "Good morning, Bob. What brings you two in so early?"

"Morning, Pastor," Bob replied through a clenched jaw. "I think it's time we stop avoiding things and get on with what needs to happen. I believe you have had enough time to respond to my concerns. More time than I would ever give to a member of my team."

"Well," I replied, giving him the eye contact he sought, "That is an entirely different situation than the one we have here, isn't it, Bob?"

Daisy flinched. I heard a sharp intake of breath from Janice's side of the door.

Bob considered for a moment, and then continued, "Be that as it may, it is time to clear things up. There are a lot of people who are growing more and more concerned about your performance as the pastor of our beloved East Fork First United Methodist Church. As such, they want me to . . ."

"Excuse me, Bob," I interrupted, softly, "who are they?"

"What?"

"Who are *they*?" I asked again, so quietly that Bob had to lean closer to hear.

"Who are who?"

"You said that a lot of people who are growing more and more concerned about my performance. Who are *they*?"

"People. What does it matter? People who are talking."

"I would like some names, please. If I am going to be accused, it seems it would be fair for me to know by whom."

Daisy's eyes were bugged nearly out of her head.

Bob glared. "I think that is beside the point of this meeting," he said, clipping off each word one at a time. "Can we get on with this?"

"Sure. Go ahead, Bob. But I'm still going to want those names."

"I am trying to be fair and proper," Bob continued, the red creeping from beneath his collar and threatening his cheeks. "I would think you would appreciate that."

"Oh, I do, Bob."

Bob was clearly getting ruffled, but was honestly trying not to display his anger. I could have been more cooperative, but was no longer willing.

"I have asked Daisy here to call an emergency meeting of the, what is it? The pastor/staff personnel committee?"

"The Staff Parish Relations Committee," Daisy squeaked out.

"Okay. Good. Thank you, Daisy," Bob said. "Anyway, I understand that's the committee that is supposed to deal with this. I have asked for a meeting tonight, so I can make my concerns clear."

"Sorry, Bob. That can't happen."

"And why not? I suppose you have something more important on your agenda?"

"Yes. That's right. I do."

"That is not acceptable!" The upper rim of Bob's right cheek, the only part of his lower face that was not yet engulfed in red, twitched.

"Sure it is Bob. I am to be given appropriate notice of any meetings, and less than a day is not appropriate. I will not attend."

"Then we'll meet without you. It would seem that you would want to be present to defend yourself, but then I guess you're not being there will just make the job easier."

"No, it won't, Bob. There isn't going to be an SPRC meeting, at least not tonight."

"And why is that!" Bob shouted.

"The SPRC committee cannot hold a meeting without me, unless they have arranged ahead of time for the district superintendent to be present instead. Daisy," I said calmly, smiling at the quivering lady, "has the DS been asked to have a meeting about this?"

"No," she said, with a hint of a grin.

"Well, there you are," I said, "No meeting."

"All this does is cause unnecessary delay! We need to have a meeting so I can get this thing settled!"

"Well, that's another thing, Bob. If and when there is a meeting of the SPRC, you will not be there."

"What do you mean I won't be there? It is my meeting!"

"No, Bob, it is not your meeting. If there is a meeting, it belongs to the church, not you. And the SPRC meetings are the only meetings we have that are closed. There are private and sometimes delicate personnel matters to attend to, so all parties are protected by keeping the meetings closed. Sorry."

"This is insubordination! I promise you, before this is over, I will fire you and this church will move on just fine without you!"

"Bob, I hate to be such a contrarian, I really do. But it is only fair to tell you that no one in this church can fire me. How about that? The only people who can move me, or fire me come from the Lower Michigan Annual Conference."

Bob looked about to pop a blood vessel, but I kept talking.

"The bishop is the only one who can move me. The Board of Ordained Ministry does the disciplinary stuff—forty-one people on that one."

"This can't be right!" Bob was nearly screaming now. "This is outrageous! If you think that you are going to hide forever behind a bunch of red tape, then you don't know Bob Williams very well."

"I am not looking to hide, Bob. It's just that there is a right way to do things, and this is not it."

"I'll figure this out, you can count on that!" Bob yelled and leapt to his feet.

"Oh, I'm sure you will," I replied. "Let me help you out. Janice," I said, not too loudly, "would you please bring a copy of the most recent *United Methodist Book of Discipline* in here for Mr. Williams? I really am not trying to confuse things, Bob. All the appropriate procedures for charging a pastor with incompetence are in the book. Study up, and when you're really ready, we'll get this thing started."

Within a few seconds Janice opened the door and walked in carrying a very thick book. Bob started to push past her and, thinking better of it, turned around and snatched the book from her hands and then stormed out of the building. Daisy sat right where she had been the whole time, visibly shaking.

"Daisy," I said, "remember when we talked you into taking this position because we told you it isn't too hard and everybody pretty much gets along?"

She nodded.

"I'm sorry, Daisy. I really am. Thank you for putting up with all this."

I bent down and kissed her on the cheek. I don't usually do that kind of thing, but I did it anyway.

Daisy stood up and straightened her dress. "That guy's a real wiener," she said. "Goodbye, Pastor. Goodbye, Janice. Please let me know what's next. I don't know what I'm supposed to do, but I will show up."

When Daisy was out of earshot, Janice said, "I must say I didn't see that coming. I don't think he's used to having his ear's boxed like that, and with witnesses, to boot."

"It's coming to a head, Janice. All I did was buy some time and *poke the bear*. The gloves are off now."

Chapter 17

The next evening I walked into Carl's little church at about 5:45. Carl was already hard at work, trimming around the base of the now-gleaming floor. The sanctuary was really shaping up. I imagined that someone who had seen only the *before* and the *after* would be pleasantly shocked at the difference.

"Evening Carl. Kind of stunning, walking into this place these days. Looking great."

"It is, isn't it," Carl replied, pausing to look around. "It's getting exciting, how quickly it is progressing."

"Well, there's plenty to do yet on the downstairs and outside," I chattered out. I realized that when he said, 'how quickly it is progressing,' I heard, *our time is almost over.*

He ignored my jitteriness and went back to work. I joined in. What Carl had said earlier was true, no matter how upset or tense I started out, when we settled into working the wood, slowly bringing sacred space back to life, a sense of calm and connectedness always came over me, and before too long, I would find myself praying.

After a few minutes I said, "You know, it just occurred to me that I have never heard the name of this place. What are you planning to call it?"

"Don't know," he replied.

"Surely you've thought about it. Naming is one of the best things."

"Oh, sure, I've thought about it. But, I haven't been told the name yet." He smiled.

I smiled.

After another twenty minutes of silence, I couldn't stand it anymore, so I said, "About the way things ended last time…"

"You did leave a might quicker than usual," he said.

"Yeah . . . kinda hit a nerve, I guess."

"That happens. So, what have you made of it since?"

"Well, I think that particular conversation set off a chain reaction of emotional responses I have been trying to avoid."

"Yeah, we hate those darn feelings sometimes, don't we," Carl said.

"Yes, and I didn't really think I was like that. I like to see myself as a real *renaissance man*, you know? A perfect blend of intellect and spirituality and common sense, fully self-aware and highly functional. I learned that the truth of it doesn't quite fit the model."

"How so, specifically?"

"After going back and forth between self-flagellation and defensiveness, I realized that I have been anything but self-aware. I have above average abilities in many areas that a pastor needs, even excellent here and there, but along the way I lost a big chunk of who I really am. Worse yet, I think I lost a big chunk of what God wants me to be."

"Tell me about that."

"I am not talking about the expectations that God has for all Christian men. I haven't even taken a real hard look at that lately, and maybe I'd better not right now. I'm not sure how much more disappointment I can take. Anyway, I am talking about the job that God has given to me in particular. To be clergy in Christ's Church."

"I get it. Tell me what you discovered."

"Just like you knew I would, I spent a lot of time meditating on the differences between the kind of pastor that I am and the kind of pastor God called me to be. And, being as precise and academic as I surely am, I gave myself a report card."

"That's a brave thing to do, and very difficult to do accurately. We rarely see in ourselves what other people see, and almost never what God sees."

"I thought I knew that, but this has made me realize I really didn't."

"Care to share your grades?"

"Yes. I thought I would dread this so much I would probably just throw it away, but I find I really want to share this and get it out in the open."

"Have you shown anyone? Your wife?"

"No, just God. I think this will affect Jenn so much that I want to be as sure as I can I am not going down a wrong path."

"Good thinking. Okay, let's see it."

I handed Carl a twice-folded sheet of paper from my back pocket and held my breath. It read:

God's Expectations of Me as Pastor

Present Grade
- Spreader of the Good News............*Good*
- Teacher of the Word......................*Excellent*
- Caretaker of the people.................*Excellent*
- Reliever of suffering.....................*Good*
- God's bold, prophetic voice........***Utter Failure***

I tried to look calm and cool, but my insides were really jumping. I have never wanted anyone to know when I was angry or hateful or disappointed. I especially never wanted to expose my fears. And I was terrified to admit I lacked the ability to handle anything and everything. I must always be the best and the smartest and the most accomplished. I must *be in control!* I must *succeed!* And, the one I had never admitted even to myself, everybody must *like me!*

As always, Carl took his time. He took his time and, it seemed to me, the time of three or four other people as well.

Finally, he looked away from the paper, folded it twice on the lines, and handed it back to me. All he said was, "Bingo."

"I take it you agree with my self assessment?" I asked.

"Yes, I do. If anything you have not credited yourself high enough on *Spreading the Good News* and *Relieving Suffering*. From what I have learned, I would say that you are quite gifted to be an effective clergy-person, both preacher and pastor. Exceptional, really."

"But?" I asked.

"But nothing, except what you already know. Among other things, but, I would venture, outweighing all the other things, God has called you to be a prophet. This is no minor matter. Only a very small percentage of those called to a life of full-time, professional ministry are called mainly as prophets. Many have their prophetic moments, but the one who can rightly be called Prophet is rare. And you are one of the few."

"Am I? Am I really?" I asked, a strange mix of anger and self-doubt flooding my voice.

"That you are called and chosen is clear to me, and I am not wrong about this."

"How can you be so sure?" I asked.

"Just trust my judgment on this. You are not the only one equipped with gifts from God. One of mine is discernment. It is not as flashy as prophecy, but quite helpful nonetheless."

"Can one be a prophet, and still be an utter failure at being God's bold, prophetic voice?" I whispered, the full magnitude of the question finally hitting my conscious mind.

"That would seem to be the question of the day, wouldn't it," Carl responded gently.

"What's your take, Carl? And please don't answer with a question or an assignment. I really want to know."

"Fair enough. Suppose a twenty-three-year-old man shows up at the Detroit Tigers' spring training, seemingly out of nowhere. Nobody has ever heard of him. The manager and the coaches let him on the field and it is immediately obvious that he can run faster than all the Tiger players. He can throw farther and more accurately than anyone they have ever seen. He catches every fly ball hit anywhere near him. They let him hit in batting practice and every swing is a scorching line drive or a home run deep over the fence. They have never seen anything like it. All they can think about is getting him signed to a contract. Is this man a major league baseball player?"

"No. He may be good enough to play in the major leagues, but so far he is not."

"Okay. Good. Say they sign him to a major league contract. Then, he practices with the team at spring training. Then he plays in preseason games. Then they put him in the lineup on opening day of the regular season. Then he has his first major league at bat, in a real game. Exactly when did this man become a major league baseball player?"

"I don't know if anybody has ever written a technical answer to such a question."

"There you go. That is one critical point, right there. Go on."

"But, in my opinion, he was not a true major league player until he had that first at bat. Until then, something could have gone wrong to stop him from ever playing."

"Good answer. Now, let's be clear, I have no idea what the right answer is. There is no clear definition. But, I tend to agree with you."

"Okay, and your thoughts, like I asked?"

"Right. In my opinion, you have been called to be God's Prophet, and you are God's Prophet. You are in the game. You have been lavishly equipped and you have been given a pulpit and a congregation and a forum. And, I know that you have at times preached and pronounced the genuine Word of God. Am I right?"

"I'm not used to saying such a thing about myself, but yes, I have."

A Dragon in the Church 103

"Good. I agree. Now, play the game a little more. What is the Tigers' management expecting from the new player?"

"They will expect him to hit better than most players, a good batting average, maybe over three hundred. And, some home runs, thirty or more. Drive in runs, play good defense. Maybe, as time goes by, they'll hope he is named an All-Star. And, of course, they hope he will help them win a lot more games."

"Exactly. Because, they hope he will live up to his . . ." Carl said.

The phrase hung in the air. I let it hang. So did Carl. I caved first. Carl was still the undisputed champion of waiting.

"Potential. They hope he will live up to his potential."

"Yes. And live up to his gifts, and his abilities, and his promises."

"Promises?"

"Yes. Promises. Vows. Tell me, when you acknowledged God's call upon you to be his Prophet, what kind of prophet did you promise him you would be?"

"You already know. Bold. I promised God that I would turn my life over to him and that anything he asked me to do I would do. I promised God—not the United Methodist Church, but God—that I would go wherever he called me to go and say whatever he wanted me to say. I promised God that I would not count the cost or worry about how things would turn out for me, but instead would be God's voice, God's mouthpiece, maybe even God's warrior in the world. That is the promise that I made, okay! And we have already established at great length and much pain that I have been anything but the 'bold, prophetic voice' that I promised to be. I have turned into—honest to God I am not sure when or how it happened—I have turned into a . . . professional. That's what I am, a professional! I let myself get swallowed up *in* the system and *by* the system. I learned to please the powerbrokers. I solve problems. I settle conflicts. I whitewash the stupid things we do, so that I can report each year that we are still successfully doing stupid things. I spout fancy theories and explain how the positions of the church are pleasing to God, whether it's true or not. I coddle lazy Christians, self-centered people who see the main duty of the church to be the continuation of their own personal comfort and happiness. I suffer petty nonsense and smooth it over, so that people will keep coming to church and keep filling the offering plate. And every year someone tells me that I have done a fine job and all I need to do is 'keep it up.' And I bought into it. I gave my life, my very self, not to God as I had promised, but to an illusion of what the church wants to be, but is not."

I felt my voice rise and heat flow into my head. "And on top of all that, I let my delusion get all over my wife. I love Jenn so much and I cut her out and left her in the cold! I sacrificed her to my quest to be the ultimate professional."

I stepped closer to Carl and got my face way too close to his. "I gave away the very things that make a man a man . . . a Godly man . . . even a true man of God. So how is that, Pastor Carl?" I swear I wouldn't do it, but I felt my fingers clench into fists. "A complete enough answer for you? Or did I exceed some word limit?"

I found my breath coming hard. Carl backed up not one inch. He leaned in even closer to me, his shiny forehead level with my eyes.

He smiled and whispered, "No. No, that was real good. Just fine."

"Just fine! What the heck does that mean, just fine?"

"It means we're getting close to where you need to be."

"*We* are getting close?" I replied through a heavy layer of sarcasm.

"Well, mostly you, but I am your friend, so that counts for something."

I felt the starch come out of my spine, my hands went limp and I backed away. Anger left me, replaced by calm. It was peace at a time when peace made no human sense at all. And yet, peace it was. "Yes, my friend, that does indeed count for something. In case I get so wrapped up in myself as to forget to say it later, I am your friend, as well."

"I am grateful that God put us together," Carl replied. "And, the next time we meet, I believe that this chapter of our friendship will be completed."

"What do you mean?" I had a sudden fear that I was about to be dumped!

"Oh, there will be a new chapter, I am quite sure. But this process of getting you back to understanding God's claim on you is almost finished. Once you've got it, there is no time to beat a dead horse. It will be time to ride the live one."

I stared at Carl for several seconds, battling to keep a straight face, but I lost.

As I burst into laughter, Carl giggled and asked, "A little too far with the whole dead horse/live horse thing?"

"You think?!" I guffawed.

"Yeah, it sounded way more impressive in my head."

"I appreciate the effort, and the point. What now?"

"Only one thing, really. Next time, all I need you to do is tell me what you're afraid of."

Chapter 18

When I got home, I small-talked my way past Jenn. She was biding her time, hoping, I'm sure, that whatever was coming would be an improvement on the way things had been. But, my wonderful wife, always more devout, more trusting in God and more intuitive than I would ever be, didn't allow her curiosity or her anxiety to overrule her wisdom. She seemed to know that time was needed for whatever was cooking, and she was strong enough to allow it. I loved her all the more, and had to work hard to stifle my immediate desire to make everything up to her, at least until I figured out what that was going to look like.

I got to my office the next day, fully expecting the pressure in the cooker to be rising. I was right. As I sat at my desk, Janice walked in and set a hot cup of coffee on my desk. There was also a small *Happy Birthday* paper plate, with a gigantic, homemade chocolate-chip cookie.

"Is it my birthday?" I asked, trying to appear cheery and unaffected.

"No, those were the only small plates left in the pantry. I just thought you might enjoy fresh coffee and a cookie, before I ruin your day."

"Pull up a chair," I said. "Let's share coffee and a cookie."

She retrieved her own refreshments from her desk and sat down.

"Let's pray," I said.

Janice raised an eyebrow at me, as I am rarely so formal in the office.

"O Holy God," I said, "Thank you for coffee, cookies and friendship. Amen."

A Dragon in the Church

"That's it?" she asked. "I was expecting something momentous."

"Nope. Just for peace enough to enjoy a cookie."

We ate.

We sipped.

We ate.

Janice could no longer take the silence. "Damn fine cookie," she said.

Coffee came out of my nose. After I got cleaned up and recovered from the best laugh I had had in a long time, I looked at Janice and said, "This is not on you. Just tell me what is going on."

"No offense, Pastor, but this is on me if I choose it to be."

"Yes Ma'am."

"Bob is on a mission. You 'poked the bear,' just like you said. He is demanding meetings with just about every committee and powerful person in the church. He's on the agendas of the Trustees Committee, the Music Committee and the Church Council. The terms 'district superintendent' and 'bishop' are being thrown around a lot. He tried to get on the docket with the Worship Committee, until someone told him that you have total say-so over worship. He scrapped that, and said he would have to 'look it up in the book.' I don't know if it was such a good idea to give him a *Book of Discipline*. He's probably got lawyers going through it. Anyway, the Chairs of those committees are flying around asking everybody and his sister what's going on. 'Why is Bob Williams on the warpath?' Everyone is talking about 'trouble in the church,' or 'trouble with the pastor.' There is no more keeping a lid on this."

"No, but that's all right."

"All right! How is this all right?"

"Janice, often times things don't change until they've been stirred up first. If God wants change, then this may be the necessary pot-stirring."

"Well, you can go ahead and be extra happy, then, because the stirring is well underway. I'm not so sure that I can relish what is about to happen."

"Don't misunderstand me, I don't relish it either. But, what follows chaos is either what God wants, or it is not. I don't think that Bob is concerned with what God wants. So, he must be stopped from dictating what the church does next."

"From what I saw the last time you and Bob were together, I think maybe he is in for the surprise of his life. Pastor, I think you can take him!" Janice eyes glowed fiercely, as she rose to the challenge.

I felt my own blood begin to run hot—personal power being concentrated to meet Bob's challenge. But as I started to offer some brave words, a knot caught in my throat. Something was wrong.

"I have to make a couple of calls," I lied. "Let's get back together in twenty minutes."

"Sure . . . okay," Janice said a bit quizzically. "I'll be back in twenty."

She closed my door. I pushed a few buttons to make the phone beep, picked up the receiver to get a line, and hung up. Then, I prayed.

Fifteen minutes later, I told Janice, "I have to prepare some things. It might take all day. Let's you and I meet here at 9:00 a.m. tomorrow to formulate a response. Will that work?"

"Yes sir. See you at 9:00 sharp."

I set out on a long drive, maybe to find a quiet outdoor spot to pray and meditate. Something that I did not exactly know or understand was about to rapidly unfold. And, whatever it was, I felt certain that it had to happen in a very particular order that I had not yet figured out. Maybe Carl could help me unravel the next mystery. Oh yeah, Carl. He would be waiting to hear an answer to *what am I afraid of?*

Later, I told Carl, "I spent the afternoon laying low. A full-blown, get-rid-of-the-pastor movement is underway, and I have to decide how I am going to respond. I can't avoid it. As I see it, I have three basic choices of how to address this . . ."

"Oh, I doubt that," Carl interrupted quietly. "There is generally only one correct choice. The others are wrong options, in place mostly as distractions."

"Yeah, that's a nice theory, but this is very complicated. There are a great number of factors involved and several different perspectives. To move too quickly without good information would be a mistake. I don't like mistakes."

"No, you don't. So, how is the no-mistakes approach working for you, lately?"

"Lately? Not so good. But, that's because I have made some mistakes, assuming things that were not accurate. So I think if I double up on gleaning good information before . . ."

"Tell you what," Carl interrupted again, only not so quietly this time. "Let's proceed with our original plan, not because I don't want to address this topic, but because this will address it. Okay?"

I must have looked perturbed at being knocked off my rant, because Carl added, "Can you just trust me one more time?"

I counted to ten. I counted to ten again, and then replied, "Sure. Okay. Go ahead."

"All right, then just tell me, what are you afraid of?"

"This was hard. I'm not sure what you want me to say. I have fears, of course. I am afraid that people I love might not be saved, you know. I always say that I don't judge who is saved and who is not, but still, there are people I love who deny God. That scares me."

Carl continued to be Carl, patiently waiting for me to form my thoughts and construct sentences, being no help whatsoever.

"I'm afraid that horrible things will happen to Jenn, or Lisa, or my mom, or my sister. Myself, too, but them first. It scares me to think of them suffering. I'm afraid that I might wrongly teach God's Word and lead someone astray. I am afraid that I might be a disappointment to God. And, I am afraid that I will be a disappointment to Jenn. I'm not sure what else to say. . . . bats. Bats freak me out, especially if they're trapped in the house. They get all confused and go straight for your neck."

"Okay, thank you for trying so hard, but let's narrow it down to the point at hand. What are you afraid of that stops you from being the bold, prophetic voice of God that you know you are intended to be?"

"I don't know what you mean! What are you looking for?"

"Yes, you do. When you have the inclination to be bold, but you do the careful thing instead, what are you afraid of?"

"I just want to get it right. I want to be a really good pastor. What's wrong with that? If I screw up, people will leave the church. Money will dry up. Services will have to be cut."

"Now you're getting there. Keep going."

"The United Methodist Church put me here to do a job. God called me, but the church affirmed my call and educated me and ordained me and gave me a church to serve, and a lot of rules to follow. If I don't do it a certain way, it all falls apart."

"What does it mean to fall apart?"

"Angry people. Lost membership. Lost attendance. Bad year-end reports. Warnings. Blame. If it gets bad enough, I probably get moved—to a worse appointment, not a better one."

"Warnings? Blame?"

"Yeah. Bad reports. Criticism. Complaints. Meetings with the district superintendent, maybe the bishop. Loss of credibility. Whatever."

"Failure!" Carl shouted, waving his arms in the air. I'd never seen him wave his arms.

"Yes, failure. I don't want to fail. How is that bad?"

"Because if you fail, people won't . . . what?"

"I don't unders . . ."

A Dragon in the Church 111

"Because if you fail, people won't . . ."

"They won't respect me! They won't say I am good and smart and better than the rest. Okay!? They won't like me! Does that make you happy?"

"Yes. That makes me happy. Very happy."

"What! I was being sarcastic. I'm about ready to have a stroke and you're happy? Why the heck are you happy?"

"Because my job, this particular job, is nearly finished. And, quite successfully."

I sat with a thump and caught my breath and shook my head. "Well, Most High Reverend Master Carl, maybe you could let me in on your insight. Because, I am at a loss."

"God has blessed you richly. He has given you as many tools to do effective ministry as I have seen in any one person, man or woman. So much so that you have been called to more. To be a Prophet of God. Is that somehow lost on you?"

"No," I whispered, "it is not. I knew it once."

"Exactly. You knew it once. In fact, you know it now and have all along. That's why you have become so miserable. A part of you has been very aware that things are not as they could be or as they should be. And that is why I am so happy."

"In short words, please."

"Because now not just a part, but all of you, knows what's wrong. Your conscious and your unconscious are finally back together. Now you won't be able to live with yourself until you do it right. I know you. I know you better than you realize. You are now officially stuck on the right path."

"Then how come I feel so limp and unfocused?"

"Focus is but a target away, my good friend. Would you like to recognize your target?"

"Is it too late to say *no*?"

Carl laughed from deep in his belly.

"Yes. It is much too late to say *no*."

"Well," I said, "go ahead on, then."

"It is simple, really, now that you are ready. You have been called to be a man of God. Most men, but especially those called to the greater tasks, have something deep inside that craves the challenge, the quest, the impossible dream. You have felt this in your lifetime, right?"

"Yes. Actually, I have. Sometimes it is even hard to control, when I am about to do the wrong thing in the heat of the moment."

"That is the secret. It is not to be controlled. It is not to be choked back or minimized, that has been your great mistake. It is to be channeled and focused and directed, but never controlled. This is the curse of modern man."

"Modern man?"

"Yes. Polite society, whitewashed and systematized and full of well-intended rules, has rejected the idea of the mighty man of God, or mighty woman of God, I might add. God has not asked you to be a highly professional, polished administrator and motivational speaker. God has asked you to be his Prophet."

"But, I live in this modern, post-modern world. Part of me yearns for an earlier, simpler time. I want to set out on the daunting quest, the impossible task. I want to answer God's call to action. Who doesn't tingle at the thought of riding off in search of the dragon that is terrorizing the kingdom, and to meet the dragon and defeat the dragon and ride triumphantly back to the castle with the dragon's head on a pike, while the townspeople cheer and the king stumbles all over himself trying to think up a suitable reward? I want to think that I could be that guy."

"But?" Carl asked.

"But, this is today. The communications age. The technology age. A time of systems and committees and reports and politics and money. Dealing with problems today is not like battling dragons. It is more like slapping at gnats."

"Oh, you are so close, my friend. In the last few minutes you have said three things that were completely wrong. Once we clear those up, you will see clearly."

"Oh great, I get to hear some more about how wrong I am."

"Yep."

"Okay, this is me letting go and letting God," I said through a tired smile. "What do I need to recognize as *wrong* to see the light."

"You said that you were afraid to disappoint God. You are not. You have found it far easier to disappoint God than your congregants or your supervisors or your church rules."

My smile disappeared.

"Also, you said that you were afraid to disappoint Jenn. You are not. Your dedication to your career and the people in it has allowed you to find disappointing Jenn acceptable."

"Now, wait a minute before . . ."

"It is true," Carl interrupted, "and I'll tell you why. You have full faith and surety that God and Jenn love you and will continue to love you, no matter what. As such, you will risk stretching their love, even counting on it to support you in your efforts, where you would not take the same risk with those whom you assume will turn on you if given a reason."

I nodded again. I could not risk speaking and losing control of my face.

"The third thing that you are wrong about is dragons. The world today is filled with dragons, probably more than at any other time in human history. The problem is not that there are no more dragons. The problem is that we have lost the ability to recognize them. And, further, the dragon that God wants you to slay has been staring you right in the face for years."

We sat quietly for two minutes that seemed like ten. Once again, Carl waited, but this time he was red in the face and puffing a bit. He seemed about to spring into action.

"Carl?" I said.

"Yes?"

"Where's *my* dragon?"

Chapter 19

When I left Carl I drove straight home. I wanted desperately to find Jenn and share my new insight with her. I was still frightened and more than a little confused, but I finally had a grasp on what had been going on with me. It was a tenuous grasp, at best, but it was there and it was already growing and taking shape. I could see where and how I got off course. I wasn't at all sure how to fix it, but that suddenly seemed possible. All the way home, I fantasized about sweeping her up in my arms and explaining as best I could between kisses and tears and laughter how much life had just changed and how dramatically different things were now going to be. In my excitement, I even imagined there might be a quick trip to the bedroom mixed into the festivities. But, as I burst through the door and ran into the living room, I saw her. My darling wife. My beloved partner in life. She was curled up on the couch reading a book. When I interrupted her space, she looked up and smiled thinly.

"Oh, you're home. Hi, Honey. Did your time with Pastor Carl go well, tonight?"

She reached down with one hand, took hold of her ankles and pulled them more tightly beneath her. My inspiration did not waiver, but my exuberance quickly turned to sadness. I had reached a turning point, but Jenn had not. I was already different, but Jenn was not. In being forced to confront the reality of my circumstances, I was now intensely, crushingly aware that Jenn had been operating through a murky veil of hurt and anger. Far worse, she was steeped in disappointment. Disappointment in me. I stood there feeling incompetent and clueless. I had no idea the depth or breadth of her despair, or how to even begin dispelling it, and yet just a minute before I was assuming that her enthusiasm and willingness to move forward would automatically match mine. Sometimes, I am such a stupid man.

"Yes," I finally answered. "Very well."

"Good," she said. "I'm glad."

"I don't mean just *good*, like usual. Real good. Decision time good."

"Oh, really?" she asked. She perked up a bit, but then caught herself and settled back down. *Protecting herself*, I thought. For years now, most of my *decisions* had worked against her and our marriage. *Decision time* probably seemed to her more scary than hopeful.

"Yes," I started. "I am not sure how to explain. It took me weeks to figure out, with Carl's help, so maybe I had better start with some context." My mind raced with rhetorical strategies and possible outcomes and called upon our shared history for clues to successful approaches. "Okay. Yeah. Okay, let me start at the beginning, so this will make good sense when we get there."

I sat down across the room from her.

Jenn methodically and purposefully and—it seemed to me—painfully, closed her book and set it down beside her. She pulled her feet even tighter underneath her. Her face became a carefully controlled mask. She was ready. Emotionally prepared to receive whatever drivel I was about to manipulate her with. I thought, *She still loves me. She still wants to protect the marriage. But, she can hardly stand the sight of me right now.*

"Go ahead, dear," she said.

In that moment, I decided that it was time for the new me to debut. Right then.

"I love you," I started.

"I love you, too" she replied evenly.

"Please don't respond, yet," I pleaded. "I need a minute."

"Very well."

"I love you and Lisa more than anything else in this world. The only thing I love more is God, and even then, if I'm honest, I tend to love you more passionately. I have wanted very much to live a life that fully expresses that love."

Jenn sat quietly, as instructed, waiting for whatever would come next.

"I have wanted to love God and love you the way a committed, courageous Christian would. And, I have failed miserably. I have many times sided with convention and people's expectations and the human rules of the church, and against God. God has called me to be someone unusual and unique, someone willing to speak for God no matter the cost. Instead, I have caved in to worries about my career. My status. My so-called success. Even my popularity. I have fallen to my knees, apologized to God and begged his forgiveness. I am sure that will have to happen many more times in the near future."

Jenn's eyes were wide open, now. She looked as if she was afraid to blink, or breathe.

"And in the same way, I have failed you, repeatedly. I have sided with my career and peace in the church and conflicts resolved and compromises made and against the proper display of the great love I have always had for you. I have failed to be a truly Christian man, while you have remained an exemplary strong Christian woman. I have seen you belittled and beleaguered and even attacked, and I have not defended you. I have not rescued you."

Jenn sat bolt upright now, both feet on the floor.

"You have been forced to live with one of the most debilitating emotions that one spouse can have toward the other. Disappointment. You have tried and tried to not feel it, yet you do."

Part of me was still hoping that she would say it wasn't true, but she did not.

"Jennifer, I asked you to marry me. You said *yes*. You knew that I was going to become a pastor and that our lifestyle would be dictated by that choice. Still, you said *yes*. You knew that we would not be rich and that my career would sometimes pull you away from yours. You knew my time and energy would always be pulled in many directions. But, you said *yes*. Your faith was stronger than mine and still is today. I didn't always know that, but I have for awhile.

"But I also promised that I would be your husband. That I would love you and honor you above all others, except God. That I would nurture you and support you and even, if need be, defend you and protect you. Especially, I know now, against those who would attack you and tear you down. Jennifer, I have never once stopped loving you. But, in recent years, I have routinely failed you. I have not lived up to my promises to you or God and I sincerely apologize.

"I will apologize again, and probably a few more times, but then I will stop apologizing. If you will allow me, if you can open up to the possibilities, if you can risk it one more time, I will move on to being the man that God intends me to be, and that you deserve me to be. Jenn, I am about to make some radical changes in my own behavior. In the church, I will say and do exactly as I believe the Holy Spirit is leading me to do. I will not attack my enemies. I will love them. But I will also speak the unadulterated truth to them. I have no idea what the results will be. The results no longer matter. The results are up to God. But, there will be turmoil and conflict. Those used to winning will dig in and fight harder, assuming they will win again. Our security and stability could be threatened. I could even lose my position. We will certainly endure a great deal of tension."

Jenn appeared to be willing herself to sit still and finish listening.

"Because of all this, I am stating clearly, *I need you*. I need you at my side, in the church. The battles will not be pleasant, but I make you this promise. If anyone even begins to demean you, I will be your husband first and the pastor of East Fork First United Methodist Church second. There will be some shocked people at first, but they will learn soon enough that while, as the pastor, I am fair game, my wife is not. The consequences be damned, I will not rest until the disappointment leaves your eyes. So I ask you only this; Jennifer, can you find it in yourself to trust me one more time?"

Jenn still didn't move or respond. She seemed to be studying me, like she was looking at me for the first time.

"Yes," she said, rising to her feet. "I have been waiting for you to reignite for quite some time now, and I am more than ready. For me, this is the culmination of many prayers. I am not afraid of anything that might come. When God is with us, who can be against us?"

"Well, the list is actually quite long," I said, chuckling and enveloping her in my arms. "There will be many against us."

"I know," Jenn whispered, "but they will not win. Even if they run us down and push us out of here, even if they think they have won, simply obeying God will be enough. And another thing, not quite so important, but almost."

"What's that?"

"Welcome back."

Later, as we were snuggling, I said to Jenn, "I know this will sound silly and childish, especially to a sophisticated woman such as yourself . . ." She snorted, then giggled. ". . . but as Pastor Carl and I were trying to piece this thing together, I finally got a handle on what has been holding me back when we started talking about dragons."

"Dragons?"

"Yeah, you know, the old idea about going out on a mighty quest, good versus evil, facing danger, rescuing the village and all that."

"And slaying the dragon that is holding the helpless damsel hostage?" she added, more than asked.

"Well, yeah, kinda," I replied, suddenly feeling foolish and chauvinistic. "I didn't say the damsel had to be helpless. I know it sounds like a bunch of little boys sitting in a tree-fort, dreaming about being heroes."

"Yes, it does," she answered. An uncomfortable silence surrounded us. A concept that had finally gotten me stirred up enough to face suffocating challenges was being exposed as nonsensical. I was already thinking up a way to extricate myself from the room, when my beloved wife added, "It's a shame that you boys give up on that when you become men."

"Huh?"

"Come on, Honey, you're supposed to be the expert on all this human relationship stuff. Did not God call on many biblical characters to be in some way, mighty? Does not God tell us to 'fear not?' God has plenty of wimps at his disposal. It seems to me that God is seeking a few heroes and heroines, and finding the pool of such people lacking."

"You've thought about this stuff?" I asked.

"Sure. You don't think I want to be and do all that God is asking of me?"

"Well, yeah, I do think that. I guess I didn't realize that you might wrestle with such things, because you seem so good at it."

"I still struggle daily with what God really wants from me. And, from *us*. We are a team, are we not?"

I smiled and said, "Yes. Probably more so than I have ever fully realized."

"So, now that we know that it is okay for you to quest, and it is also okay for me to quest, tell me about your dragon."

"My dragon?"

"As excited as you are, surely you have identified your dragon."

While feeling the habitual urge to mitigate and intellectualize and sanitize everything that I was about to say, I gave myself an internal slap in the head and plunged forward. "I have, actually, and I am anxious to seek it out and cut off its head."

"Go on," Jenn encouraged. "Who's your dragon?"

"My dragon's name is *Agendor*."

"Okay. Agendor?"

"Agendor is so complicated and intricate that it is almost impossible to know where he is. It is even harder to know what he is doing. Our whole society is swimming in multitudes of belief systems, written and unwritten rules of behavior, agendas of all kinds and persuasions, and the incessant drumbeat of individualism, personal rights and complete disdain for anyone who would suggest that anyone is wrong about anything. We demand to do as we please. We demand that no one criticize us, no matter how outlandish our behavior. We demand that every idea, every philosophy, every belief, every lifestyle be treated as equal to any other. Except, of course, the established Christian Church, which one may freely despise and denigrate. It is the way of the world around us. Each person is entitled not only to the truth, but to their own personal truth. And, we are all expected to honor that, whether it makes any sense or not."

"All right, I think I'm halfway there," Jenn said, looking at me with great intent.

"The worse thing is that we have let Agendor into the church. Many people are not in the church at all, of course. But, most who *are* bring Agendor with them. They want to hear only what they want to hear, they want to pick and choose to believe only that which suits them, and, worst of all, they expect the church to serve them. They want God to serve them. If the church does not make them happy, then the church had better change. Or, they will move on and find a church that will tend to their happiness. So, we in the church are constantly mediating. Keep 'em happy. Tone down controversy. The list of things that a preacher must not say, and the list of ways that you had better not say it, is like a three hundred and sixty degree minefield."

A Dragon in the Church   121

"I get you," Jenn said. "Believe you me, I have experienced the church in ways that make this easy to believe. But, it isn't completely true, is it?"

"No! Not at all. There are good and wonderful people doing good and wonderful things all throughout the church. Some of them are even doing what God has called them to do. And, many others are doing good things of their own choosing, which is not exactly how God asks us to operate, but still with every good intention. The church is full of wonderful people and things!"

"But . . . what?"

"But God is much too rarely in charge. We are in charge. We insist on it. We battle things out in meetings and conferences, instead of finding our way on our knees. We make resolutions and take votes and write legislation and compile books full of rules. All the while, the self-centered go on fighting and politicking for their own victories, and the well-intended go from one good thing to another, assuming that God will be pleased. And the atmosphere, the society, the culture, the church subculture and sub-sub-cultures in which we do all these things make up such a complicated mass of moving targets, expectations, rules, demands and sensitivities, that it becomes almost impossible to even identify the problem. Information overload, the instant, public expression of opinions and emotions, the twenty-four hour news cycle all add up. The complex, suffocating, self-perpetuating web of red tape and constantly changing unknowns that is today's society, and today's church, is so pervasive that we stare at it all day and yet never see it."

"Agendor."

"Yep. The dragon cannot be fought because it cannot be seen. And, it cannot be seen because it is everywhere."

"So, what is your quest, then?"

"The hope, the solution, is God's will. God's agenda. No matter how complex we humans make things, life can always be simplified and made right by seeking God's will. It's so simple.

We were created to be in relationship with God and live according to God's Word, Will and Way, and yet we are ready to run in almost any direction except back to God."

"But, that can change, can't it?" Jenn asked.

"Yes. Even today many more people would respond to God's will if they were just clear on what it is. Discerning that for themselves is beyond most people, because of all the competing hype that can be so attractive. Even though we insist that we must always make our own decisions, most cannot see that the key decision is to decide for, and not against, God. As he usually does, God has sent a human being to bring his Word to the people in this particular place and time. To make clear what God wants, to cut through the web of confusion. In this church and this town, God has sent me. And, I have failed. Agendor has swallowed me up."

Jenn lay quietly in my arms. We did not speak, or move. I clung tightly to her, soaking up her warmth and her strength. A bit of fear lingered nearby, as I contemplated the implications of all that I just said. I alternated between short, silent prayers for help and wisdom, and giving thanks for the gift of Jenn. Then, she interrupted my thoughts.

"Nathan Lee Martin, today is a new day."

"Yes, Jennifer Marie Pool Martin, today is a new day."

I wept, and with each cleansing tear I grew stronger.

Chapter 20

"Janice, first I want to thank you for being such a help so far, and for the help you're going to be in the future. Your devotion is important to me, and it helps a lot."

"Well," she replied, "some of it is personal. I like you and I think that you are a good pastor. Also, I think you are trying to do things the right way. Bob is trying to solidify his kingdom, and I am sick of it."

"Thank you," I said, "and that brings me to what I wanted to clarify first. I have become aware that this mess is becoming a personal battle. Bob is trying to take me down and I am trying to beat him at his own game."

"Sounds about right."

"Except that it is not right, not really. I admit that I have been ready to go down that road, but I can't let myself. And, especially, I must not drag good, devout people down that road with me. You, for instance. So, I really need your help, but only in specific ways."

"I'm listening."

"Everything we do and say needs to be, as much as we are able, done according to God's Word. If I come out looking like the winner in this thing, I have failed. If God's church is back on track, operating like God wants it to and to his glory, then God's kingdom has won, and that is good."

"Okay. How do we go about that?"

"I'm not completely sure, yet. But I know that we need to be open, transparent and honest. No secrets regarding the life of the church. Everybody involved gets all available information, even if it's stuff we wish Bob didn't know. Every statistic, financial report, regulation and procedure of the United Methodist Church is knowledge that everyone will have."

"I guess that's my job."

"Yes, and I know you will do it well."

"It won't always be easy. I'm going to feel like I'm on Bob's side, and I won't like that."

"I know. Just think of it as being on God's side."

"What else?"

"You must be completely honest with answers to specific questions."

"And you?" she asked.

"For the first time in a long time, I am going to respond to every person in the church with what I honestly believe to be the response God wants me to have. No more politics. No more conflict resolution. No more communications strategy. No more being afraid to rock the boat. Just straight-forward statements of *this is what God wants you to hear*."

"Pastor, that sounds absolutely terrifying. I can't imagine the responses you're in for."

"I am terrified. I'll admit that. But not in the way you think. As of now, I am no longer going to fear the reactions of others. I am ready to ride it out wherever it takes me."

"Then what are you afraid of?"

"I am terrified that what comes out of my mouth won't please God. I will have to discern what God wants very rapidly. That scares me because, to tell you the truth, I'm a little rusty. And sometimes, with certain big things, I will even have to wait for God's direct instruction. That takes prayer time that some folks will not want to allow."

"Then I have my next job," Janice said, firmly.

"How's that?" I asked. "I think you're getting ahead of me."

"I will be open and honest, and when you need time I will make them wait."

"All right," I said, "I guess there is nothing delaying this brave new world, is there."
"Guess not," Janice replied. "Pastor?"
"Yes?"
"Nice knowing ya!"
About an hour later I was still sitting in my office, playing scenarios through my head.
Janice stuck her head through the doorway and said, "Here comes your first opportunity. Berta and Virgy Lou are headed your way, both mad and both expecting you to choose her side."
"Oh boy!" I said with a heavy dose of fake enthusiasm.
"Pastor?
"Yes, Janice, what is it?"
"May I have your permission to listen, pretty please?!"
"Will my answer make a difference?"
"Only in how guilty I do or do not feel."
"Let's go with 'don't ask, don't tell.'"
"Deal. Do you want me to hold them off a bit?"
"No, send them right in and we'll see what happens."
As Janice showed the two powerful church ladies into my office, there was a certain amount of jockeying for position as to who would sit in which of the only two chairs available. There is no discernible advantage between the seating choices, which is what caused the indecision. Neither could decide which seat would imply a place of superiority, and so neither knew how to act. At last, they sat.
"Good morning ladies. It's a pleasure to see you today. I trust things are going well."
Berta Lou jumped right in. "Things are decidedly not going well, Reverend Martin. Perhaps I should be referring to the various rumblings that I hear all about the church, but my immediate concern is more specific. Despite clear communication of the facts at hand, both verbally and by the provision of clear signage, the food people have seen fit to once again disturb fragile materials belonging to the Crafty Ladies

Quilters Group. I do not need to remind you that the quilters' work is one of the primary ministries of this church, providing financial benefits, reputation enhancement and growth of the artistic culture in our community."

Virgy Lou sniffed and said, "Look up *fine arts* in the encyclopedia and you won't find quilts."

"Opinions being what they may," Berta Lou retorted, "the problem here is a matter of fact and procedure. Once again, the cooks have given themselves permission to improperly remove quilting supplies from the yellow, multi-level, wheeled storage rack that is properly designated to the sole use and control of the Crafty Ladies Quilters Group, and replace them with boxes upon boxes of Styrofoam containers that I ought not have to remind you, Reverend, are banned from use by United Methodist churches, anyway!"

"Oh, come now, Berta Lou," Virgy Lou interrupted. "When you had the party for your and Howard's fifty-fifth wedding anniversary, this place was swimming in Styrofoam! You just don't like anyone else using anything around here unless you have already rejected it!"

"That rack belongs to the Quilters and no one else!"

"It . . . does . . . not!" Virgy Lou was loading up for bear. "That cart was paid for with memorial money from Aunt Lorraine's funeral! God rest her soul. I am glad she has not been here for 18 years of bickering over what was given in her name! For over twenty-five years she was head of the Community Dinner Committee, and I took over from her! She would *never* begrudge the use of any church facilities or equipment for the Community Dinner. It is the biggest event in this church every year! She loved The Dinner!"

"Now, Virgy Lou, calm yourself." Berta Lou spoke slowly and quietly, as one might address an upset child. "I know that *our* Aunt Lorraine loved The Dinner. Everybody knows that. I love it, too. However, as I have so clearly and carefully informed you many times, if you would simply check the Book of Memorials for that date eighteen years past, you would find . . ." Berta Lou was quickening her cadence and beginning to quake. ". . . that the entry says, 'One yellow, multi-leveled, wheeled storage rack . . ." Her voice was getting shrill now. ". . . to the Crafty! Ladies! Quilters! Group!!!"

The two women leaned toward each other and settled into a glaring death match.

"Excuse me," I said.

They both started, having forgotten my presence.

"You came to me for this discussion, did you not? May I offer something?"

"Yes, of course," whispered Berta Lou.

"Yes, of course," whispered Virgy Lou.

"Let us pray. Dear God, we come to you in a spirit of awe and wonder and gratitude. You are majestic and powerful beyond our ability to comprehend . . ."

It was at about this point that they quit staring at each other and assumed prayerful poses. Every pastor knows that the way to instill at least short term order is to start praying.

". . . and yet you are so personal as to care about each and every one of us, including those of us in this little room. We ask that the Holy Spirit help us to decide in ways and behave in ways that are pleasing to you and are positive forces in the growth of your Kingdom. Amen."

Both of the combatants whispered half-hearted *Amens* and moved their stares to me. Habitual responses containing "positive 'I' statements" and "collaborative, third choice solutions" flooded my mind. However, I had just in the past few hours promised God a new day and a new me. Go time!

"Well?" Berta Lou asked.

"Well?" Virgy Lou asked.

"As I see it, one of the reasons that you have such a difficult time forming a lasting agreement on this issue is that you are both cut from the same cloth. You are a great deal alike."

Both started their heads shaking, preparing to protest.

"Hang on," I said, "let me finish. You are not exactly alike, of course, but you are both strong capable women. Is that fair to say?"

"Maybe," one murmured.

"Perhaps," the other mumbled.

Neither wanted to credit the other, but enjoyed her own compliment.

"Okay. You are both well-educated, and from the same prominent family here in East Fork. Right?"

They nodded.

"You are both good organizers and have long been in charge of important church functions. Is that not so?"

"Well, yes," they both exclaimed.

"And, you are both aware that certain things would collapse around here without your vigilant leadership. Am I right?"

"I think I see where you are going, Reverend," said Berta Lou. "God has given each of us many gifts, and we should not be working at cross purposes. If we find a way to be supportive of each other, both of our ministries will flourish even more."

"Yes, I see, too," chimed in Virgy Lou, not wanting Berta Lou to be the only newly-enlightened one. "Perhaps we have been silly to squabble. Berta Lou, I have a thought. How about we do a fund-raiser and buy a second rack! Then we could concentrate on our work."

"Well," Berta Lou responded, "an important consideration would be space for the second rack, but I think the old broom closet has fallen into disuse since the new shed was built out back. I'll bet we could redo that room to get the space we need!"

I had just worked the kind of miracle that I had been doing for years. We found a mutually satisfactory way out of a seemingly unbreakable logjam. Two longtime members, two longtime givers, who were angry were now happy.

"Ladies, I think that as far as it goes, this is a good solution. Both the quilters group and the Community Dinner are important ministries and I agree with Virgy Lou (the first time I ever said that name out loud without the feeling that I was about to burst out laughing), you have been silly. But what is sillier still is that you have both spent years trivializing your God-given gifts, more motivated by your desire to win and get your own way than by the good that your ministry and your witness for Christ might actually do. The quilting and the Community Dinner are good ministries, but as the capable, educated, natural leaders that you both are, God would want to know why you have failed to do more. You might alleviate hunger or teach illiterate people to read or help wipe out a disease or, heaven forbid, evangelize! When have you last told someone about Christ your Savior or invited anyone to church? Ever? The Bible tells us that to whom much is given much is expected. You, Berta Lou, have been given much. You, Virgy Lou, have been given much. And yet you are about to walk out of here happy and satisfied that, finally, after so many years of personal hurt and frustration, you have your very own yellow, multi-leveled storage rack. God loves you. And, while you might not believe it right now, so do I. It is my job to tell you, God hopes for more from you both."

I stopped talking. Crushing silence.

Finally, Berta Lou said, "I have been a member of this church for as long as you have been alive, and no one—not a pastor, not a DS, not a bishop, not a Church Council Chair—has ever spoken to me in such an accusatory and disrespectful manner. If you think you are going to get away with . . ."

"I guess we can see," Virgy Lou almost shouted, "where all the talk is coming from. We have been here for many years before you got sent here and we will be here for many more after you are sent away. If you think we're going to sit here and . . ."

"I'm sorry," I blurted out. "I'm sorry."

Berta Lou and Virgy Lou froze, calculating their next move. Finally, Berta Lou said, "I would think that you would be sorry for talking to us in such a fashion. I suppose we can try to consider pressures and . . ."

"No, I think you misunderstand," I said. "I am sorry that it took me over four years to finally tell you God's truth. I should have done it sooner."

"Come Virgy Lou. We have people to see."

"Come Berta Lou. We have calls to make."

As they exited my office together, I sarcastically thought, *Success! I have finally united Berta and Virgy Lou, by giving them a common enemy. Me!* If I hadn't already, I had now officially grabbed the tail of the dragon and then poked it with a stick.

Janice stuck her head through the door and said, "That was smooth."

"Yeah" I replied. "Like butta."

"Well," Janice continued, "I can give you more news now or I can let you process what just happened, but only for a few minutes."

"Give it to me now. It seems I'm on a roll."

"The dam has broken. Ten minutes ago I got a call from Annabel Ustis. She asked me to give you what she called 'proper notice' that there will be an emergency meeting of the Finance Committee on the night after next at 7:00 p.m. She added two things. She said that this notice is more than forty-eight hours, and she said she was sorry. Then she asked if she needed to deliver the notice in writing."

"No, I don't need it in writing. Please call her and thank her for tending to her duties in such a dedicated manner, and tell her that I will be at the meeting."

"Then you are going to want me to call Jack Conwell, too."

"Okay," I responded, "can I safely assume that there is also a call for an emergency Church Council meeting?"

"Yep. The next night at 7:00 o'clock. Over seventy-two hours notice. I got that call five minutes ago."

"Sounds like our friend Bob is working the phones."

"Sure does. He is listed as the only agenda item for both meetings."

"That's fine. Let Jack know that I will attend."

"Will do. Pastor Nathan, are you okay?"

"Yes, strangely, I am okay. Some things have to happen and the time is now. There's one thing we can be sure about the next few weeks at the East Fork First United Methodist Church."

"What's that," Janice asked through a wry smirk.

"It isn't going to be boring."

Even though it was early in the day, I quickly put a few things in order and left the church. Once again, I needed time to think. While there still seemed to be only a few main players involved in the unfolding drama, the rank and file congregation was surely getting wind of what was going on. The texts and e-mails would soon be flying, with dozens of different versions of what was going on.

I parked near a favorite walking trail and took a hike. As I walked, I prayed and listened. Eventually, I had cleared my mind and stopped thinking about anything in particular. My first surprise was that serenity had snuck up on me when I was not looking. *Why am I not more frantic?* I wondered. I chuckled at the recollection of the old joke, *If you are not panicking, perhaps you don't fully understand the gravity of the situation.* Still, I had a few moments of peace. My second surprise was a clear prodding from God. The phrase "I told you, I've got this" tumbled through my mind. I reminded myself to do only the job God gave me.

I decided to goof off until I could see Carl at 5:30. He was the best I had ever met at cutting through the mustard and getting to the meat of things. Suddenly I was famished and in need of a thick cheeseburger with lots of mustard. I turned around and headed back to my car, now at least three miles away.

I would have time to drive a town or two over and have an anonymous feast at a diner in some other pastor's town. By the time I had my work bee/therapy session/strategic planning meeting with Carl, Jenn would be home and I could update her. Thoughts of eating alone, meeting with Carl and working alongside Jenn made me happy.

A few hours later I approached the little church at the crossroads. *Maybe "crossroads" ought to be part of the name,* I thought.

"Evening, Pastor Carl," I said as I walked in.

"Evening, Pastor Nathan," he replied. "So how are things?" Carl seemed more concerned than usual, like he was expecting trouble.

"Things are weirdly fine," I said, "and I am going to tell you all about it. But first, let's have a look at this wonderful place."

Carl nodded and said, "Excellent."

We walked about. The woodwork in the sanctuary was quite spectacular. We did not want to over-compliment our own work, but the change was stunning. The pews had been repaired and refinished. The walls and floor had the deep, rich shine of lovingly cared-for wood. The windows had been repaired, albeit with plain, clear glass. But, they were water tight and now in excellent condition. The old metal ceiling had been patched and sanded and restored as closely as possible to a natural state. It looked pretty good and would only improve with age. The chancel and altar area were still a mess. We were about to tear up the threadbare, musty carpet and see what was underneath. Still, the progress was phenomenal.

"This is going to be a very special place," I said to Carl.

"Yes," he replied. "Wonderful things are going to happen here."

"What still needs to get done?"

"Well, this is obvious right here, new carpet and probably some repair work underneath. I'm not planning on doing much to the pulpit, just some refinishing. The cross I plan to give a good dusting, and leave it be."

"Yeah," I said, "I think that is best, too. That old cross will outlast a few more generations. What about the rest?"

"I think we'll put the bathroom in good working order and clean it up. Downstairs I want to make sure that the plumbing and wiring is good, make sure the cupboards are in good repair."

"What about fixtures and appliances?"

"I think that's up to the congregation, once there is one. Right now, it feels like I am supposed to get the sacred space in order. A place to worship and pray and teach and preach the Word of God. Once there is a church family here, God will tell us what else we need to do."

I looked at Pastor Carl and marveled. He seemed to live out an authentic and genuine faith as easily as he breathed the air. *Why is it such a daily struggle for me?* I wondered.

Out of the blue, Carl asked, "So, what's up with the adventures at your church?"

I snapped out of my contemplative state. "The pressure is building and the volcano is about to blow," I replied, with a giggle.

"You seem pretty comfortable, given what you just said," Carl observed.

"Yeah. Some of it is just fatalism, you know? If you can't run and you can't cry, might as well laugh."

"That can happen."

"I feel like I have gotten off the sidelines and back into the game. It even feels like God is communicating with me more clearly. Maybe I am just listening better. Anyway, I am okay with whatever is coming."

"Good. Sounds great. How about your wife? Okay there?"

"Better than okay. Jenn is such a gem. We are standing shoulder to shoulder, and I haven't felt as confident in our marriage in years."

"Well, it sounds like things are looking good."

"Oh, no," I corrected Carl, "there are so many controversies brewing that I think we can count on multiple disasters!" As I stood there grinning, Carl took measure of the *me* that was now standing before him. He didn't say anything, so I added, "I think so much change is needed at the East Fork First United Methodist Church that God has to start with a monumental 'stirring of the pot.'"

"Excellent," Pastor Carl said.

Then he started yanking at a corner of rotted carpet.

Chapter 21

It was 9:45 as I arrived home. Usually at this time, Jenn was in pre-bedtime relaxing mode, curled up with her latest favorite book. This night she had only been home a few minutes herself and was rustling up a snack to replace a missed supper. Even though I had already filled up on a bologna sandwich and a bag of Fritos, I decided to do the right thing and join in with reheated goulash and Italian bread dipped in olive oil.

"Officially, I have declared this to be a snack," Jenn said as she sat down. She laughed as she gestured to our mounded plates.

"Of course it's a snack," I added. "After all, it's almost ten o'clock."

As Jenn crammed a heaping forkful into her mouth—she has always been what is known as a *good eater*—I said, "I love you very much. I just want you to know that."

She opened wide her mouth full of semi-masticated food and asked, "How much?"

We laughed heartily together and it felt great. Truth is, we think we are really funny, despite the continual reactions of others that would seem to indicate otherwise.

"More than I can either imagine or contain," I said.

"You don't have to try so hard," she replied. "I am already in a good mood." She laughed again, but then she added, "I love you, too . . . always have, but it sure feels better lately."

"I'm glad, because we are about to share some memorable experiences."

"Good. Let me finish this fine cuisine, then I want to hear all about it."

Shortly, we sat down in our designated recliners. "The gloves are off and the action has begun," I said. "Meetings are being called, two for this week. The word is being spread. People are talking even when they don't know what they are talking about. Typically small meetings will have to be moved to Fellowship Hall. Suddenly everybody is interested in what the Finance Committee or Church Council is doing."

"Are these meetings proper?" Jenn asked.

"Close enough, I guess. Anyone can sit in on meetings of all groups except the Staff Parish Relations Committee. But, they have no vote and no voice, unless they are recognized by the particular Chair. And, the committee can only act within its own scope of authority."

"So, then, what does the Finance Committee have to do with anything?"

"Technically, not much, unless someone is going to allege financial wrong doing or improper business practices."

"Is that going to happen?"

"Who knows? Bob and his cronies might say just about anything, but I don't think so. Bob wants as many forums as he can find. He has gone to war. His chief weapons are influence and persuasion. Proper process won't matter to him. He figures that if he can get enough people turned against me that eventually there will be a way to get rid of me, no matter the rules."

"And," Jenn interjected, "he's probably right about that."

"Yep. It usually does work that way. But, this is a God-thing, so who knows?"

"Do you have to participate in these quasi-meetings?"

"No, but there is no sense hiding or postponing. I think a day of reckoning, or maybe a day of transition, is supposed to happen. If this is the buildup, fine."

"What do you want from me, my love?" Jenn looked at me with wide eyes and an obviously open heart.

"I want you to choose. It has to be your choice."

"Between what?"

"Will you be *damsel* or *warrior princess*?"

"Do you really have to ask that?" she said, with more than a little hurt and annoyance creeping into her voice.

"Yes, I do. I feel guilty for having repeatedly let you down. I want desperately to make that up. At the same time, I am not sure how much to protect you or how much to include you. I need you to be clear with me which way you want this to go."

After a long hesitation, she finally said, "I think I like this new straight-forward honesty thing, but it is going to take some getting used to. Okay. You are in several precarious situations and it does not help if I expect you to read my mind. And, I appreciate that you are trying to get this right."

"Thank you. I'm not going to tip toe around you, and I'm sure I will annoy you once in a while, but I don't want to disappointment you again."

"Fair enough. I do not need you to protect me. What I need is for you to include me in whatever you are trying to do. We are in this together. I will hold up my end."

"I love you. And, be aware that this is going to be rough. You and I have a new understanding of things; the people we are dealing with do not. There is nastiness on the horizon."

"I know. And, I'm ready. I have wanted to fight back. Now, I still do, but I want to fight for what's truly right. If we stick together, I can handle anything that comes."

"I promise. You and me, side by side. Whatever happens."

"Then *warrior* it is. You can drop the *princess* part. That just sounds silly."

Chapter 22

Fortunately, my first appointment the next morning was with one of my favorite couples.

"It's 10 o'clock," Janice called through the doorway, "Frank and Sylvie are here."

"Thank you, Janice. Send them in."

Sylvie led the way into my office. I've described her as short, squat and dumpy, but somehow she was a beautiful ray of sunshine at the same time.

"Morning Pastor," she said, with a gorgeous smile. She walked over to where I stood and took my right hand in both of hers. She squeezed, gently but firmly, and pumped my hand up and down in tiny arcs. "You are a good man," she said, "and outside of my Frank I have only met a few." She turned and took her place on my counseling couch.

"Good morning, Pastor," Frank stated plainly, but with an uncommon air of respect. He sat down next to his fiancé, ready for pre-marital counseling.

"So, how have the two of you been since we last talked?" I began.

"I am loving this man almost as much as I love the Lord. I'm near drowning in the stuff!" she said through giggles and a slap on Frank's knee. I'd heard her use exactly this line before, but she meant it every time.

"Now, calm yourself, Sylvie," Frank said, patting her on the shoulder. "You'll scare the poor pastor!" Frank's smile nearly split his rugged face.

Same patter. Same exchange. Two people who had seen the dark side of life for much too long, ecstatic to finally love and be loved.

"Don't scare the poor man," he repeated. "Besides, everyone in seven counties knows that you don't love me half as much as I love you."

"I thought it was only six counties," I said with a smile.

Frank grinned and said, "I called up my second cousin Rodger Skinner, from way over in Oceana County, and told him God must have mistaken me for someone special to give me such a woman as Sylvie, to be my wife. Rodger's is known far and wide as a blabbermouth so I'm sure the whole county knows by now!"

Sylvie beamed and punched him in the arm.

"Where shall we begin?" I asked.

Uncharacteristically, Frank took charge. "I'm fine. Sylvie is fine. We are more than ready to get married. I'm so ready I can hardly think straight, but for some reason Sylvie seems awful calm."

"Oh, be quiet, you silly man. You see, Pastor, I have been a little over-giddy lately and Frank enjoys pointing that out to everyone who will listen, and half of them who won't. The man belongs in the funny papers."

"Anyway," Frank went on, taking back the reins. "We're fine. What we hear is that rich bastard Bob Williams is coming after you. That true?"

"Don't use that word in front of the pastor," Sylvie chastised.

"The only other words I got to describe Williams are way worse."

"Oh, well, go ahead then."

I said, "I don't think I had better say it just that way, you understand, but yes, he has taken the first steps to try to get me removed from this church."

"Why?" Sylvie asked, already fighting tears.

"Don't matter why," Frank declared. "Rich folk think God gave them the right to decide what's gonna happen for everybody else. Bob Williams sure as heck didn't consult us on what we think ought to happen to our pastor, now did he?"

"No," he did not, Sylvie agreed.

"I told you, Sylvie. You're the finest woman I know and I don't want to get contrary with you, but I told you. You go to church with rich people and there's going to be trouble. We should have gone back to the Rolling River church where the people are more like us."

"You mean the one where the pastor got caught by his own wife, dallying with the choir director, right in the church? That Rolling River Apostolic Church?"

Frank took a sly look at me and said, "Well...there is that."

We all laughed.

"I love you two," I said. "You bring me joy in hard times."

"That's what I've been trying to say," Frank said. "We lo ... you tell him, Sylvie."

"We love you, too, Pastor. And we want to know what we can do."

"A minute ago you called me *your* pastor. That's what I need. To know that God has let me serve the likes of you makes everything else worthwhile. You just hang in there and stick with the church, and you'll be helping me plenty. And pray. This whole thing needs prayer."

"We'll sure do that," Sylvie said.

"Pastor," Frank said, "if you were to ever decide on a different strategy to deal with Williams, I know some guys . . ."

"Frank! That's not funny," Sylvie blurted with genuine alarm.

"Some guys who live so far off the grid that hardly anyone even knows they're alive."

"You stop that right now! Pastor is going to think you're serious!"

"Okay, okay. I guess I'm not as funny as I think I am. Sorry Pastor."

"It's fine, Frank. It's fun to kid around. Now, let's talk about the wedding ceremony."

We made arrangements which were a little more grand than Frank found comfortable, and a little less grand than Sylvie had imagined. Both were very happy and it seemed to me that it would be a simple, loving affair, my favorite kind of wedding.

"Pastor," Sylvie said as they were leaving, "we love you and we are on your side."

I hugged her and said, "Thank you. That's more encouraging than you could guess."

As Sylvie exited to the hallway, Frank surprised me by giving me a big bear hug, slapping me loudly, three times on the back. Just before he let go, he whispered in my ear, "I really do know some guys."

Chapter 23

"Do you want to go in, or do you want to head for the border?" I asked my darling wife.

"I don't know about you," she replied, "but I'm going in. I'm done with waiting."

We were sitting in our car, in the furthest parking place from the church door. It was finally time for the specially-called, emergency meeting of the Finance Committee. The meeting was so special and so emergency that it was being held after dark. I assumed that the time was chosen, certainly by Bob Williams and no one else, to afford the greatest attendance of suddenly interested church members. A typical finance meeting was attended by, maybe, the five members of the committee. As usual, Janice would serve as non-voting secretary/treasurer. Annabel Ustiss would chair the meeting. Resident skinflint Sid Colms and Dosie Wainright would be present and voting. Jeremy Clark, the sixteen-year-old who was the most effective member of the committee would also be the main topic of debate. One of my chief concerns would be to protect Jeremy from unfair treatment. The fifth vote on the committee was mine.

"Then, let's roll," I said.

"Isn't that what they say right before embarking on a suicide mission?"

"Yes."

As we moved toward the church building, we weaved our way through maybe seventy-five closely parked cars.

"Please tell me that there is something else going on here tonight," Jenn said through a wicked chortle.

"Nope. Just the *you and me* show."

Jenn and I entered the Fellowship Hall, the largest meeting room in the church, and paused momentarily to get the lay of things. Someone had set up the room theater style, with at least a hundred folding chairs lined up in rows, separated by a center aisle. At the head were two eight-foot tables end to end. Annabel sat near the center, and was flanked to her left by Sid, Dosie, Jeremy and Bob Williams. Annabel's right side was left conspicuously empty, except for Janice, who sat at the very end of the table, at a ninety degree angle to the others. She had her laptop plugged in and was prepared to take notes.

I took Jenn's hand in mine and strode purposefully to the front. We stopped at the front row of spectator seating. I was hugely relieved to find Frank and Sylvie sitting on the aisle.

I bent down and quickly whispered in Frank's good ear, "I need you." He was still looking at me quizzically when I straightened and said, loud enough to be heard by most everybody, "Frank, I would sure appreciate it if you would allow my wife to have your seat. Only the members of the committee are allowed to sit *at the bar*, and tonight the bar is that long table up there. Do you mind?"

Frank is a simple man, but he is a long ways from dumb. Almost immediately his eyes lit up with recognition, and he replied, even louder, "No problem, Pastor, your wife should have a good seat, even if she's not on the Finance Committee."

He stood and motioned Jenn into his chair. Sylvie was still seated and she took Jenn's hand without a moment's hesitation. Frank looked highly satisfied to be in on the drama, but suddenly realized that he had nowhere to sit.

An elderly women sitting next to Sylvie stood up with considerable effort and stated, loudly and with theatrical flair, "You'd better sit back down next to Sylvie. I wouldn't want the two of you to shrivel up and die from being more than ten feet apart."

As the laughter died down, a young man in the second row motioned the woman to his seat, then sprinted for the back rows.

The game of musical chairs completed, I walked around and took my seat at the head table. I stared at Bob Williams. Jeremy stared at Bob Williams. Dosie stared at Bob Williams. Sid stared at Bob Williams. Annabel sat frozen, face forward, obviously terrified. As it dawned on them what just happened, the people in the front rows turned and joined the staring at Bob Williams. Soon everyone in the room except Annabel and Jacob Turnbaugh, who was already sleeping, were staring at Bob Williams.

Bob attempted to maintain a cool façade. He tried to appear unaffected. But he started to crack. He started to waiver. Finally, he asked, "Annabel?"

"Pastor's right," she said.

With slow, methodical movements and an unsuccessful effort to affect an *I don't really care* look, Bob Williams stood up and moved away from the table. As he sought a way out and a place to sit, a man I knew to be on one of the Williams' many payrolls scooted up and placed an additional folding chair at the far end of the first row, opposite from Jenn. Bob sat with all of the dignity he could muster, and glared at me with fire in his eyes.

Good, I thought. *I've already got him off his game!* I was starting to gloat when I heard Annabel, clinging desperately to her prepared agenda, say, "Pastor, before I call this meeting to order, will you please offer a prayer?"

Perfect timing. Just what I needed.

"Let us pray," I said in my *preachin' voice.* I prayed earnestly, "Dear Holy God, we come to you in a spirit of gratitude and wonder; that you could be a God so powerful and majestic as to create a universe, and yet so personal as to care about each and every one of us. You gave us your church and asked us to use it to be your voice to the world and your hands and feet in a world in need. We try to do that in ways that would be pleasing to you. In this world, money is one of the key ways that things get done. The good people on this committee have dedicated their time and talents to oversee church finances. I thank you for them, and ask that the Holy Spirit help us to make wise decisions on how to

A Dragon in the Church 145

best use the resources you have provided. Let us always remember who you are and whose we are, that we might act according to your Word and your Way. Help us all, especially me, to not get caught up in our ways, but to turn ourselves over to yours. In Jesus' name we pray, Amen."

"I want to welcome everyone here, this evening," Annabel began, reading from a prepared script. "I am gratified to find so many members and others connected to our church who are interested in our financial operations."

The crowd laughed and the suddenness of the sound seemed to catch Annabel off-guard. She has virtually no sense of humor and obviously did not understand the reaction. Still, she returned to the script.

"According to our *United Methodist Book of Discipline*, visitors are welcome to this meeting, without voice or vote. Only the members of the committee can speak and vote. Janice, as treasurer, can speak but not vote. No one else may speak unless invited to by the Chair, that being me. Bob Williams has requested an audience with the Finance Committee. He is the only non-committee member invited to speak. However, he has no vote. So, to everyone else, please do not speak unless recognized. This will be a meeting of limited scope, called to deal with specific concerns about the structure of the Finance Committee. Therefore, we will dispense with the reading of minutes or financial report, and proceed. Are there any questions from members of the committee?"

There was only a shaking of heads. It appeared that Dosie was decidedly uncomfortable with the whole situation. Sid just sat and glowered, which was standard demeanor for him. Janice was perched on the front few inches of her seat, looking to be on high alert. Jeremy was positively excited. Annabel stuck to her notes. She had clearly spent a great deal of time and research getting ready for this event. I looked out at Jenn, sitting tall with eyes trained straight ahead. She was ready for whatever might come her way. As for me, I was simply trying to not reveal any emotion at all.

"Hearing none, I call this special meeting of the East Fork First United Methodist Church Finance Committee to order. As we are here to deal with specific concerns, I guess it only makes sense to hear what they are. Mr. Williams, would you please, as succinctly as possible, address the committee with your concerns."

"Thank you, Annabel . . ."

"Although we have known each other for a long time, in this case I believe that 'Madam Chairperson' would be more appropriate, Mr. Williams." Annabel's jaw had a determined set that I had never before seen.

"Huh? Okay . . . sure . . . Madam Chairperson."

"Proceed."

Bob gathered himself and turned to the crowd. "As most of you know, I have been an active member of our church for many years, as were my parents and my grandparents before them. It is only out of my love for this place and the people in it that I . . ."

"Mr. Williams," Annabel interrupted, "please address the committee. We are not here for speeches. Also, we all accept that you have standing in the church and the community. Please get to your points."

I relaxed slightly and settled back into my chair. Evidently, Annabel was in control.

Very well," Bob replied, his annoyance now becoming obvious. "I have grown beyond concerned regarding the performance of our pastor. In the attempt to be fair, open and honest, I have communicated directly with Reverend Martin, both verbally and in writing. I detailed my concerns and made suggestions for improvement. Instead, things have merely become worse. I have copies of my initial communication.

Would Madam Chairperson (the words stuck in Bob's throat, creating a faint air of sarcasm) allow me to read the list aloud?"

"Perhaps it would be better for the committee to read it silently, first," Annabel said, "so that we can decide what will officially come before us. May we have the copies?"

"Yes, of course." Bob approached and handed over several copies of his document.

As I began to read, which was not really necessary as I had read every accusation at least a hundred times, I heard scuffling sounds, and murmuring. I looked up to see that copies of the memo were being passed out, from the back to the front, to everyone in the room.

And so, Bob will have his forum. No matter what the committee decides to do or not do, Bob has accomplished a full-frontal attack. He is clever, I'll give him that. My thoughts were interrupted by concern for Jenn. Just after she received her copy she looked at me and, almost imperceptibly, nodded. I understood: *Game on!*

There was a long pause filled with awkward silence overlaid with continued mumbles. I first assumed that Annabel was letting the slow readers finish, but then it appeared that she was not sure what to do next.

Suddenly, she said, "I declare a short break, so that the committee can meet in private and decide how to proceed."

Someone in the audience shouted out, "Can you do that? It's our church, too!"

Annabel was now majorly flustered and beginning to panic. As I was formulating my rescue, help came from an unexpected source.

"This committee can choose to enter private session by a seventy-five percent vote of its members," Jeremy reported loudly. "As we have only five voting members, that would require four votes. As such, I move that the committee adjourn momentarily, move to another room for no longer than five minutes to make necessary decisions, and then reconvene here."

"Second!" came immediately from Dosie.

Annabel looked on in obvious relief.

"Discussion," I whispered in her direction.

"Oh yes. Any discussion?"

"I don't see why you can't say whatever you need say in front of us," David Peterson yelled from the fourth row, "we have a right to . . ."

"Please stop talking," Annabel interjected with some ferocity. "You have not been recognized. Is there any discussion within the committee? Hearing none, those in favor of the motion as given, so signify by saying *aye*!"

Five *ayes* and a short walk later we were in a Sunday school room.

"What in heaven's name am I to do with this?" Annabel exclaimed. "Nobody told Bob he could pass out that list! What does he think he's doing?"

"It's all right, Annabel," I began, "it's not your fault. Bob is good at this stuff and when he wants his way he is going to find some method to get it."

"Can't we just tell him to shut up?" Sid asked.

"We could," I responded, "but it wouldn't help. In fact, it would make him look like he's right and we're hiding something."

"Okay, we only have a couple of minutes," Annabel said. "And by the way, thank you for the quick thinking, Jeremy."

"You're welcome," he replied.

"What do we do?" Annabel asked, and all eyes turned to me.

"Pick out only those things on the list that actually concern the Finance Committee and make Bob stick to those. When he's done we take any action we decide. Then, adjourn."

"What about that handout?" Dosie asked. "He had no right to do that."

"No, he sure didn't," I agreed. "But, he did. There is no way to un-ring that bell. If we try to take them back it will get much worse."

"Okay," Sid said, "but he's getting away with murder."

"Well," I added, "sometimes people get away with murder."

"Let's go," Annabel reasserted herself. "Time's up."

As we walked back into Fellowship Hall, we saw several cluster groups gathered together, all talking at the same time. As we took our seats, people returned to theirs and prepared for the next round.

"I call this meeting back to order," Annabel started, "and we have decided how to proceed. Mr. Williams?"

"Yes, Madam Chairperson?"

Bob's countenance had changed dramatically. He once again appeared cocky and bold. He obviously felt that he was scoring some big points.

"You may address items one and three, only. The rest have nothing at all to do with the work of this committee."

"Very well, one and three it is," Bob said, smiling and bowing slightly.

He was so far ahead on the informal power front, that he was now less worried about the formal route to victory.

Number one problem, he read. *A teenage boy has been allowed a seat and a vote on the church's Finance Committee. This is unprecedented and irresponsible. Solution: by the next regularly scheduled finance meeting this situation will be rectified by removing the boy from the committee or, at least, rescinding his right to vote.*

"I would think," Bob added, "that the concerns about this would be self-evident, but let me elaborate."

"Excuse me," I interrupted, "may I have a word?"

"When I've finished," Bob replied, "you'll get your . . ."

"Yes!" Annabel fairly shouted, "you may speak."

Bob bristled, but held his tongue.

"I merely wish to point out that the *teenage boy* is sitting right here, and he is a fine young man named Jeremy Clark. Please tread carefully, Mr. Williams, and see that Jeremy is treated with due courtesy."

"Yes, of course," Bob said, stammering. "I certainly mean no disrespect. From all I have seen and heard, Jeremy is indeed a youngster of good character. I am not accusing him of any wrong doing, at least not of his own making."

"Chairperson Ustiss, may I speak please? It seems that everyone is a little too comfortable talking about me as if I were not here."

"Yes, go ahead, Jeremy."

"Thank you, Pastor, for being concerned about me, but I really don't need protection. I'm good to go. I move that we drop this topic and move on to something else. If someone would second that, I'll explain during discussion."

"Second!" came quickly and sharply from Dosie Wainright.

"Discussion?" asked the chair.

"Annabel! This is highly irregular, I have not finished."

"Hold your water, Mr. Williams. You have no voice in the discussion of a motion."

Annabel was beginning to enjoy parliamentary procedure.

"Jeremy?"

"Thank you. This matter should be dropped because this body is not in a position to take any kind of action on it. I serve on this committee properly elected by Charge Conference vote, a vote at which all church members have the opportunity to participate. The Charge Conference decides how many, and what types of people will serve on the Finance Committee. And, the Charge Conference then elects individuals to fill those spots. I was properly elected and there is no prohibition based on age. In fact, the *2012 United Methodist Book of Discipline* encourages that a full-voting-rights member of the Church Council—a body with responsibility and authority superior to the Finance Committee—be a youth between twelve and eighteen years of age. I am sixteen. Even if I were to be charged with wrong-doing the matter would belong to the Charge Conference. If you want to check this stuff out, you can look at paragraphs 252 and 258 in the *Discipline*. Right now, this discussion is totally inappropriate and indefensible. That's why I suggest we get off of it. Now, I do the other thing that I have to do. I recuse myself from any further discussion on this matter. Please let me know when we have moved on to something else. I'll be in the hallway."

Jeremy walked out.

In the stunned silence that followed, Annabel finally looked at me and said, "Pastor, is what he said accurate?"

"Every bit."

"What do we do now?"

"You can call the vote on Jeremy's motion to drop this," I replied. "If it passes, we are done with this issue. If we defeat it and take other action, we could face appeal and reversal, for all the reasons Jeremy just pointed out."

"Any more discussion?" Annabel asked.

Bob looked ready to explode.

Annabel continued, "All in favor of the motion to drop this and move on?"

"Aye!"

"It's unanimous. Next topic. Bob, go ahead."

"Might I say that this thing with kids on important committees should be revisited?" Bob asked.

"You might, but I wouldn't bother. Move on."

Annabel was on a roll.

"Well, okay. Then you have limited me to item number three. It reads," *The directions taken by the church have been insensitive to the needs of the long-term members who have provided, and continue to provide, the great majority of the church's financial support.*

1. As soon as possible, a meeting restricted to those who have been official members of the church for in excess of ten years shall be called.
2. The concerns of this group shall be duly noted and honored in every reasonable way.

"Thank you, Mr. Williams," Annabel said. "Now, please clarify for the committee what the result of this would be. Are you suggesting that, contrary to how this and every United Methodist Church has always operated, we create a special class of people who can buy influence in the church with money and seniority? And, if so, how would that power and influence be distributed? Does membership in the club of Special Rich People entitle one to the same influence as each of the other Special Rich People, or, would the power and influence be doled out in proportion to the amount given, so that one could buy a position as an extra special, extra powerful, extra influential rich person? Could you please explain that to us?"

Bob had miscalculated. While Annabel Ustiss had for decades been an active and devoted member of the church, and Chair of the Finance Committee, she was a woman of modest means. *I wonder how he'll dig out of this one?* I thought. I stole a quick look at Jenn. She was having a great time.

Bob looked at Annabel, then the rest of the committee, then out at the crowd. He turned back to the head table and said, "I'm sorry, Madam Chairperson. In my frustration and great love for this church, something that is obviously shared by you and I and the great majority of folks here tonight, I made a bad suggestion without thinking it through. You are right, of course. This proposal would cause more trouble than it solved. May I simply withdraw it?"

This guy really is good, I thought.

"Yes," Annabel replied. "Yes, and thank you. I guess we can find reason once in a while, after all."

"And thank you, Annabel, for all your hard work and leadership," Williams continued. "You have seen us through a difficult evening with great diplomacy and aplomb. Thank you."

Real Good.

"We have dealt with all before us, this meeting is adjourned. Thank you, Mr. Williams."

As the crowd filed out, small groups formed in the hallways and the parking lot. The real decision-making was about to start.

We drove home in silence, fully expecting to be talking late into the night.

Finally, as we sat down in the living room, firmly ensconced in our safe spot, I asked, "So, what do you think?"

"That was not at all what I expected," Jenn started. "I went in loaded for bear and didn't get to say a word!"

I chuckled with her. "Yeah, it's hard to let others carry the battle, isn't it?"

"Yes. I have to admit, there is a part of me that needs to get in on it. But, still, it was quite a night. Where did the new Annabel come from?"

"She has always had a tough core to her," I said, "but I think in the end, Bob just plain offended her and she decided which side she was on, and it wasn't Bob's."

"That's for sure. He took a few lumps tonight, didn't he?"

"He did. But, he is still ahead on points."

"You think so?" Jenn asked. "He seemed pretty embarrassed to me."

"Oh, he was plenty embarrassed. He's not used to people pushing back. But, he accomplished what he set out to do. And, he's got things set up perfectly for his next move."

"How so?"

"For one, he took a forum with a tiny audience, where he had no right to argue most of his points, and turned it into a big crowd and got his talking points to all of them."

"Well, that is certainly true," Jenn agreed. "Bob's not too concerned with rules or fair play, is he?"

"No, and that is very frustrating. It's like he gets to use all of his weapons and we have to fight with one arm tied behind our backs."

"But," Jenn said, "our whole point is to demonstrate God's Way, right? It's not so much trying to beat Bob at his own game, although, I am confident you could do that, because you're such a smooth talker," Jenn added with a smile and a smirk. "But isn't it truly about changing the game? Trying to win for God, even if we have to suffer defeat ourselves?"

"There you go again," I said, "the true source of wisdom around here."

"I'm learning, just like you. So where are we now?"

"Hard to say, exactly. Bob has sown seeds. I promise you that all those little meetings clustered in the hallways and the parking lot were buzzing in every direction. A few are laughing at Bob, but a lot of them are reading that stupid memo and thinking, *Hey, yeah, I don't like that either,* and, *holy cow, I didn't even know about that.*"

"And you and I are all over that thing."

"Yes, we are. At least it makes some sense that I am on the hotspot. I am the pastor, after all. But I really see red at the way you get dragged in. I want so badly to put a stop to it that I think that's where I am going to lose my cool."

"Then don't. I can handle whatever they've got to dish out."

"Thank you, my love. But, I am still going to be on guard."

"And, I am glad for that. What's next?" Jenn asked.

"There will be a great deal of side-taking. It's just what people do. The people definitely operate from a *you're either all for me, or you're all agin' me* mind-set. Bob knows that, and he is trying to make the battle lines very clear and obvious. He wants to force people to decide whether they're on the *pastor can stay* or the *get rid of the pastor* side, because then he can work toward influencing their choices. That's how he is going to build his army."

"So what happens if we refuse to play his game?"

"Hard to say, but I think that is what we need to find out."

The phone rang.

"I'm surprised it took this long," I said. "We're bound to start hearing from both sides of this thing."

After the third ring, Jenn asked, "Do we answer?"

"At first, yes. After a while we'll decide." I picked it up. "Hello, this is Pastor Nathan."

"Good evening, Pastor. I hope it is not too late to be calling you. This is Condi Cloverton."

"Hi, Condi. Don't worry about it. As one might expect, we are nowhere near going to sleep right now."

"Yes, I assumed as much. I purposely avoided tonight's meeting. I do so dislike this kind of unpleasantness. But, I have received four calls in the past forty minutes, all wanting to know my opinion of what is being said about the music program. Pastor, I don't know what to do with all this. All I want to do is honor God through my music. Can't that be enough?"

I was about to offer a comforting speech on dealing with conflict and several useful methods of coping with it. What actually came out of my mouth was, "No. It is not enough."

After a long pause brought on, I assumed, by the shock of hearing such an unexpected answer, Condi said, "I don't understand. What are you saying?"

"Condi, you are a treasure. God has given you talent and ability way beyond what regular folks can even dream of. And, for the most part, you have used it well."

"For the most part?" Condi questioned, a hint of shrillness coming through.

"Yes. It is important to recognize, Condi, that because God didn't gift you like *regular folk,* he expects you to be something more than regular. The reason that you cannot simply make music and avoid the rest is that you are, whether you like it or not, the very face of worship in our church. At least that is true for the many music lovers. That's why they are calling you."

"If that is so, what is it that they expect from me?"

"Leadership. Guidance. Inspiration. Comfort. Their understanding of worship music is being stirred up. They may agree with Bob Williams that only traditional music is acceptable in our church. If so, they want to know what to do. They may disagree. We have a whole service filled with people moved by contemporary music. Those people probably feel that they are being attacked and diminished by their own church family."

"Why does that have to fall on me?"

"Two reasons. One, many of those people are not going to talk to me right now. I am a hot potato. I'm radioactive. Even those who would support me don't know what to say. Two, you are the face of music in this place. You are the expert. You are the leader. You are the one who *knows*. It is what comes with the great talent God gave you."

"I think the people already know what I prefer."

"And that is the point. Right there. God wants to be praised and worshipped and loved, by all of his people and in all the ways that they might think to do so. With music old and new, traditional or contemporary, classical or popular, slow or fast, contemplative or joyous, God can be loved. Your preference is secondary. So far, you have been quietly accepting that others might make a different style of music, while at the same time being dismissive of it. God wants you to do more. God wants you to help everyone, not just certain types, grow closer to him through music. That is what God wants you to know. Do that, and you can simply ignore all this political maneuvering. It will not be your problem."

"I do not know how to respond to what you have said. This is not what I expected to hear from you."

"I understand, and I . . ."

"I have to hang up now," she said. Then, she did.

After my conversation with Condi, Jenn and I talked for a while longer. The pressure was building. Any pastor will tell you that one of the most difficult parts of the job is the inevitability of soaking up the emotions of others. There is enough of it in the course of typical events like marriage counseling, visits to the sick and dying, funerals, committee conflict and such, but when the whole church is in an uproar it becomes overwhelming. The uncertainty of Condi's response had me a bit flustered. Then, in quick succession, I had three more calls. All of the callers just wanted to check in and "see how I was doing." One of them was sincere. The other two were fishing for new information, new gossip that they could then share as someone who was really in the know. I got out of those conversations as quickly and as smoothly as I could. Then, I recorded a new voicemail message, directing all inquiries toward the church phone number, during office hours, and turned the ringer off.

Jenn and I agreed on a strategy. Instead of trying to deal with every call, we would consolidate important responses into general messages, via e-mail, the church website, etc. I made it clear to Jenn that she was not to get dragged into negative conversations. Her involvement was to be strictly limited. She was the pastor's spouse and not answerable to the church or anyone in it. Despite Bob William's nonsensical claims on her and her time, Jenn did not owe the church anything. She would be involved in the unfolding drama, but only as she saw fit.

We prayed together. It had been a long time since we had done so. We prayed various things, but in the end we asked for the strength and the insight to discern what God would have us do. And, do it. No matter the cost. No matter the results. No matter the changes that events might bring. We both felt better.

Before we went to bed I made a decision to do something that I had not done even one time since I was appointed as a pastor. I left the phone and my cell phone off for the night. If someone chose to die in the next eight hours, somebody would simply have to come and bang on the door. We needed to sleep.

Chapter 24

"Morning, Janice."

"Morning, Pastor. How you holding up?"

"Pretty good. Things are popping, but I'm okay."

"How about Jenn?"

"Even better; she's a rock."

"Yes, she's quite a lady. I miss her."

"Well, she'll be back in her pew this Sunday."

"Really? I would have thought she would move over another couple of counties."

"Nope. Not Jenn. We've worked out our troubles. She's ready for anything now."

"Good, I'm very glad to hear it. The pastorate wrecks far too many families as it is."

"Well, it isn't going to get us, I promise."

"Good news . . . and then there is this."

She handed me a sheet of messages. There were at least twenty.

"I'll get to work," I said.

I sat down and returned some calls and vetoed others. As I had predicted, the reaction thus far was a mix of support and questions. There was no communication from Bob or any of the church leadership. It seemed that the principal actors in the drama were content to wait for the emergency meeting of the Church Council scheduled for later that evening. I cleared up some routine matters—the business of the church did not stop during disputes—and left the church to find some uninterrupted time. I had an especially important sermon to prepare. Despite the hubbub going on, Sunday would still arrive soon enough.

The next big meeting was scheduled for 7:00 p.m. I told Jenn I would be back at 6:15, and ran out to have a quick visit with Carl.

"Pastor!" Carl exclaimed, more excited than usual. "I didn't know when I might see you again. I hear things are happening in bunches."

I wondered what, or who, his source might be, but answered anyway. "That's for sure. In fact, I only have a few minutes now. Another big gathering tonight. It's supposed to be a Church Council meeting, but I've been told the crowd will be large. But, I wanted to check in with you. Your help has been so valuable to me."

"You sure I haven't just caused you trouble?"

"I'm sure. Jenn and I are a team again. If I was me, I wouldn't mess with us. Wait, that doesn't make sense."

"I get the gist," Carl said through a smile, "and I'm glad."

"Me, too. I think we are honestly prepared to accept what comes."

"Excellent. Now you're talking."

"Thanks. It feels good. Say, you've been working. The place looks even better."

"I've been cleaning up. There is still considerable detail work, but the big stuff is done. I never use any timetable but God's, but I'm thinking three weeks or so might do it."

"Wow. What then? Is there any way I can help you get a congregation going?"

Pastor Carl grew silent and looked around the increasingly beautiful little sanctuary. I was surprised by my own patience, despite the minutes ticking away.

Finally, he said, "As soon as I know what the next move is, I'll let you know how you can help. I've been putting in extra prayer time, asking for direction. I confess to some anxiety. Who knows, but it only makes sense that my next job would be building up a church inside this building."

"Seems like," I said.

"Well," Carl said, "Like you, I'm ready for whatever God brings. You'll be the first to know, after me that is."

"Just the kind of solid wisdom I needed to hear. Thanks Carl. I'm off to do this thing."

"I'll be here, working and praying for you."

I started to leave, but turned back. "Carl, have I told you that God loves you . . . and that I love you, too?"

"No need," Carl said. "But, I will tell you this. I am eternally grateful for both of those things. Now get on to your work."

With that, Carl turned and resumed sweeping.

Chapter 25

Once again, Jenn and I entered the church, hand in hand. The Fellowship Hall was jammed with nearly two hundred people. Standing in the back was a local newspaper reporter, with photographer. The business of the East Fork First United Methodist Church was about to go public. As we neared the front of the spectator seating, I was warmed by the sight of Frank and Sylvie, sitting on the center aisle of the first row, protecting the empty seat between them. *They came hours ago, just to save a seat for Jenn,* I thought. *Thank God for such people.*

I dropped Jenn off. After she sat, I kissed her forehead and whispered into her ear, "You and me baby."

She whispered back, "You and me and God makes three. Or is it five?"

The council members must have thought I was nuts, laughing as I approached the table.

The Church Council is the highest committee in the church. It is made up of the Chairs of the other major committees, the lay leader of the church, and several others who were voted in at-large, including at least one young adult and one teen. As the only teenager actively involved in church affairs, Jeremy Clark was on the council. The other council member was me. The chairperson was Jack Conwell. There were fifteen voting members in all. As such, the head table tonight was actually four tables arranged in a crescent, with sixteen chairs for the fifteen members plus Janice, who once again served as the non-voting secretary. Every chair was filled, except mine. As I took my seat, I noted that Bob Williams was in the front spectator row, directly in front of me. No coincidence there.

Jack called the meeting to order. He is a reasonable and capable man, prone to following appropriate procedures. He is not easily pressured by others.

After my opening prayer, he said, "I am speaking to the voting members of the council, when I say that this meeting has been called to address only specific concerns. We will not be dealing with regular council business at this time. Nor will there be any new business. The only item on tonight's agenda is a request made by Mr. Robert Williams, for an opportunity to bring concerns about the performance of our pastor, the Reverend Nathan Martin. We have an unusually large audience this evening, to say the least. Let me thank all of you for being here, but also remind you that this meeting is open for observation only. Only Church Council members and those invited by the Chair will speak."

"Excuse, me, Mr. Conwell," I interrupted.

"Let's just stick with Jack," he replied. "The less this sounds like a trial the better."

"Thank you, Jack. I would just like to have it on the record that I will recuse myself from any votes that might be taken tonight, for reasons that I think are obvious."

"Yes, of course. Thank you."

"Also," I continued, "I would like to give up my voice as a member of this body, in exchange for the right to respond to accusations made against me."

Jack looked at me thoughtfully. Then he spoke. "That may be appropriate, but let me do a little clarification first. This may all become moot. Mr. Williams?"

"Yes," Bob answered. "How about you call me Bob and I call you Jack?"

"Fine. Bob, let me say that I don't want to be here. And, I am not sure that we should be here. I only scheduled this meeting because there seemed to be so much excitement going on. Bob, why are we here? The Church Council has nothing to do with this type of thing."

"Technically, that is true. But what I am asking concerns the whole church, and I think that everyone has a right to know what is happening. The hope is to be open, honest and transparent with our own congregation."

"Okay, but why here? Problems with the performance of a pastor belong to the Staff Parish Relations Committee."

"Yes, exactly my dilemma," Bob said. "According to the *Book of Discipline of the United Methodist Church*, only a bishop, a district superintendent, the SPRC Committee or the pastor him or herself can initiate a change in pastors. I want Nathan to be moved out of . . ."

"Stop, please," Jack said sharply. "Call me Jack, but let's stick with Reverend Martin when referring to our pastor."

"All right. Okay. I want Reverend Martin to be moved to another church. I am not out to get him. I do not want to bring charges against him, although I believe we could."

"Stop trying to make a case and answer my question. Why are we here, Bob?"

"As I said, I think the membership of the church is entitled to be included in this process. But, only the SPRC can initiate a request to move a pastor. And, also by the *Book of Discipline*, SPRC meetings are closed to only the committee members and the pastor, and occasionally the district superintendent. So, the people are shut out."

Jack responded, "So, is it your intention then, Bob, to simply rewrite the *Book of Discipline* to suit your own views of things? It seems to me that our denomination has written rules on how to do these things, and you want to change or ignore them in favor of some set of rules of your own choosing. Am I being accurate here, Bob?"

"Well, not if you are going to put it like that."

"How else shall I put it?" Jack asked. "This committee can take no action on this, you just said it yourself. Is this just some sort of a show?"

"Excuse me!" Jenn interrupted. "May I speak?"

Jack looked at Jenn for a moment, then said, "Yes, Mrs. Martin, if your accuser can speak, certainly you can, too."

"Thank you. Could we stipulate that this meeting is informational only, so the Church Council can be kept informed as to goings-on in the church. By extension, the church body will be informed. Then, if so led, the council can vote to ask the Staff Parish Relations Committee to consider the matter, so long as the request in no way suggests how the SPRC should rule. That way we can move on without further delays and without further posturing by those who are trying so desperately to have their accusations heard."

Jack responded, "I must confess, Mrs. Martin, that I am a bit surprised to hear this particular solution from you."

"Me, too, and, call me Jenn."

The crowd laughed.

"I don't know. Reverend? What do you think? Can we do this? And, even more important, do you want to? I won't force you to go through something that is not required."

"My wife is almost always right about such things."

"Very well, I'll let it go forward. Bob, as you have seen to it that everyone has a list of your complaints, let's address them one at a time. We will stick to the list."

Bob stood and turned to face his audience. He cleared his throat and prepared to speak.

"Janice," Jack Conwell said loudly, "would you read item number one, please?"

Bob started to rebut, thought better of it, and sat down.

Janice looked at me, tears rapidly filling her eyes.

"It's okay," I mouthed silently.

She began, *Number one: A teenage boy has been allowed a seat and a vote on the church's Finance Committee. This is . . ."*

Bob jumped up. "Uh, Jack, I think this one has been dealt with already. Could just move on?"

"Have you removed this item from all of the many handouts you have distributed?"

"No."

"Then please sit down and stop interrupting. Go on, Janice."

Number one: A teenage boy has been allowed a seat and a vote on the church's Finance Committee. This is unprecedented and irresponsible. By the next regularly scheduled finance meeting this situation will be rectified by removing the boy from the committee or, at least, rescinding his right to vote.

"What do you have to say, Reverend Martin?" Jack said, granting me the floor.

"Jeremy was properly voted into his position by the people of this church, at last year's Charge Conference. No rules were broken. In fact, Jeremy sits on the council, as well. The *Book of Discipline* recommends a teen on the council. He is a delight. He is smart, prompt and well informed. There is absolutely no wrong-doing here. Period."

"Bob?" Jack asked.

"Evidently, that is all true. That's why I tried to stop you."

"I know."

Bob pushed on, "Anyway, I'm still against a kid . . ."

"Personal opinions do not hold up against properly instituted policy. Janice, the next complaint, please."

Under the direct influence of the pastor, the music program of the church has moved in unfortunate directions. Guitars, drums, untrained musicians and music of a less than sacred nature have been integrated into the various functions and services of the church. Immediately, all control of the music program at EFFUMC shall be turned over to Music Director Condi Cloverton, including the choice of hymns to be sung during worship services. Condi shall be instructed to return the church to its well-earned reputation of offering the best of sacred, traditional Christian music. The pastor will cooperate in any manner needed to carry out this mission.

Jack turned to me once again. "Reverend Martin, what is your response?"

Before I could speak, the back door of the Fellowship Hall burst open with a crash. Jimmy Clouse walked in, carrying the largest of his many drums. He was followed silently by several others toting each piece of the set. Next came Jolene and Samuel and Nick, each with a guitar. They were followed by Cassandra and Tim, the lead singers, and then the rest of the praise and worship team. They quietly circled the perimeter of the room, in some spots barely squeezing past the packed assembly. They said not a word and carefully avoided looking at anyone. Behind them streamed people, individuals and families. Many were young by church standards, but not a few were old. I was especially taken by Lela Griffin, all ninety-three years of her, struggling a little, but keeping up. Except for a few of the children, no one made eye contact with the seated crowd. But, they did carry signs. *Jesus is my Lord,* one read. *Praise God!* another. *This is my church, too; My children come to church now; "I love you" comes in many languages; God loves me . . . and you.* A husband carried a large sign that read, *God loves classical music!* The wife followed with, *But I think he's partial to the new stuff!* Over a hundred people filed in and filed out. Not a word was said, not a note was played, but the people of the *contemporary worship* service had just had their say.

"Mr. Chairman," Bob started his complaint, "why was that allowed!? I thought the people weren't being allowed to speak during this meeting."

"Well," Jack replied, "I suppose technically you are correct. Still, once someone has put information out there, it is hard to take it back. Right, Bob?"

Some of my supporters started waving their copies of Bob's infamous handout in the air.

Bob's voice dropped almost too low to hear as he said, "I suppose," and sat down.

"Well, Pastor," Jack said, "sorry for the delay. Please speak to the music question."

"Actually, I am a little verklempt," I started.

They laughed. I love it when they laugh.

I answered, "I love classical music and the old tried and true hymns, myself. I am more of a words guy than a music guy, to be honest. So the strong theology in the hymnal lyrics are great for me. And I must say that, here at East Fork First, we have a stellar traditional music program. However, I must object to the term *less than sacred* to describe new music in new styles. Every generation tends to decide that their music is the best or the most sacred. Unless you want the church to live and then die in one generation, room has to be made for new expression."

"Thank you. Bob, what would you like to add?" Jack asked.

"I believe that I represent the great majority of people in this church. The people who have loved this town and this building for many years don't want to see their own church hijacked! While I understand that new generations of young people like their own music, isn't it the job of the church to guide them toward what is best and what is right! Just because they like something doesn't mean it is the thing to do. What about the church's obligation to hold on to what is right and teach the young to like it!? And I think this church I love so much should do what it has always done. Bring the very best to our community. God has blessed us with someone like Condi Cloverton to do just that. Most will learn to like and eventually even cherish true, sacred music. For those who don't, there are other kinds of churches for them. They should find one."

Half of the crowd applauded boisterously. The other half sat silently staring at those who clapped. The room had suddenly gone schizoid. As I contemplated this, I saw Condi Cloverton leave out the side door.

"Okay, let's have order!" Jack shouted. "That's enough demonstrating from all parties. Unless a member of the council wishes more information on this topic, I suggest we move on."

I saw Bob subtly nod to Craig Jenkins, an at-large member of the Church Council.

"Jack, may I say something?" Craig asked.

"Sure, go ahead."

"This next one, the one about having a special meeting for long-time members and giving them special say-so. I would like to move that we just rule that one out of order and move on."

"Is that a motion?"

"Yeah. I move that item three on the list be ruled out of order."

"Second!" came from several relieved council-members.

Bob sat with his arms crossed, a smug look on his face. *He's doing damage control,* I thought.

"Any discussion?"

"Yes," I answered, "I would like to hear it read before we decide."

"What's the point?" a suddenly less-smug Bob Williams blurted out.

"You have not been recognized, Bob." Jack said. "As it is Reverend Martin being accused, we can be fair enough to let him have some say in what gets heard. Janice, would you please?"

She read, *Number three--The directions taken by the church have been insensitive to the needs of the long-term members who have provided, and continue to provide, the great majority of the church's financial support. As soon as possible, a meeting restricted to those who have been official members of the church for in excess of ten years shall be called. The concerns of this group shall be duly noted and honored in every reasonable way.*

"Thank you, Janice," Jack said. "Pastor?"

"Oh, I think that is way out of order."

A Dragon in the Church 169

Even Jack grinned before asking, "Any further discussion? Hearing none, those in favor of ruling item number three out of order, please say *aye*."

"Aye!"

"It's unanimous. Next item, please."

Janice read aloud, *Number four—The pastor has routinely preached sermons on topics and subjects that are not desired by the majority of the membership. Topics such as, but not limited to: abortion, homosexuality, anti-patriotism and God's so-called "preference for the poor" make good examples. The pastor is now advised to stick with sermons that the membership find positive and suitable to Sunday worship. If the pastor fails to demonstrate improved judgment on this matter, a committee should be formed to preview his choices ahead of time, with the power to rectify any inappropriate situations before they get a chance to occur.*

For many, the only regular contact had with a pastor is as preacher. To openly question the competence of the preacher, and the preacher's right to decide what is to be preached, is not something that happens often. No doubt some in the crowd disliked some of what I preached or, perhaps, most of it. Just as surely, some in the crowd would vehemently disagree. As such, the sudden quiet underlined the interest that was at once intense, nuanced and ambiguous. Bob Williams sat and stared directly at me, trying hard to get my eyes to lock on his. So, I obliged. *Gotcha!* his eyes screamed at me. Right then, I hated him.

Chairman Conwell spoke. "As the charge has been leveled against Reverend Martin, I believe it best to give him the first response. Nathan, what would you like to say to that?"

I said, "Thank you, Jack. I appreciate the opportunity to address this topic directly with the good folks here at East Fork. Preaching is, of course, one of the most important things that a pastor does . . . the exposition of Holy Scripture and all . . . which is really what preaching is, after all . . . very important . . ."

"Yes, indeed," Jack said, "But how do you respond to Bob's accusation? This is your chance to respond."

"Yes, certainly," I said.

But I had no idea what to say. Bob picked up on my uncertainty. He smelled blood.

"It appears . . ." he started to say.

"Be quiet! My husband has the floor. Unlike some, he is careful about what he says."

The room filled with an odd soup of giggles, oohs and ahs.

"Just say it, Honey," she said even louder, coming to my side without leaving her chair.

Finally, I found my voice. "When I have my preacher's hat on, it is not my job to please the people. Not the people in general, and absolutely not whoever might have decided to put themselves in charge of God's Word. My job is to preach the Word of God as accurately and completely as I can, regardless of what people want to hear. And, my job is to help us all live into God's Word in new and better ways. Usually, we find the process positive and uplifting and inspiring. Sometimes it feels like a slap in the face as it reminds us how far we have fallen short. Either way, the only one I seek to please is God. Period.

"I might add that, according to United Methodist rules, there is no one at East Fork First UMC who can tell me what to preach or how to preach it. That responsibility rests on my shoulders alone. Don't think that the task does not sometimes weigh heavy on my soul. It does. The Church Council cannot change that, nor the Trustees, nor the Worship Committee, nor even the Staff Parish Relations Committee. It is also important to point out that Bob Williams does not serve on any of those properly elected bodies. He has presented me with instructions on how to preach, and warnings about what will happen if I don't perform to his satisfaction, with no authority of any kind. Except, of course, that he is rich. And, he is a bully. This church will not be run by bullying. At least, not while I am still the pastor here."

"And that may not be a whole lot longer!" Bob blurted, a whiny catch in his voice that I am sure he would like to get back. "That's why we're here!"

"You do not have the floor, Bob!" Jack shouted.

"Thank you, Jack," I said, "I am about finished. With respect to the council, let me state as the sole authority on matters of preaching in this church, that this matter is closed. Move on."

"Very well," Jack said, trying but failing to suppress a grin. "Moving on."

Bob stood. "Can he do that!?"

Jack responded, "Looks like. And if he can't, I can. Moving on. Janice?"

"Number five—*The church has been embarrassed by the fact the pastor cannot influence even his own wife to attend the church. Barring medical emergencies and unusual circumstances, the pastor's spouse—who, after all, benefits from living in the parsonage owned and kept up by the church—shall regularly attend Sunday services. It is also reasonable to expect that church participation of the spouse, additional to Sunday services, would be evident.*"

"Thank you, Janice," Jack said. "Reverend Martin, your response?"

"I choose to defer the floor and my time to the person most involved in this particular matter, Jennifer Martin."

"I object!" Bob Williams yelled out, jumping from his seat. "I object!"

"This not a courtroom and I am not a judge," Jack explained. "What is it now?"

"The whole idea of this meeting is to deal with problems that we have with the pastor. I just think that we can only deal with Nate, excuse me, Reverend Martin. His wife is not an employee of the church. He is, so . . ."

"I object!" I shouted. "I am not an employee of the church."

Dead silence. Everyone stared. Nobody moved. The pause grew long. Finally Bob, perhaps sensing a victory, recovered and said, "Did you just quit?"

"No, I certainly did not."

"Let me clarify, if it is okay with you, Mr. Chairman?"

"Jeremy? Sure. Please do."

"According to United Methodist rules, the pastor has an unusual relationship to the church. The pastor does the work required of a pastor: teaching, preaching, counseling, bookwork, meetings, raking leaves, whatever. And, the church pays their salary and benefits and provides housing. So, it sure looks like an employer/employee relationship. But, the church did not hire, and cannot fire, the pastor. The pastor did not choose the church, and cannot decide to move to another church. A minimum salary is dictated to the church, although we pay Pastor Nathan more than that. His job description does not come from this church, either. And, according to the IRS, the pastor is an independent contractor. The church does not withhold taxes from his pay and we don't pay half of his Social Security, like you do for an employee. The pastor has to pay the whole thing, like a business guy. So, it is at least as accurate to say that he is not an employee of the church as it is to say that he is."

Extended silence was interrupted by a shout from the back of the room, "Hey, Williams! You been trying to kick the kid off committees, and he's smarter than the rest of you!"

The room erupted in tension-relieving laughter.

"The Chair sees no reason to pursue this particular line of discussion any further. I believe that Jennifer Martin has been dragged into this and has a right to respond if she wishes."

Oh, she wishes, I thought. Jenn stood and turned to face the crowd. Unhurried, she surveyed the room as she formulated her remarks. She had soaked up a lot of pain in recent years, without pushing back. Finally, it was her turn. Someone scooted up and handed her a cordless microphone. The silence was complete. Those who loved her, those who hated her, and those who knew her not at all, wanted to hear what she had to say. *She was about to speak.*

"Good evening," she began. "I'm Jennifer Martin. I don't know all of you, so I am sure that you don't all know me. I wish we could meet under different circumstances, but here we are. I am grateful for the chance to speak. There are some things that need to be said."

If complete silence can somehow become even quieter, it did. Collectively the entire crowd seemed to be holding its breath.

"I love God. I love the Father. I love Jesus. I love the Holy Spirit. That is first. Almost equally, I love my husband. To you he may be Pastor Nate or Reverend Martin, but to me he is my love. My one and only. So, you will have to excuse me—or not, I suppose—when I say that when I hear some of the things being said about him in recent weeks and still tonight, my first reaction is to gouge someone's eyes out."

The crowd gasped.

"You don't need to be afraid," she said through a smile. "I would never do that. As a Christian woman, it is against the rules."

A little nervous laughter mixed in.

"I try to always work past my anger and get on to more peaceful responses. But, I wonder if anyone understands that a pastor is a human being, with loved ones and a family made up of human beings. We are not your punching bags or your appliances. We are people, just like you. We laugh, we cry, we try, we succeed and we fail. And we hurt. So I will ask everyone here, whether you are pro or con on any of this, to treat my husband with respect. He is a good Christian man doing only what he thinks is right. Even if you want another pastor, remember that a good man stands before you."

Jenn paused and perused the crowd. Most were waiting expectantly. *Was this all she had to say?*

"As for the demand that I attend on Sundays and participate in other church activities, I am very tempted to give the obvious answer, which is that it is none of your business. I am under no obligation, like it or not. However, that is not the real story. I love church. I love to worship and fellowship with others. Ever since we started this life as pastor and spouse, I have just naturally and gladly participated in the churches that Nathan has served. As most of you know, I once participated here. But, it was not because I had to or was supposed to. It was because this was *my* church, just like you come here because it is *your* church. And, I was perfectly happy with that, despite the fact that from the very beginning, I was treated more coldly here than I had ever been anywhere else."

Silence gave way to murmuring and sideways glances, as individuals in the crowd checked to see what their reaction ought to be.

"I understand that it is uncomfortable to hear such a thing said out loud, but it is true. For a while it wasn't too bad, and I could not tell exactly what the problem was. But, unfortunately, the time came when clarity only made things worse. You might remember my husband's short-lived attempt to create open communication by setting up an e-mail account specifically for the members of the congregation to make comments and ask questions." Jenn turned to face me, and said, "Thanks Honey . . . great idea."

Laughter intermingled with the low-grade wave of murmuring that was still in the room.

Jenn went on, "As you are wondering how I could dare to label your church as *cold,* let me share a few of those e-mails with you. I know who sent each one, even though none of them had the courage to identify themselves. Not one. However, unlike you, and you know who you are, I will not criticize you in public, at least not by name."

Jenn unfolded a piece of paper that she had been holding in her hand. The buzz stopped. I could barely breathe. It had been such a painful realization that I had failed to be my beloved wife's advocate or protector—her *hero*, really—that I was petrified watching her stand up to the people. Still, she had insisted that it was what she must do.

"There were several written to my husband, your pastor, on other matters. I am reading only those that involved me. One at a time, they are:

The pastor seems to be friendly enough, but his wife could stand to get her nose out of the air—as if she has anything to be proud of."

"I am sorry," Jenn continued, "if I have ever seemed snobbish in any way. I certainly do not mean to be. And, as is true for most, I imagine, I have things in my life that make me feel proud, and things that I wish I could change. Is that different from any of you?"

She continued, "*Perhaps the pastor's wife thinks that skirts that might have fit her once still do. It's indecent. Get some bigger clothes or lose some weight!*"

An unidentified "Oh my!" was heard above the quickening murmur.

"I hardly know what to say," Jenn said. "It was a gut-wrenching and humiliating thing to hear, especially from a woman who hasn't seen the underside of 200 pounds in decades."

The room erupted in laughter and angry retorts, some whispered and some shouted. *You tell her! Are you kidding me? Did she say that! Cat fight!* The loudest was, *That's out of line!*

Jennifer waited for the hubbub to quiet down. Then she said, "Yes, it is out of line, isn't it? I apologize. Truly. That is, however, exactly how it feels."

In the fourth row, two seats from the aisle, a fat woman started to cry.

"The next e-mail—and these all arrived in one day, by the way—reads, *I was running the Sunday school for years before* you two got here, and I will still be running it when you're gone. The pastor's comments are part of the deal, but the pastor's wife should just butt out."

All eyes sought out, and found, Margaret West.

"The hardest part about this may not be what you think," Jenn said. "Sure, being told to butt out is difficult, especially coupled with the expectation that I should participate. We clergy families are moved about by the United Methodist Church. If you think it is weird to be told by someone else what pastor is coming to your church, please try to imagine what it is like to be told what church you are going to serve, and what town you now live in, and in what house you will now stay. Without even knowing how long the stay will be. You have to leave people you love and you arrive in the new place as an outsider who is suddenly supposed be an insider and some people want you there and some don't, and some are already mad before they meet you and some are excited that you've come. And, you don't know which are which. And, you're supposed to be and act like a hundred different people want you to, only they have a hundred different opinions about what that is. And, this is rich, they only tell you what you did wrong after you've already done it. How do you suppose that feels?!"

The words were flying now. Jenn no longer consulted notes. She went on, "And so you are told, to win an argument or to make a point, *I was here before you were sent, and I will still be here when you are sent away. You'll never be one of us."*

No one said anything, so Jennifer continued. "Much of what has been said so far is expected. It happens, so you try to deal with it. But, this last one brought things to a level that I could not tolerate. So I became affiliated with a different church. A church where I would not be *fair game*. It reads, *I wonder if the pastor's wife has ever repented or apologized for her ways as a young woman. Should we have someone who sets such an example teaching our children? It's not as if people don't know."*

"I wrote that! And, I'd do it again!" The shout came from Berta Lou. "I'm sure we're going to hear a sob story of what a difficult childhood she had and . . ."

"Sit down and be quiet!" shouted Jack Conwell. "You have not been recognized. Sit down!"

Berta Lou glared at Jack and moved not a muscle. She was deciding what to do. Berta Lou Gallagher was not used to be told to sit down, much less to stop talking.

"I yield the floor to Berta Lou Gallagher," Jenn said. "Let's hear it."

"Are you sure?" Jack asked. "I won't allow anyone to get beat up on my watch."

"We came here to settle some things. Let's settle."

"Very well," Jack said, "Go ahead Mrs. Gallagher."

Berta Lou appeared to be anything but settled. She was confused by Jenn's action.

"As I was trying to say . . . what I mean is . . . we . . . East Fork First United Methodist Church has always had standards. Yes, we all make mistakes. However, when it comes to proper clergy, and by extension the clergy family, we have a right to expect our standards be met. We all know that Mrs. Martin has a child, a *step* child to our pastor, that was born out of wedlock."

The gasps and questioning eyes around the room made it clear that *we all* didn't know that.

"And," Berta Lou went on, regaining her momentum, "she behaves as if it is just the most wonderful thing in the world. I have neither seen nor heard one bit of repentance or apology. It is right of us to expect more from our pastor, and his family. I might also add, as a recent victim of his hypocrisy, that it is obviously easier for Reverend Martin to chastise and criticize and humiliate one of us, than he ever would his own wife."

Jenn responded, "My daughter's name is Lisa. She is a grown woman now. A fine, productive, happy, Christian woman. And she was born out of wedlock, just after I finished high school. It was not how it should have gone. But once it happened, I loved her and worked hard and raised her on my own and finished my education and became a teacher and married a fine man. I was contrite. I have repented. I have apologized. To God. To God who loves me, forgave me and made me new. I will however, never, apologize to the likes of you."

Things happened fast after that. Berta Lou started hollering at the top of her lungs about *how she never . . . and after all these years, if you think I'm going to put up with . . .* and such. And, people joined in. Some cheered Jenn's direct (too direct?) honesty. Others shared Berta Lou's outrage. A shouting match didn't take too long to turn into complete chaos.

Jack screamed, "Order! Order!" for quite a while. Eventually he just switched to "We are adjourned! We are adjourned!"

But no one showed any signs of leaving, or shutting up. Smaller groups started to form, as the arguing got more personal and sides were taken up like armor and weapons.

Frank delivered Jenn to me and yelled, "Get her out of here, Pastor, before she gets hurt!"

I hugged Sylvie and Jenn hugged Frank. Then I yelled *let's go!* a couple of times and dragged Jenn toward the rear exit.

Halfway to freedom, or at least relief, we ran square into our buddy Bob. He was grinning from ear to ear. He moved close and stuck his face in ours. His always-ridiculous mustache was too long on one side, and he had obviously had onions in his supper.

"Way to make peace, Pastor!"

He could not suppress his outright laughter, but made sure that only Jenn and I could see it.

"Once the shouting stops," he shouted, "I'd say it's all over but the paperwork! Your precious bishop is going to love this!"

I knew it would be best to just leave, without any kind of retort, but my body wouldn't move and my mouth wouldn't stay closed.

"I might get blamed," I shouted right back, "but you did this. How can you bring so much hurt to a church you say you love?!"

"You'll be gone. Your kind will quit. We'll recover and be what we want to be. Face it Nate, any way you look at it, it's a win!"

"A win for who? The Church? God?"

"A win for me. You thought you could play with the big boys. I taught you different. The winner writes the history, buddy. The blame falls on you. I was going to offer to let you resign quietly, but after tonight, I don't think so."

"You are a pathetic little man!" Jenn spat out. "You will never be the man my husband is."

"I sure hope not, Jenny."

The sarcasm dripped from his lips. The rest of the world roared around us and only the three of us would ever know how Bob now behaved. In a few moments he would be back to polished Bob, local business leader and pillar of the church.

"I try not to be anything like a loser," he continued.

"You are just plain evil," Jennifer said.

"And you, Jenny, once a skank, always a . . ."

Chapter 26

At the police station, waiting for the completion of paperwork, all I could remember of that crucial moment was the feel of my fist against Bob's face. I hadn't hit anybody since I was fifteen, and Jared Warner called me a sissy in front of the cheerleaders. Now, I could still feel the impact of catching Bob between the corner of his mouth and his nose. A face is hard there and it hurt my hand, but I could hear the crunch as something gave way. It was simultaneously sickening and exhilarating. I know I caught him by surprise. I never saw it coming myself. Bob went down hard and fast. He screamed in pain and, becoming aware of the converging crowd, screamed again even louder.

Just so no one would miss the latest plot twist, he added, "He hit me! He hit me! The pastor hit me!"

Like I said before, the guy is good. The ambulance was called. The police were called. A ride to the emergency would have sufficed, but the charging arrival of first responders is much better theater. I probably should have helped or apologized or explained or something. But I did not. Jenn and I stood off to the side and watched. What was there to say?

The EMTs walked Bob out, headed for the hospital. The police arrived. An officer approached me. The once-unruly crowd moved not a muscle and said not a word.

"What happened?" the officer asked.

"Bob Williams insulted my wife, and I decked him," I said.

"That's it. It's that simple? Did you sneak up on him or hit him with anything?"

"No. That's it. We were talking face to face. He said something that I didn't like, and I hit him. Once."

"Okay. I am going to have to arrest you. You know that, right?"

Handcuffs. Miranda rights. The *perp-walk* to the back seat of a cop car. All with an audience of two hundred of my *flock*. And one wife. Who watched the whole thing, looking at me like she used to. Which felt great. And confusing. And wrong. Very wrong. Or not.

Jenn had gone home for the check book and come back to do what I am sure she had always hoped to do one day—bail me out. Now, we sat waiting to see what would happen next. I had been printed and photographed, but not much else. We had been sitting for a couple of hours since the last action. It was late. We were exhausted and shell-shocked.

"So much for taking the high road," Jenn said.

I laughed. I couldn't help it.

But I said, "I know. I am sorry, Honey. I don't know how I lost control of myself."

"I meant me," Jenn replied. "I went in there to be the reasonable one, the cool one, the good one. And then I started flapping my gums."

"It's all right. You had plenty of reason to be upset. And, besides, I think I provided you with good cover. I don't think they'll be remembering much but the ending."

"It *was* dramatic," she said. "A real unpredictable twist."

Jenn chortled a little and snuggled as close to me as the bolted-down chairs would allow. We sat in silence for a time.

"Although," I said, "a few people might find that whole, two-hundred-pound, fat lady thing quite memorable."

We laughed from our bellies.

"I know," she said. "That was way wrong. It really was."

"Yeah," I replied, "we got some wrong on us tonight. But, the good news is, I think we are looking at a future that is wide open from here on out."

"Looks like," she said quietly. "But, we'll face it together."

"No doubt."

I had just started making up a story about a United Methodist pastor and his devoted wife turning to a life of crime and adventure, when visitors arrived. Not cops. Not lawyers. It was Bob Williams. His nose was grotesquely bandaged and he had rough, black, blue and yellow terrain on the left side of his face. I felt a rush of genuine shame. I did that to another human being. It was still hard to imagine. And, Bob was not alone. He was with his mother.

Bob's mother is not a woman to be trifled with. She is brusque, straightforward and used to getting her own way. She had once been very active in the management of all of the family businesses, including the East Fork UMC. When I arrived, I was told that, upon her husband's death four years earlier, she had turned her various powers over to Bob. She then moved from her undisputed spot in the front pew, to the widows' pew in the back. To most of the locals, Robert Williams Senior and his son Bob (never to be confused with Robert) had built an impressive business empire. Only a few knew that Mother Martha had always been the power behind the throne. Immediately, she took control.

"I want to understand clearly what happened here," she demanded.

"Hello Martha," I said. "I am really sorry to bother you with such a mess. I believe you know my wife, Jennifer."

"Yes. Of course. I hope you are both doing all right, considering. Now, I have heard Bob's perspective on this. You will find it important to help me understand clearly."

"Very well. Your son and I have been doing political battle in the church . . ."

"I am aware of that."

"Yes. Until now, we have been able to be civil and try to work things out through channels. Tonight, things took a different turn."

"Please be specific."

"Mother, please."

"Bob! Go on, Reverend."

"Specifically, Bob had been publically building a case against my wife and her performance, or as he sees it, her lack of performance, as a proper pastor's wife. So, I was already somewhat angry, but in control."

"What changed?"

"The meeting had broken up into raucous discussion. In the middle of the crowd, but privately, due to the noise, the debate continued. Some things were said."

"You did not assault my son because *some* things were said! What was said?"

"Bob called Jenn a *skank*. I punched him in the face."

Martha Williams took her time to respond. When she did, she questioned Bob. "Why did you call Mrs. Martin a *skank*?"

"Mother, please, I think this would be better discussed alone."

"Why? You evidently think it fit to attack people in public. Which is something, by the way, I never once saw your father do. He was tough, but he was decent. So, tell me, right now. Why is Mrs. Martin a skank? Surely you based that on something."

"Sometimes people comment that her clothes are too revealing, too short or too low."

"That's it?" Martha asked incredulously. "That's your reason for calling a pastor's wife a vile name like *skank*?"

"No! She had a baby right out of high school and didn't get married, okay!? She had a baby and her daughter doesn't belong to Pastor Nathan."

Martha said nothing.

"People talk, Mom. They don't think our kind of church ought to have that kind of influence, especially from the pastor's family." Still getting no response, Bob plunged desperately on. "People say if she was sorry, if she apologized and repented and stuff, maybe it would be okay. But she acts as if everything is just fine."

After more painful silence, Martha turned to Jenn and asked, "How old was your daughter when you and your husband first came to East Fork?"

"Thirty-eight."

"Is she a productive citizen?"

"More than that. She's top-notch. And, other people say that, not just me."

"Well done, Mrs. Martin. Well done."

"Mom!"

"Pastor," Martha went on, "exactly why did you hit my son? Please be honest."

"I love my wife and our daughter. Bob demeaned Jennifer, so I popped him. That's the whole truth of it. It wasn't exactly a decision."

"Are you proud of it?"

"No. I teach peace and then I do this. Not good."

"Are you sorry you did it?"

I didn't look at Jenn. I was afraid to. I didn't look at Bob. With more than a little hesitation, I looked at Martha and said, "No. Maybe I should be, but I am not the least bit sorry."

Martha's face softened. She smiled a world-weary smile, and said, "Good. And if any other man does what my son did, pop him too. God made men to be men."

"Mother! For heaven's sake, what are you saying?" Bob more whined than asked.

"I am saying, young man, that I am going to settle this. Don't make me remind you whose name is on the deed of every

Williams property. Right now I'd be happy to sell everything and leave the money to a gold fish."

Bob shut up and began studying the tops of his shoes.

"There will be no charges. As soon as my son explains that he made a mistake, and he was not assaulted after all, you two should be able to go home. Do you understand me, Bob?"

"Yes, Mother."

Martha continued, "I am sorry, Reverend. I am sorry, Mrs. Martin. This should not have happened. The Williams family has always been tough, hard competitors. We like to be successful. Sometimes when we win, others lose. Life's like that. But, we play honest and fair. Tonight my son forgot that. Reverend Martin, I am not at all certain if you should continue to be our pastor. I have reservations myself. However, there are ways to express concerns and there are ways to fight dirty. To attack a pastor through his wife? It just makes me want to cry."

"Thank you," I said, "I appreciate that."

"Thank you," Jenn said.

"Very well," she replied. "I have apologized for my family. I don't care whether Bob apologizes or not, but he is going to fix this."

"What do you mean *fix it*," Bob asked, his whine becoming more pronounced.

"This Sunday morning, the Reverend is going to give you five minutes to address the congregation. You tore this woman down in front of hundreds of people, and in front of hundreds you will build her back up. And lest you worry about whether your effort will satisfy Reverend and Mrs. Martin," Martha said, closing in on Bob, "The one you had better satisfy is me! Speak well, Son, or pay the price."

She moved until her forehead was inches from his bandaged nose.

"And you listen to me, you snot. You remember that big, showy fiftieth anniversary party you threw for your dear departed father and me nine years ago?"

"Of course. It was a special night, real special."

"Yes," she said, softening noticeably, "it was. It was also only our forty-ninth year of marriage. We had to add a year right after you were born. People used to remind us of that once in a while, until we got rich. Then they found it wise to leave it alone. Robert . . . Son, sometimes people screw up. God gives them another chance. So should we. Fix this."

With that Martha Williams walked down the hall without a look back, and disappeared. Bob started to speak, thought better of it, and followed her at a safe distance.

Ten minutes later an officer said, "I shredded the paperwork. Just go home."

We went home.

Chapter 27

By the time we arrived home, physical and emotional exhaustion was setting in. It was 2:30 a.m. and it seemed as if we had been up for three days. We made it into bed and snuggled up to talk, but sleep was coming on fast.

"We'll talk about how wrong this is later," Jenn whispered. "Right now I'm fading fast, but in a few hours, I am going to make you glad you're a man. You are my hero, you know."

"I know that I want to be. And, to be clear, what I am glad for is that you are my wife."

"And I'm glad, and blessed, that you are my husband. So that works out nicely."

"Quite a night," I said.

"Yeah, quite a night. That'll get a whole chapter in the book."

We laughed and faded out.

Come morning, she whispered, "It's Friday. Sunday's coming."

"I'm thinking we're going to have an unusual Sunday," I said. "What do you think?"

"I think, let's get out of here," she said.

I canceled everything and we and took off toward northern-lower Michigan. We drove and we talked and we laughed. We cried some, too. Things were happening so fast, that we could not even keep up with the *what ifs*. We were driving ourselves nuts with all the possibilities. *Was my formal ministry over? Could I, would I even want to, stay on at East*

Fork First? Another United Methodist Church? A different church entirely? Could Jenn find another teaching job? Could I master the art of making of french fries?

Eventually, Jenn said, "Did we or did we not claim that we would do whatever God wanted, no matter the cost?"

"Yes," I replied, "we did. I'm not real sure how well we're doing, though."

"True, we've both fallen short, for sure. But, so did King David. At least you haven't matched his whole Bathsheba/Uriah thing. Right?"

"If it helps you to think that," I replied.

My arm hurt for hours. The woman can punch. We agreed to stop obsessing and stopped at the Apple Tree Inn in Petoskey. We had stayed there before, enjoying the nice accommodations and a beautiful view of Lake Michigan's Little Traverse Bay. It had been a place of solace and tending to our marriage. Saturday morning, I sat with Jenn on the balcony, enjoying the morning view and the company of the woman I loved so much it was hard to contain.

I said. "Let's quit trying to figure things out ahead of time and see where God takes us."

She responded, "K-Sarah-Sarah, whatever will be will be. I'm in. Let's stay here until they kick us out. Then we can head home and talk about what happens in church tomorrow."

"Great," I said, "Let's order breakfast."

Chapter 28

Pastors are all the time trying to find ways to increase attendance on Sunday mornings. The church building at East Fork First United Methodist Church has seating for an overly optimistic nine hundred. In reality, our typical Sunday turnout was about four hundred at the 9:30 traditional service, with another hundred and fifty or so at the 11:00 contemporary service. Over the years I had tried different music, guest speakers, drama, ambitious visual creations and many other strategies, without much change in participation. Who knew that all I had to do was create a juicy enough scandal for word-of-mouth to take over? On this particular Sunday, the place was packed. Standing room only. Late-arriving regulars approached *their* pews, only to find them already occupied with people they didn't even recognize. I thought we might have to get the automatic defibrillator out. Indeed, more than one quavering voice was heard to call out, "You're in my spot!" The ushers scurried about and set up chairs in the lobby. The extra seating absorbed the overflow and we got everyone situated.

Ten minutes before start time, the place was filled with a loud and constant buzz of conversation. Many church folk, especially those of a certain age, think they are whispering when they are not. I would have been absolutely thrilled had I thought that all of that excess energy was in anticipation of the praise and worship of God, but I knew it wasn't. Most of them, probably half of the regulars and ninety-five percent of the irregulars, just wanted to get the latest scoop. Churches always have to navigate a certain amount of controversy, but *a senior pastor physically decking a leading member of the church in front of two hundred people!* That's not a story you get to watch unfold every day.

Five minutes before service—wearing a black clergy robe and bright red/white/black stole (I often joke that I got into the ministry for the outfits)—I moved into the lobby and prepared to *process* into the sanctuary. I stood behind the day's acolytes (the wonderful grade-schoolers who so love to light the candles) and tried to focus. I knew that Bob Williams sat in the front row, waiting to make the speech that Mother Martha had commanded. Across the aisle, also in the very front, sat the lovely Jenn Martin. It was not a relaxed Sunday. T-minus three minutes.

"Good morning, Nathan." The voice came from just behind my right shoulder.

I turned and said, "Good morning. Welcome to our worship service, Reverend Halliday."

"Please, I'm still Judy. It's good to be here," she replied. "I thought maybe I should drop by this morning."

"How fortuitous! It just so happens that we are planning some special events today."

"So I heard. I'm just here to take the temperature of the congregation, so I know what is really happening, and what is not."

"I understand. Would you like me to fix you up with a seat down front, Judy?"

"No, I am keeping a low profile. I'll just stay back here."

The music started. The acolytes led the way. I followed down the aisle. And the district superintendent of the Gateway District of the Lower Michigan Conference of the United Methodist Church headed for the last empty folding chair. *Curiouser and curiouser,* I thought.

As I approached the chancel (the area at the front of the sanctuary that contains all the worshipping stuff) I smiled at Jenn. She smiled back. I also glanced at Bob, who sat unmoving. I entered the pulpit and looked out over the bulging, buzzing crowd. I had daydreamed often about the problem of too little room to accommodate all the people. But in my daydreams, they were all seeking God and God's Word. Not so today.

According to the morning bulletin (which really ought to be called a *program*) I was to start with a prayer and then have the lay-reader lead the congregation in a responsive reading known as the *Call to Worship*. Although most of the people in the pews would neither know nor care, the Call to Worship served as the official opening of our worship service.

I prayed, "Oh good and generous and holy God, we gather together as your children, the Body of Christ. We come seeking you and your Word. We sincerely hope that we can take even a bit of the great love you send down to us, and return it to you in ways you will find pleasing. May the Holy Spirit help us to understand what we have not understood, and to be more able and willing to live as Jesus taught us."

I didn't say the same prayer every week, and I never wrote it ahead of time. Typically, I would stop with something similar to the above and say an *Amen*.

This day, I felt the need to go on, "Let us not be distracted from our purpose, to live out your most basic instructions to us; to love you, God, and to love each other. Amen."

The temporary quiet for prayer time revved back up to a steady hum. The regulars positioned their bulletins, getting ready to stand and read their responses.

Instead, I said, "Please remain seated. We all know that today is an unusual Sunday. That is, unless this just happens to be a perfect storm of people deciding that it is time to get back to attending church."

Most of the regulars laughed. The rest did not.

I continued, "We cannot avoid dealing with some issues, but I will not allow that to spill over into our worship time. So, we will deal with a couple of topics right now. Once that has been done, and all that needs to be said has been said, we will proceed with the Call to Worship and the rest of our service. If we cannot then concentrate on worship, I will close the worship service immediately, and go home early. If that happens, would somebody please call Applebee's and Ramona's, and let them know that the after-church rush will be early and for once we will be arriving before the Baptists."

After the welcome laughter died down, I said, "Bob Williams has asked to address the congregation. Bob?"

Bob moved to the lectern, on the opposite side of the chancel from me. He laid down some note cards. He seemed reluctant to begin, but begin he did.

"Good morning. Many of you were present at the Church Council meeting this past Thursday. Most of the rest of you, I am sure, have heard about events that happened during and after that meeting. I am also sure, however, that not very many people know the whole story. It is no secret that I am personally disappointed and dissatisfied with some of the things that Reverend Martin is doing. I have become convinced that our church would be better off if he moved on. It was in that spirit that I brought my concerns to the attention of the entire church, which is, I think, as it should be . . ."

I sat quietly and as still as I could in my high-backed, red velvet clergy chair. I was never more aware of how visible and exposed a position I was in. *Is he just going to attack me here, too? I* wondered. This was represented as a chance to apologize, but Bob seemed to be building his case once again. Just as I was wondering what I could say to force the issue, I saw Martha Williams stand up in the very back row. Bob saw her, too.

"However," Bob said so much more loudly that several in the audience started, "I made a horrible mistake, for which I want to apologize."

Martha sat back down.

"I got carried away. I used poor judgment. I behaved in a way that a good, Christian, church-loving man ought never to behave. And, I am ashamed. So, I come before you to publically repent and ask for your forgiveness. I went past my legitimate concerns with Reverend Martin and made personal attacks against his wife. In front of many of you good people, I accused her of not living up to her duties as our pastor's wife. Some of those duties, I pretty much made up myself, just so I could make my case. I feel so foolish. I went on to imply that she is a woman of low character. Others chimed in, but it was my fault. I apologize to you, Mrs. Martin. I hope one day you will be able to forgive me."

Jenn sat as a statue, showing no change or response.

"And," Bob continued, working up a *preacher's voice*, "I apologize to my church family. I want to represent our church well, and I am crushed by my own failure. I am so sorry."

He had the crowd with him—people love a good admission of guilt—but they clearly expected more. Bob had not yet touched on the hottest of the potatoes.

"There has also been a lot of buzz about how the meeting broke up," Bob went on. "Pardon the pun," he said, reaching up to touch his still heavily bandaged nose.

He got a good laugh. I hate when he gets laughs.

"The big talk, unfortunately, is that the pastor of our church punched a member in the face. Admittedly, that is something that you don't hear about every day. So, I stand before you this morning to tell you . . ." Bob paused for dramatic effect, "that I had it coming! I spoke harshly about a good man's wife, a good wife, and I got punched. I know we don't support any sort of violence, but maybe there is a time when it is not so wrong for a man to defend his wife. There will be no charges brought in this matter, and I will hold no grudge."

It started very slowly, but someone started to clap . . . and then another . . . and then two more. Reluctant at first, the congregation gradually came to a steady applause. There were many who did not join in, including some whose judgmental glares tried to shut up those who did. But, in the end, there was applause. When it died down, Bob said, "I also implore all of you in this church to not hold the incident against Reverend Martin. I would rather it not come up again, but if it does, blame me. If I could, I would give the same advice to the powers that be from the United Methodist denomination."

Bob's eye's scanned up and all the way to the back of the lobby. *How does he know that the district superintendent is back there?!* I wondered.

"Thank you once again, Reverend Martin, for allowing me this time. And, again, Mrs. Martin, I am very sorry." Bob took one step from the lectern, and then returned, saying, "One last thing, Reverend Martin, I'll never say something like that again, but if I do, you have my permission to give me another smack!"

There was laughter mixed with scattered applause.

I replied, "Thank you, Bob . . . I just might take you up on that." Dead, stone-cold silence. Jennifer's eyes nearly popped out of her head. Bob paused and met my eyes with his. His right eyebrow raised almost imperceptibly. As he exited the stage, he allowed just the tiniest shake of his head. I had just laid a bomb and stepped on it.

"Just kidding, of course," I said. "I do apologize for resorting to violence. And, Bob, I very much appreciate your testimony and confession. I have a confession of my own to make. I have recently been keenly aware of my failure to be the husband that my wife deserves. I don't mean that I have done anything horrible. But most people don't realize that a pastor is caught between a rock and a hard place when trying to balance the needs of the congregation with the needs of family. I have tried so hard to serve the congregation, that at times I have not supported my own wife. I have let her suffer hurt and loneliness and criticism here in the church . . ."

I was immediately aware that I had wandered into dangerous territory. My initial efforts to apologize and reclaim the empathy of the crowd was working (a man admitting his mistakes and apologizing to his wife; who doesn't love that, right?) but when I diverged into the congregation's treatment of Jenn, the uptick in defensiveness was palpable. Still, this is what I had come to say. And, it was a lesson that I was convinced God wanted heard.

". . . without coming to her defense. I have valued peace in the church more than I valued the best care of the wife God gave me. I was in that frame of mind, wanting very much to fix that, when the incident with Bob occurred. But, it was wrong. I will not do it again. I will do my best to care for you, the church. And, when faced with a choice of smoothing things over in the church, or supporting my wife, I will from now on choose to support my wife."

Only the lay-reader, Condi and I could see it, but Jenn smiled.

I concluded, "I hope that makes good sense to most of you."

"You and me both, brother!" Frank had sprung to his feet. "As soon as I finish marrying Sylvie, I'll stick up for her even more than I do now!"

Praise God for Frank. There followed a *pregnant* pause. What next? Would this be chalked up as an outburst by one of our less-sophisticated members, or would it make sense to others? Condi's husband Kevin Cloverton was rarely heard to speak more than two or three words in a row.

He stood and said calmly, but loudly, "God first. Then Condi. Then the kids. Everything else is tied for fourth. And, unlike everyone else here today, I am not apologizing."

I had a clear view of Condi, sitting at the organ, waiting to get back to her beloved music. As she gazed out at her husband, her eyes misted over and her chin started to quiver.

"Me, too," Harold Garner said, standing.
"Me, too."
"Me, too."
"Me, too."

Soon, at least twenty husbands were standing. It wasn't a landslide or an avalanche, but in a church where speaking out loud during the service was viewed as deviant behavior, such a display was touching indeed. I was willing to suffer the cost of blunt talk in God's name, but I won't pretend that I was not grateful and relieved to receive some support.

"I hope we have pleased God already this morning," I said, "but we have spent enough time on this. Let us begin our worship service with the reading of the Call to Worship."

In the farthest corner in the way back of the lobby the Reverend Judy Halliday, district superintendent and my immediate supervisor, stood and snuck out of the church. *What the heck is that supposed to mean?* I wondered.

We got through the rest of the worship service without any more unusual happenings. In fact, it was a nice, positive service. My sermon on unity was well-received. I think the decidedly mixed emotions in the congregation created an atmosphere ripe for contemplation of getting along. Still, the people clustered and talked after the service. The official *fellowship* time of coffee, cookies and red punch was lightly attended, but in hallways and corners and spaces between parked cars, dozens of debates raged on. After hanging around just long enough to avoid accusations of running away, Jenn and I ran away. We got in the car and took off. We did not go straight home.

"That wasn't a typical service, now was it?" Jenn commented.

"No, it was not," I replied.

We laughed. There was precious little that was typical any more.

"So, what's your take?" Jenn asked. "Where do we stand now?"

"More than any time so far, I honestly do not know," I said. "Up and down. Bob scores, we score back, no one scores, and we all look like the gang that couldn't shoot straight."

"I wanted to say something," Jenn said, "but that Bob is so smooth, all I could have done was thank him for saying nice things about me, after trashing me. Do you think he means any of that, or is he just being strategic?"

"I tend to think he's just playing his cards the best way he knows how, but even on that I can't be sure. He sure sounds contrite when he wants to."

"Yeah, he does," Jenn agreed, "and I bet that if you didn't deal with him as much as we do, if you were just someone sitting in church today, he would seem like a nice guy who screwed up and sincerely feels bad about it."

"Hey," I said, "maybe part of him really is."

"Yeah," she said.

After a bit of contemplative silence, I asked, "So how bad did I bomb out today? That *maybe I'll hit you again* crack went over like a fart in church."

"No, Honey, a fart in church usually leaves people wondering who did it."

I giggled, but said, "No, really. How bad was it?"

"Pretty bad, at first. But your admission that you struggled with how you, used to, treat me, got you up off the mat. Then, when you started to blame the church for treating me badly, the focus-group meter plummeted again. But, in a determined flurry of never-say-die perseverance, the *I'll side with my wife from now on* declaration got you back on your feet. Frank's pronouncement was a fifty-fifty pick'em, until a couple dozen other masculine husbands took the high ground with him. I would say that we lost a little ground, but not much."

"Are you having fun with this?" I asked.

"Yep."

"Okay," I went on, "how about our pledge to speak for God? Did we do that today?"

"Yeah. I think so. I admit it is hard to tell, but I think so."

"I hope so." Then I added, "Did you know that Judy Halliday was in church today?"

"The DS? Really? I didn't see her."

"That's because she got up and walked out, just before the Call to Worship."

"Well, what the heck does that mean? Why was she here in the first place?"

"Now, aren't those sixty-four thousand dollar questions."

We drove about ten miles without saying a word. "It's still Sunday, right?" Jenn asked with a smirk.

"We only left church an hour ago."

"If it's not against some secret blood-brother spit oath, how about you turn around and show me that church that's been taking up your time? Maybe your little friend Pastor Carl will even be hanging around. I think it's time I met the guy. You say he's good at figuring out stuff, so maybe he can help make sense of this."

"Why not?" I answered quickly. "I have been wondering how and when you two should meet. Today's as good a time as any. I have no idea if he would be there, though."

"What's to lose? We're just driving. Let's go."

We pulled into the gravel parking lot of the no-name crossroads Church of True Followers of the Father, the Son and the Holy Spirit (the name was still in need of refinement).

"Looks like he's not here," I said. "He always parks on the west side of the building."

"Too bad," Jenn replied. "My curiosity is all wound up. Can we peak in the windows?"

"Oh, we can go in. It's never locked."

"Really? It's been awhile since we saw a church that was always open."

"There isn't much that's usual about this place," I said. "Let's walk in the front and pretend we're going to church."

"Wouldn't have it any other way," she said. "Lead on. You can play usher if you want."

"You are a funny lady," I said. "I just like to see a church like a first-time visitor might."

"Yes, dear. I know."

We walked up the short staircase to the front door. I was tempted to start explaining things, but I decided to hush up and let her react on her own. After all I had experienced in this place, I admit I really wanted Jenn to like it. I was surprised at how nervous I was. Even if *quaint* was the best adjective that she could use, I would be happy. As expected, the knob turned easily and the door opened wide. Three feet forward, and we were in the sanctuary. I let go of her hand, jumped in front of her and turned.

"Welcome to our church," I said, pretending to hand her a church bulletin. "Is this your first time worshipping with us?"

"Shush," was her only response. Jenn walked around me and slowly moved about the room. She ran her fingers along the walls. She smelled the wood. She bent over and touched the floor. For long moments she stood at the windows and looked out, first on the east side and then on the west. She sat down in the back pew, on the right of the imaginary preacher she seemed to see in the pulpit. She moved to the front pew, this time on the left. For ten minutes she soaked up whatever it was that engulfed her. Before my time with Carl, I would have never been able to stop explaining long enough to let this happen. Jenn got up and moved behind the pulpit. As I saw her looking out over the empty pews, I would have sworn that she was seeing a gathered flock of Christian men and women, come to church in search of more. More intimacy. More insight. More worship. More praise. More love. More love from God. More love to God. More love for each other. More love for those we have not met yet. I was glad Jennifer did not want, nor expect, me to speak right then, because right then I could not. She moved from the pulpit to the heavy, permanent cross hanging on the wall. She put her hand on the wood. She bowed her head. Long moments later I heard her say, "Amen."

I added my own.

Then, she turned around and walked toward me. Her eyes became clear again and her smile quick and natural. It was if she had just left a realm that had totally consumed her, and returned to the present time and place.

"Sweet," she said with a giggle.

"It is, isn't it," I said a bit too exuberantly. "Do you like it, Jenn? Do you really?"

She smiled, wrapped her arms around me and kissed me.

"In this place," she began, "I want you to call me *Jennifer*. And I will call you *Nathan*."

"Sure. Of course. Why?"

"This is holy space," she replied. "It just seems right to bring our best, most complete selves to God in such a place. Don't you agree, Nathan?"

"I do, indeed, Jennifer."

Jennifer said, "You and Pastor Carl have worked so hard to bring this building back to life, surely there must be a plan. What is Pastor Carl going to do with it?"

"I don't know. I don't know because he doesn't know."

"He doesn't know? How does he do all of this and not know what the goal is? He is going to start a church here, isn't he? He's got to!"

"Pastor Carl would tell you all he has *got* to do is whatever God has put in front of him right now. Honest to God, I have heard all kinds of people talk about abiding in God and waiting for the Holy Spirit to move and all that—heck, I've preached it myself—but I have never known anyone who actually did it. You'll believe it better when you get to know him, but he is absolutely content to fix up this building, no matter the time or the cost, without an inkling of what will come of it. Once it's done, it won't matter if God tells him to start a church in it, live in it, or burn it down. He'll do exactly as he's told and not worry or question it a bit."

"Well," Jennifer said, "he's a better Christian than I am. I don't think I could stand it."

"He is more connected to God than anyone else I've ever known."

"Surely God will want something special to happen here," Jennifer almost pleaded. "It feels so powerful."

"Yes, I sure think so," I answered. "Carl would tell me to not get ahead of myself, but I am certainly excited to see what God does next. Whatever it is, I'll bet it is going to be . . . what is that high theological concept you used a minute ago? Oh yeah, I remember. *Sweet.*"

"So, when am I going to meet this mysterious Pastor Carl of yours? I am intrigued."

"I have never seen him anywhere but here and at the ministerial association meetings. Every time I suggest we get together for lunch or something, he is busy or on his way somewhere. Still, I've never known him to miss a weekday. Want to come with me tomorrow?"

"Sure do. I thought you would never ask."

Chapter 29

Despite all the goings on, the day to day work of the church continued. I sat at my desk and pondered an almost impossible task. Our once-a-year Church Conference was only four weeks away. Preparing for it is a major chore in the best of times, and this was nowhere near the best of times. It is a meeting that is required yearly, called into session by the district superintendent. Dozens of forms and reports needed to be prepared, including membership activity, attendance, finances, reports on the past and plans for the future. The salary of the pastor is to be set and people nominated to all of the leadership positions in the church voted upon. It is the one time during the year when the entire membership of the church is invited to come and vote on important church business. Of course, getting any more than five percent of the membership to attend wasn't likely. About the only thing that would greatly increase that number was a good controversy or scandal. *Should be a full house this year,* I mused.

I am always responsible for certain reports. Most of them, I find pretty simple. The difficult one, the one I was finding impossible to deal with right now, was the *Nominating and Leadership Development Committee* list of nominees. In other words, it was my job as the Chair of the committee to put together an entire slate of Chairs and members for each of the many United Methodist committees. This includes trying to remove people because they have already served too long or are not doing their jobs to the benefit of the church. It also includes trying to discern the best people to fill open positions, and talk them into accepting them. It is at this time of the year that I feel the full weight of the bureaucracy, excessive institutionalism, and outmoded rules of the United Methodist Church contributing to the *dragon* that stultifies and distracts us from being God's Church.

Anyway, I always procrastinate at nominations time. And this particular year, I was facing a congregation filled with equal parts supporters and enemies. For the tenth time at least, I picked up my stack of nominations forms, committed myself to getting them completed, failed to start, gave up and threw it back on the pile.

Janice stuck her head through the doorway and said, "Call for you on line one. Vonnie Lawson wants some details on the Spaghetti Supper fundraiser this Friday."

I thought, *Why in heaven's name would Vonnie need me to answer questions about an event that is being run entirely by people who are not me,* but I did not bother Janice by saying it out loud. We both knew that Vonnie would accept no information, no counsel, and no visitations from anyone except the *Senior Pastor.* Nothing but the best for Vonnie Lawson.

"Good morning, Vonnie, how might I help you this morning?"

"I hope you still have time for church business, Pastor," she began, "what with everything else going on."

"Of course, how might I help you?" I repeated.

"My husband and I are considering having our supper at the church on Friday, and I would like some information."

"Yes, it is a fundraising event for the next mission trip to Haiti. I believe there are eleven people going this year, to continue work on the new orphanage and medical center. Admission to the Spaghetti Supper is by free-will donation. It runs anytime from 5:00 to 7:00."

"How much is expected?"

"Anything you choose to give for the cause. One dollar or twenty. Whatever you wish."

"You can't make any money at one dollar and twenty is far too much for pasta. They should set a price."

"Still, that's how it works."

"Will there be ham?"

"I believe the only entre' is spaghetti. It is a fundraiser."

"My husband does not care for spaghetti. They should have something for people who don't like spaghetti. What else are they serving?"

"I am not sure. The last time there was salad and garlic bread. Then, desserts were auctioned off."

"You have to bid on dessert? How much is that?"

"It really depends on the bidders, Mrs. Lawson. It's an auction. Sometimes people pay thirty or forty dollars for a pie . . . it's for the orphanage in Haiti. I think helping others is more the point than the menu."

"I am not sure this sounds right to me. Besides, I think we should take care of our own people around here, and not half way around the world. Please let the spaghetti people know that we will be having chicken at Dora's Diner."

"Yes, Mrs. Lawson, I will let them know."

I hung up and my head hit the desk.

Janice walked into my office and asked, "Nothing like that good, old-time Christian love and concern, huh boss?"

I smiled. "Yeah. Back when I used to lay awake at night and dream of being a pastor, this is exactly what I had in mind; *will there be ham at the spaghetti supper?*

"Go for a walk, somewhere not around here," Janice instructed. "After that you are supposed to be at the ministerial association meeting. That will kill some time. Don't pretend that things are normal right now. They're not."

"Excellent counsel, Janice. I will stop back after."

I made my way out of the church, and out of town. Later, I arrived at the regularly scheduled meeting of the East Fork Area Ministerial Association. All the regulars were accounted for: Pastor Stan from the Church of God, the Episcopalian Reverend

Catherine Thorne, Father Fred and me—but no Pastor Carl. I was disappointed. I assumed he would be happy to meet Jenn, but was not entirely confident. I kind of wanted a chance to feel him out on the subject.

"I really wish I could get some of you guys to attend my Thursday night class on *Surviving the Tribulation: 7 Years of Hell on Earth*," Pastor Stan said. "It has been a powerful time of God's Word properly explained. Last week . . ."

"I am sorry to interrupt," I said, "but I would like to share some discussion about some things that are going on right now. Stan, none of the people in this room are going to come to your tribulation teaching. We do not agree with your biblical analysis on this, and probably never will. It is your right to do so, of course. Who knows, maybe you are right about some of that stuff. But, I think it takes our attention away from helping people to become Christians and learn to live a Christian life. So, please, let's talk about something else. Okay?"

Pastor Stan appeared stunned. He said nothing, until after an uncomfortable pause he finally mumbled, "Okay."

"Thank you, Reverend Martin," Father Fred began, "I couldn't agree more with what you just said. And, I might add, I think that the focus on Christ and the Christly life would be greatly enhanced if we ended our differences in doctrine and praxis by returning to a completely united Church, by . . ."

"I am so glad that you have found a point of agreement, Father. I really am. However, to keep explaining to the rest of us that we are not really part of the Church is simply not going to help. I love the Roman Catholics. I know that Catholics can be, and often are, every bit the saved, Christ-loving followers of Jesus that I could ever be. But we Protestants do not agree with your historical claim to being the one and only Christian Church. I know that you are convinced otherwise, but to ask us all to become Catholic falls on our ears as offensively as if I suggested that Roman Catholics can only be in the Church if they become United Methodists. We do not claim that. We do our best. You do your best. We can be the Church Universal by acknowledging and respecting each other's efforts to understand and obey God. Efforts to banish some churches in favor of others will not help. Again, could we please talk about something else?"

Father Fred sat silently, his face carefully blank. No one said anything for at least two minutes. I could see the others straining with what to do and what to say. Thanks to my Christian/Zen/Mind-Master training at the feet of Pastor Carl, I did not crack.

Finally, Pastor Stan smirked and said, "What do you have to say today, Most High Reverend Catherine Thorne?"

"I admit," she replied thoughtfully, "that each of you could probably offer a pretty good version of what I usually say in this type of exchange. I am also, however, intensely aware of how crucial certain issues are in the Church today. Am I not to advocate for what I believe to be correct? What is your response to that concern, Reverend Nathan?"

"I find what you just said to be very refreshing. You tend to talk about things that are, indeed, crucial topics in the Church today. Until now, you have pre-decided what is right, fought for it, and allowed no dissenting opinions. For you to stop and ask, 'How should I talk about this?' is a tremendous beginning to fruitful talk. The Church's response to feminist and LGBTQ issues is important and multi-faceted and theologically complicated. To simply choose up sides and fight is not going to get us to what God wants."

"All right," Reverend Catherine Thorne replied. "For argument's sake, let's buy into your new straight-talking persona for the time being. What is the 'something else' you would like to talk about?"

All three of my colleagues looked at me expectantly, waiting, I'm sure, for some profound nugget of wisdom.

"I'm wondering a lot lately about whether it is possible to practice solid, relational, God-connected, God-loving Christianity in the Church. It seems that our whole society is enveloped in multitudes of belief systems, written and unwritten rules of behavior, agendas of all kinds, and the incessant drumbeat of individualism, personal rights and complete disdain for anyone who would suggest that anyone is wrong about anything (I decided to leave the whole *personal dragon named Agendor* thing for another day). The worse thing is that we have let these attitudes into the church. People hear only what they want to hear. And, they believe only that which suits them. Worst of all, they expect the church to serve them. They want God to serve them. Or, they will move on and find a church that will tend to their happiness. Add in all kinds of bureaucracy and paperwork and hierarchy, and it seems like living a God-filled life actually takes a back seat *in the Church!* So, I want to ask you, as colleagues, two questions. One, do you get what I am saying? And, two, is there some way to fix it?"

"Yes, I get it," Stan said.

"Me, too," added Reverend Catherine Thorne.

"I hesitate to criticize the Church," Father Fred began, "but in the honest and confidential spirit of this conversation, yes. This kind of thing drains me sometimes."

"Thank you," I said. "Could we maybe spend some of our time trying to figure out how to reclaim the Church for God?"

After two hours of clumsy, halting—but highly encouraging—discussion, I returned to my office. I had seventeen phone messages and fifty-eight emails, just since I left for lunch. I combed through them, looking for those that could be answered. Since the entire congregation had become embroiled in the growing controversy, the communications stream had become overwhelming. Most just wanted to let me know of some additional example of dissatisfaction I might have missed. And, quite a few wanted to let me know they supported me as their pastor, and were mystified as to what all the hubbub was about.

To be a pastor, or a member of a pastor's family, is to live in a fishbowl. You are closely watched. Often, you even live in a closely watched house that is owned by the church. None of that is too surprising, but it is worsened by the fact that the many people doing the watching are each judging you by different criteria. The *key question being* asked and answered is, *is this pastor a good one or a lousy one?* For some, the only thing that matters to the *key question* is whatever happens to matter to them. I purposely use the term lousy, because the point isn't usually whether the pastor is *bad* as in *evil*, but rather whether the pastor is one I like or don't like. This is further complicated by comparison. *Do I like this pastor as much as my all-time favorite pastor? Do I dislike this pastor as much as my least-favorite pastor, ever?*

The criteria are both varying and secret. Some only care about how often you visit. Nothing else matters. Some only care about how entertaining your sermons are. Some only care that you get the worship service done on time. Some only care that the church runs smoothly. Some only care that nothing changes. Some only care that many things change. Some only care how well you serve the young; some only care how well you serve the old. Some only care that you agree with them on social issues. Some only care that you treat them as the important people they think they are. Some only care that the reputation of their church is held high. Some only care that you support foreign missions; some only that you keep missions local. Some only care that you bring in much money and spend little. Some only care that the church building be beautiful and impressive. The list seems unending, and yet it is very real. And, unfortunately, some only care that *the pastor has served us as a good hired hand should.*

There is another category of parishioner, however. And, every pastor has these, too. There may be only one or two. There may be a considerable number. In a few churches, these people may even rule supreme. When that happens, it is a good and wonderful thing. There are people in the church who are in love

A Dragon in the Church 209

with Jesus Christ. These are people who have let God actually change their lives, and hunger for the next change God has in store. These are the people who seek to live in more Christly ways each day of their lives. They seek God's Word and God's Way in the scriptures and through the teaching and preaching of the church. They love to praise and worship God.

When these people receive a new pastor, or live in communion with an old one, they see a spiritual leader sent to help them. Not an infallible person, certainly, but a person called and equipped by God to help them in their quest to know God. Working, living and sharing with such people is joy. And, working with such powerful Christians is strengthening and uplifting, providing the support a pastor needs to keep fighting the more difficult battles.

In none of my previous professions, before becoming a professional minister, was I ever so routinely and pettily criticized. Nor, had I ever been so affirmed, supported, complimented and loved. It is a great life, if you can survive it.

Anyway, the phone calls and emails made up a diverse and eclectic collection of information, emotions and opinions. Most I had not the time or inclination to answer. A few important ones, I did. But the email that jumped out at me was from the district superintendent. It said only, *Call me, ASAP.* Instead of letting my mind conjure up all the possible reasons for the message from the DS, I decided that ASAP meant right now. I got out my cell phone and hit #3 on the speed dial. Jenn was #1. Lisa was #2.

"Good morning, thank you for calling the Gateway District of the Lower Michigan Annual Conference of the United Methodist Church. This is Sondra, how may I help you?"

"Hi, Sondra, this is Nathan over at East Fork."

"Good morning, Most Excellent High Reverend Martin."

"You know I prefer Your Eminence."

"Yeah, but that would make you seem snooty."

Sondra had been around for years, and was not the least bit intimidated by clergy. Truth is, Sondra was a great witness, and probably did more good for God's Kingdom than most of us.

"How are you Sondra? I haven't spoken to you in a while."

"I am well, Pastor. I have been praying for you every day, just so you know."

"Thank you. That means a lot coming from the likes of you."

"We're all in this together," she said matter-of-factly.

"I like thinking that I am in this with you, Sondra," I said sincerely. "I have a message to call in right away. Is the Reverend Halliday in?"

"No, but she told me to forward you to her cell no matter the time. Hold on."

The phone rang only twice, when I heard my boss answer, "Please hold, I have to step out of a meeting." A few seconds later, she was back. "Good morning, Nathan. How are you holding up?"

"Morning Judy. Surprisingly, I am doing quite well. How about you?"

"I'm fine, but I am glad to hear you are all right."

"I am. In the end, this is God's battle. Hey, I better write that down. That *it's God's battle* thing will preach."

"Glad to hear your excellent attitude. However, there is still business to deal with."

"Always is."

"Yes. Nathan, I'm going to admit to you that I am in an unfamiliar place with this. I got a call from your SPRC Chair. Daisy Watkins?"

"That's right."

"She says that she is being pressured to initiate a request for a new pastor. She wanted to know how that is done, and how was she supposed to decide if it should be done."

"Meaning?" I asked.

"Well, as you know, the first part is clear. If the SPRC is going to recommend a request for a pastoral change, they just need to turn in an *Advisory* by the first of the year. You, of course, would have to be made aware of that, if it happened."

I put my new waiting skills to work.

"Okay, the tricky part is that usually the SPRC just decides to put in the Advisory and does it. Or, they ask for a meeting with the DS to talk about it first. I know you know this stuff, but sometimes that meeting is held with the appointed pastor present, sometimes not."

"Right," I said.

"Thing is, one way or another, this is usually done quietly. That seems unlikely here. It is clear that Daisy does not even know what the committee wants to do. And, I am not comfortable that they are acting under pressure from others within the church."

"It's all right, Judy. I understand this has become a loud and unusual situation. I am handling it by trying to stick to what I believe to be the right and Godly approach, and will accept whatever comes of it. I am sure you will do the same."

I was not entirely sure of that, but said it anyway.

"Thank you, Nathan. I have consulted with the bishop, and he believes that the only reasonable course is to call an emergency Staff Parish Relations Committee meeting, before your Church Conference comes up. He is hoping that we can bring some sense to this before it gets completely out of hand."

"Fine."

"Fine?"

"Yes. Fine."

"Would you prefer to be there, or have me do it alone?"

"I'll be there. Straight talk is the order of the day."

"Okay, then . . . fine. A week from Thursday, 7:00 p.m. at your church. You, me, and the official committee members only. I will allow no ring-leaders or witnesses. This meeting is closed, as per the *Book of Discipline*. Also according to the *Discipline*, this conversation stands as ten days proper notice. I will instruct Daisy to notify the others immediately. Good?"

"Yes. Thank you for all that you do. I know this is not an easy part of your job."

"Thank you for understanding. Nathan, I will make sure this stays scrupulously fair . . ."

"But?"

"But, what you do and say will have consequences. You might have to decide whether you want to save this appointment, or not."

"And?"

"And, no one has officially mentioned anything more serious, such as the bringing of charges. I don't think it will come to that, but it could."

"Like for slugging a member?"

"Well, yeah," she replied, "that doesn't happen every day."

"No. It does not," I said. "But then, there are new things happening all around us, no matter how hard we try to fight them off . . . pardon the pun."

"Well, being at a loss for words, how about we see what happens next Thursday?"

"Excellent, see you then."

I chuckled to myself. It sure throws people off when you don't respond exactly like they already have planned in their heads.

Chapter 30

I cleared up a little business and left the office for home. Jenn and I planned a quick supper at 5:00 before heading over to the no-name church to see Pastor Carl. Just as the garage door was closing behind my car, I heard the door on Jenn's side start to open. I waited for her to pull in and close the door.

Approaching her with outstretched arms, I said, "There's my sweetheart, come to . . ."

"Yeah, yeah," she said. "I love you, too. Look what I just pulled out of the box."

She held a newspaper in my face and, nostrils flaring and eyes nearly popping out of their sockets, impatiently demanded my reaction. I froze. All I saw was a newspaper. I assumed it contained something wonderful or horrible, but how was I to know which?

"Okay," I said, "what am I looking for?"

"The picture! The picture!"

Thankfully, she pointed directly at the picture she meant, so that I wouldn't have to sort them out. I felt like I was on Jeopardy and couldn't make the button work. There, on the front page of the East Fork Chronicle, above the headline, was a picture of me. And the teaser blurb, *East Fork United Methodist Church: Should the pastor go, or stay?* Under the picture, in smaller font, it said, *For the full story on the controversy surrounding Reverend Nathan Martin, see page A-2.*

"Oh boy," I said. "I wondered why the reporter hadn't published yet. What does it say?"

"I have no idea!" Jenn spat out. "I just pulled it out of the box! We need to read this together. Get inside, go to the bathroom if you need to, grab a couple of Diet Cokes and meet me in the living room. Move!"

I moved. As I ran into my bathroom, I saw her disappear into hers, newspaper still in hand. Perhaps not liking the visual, Jenn opened the door just a bit and threw the newspaper out and onto the floor. I found that hilarious. I thought I could hear Jenn laughing, too. I finished up, washed quickly (always wash your hands, even if your wife is starring in a rapidly unfolding dramatic scene) and ran for the pop (unless you live somewhere that it is called *soda* or *tonic*, which is silly). I got to my living room chair, just as she got to hers.

"Okay," she said, "I'll read, you listen."

"Yes'm," I said, "but first, may I serve you?"

I rubbed the top of her Diet Coke can on my sleeve, popped the top with that satisfying crack'n-hiss sound, and handed it to her with a flourish. I did the same with my own, held it out to her and said, "Here's to good news!" We clinked cans (there are some good jokes right there that I will just let go by!) and repeated, "To good news!"

Then she turned to the first page of the second section, and began to read: *For over 125 years, the East Fork United Methodist Church has stood as a symbol of faith and stability. The church is best known for its civic pride, helping the needy and one of the finest Christian music programs in the state. Staid, decent, civil and polite are all words that one might use for this fine institution. Until, that is, recent events—some might say scandal—have played out regarding the ministry of the East Fork UMC pastor, the Reverend Nathan Martin. This reporter recently attended a church meeting that was—to say the least—revealing, and—to say the most—shocking. The church council convened a special meeting, open to anyone to watch but limited in those who could participate, to address concerns about the performance and behavior of Reverend Martin and, evidently, his wife.*

A contingent of East Fork UMC members, led by prominent local business figure Bob Williams, detailed their concerns for the council, but in front of some 200 in the audience. Concerns listed included: 1) a teenage boy being allowed a voting seat on the church's Finance Committee, 2) the use of, quote, "less than sacred music" in the church, 3) the pastor's lack of attention to long-time members, 4) the preaching of controversial or inappropriate sermons, such as "abortion," "homosexuality" and "anti-patriotism," 5) the lack of participation on the part of the pastor's wife, Ms. Jennifer Martin, and 6) the pastor's unwillingness to behave as an employee of the church.

The discussions led to many emotional and volatile comments. At one point, over a hundred other members of the East Fork UMC entered the meeting room in a sort of protest, marching silently around the room, carrying signs and banners. It appeared to this reporter that the protest was being done by those in favor of modern, contemporary Christian music being used in the church! Another interesting debate was about whether a United Methodist pastor actually is, or is not, a church employee! This reporter questioned Bob Williams on this matter, who was very forthcoming and helpful to this article. Mr. Williams said, among other things, "the pastor is obviously an employee of the church, as we use our money to pay his salary and many benefits. Some people like to think otherwise, because the church does not hire or fire the pastor. The pastor is sent to the church and we have to accept whoever we get. And, a lot of the rules that we have to use come from some higher source, boards and conferences and bishops and such, instead of from right here in our own church. But, last I knew," Williams continued, "you work for whoever it is that signs your paycheck."

It would take a lot more space than this reporter has available here, but it appears the United Methodist way of doing things is quite complicated and surprising. Who is in charge? Who controls the pastor? Anybody? At East Fork UMC, nobody seems real sure.

As the complaints were made, they were not really settled so much as disposed of. There was quite a bit of putting things off or pushing things on to other committees and such. The meeting reached its crescendo over the wife, Ms. Jennifer Martin. As she was publicly criticized for her lack of participation, and evidently some behavior some of the church people didn't like, the whole affair turned ugly. Names were called and voices were raised. The Chairperson of the East Fork UMC Church Council, Jack Conwell, abruptly adjourned the meeting in an attempt to calm down the crowd. The crowd was slowly and noisily dispersing when a whole other level of conflict erupted. It took a minute to figure out what happened, but it became clear that the Reverend Nathan Martin had just punched Bob Williams in the face! This is not the church I remember from my childhood! The ambulance came for Mr. Williams and the police came for Reverend Martin!

In following up on this story, a story that is important for us in East Fork and surrounding communities to know about, I interviewed Mr. Williams. In one of the most surprising and heartwarming answers this reporter has ever received, when I asked him about getting punched, Mr. Williams said, 'Really, Alicia, it was my fault. In my fervor and commitment to fixing what ails the East Fork United Methodist Church, the church I love so much, I lost control of my temper and my manners. I spoke very disrespectfully of Pastor Nathan's wife. I won't repeat it, but it was both wrong and uncalled for. Probably the most honorable thing that Pastor Nathan did that whole night was defend his wife. I hope everyone in our church and our community will put the blame for the punching issue right where it belongs ... on me. And again, to all concerned, I am sorry.' In this reporter's opinion, if everyone could take ownership of their mistakes like Bob Williams, we would all be better off.

I asked Mr. Williams what he thought was going to happen next in this saga of "Should the Pastor Stay or Go?" He answered, 'We are discovering that the rules of the United

Methodist Church are much more complex than we knew. We have never tried to let a pastor go before. But, we will figure it out, step by step. I . . . we, just want to do the right thing and, right now, the church is in turmoil and needs a change of pastor. We will work hard to get that done.'

This reporter will keep track of this still unfolding story, for you, our readers. In the attempt to provide fair and balanced coverage, I contacted the Reverend Nathan Martin multiple times, but no response was forthcoming.

By Alicia Skiba—Regular Contributor

Jenn laid the paper down on the coffee table and took a long, slow swallow from her Diet Coke. I took a couple and set the can down on a coaster.

"Well," Jenn said.

"Well," I said.

"What do you think about that?" Jenn asked.

"What do *you* think about that?" I asked.

"I think that *this reporter* is not a very good writer," she answered. "And, I think she started about ten stories she didn't finish. And, I think she has no understanding at all about what is going on. And, I think if we were to dig deep enough, we would probably find her name on a Williams payroll somewhere."

"I agree with everything you just said," I replied. "But I am afraid that her level of understanding is about the same as ninety-five percent of our church members. Hardly anyone knows what is actually happening, or how things work. This whole thing has become one giant, emotional mess. What's true doesn't matter much anymore."

"How are you?" Jenn asked me.

"I'm a little shell-shocked. Just the audacity of the whole thing. How did moving into a church and trying to serve God and the people turn into such a circus? It seems like a comedy sketch, not something that is really happening."

"It does that," Jenn replied. "*Monty Python Explains Church!*"

"Yeah, that nails it," I said. "How about you, Jenn? This thing drags you right back in."

"I was never out, I don't think. Same as you. Incredulous. Stunned. But okay. Life is certainly filled with all sorts of new possibilities. Right?"

"Well said. I love you more than ever."

"So, husband, what would God have us do with this article? And by the way, when were you contacted by *this reporter?*"

"The answer to the first question is *I don't know*. Come to think of it, that's the answer to the second question, too. Let's grab a bite and go find Carl. He might offer some clarity of thought. How about you whip something up, while I go check my messages."

"Will do. Let's go."

Jenn was just putting the finishing touches on a couple of BLTs, accompanied by leftover potato salad, when I exited my study and walked into the kitchen.

"Well, *this reporter* was not exactly lying," I said.

"*What's that mean?*"

"She did try to make contact. There is an e-mail sent at about 4:30 in the afternoon last Friday, and another late yesterday, probably right before the paper went to print."

"So, she did try," Jenn stated matter-of-factly.

"Yeah, but the subject line read *Information Wanted*, and made no mention of the newspaper, the reporter or the topic. I have been getting so many emails that I have been barely skimming them. I missed it. Call her *any time day or night*, it said."

"Makes her sound serious about wanting your side of things. Smart. Devious, but smart. Any phone messages?" Jenn asked, while handing me my plate.

"No, not a one. I think if she really wanted to contact me she would have tried harder. I am not that hard to find."

"No, but she got to write what she wanted and you can't possibly deny she tried twice. No question she has copies of those emails."

"Score one for the press."

"Well," Jenn said through a big mouthful of potatoes, mustard and mayonnaise, "nothing has changed from a few minutes ago. It is what it is."

"I hate that saying," I said.

"I know, but still . . ."

"Yeah," I said. "It is what it is."

"Eat up, slow poke," Jenn hollered over her shoulder. "I'll be ready in five minutes. I finally get to meet this mystery pastor hero of yours . . . if he actually exists."

"He exists. I'll be ready before you are." I mawed into my sandwich.

On the way to Carl's church, we were quiet. I think that the sheer magnitude of the drama that was building around us and about us was overloading our ability to articulate our feelings.

Finally, Jenn continued, "It's the details that make it hard. So many things are happening. So many things are being said. In the end, most of it is just noise. And, that's what I let stir me up, who said what, and when. You know?"

"Oh, yes," I said, "I know."

"I know you do. I am just thinking with my mouth open. But, the thing is, if you boil it down, it isn't so complicated. We live and work in a system of complaints and self-interest and power-mongering and worn out traditions and bureaucracy and too much hierarchy and paperwork and worldly influences and so much nonsense you can't even list it all."

"Agendor," I said.

"Yeah," Jenn answered. "Nobody but you and I know what that means, but all the garbage adds up to Agendor. Simply put, we are being called to cut through all the Agendor crap and try to wrestle God's Church, at least our little piece of it, back to a God-focus."

"Slay the dragon."

"And all this angst is only about whether we pull it off here or somewhere else. Right?"

"Right."

Jenn went on, "Is that such a big deal? Sure, it's scary because we don't know what the next thing would be. Where? With who? How do we make a living? Where do we live? But, we just need to trust God. Easy. Right?"

I hesitated before giving the answer that I found curiously difficult to give. "It is if we are who we say we are," I said.

"Trusting God is easy, if we are who we say we are," Jenn repeated, out loud but mostly to herself.

The last two miles went by in reflective silence. As we pulled into the little gravel lot surrounding the little white church, Jenn nodded her head with conviction and said, "Then let's be who we say we are, disciples of Jesus Christ. Deal?"

"Sounds great," I replied.

Miss Non-Sequitur responded with, "Where's his truck? I don't see a truck."

It was just after six o'clock on a week day evening and we saw no evidence of Carl.

"Let's go inside," I said. "This has never happened before."

We went inside. No Carl. I scanned the room and everything looked exactly as it had the day before. *Where was Pastor Carl?*

"Call him," Jenn commanded.

"I can't. I don't have his phone number."

"What do you mean you don't have his phone number?" Jennifer asked incredulously.

"I mean that I do not have a phone number for Carl, or an email or any other method of making contact."

"How can that be?" she asked, still not believing me.

"I don't know. When I suggested we exchange contact info, he always had an excuse. He was *between phones*, or *taking a break from technology*. After awhile, I just accepted I would only see him by coming here. His schedule was so predictable it didn't seem to matter. I'm sorry."

"Okay, but how can we find him. Where does he live? Where does he work? You said he had a regular job."

"Sometimes he mentioned *going home* or *getting out of work*, but he never told me anything about where that was."

"So he is just a ghost? Has anybody but you ever seen him?"

"Yes, and don't make fun of me. He has been to ministerial association meetings. The other pastors have all seen him, unless they aren't real either."

"All right, all right," Jennifer said, finally giving up on the idea that I was holding out on her. "We'll just have to try again tomorrow."

"Of course. We'll try tomorrow. I admit it worries me some. His being here was something I got used to. Something I could count on. It feels like a member of my family is missing and I have no idea where to look."

"I'm sorry, Honey," Jennifer said. "I'm sure this is uncomfortable for you, and I didn't mean to make it more so. We'll find him soon. He wouldn't just leave without telling you."

"No, I don't think he would. But, I'll feel better when I see him again."

We went home. It was still early. It had been an incredibly full and eventful day. Jenn and I talked for three hours, rehashing everything that we knew and did not know and trying to distill it down to basic concepts, and arrived at a relatively peaceful place. I don't know why I am continually surprised how much easier things are when you let God worry about how things turn out. It is a lesson I have to learn over and over again.

We agreed that the next key event was ten days off. The special meeting with the Staff Parish Relations Committee and the district superintendent would be telling. If there was going to be any *official* action taken, that is where and when it would start.

"So," Jenn asked, "I've always known that as an ordained elder in the United Methodist Church you have a *guaranteed appointment*, but I never cared much what that meant. What does guaranteed appointment mean?"

"It means that, as long as I am in good standing, they have to give me a church to pastor and they have to pay me at least the minimum allowable salary and benefits. The flip side is that I have to be itinerant, meaning I will willingly go wherever they send me. That's the deal."

"What does *good standing* mean?"

"That's pretty tricky. The bishop can move somebody with the flick of a pen. Getting rid of somebody entirely is a long, difficult and rare process. First a formal complaint is made, either by or to a district superintendent or bishop. Pretty much anyone can start it. They need to be quite specific about what is being alleged. Generally, you have to show what rule in the *Book of Discipline* has been broken."

"So, obviously, there are people here who would be happy to write up a complaint. What happens to it?"

"Usually, they try to fix it without going to United Methodist Court."

"We have a court!?"

"Oh yeah. But having a trial is really a pain, so they try to fix it, talk it out, find a solution that's called a *Just Resolution*. Maybe, convince the pastor to quietly retire. The most common thing is to move the pastor to another church and start fresh."

"So the DS coming to the SPRC meeting does what, exactly?"

"Hard to say. The SPRC can say they're happy the way things are, and that's that. They can turn in an *Advisory*, asking for a new pastor. The bishop can respond with a move or ignore it. The SPRC, the DS and the pastor can negotiate a deal to fix things. Or, they can make a formal complaint, demanding judicial action."

"Can they do that to you?"

"Yes, but there isn't much that would stick. You can't bring a complaint against a pastor just because you don't like their sermons or their music choices."

"Or the way the wife behaves."

"I love you. A pastor's spouse is not beholden to the local church, any more than any other member might be. I love you."

"I love you, too, smart butt. You said there isn't much that would stick. What would?"

"Popping Williams in the nose."

"But he has taken responsibility for that."

"Doesn't matter. The victim saying, *It's my fault, I made him mad,* doesn't negate a crime. It is exceedingly rare for a clergy person to punch out a church member. And, it is exceedingly clear cut. I hit him. He was not attacking me, which would be the only legitimate excuse, and I hit him anyway. If someone files a formal complaint for that, I'm toast."

"How is the complaint handled? Who holds the trial?"

"I'd have to look it up. I know there is a bishop involved, and The Annual Conference Board of Ordained Ministry, the Conference Relations Committee of the BOM, an appointed position called the Counsel for the Church—kind of a prosecutor—and a Conference Committee on Investigation. They all do a bunch of stuff, all of which leads to a potential Trial Court. After that, there is the College of Bishops at the Jurisdictional Conference, who form a Committee on Appeals. To tell you the truth, I have no idea how it all works."

"Agendor strikes again."

"That's for sure. We never make anything easy. But don't worry about it. A trial is not going to happen. I can guarantee that."

"How so?"

"We'll be long gone before it gets that far. I am not exactly sure what God wants us to do next, but I know we are supposed to be working against all this wrong-focus nonsense, not participating in it. Pastors have been to trial before—some won and some lost—and it didn't change a thing. We will either succeed in bringing a God-focus to this place, or we will do it somewhere else."

"So where does that leave us with this next meeting?" Jenn asked.

I noticed that she was completely calm. Almost serene. *That's my partner*!

"Well, I guess the hope for change is in the *fix it* mode. The hope is that a Holy Spirit led wave will come through the East Fork UMC and make it a new place. If not, then it is whatever comes next."

Chapter 31

Despite our efforts to remain serene, the big SPRC meeting loomed more and more ominous. It wasn't that we were terrified of the future, so much as we were struggling with our own behavior and decision-making. We prayed a great deal. In fact, we prayed together more than we ever had before. Still, we wrestled with whether we were actually doing and saying the right things. Clearly, Jenn and I had both failed already—you really shouldn't punch people in the face and you really shouldn't call fat people fat in public meetings—and we wanted desperately to not fall short again. As the days slowly ticked off towards the big meeting, there were no big conflicts, no rallies, no media spreads, no new accusations. Each day seemed made up of a series of smaller events, some related to recent controversies, and some not.

Kathy Morgan came in to the office on Tuesday. She is the mother of Jacob Morgan, a rambunctious eight-year-old. Jake was well known around the church, mostly for his inability to remain still or quiet for more than a minute at a time. Kathy did her best, God bless her soul, but she had fallen into the habit of blindly defending Jacob against any and all complaints. This day she entered my office carrying a large napkin, carefully folded around something. She laid the package on the one clear spot on my desk and said, "Good morning, Pastor Nathan."

"Good morning, Kathy. How are you today?" I replied.

"I am not very happy, I'm afraid. There is a problem in the Sunday school, and I thought you should know about it. So that you can do something about it. Fix it."

"Well, I am not directly in charge of Sunday school," I said, "but maybe I can help."

"I hope so," Kathy snapped. "The problem is with the head of the Sunday school."

"Mrs. West?"

"Yes. As you know, she teaches the third and fourth graders. She used to teach the first and second grade classes, but as her daughter Sydney has gotten older, she has moved herself right up the ladder with her. I guess you can do that when you're in charge of everything."

"Well, teaching one's own children is not uncommon, I don't think," I began, "I . . ."

"Maybe not! But it depends on how fair one is capable of being, don't you think!?" Kathy asked with great vehemence.

"I can see that something is upsetting you," I said, retreating from any idea of discussion. "Why don't you finish telling me what that is."

"Fine. Perhaps I should just let the evidence speak for itself."

She leaned in and slowly unfolded the napkin, revealing two Rice Krispie treats. One was about one and a half inches square, and the other about two and a half by two and a half.

"There!" she said. "Can you believe it?"

"Perhaps you could tell me a bit more about the significance of this. I know what they are, but I don't understand the problem."

"The problem is!" she exploded, "is that, just as I was walking into the classroom to pick up Jake, Mrs. West was handing out the snacks. Guess which great big piece she gave to Sydney and which itty bitty piece she saw fit to hand to my Jake! Go ahead, Pastor! Guess!"

I considered Kathy for a moment and thought that it might help to diffuse some emotion if we talked about factual details.

"So, did the children not eat their snacks? Being we have them right here?"

"Oh, they tried! But, I snapped up the evidence right then and there. She has been doing this kind of thing for years, but I finally got her dead to rights. I grabbed these from Sydney and Jake, and got my son right out of there. Jake had to do without, to protect the chain of evidence. I can't prove that she gave another one to Sydney, but you and I both know she did."

"Perhaps..."

"*Perhaps* nothing! The evidence is right in front of you. What are you going to do about it? Or, are you not being the pastor, anymore?"

I paused and tried to take in the whole picture. Kathy was seething, breathing fast and hard, her eyes so wide I wondered if they hurt. I knew her fairly well. She was married, but her husband refused to enter the church and was somewhat distant from his family. Kathy carried on mostly alone, but had always felt that the world was out to get her. Her son was troubled and was often pegged as the *weird* kid on the block.

"Of course I am your pastor," I began, "and I can see that you are genuinely upset."

"Just take care of the Most High Mrs. West, and I will feel fine," she replied.

"I will speak with Mrs. West. I will let her know that there is some feeling that she may not be treating the children equally, so she can examine her behavior and try not to do that."

"*May* not! I..."

"Please," I said, "let me finish. I know her. She will try to do the right thing. But I must add, Kathy, that God has given us the important and difficult job of raising our children to know Jesus and to one day be strong, moral, effective adults."

She stiffened up and her eyes draw into narrow slits, as she anticipated whatever attack I was about to make.

"Jacob is going to have a challenging time growing up and becoming that kind of man, although I am absolutely sure that he can. But he will have to learn good social skills and, especially, he will need to develop positive ways to cope with the world. Everyone faces disappointment and people who don't treat us the way we wish they would. And, everyone faces losses and setbacks. Don't you agree?"

Warily, she replied, "Yeah, sure, but I am not about to let anyone give my kid any crap or . . ."

"Please stop. I am one hundred percent on your side. God loves you and Jacob. I love you and Jacob. But to love you, I have to tell you that defending Jake's every move against whoever else is involved is going to make things far worse for him. I am willing to help you help him to develop all the skills he's going to need."

Kathy stood abruptly, barely containing her anger. "I cannot believe the load you are trying to feed me. No wonder people are jumping off your wagon ten at a time. I'll tell you exactly how you can help me and my Jake. Don't ever talk to me again. And if I see you talking to Jake, I'll call the cops, not that that would be anything new for you. You have seen the last of us in this place you call a church!"

She turned, took two steps toward the door, then wheeled around and swept up the two pieces of *evidence*, and proceeded out the door. *Honesty is not real popular,* I thought, as I tried to figure out what to do next.

On Tuesday, Frank and Sylvie dropped by, just to let me know that they were still thinking about Jenn and me, and that they were praying for us every day.

"Anything you need, anything, anytime, day or night, you call me," Frank said.

"No matter what," Sylvie said, "you're doing our wedding. Even if it's not here."

A look of horror crossed her face, as she realized that she had just suggested that I might be gone soon. I wrapped her up in my very best hug and told her what a treasure she was.

A Dragon in the Church 229

"And, I like Frank almost as much as I like you."
Frank got a big kick out of that.

Then, on Wednesday, Frieda Loveless died. She was eighty-eight and had been sick with various ailments for years. Her earthly life ended with no regard to whatever the rest of us happened to be fighting about at the time. A Saturday funeral was planned. I met with the family on Friday and interviewed them for the eulogy. The service was meaningful and reverent. The flowers were lovely. A memorial slide presentation of Frieda's life made me wish I had known her better. The United Methodist Women provided one of their best-ever funeral luncheons. For decades Frieda had been in charge of potato salad, and the ladies always went all-out for one of their own. It actually felt good to simply serve as pastor to Frieda's family. For a short while, things weren't so complicated.

Sunday service was so typical of any given Sunday as to be eerie. Attendance was still on the high side. I think there were quite a few who didn't want to miss out on any unexpected action. But the service itself was smooth as silk. My sermon seemed well-received. The choir was in excellent form. Condi added a solo piece on the organ that was truly sublime. The service ended. I stood at the rear of the sanctuary and shook hands with the *shakers* and hugged the *huggers*, just as I always did. And, suddenly, that week was over, and it was time to start the *week that was*.

The only other thing about the past week I should mention is that the saga of Pastor Carl continued. On Tuesday evening, Jenn and I drove out to the little church. No Carl. Again on Wednesday. Still no Carl. I was growing increasingly concerned, but did not know what my next move should be. On Thursday, Jenn had other obligations. I was going to give it a rest and try again on Friday. But, by 7:00 p.m. curiosity got the better of me, and I jumped in the car and drove to the church. There, parked in its usual spot, was Pastor Carl's truck. I entered more frantically than usual. There he was, polishing away on some just-completed floor molding.

"Hey there, stranger" he said, before I had a chance to speak. "Long time, no see. What's new?"

"What's new is that I have finally found you!" I exclaimed. "Where have you been? I've been really worried."

"I'm sorry to have concerned you," he replied. "I had some business to take care of out of town. Family stuff. I would have told you, but you weren't here the last couple of times. I could have called. I'm sorry."

"Well, I'm over-reacting, I'm sure. You don't need my permission to go wherever you want to go. I just got used to finding you here…that's all."

"Then let's just let things be okay and move on," Carl said. "Things here are wrapping up fast. What do you think?" Carl swept his right arm all the way around, indicating the entire sanctuary.

"I think it looks magnificent, even better than I had imagined it."

"Yes," he said, "I am pleased. I sure hope God got what he wanted."

"I don't see how he could be even a little bit disappointed," I answered. "It's both beautiful and powerful. It took my wife's breath away."

Carl looked at me. His face struck me as an odd cross between quizzical and unsurprised.

"So, you brought Jenn to see the place?"

"Yes. She was so moved that she asked to be called Jennifer whenever she is here. She has never once said anything like that before, so I knew that something was working on her."

"Or somebody," Carl whispered.

"Exactly," I responded. "Somebody."

For at least two minutes we stood quietly and comfortably, contemplating the magnitude of what had just been said.

"I wanted you to meet Jennifer," I said. "She is very anxious to meet you."

"Yes," Carl answered, "I would like that, too. Perhaps the time will come for that."

"Perhaps?"

"Oh, don't take that wrong. I'd love to. But, you know me, I only operate under strict orders from God."

"But, you have been dealing with me all this time. Does that mean that you and me are together under orders from God?"

"Of course."

"Wow. I guess I never thought of it quite that way."

"It's the most natural thing in the world, listening to God and doing what he wants. We just get too used to listening to everything and everybody else. Anyway, I have a strong feeling that as soon as this molding is finished I will have done all that I am supposed to do to the sanctuary."

"I think you're right," I said. "I'm not sure if anything else could make it any better."

"I'm going to do some work downstairs," Carl continued. "I will get it cleaned up and ready for new appliances and such, but I think I am supposed to stop there. It will be up to others to tackle the rest."

"Others?" I asked.

"Yeah. People from the congregation, or something. Who knows but God?"

"So you still don't know the next step? You're probably only talking a week."

"I'll admit, I kinda thought I would have more direction by now. But, *all in God's time*."

"I have always struggled with that phrase," I admitted. "It always seemed like an excuse for not getting things done."

"Lots of people use it that way. But, I learned long ago if you wait and listen intently enough, God will always let you know what and when. Of course, sometimes he just wants you to wait. That's never easy."

"Why, Pastor Carl, I think that's the first time I ever heard you admit that following God's will might be hard for you."

"That's because you didn't know me back when. We all have to grow, that's for sure."

"But, you will be leading a congregation here, right?" I asked.

Carl might have this Zen-waiting thing down pat, but I was still floating in curiosity.

"I think so. I guess I have assumed so. I've gotten real attached to this place. We'll have to wait and see."

"Yeah, I guess so," was all I could think to say.

Chapter 32

"Carl wants very much to meet you, but he wants to wrap things up at the church, first," I told Jenn. "Then he will do whatever God leads him to do at the time. That's how Carl operates."

"Is something wrong?" Jenn asked. "It feels like I'm on a black-list."

"No, not at all. It's hard to explain. He seems genuinely excited to meet you, but will only do so when the time is right. It's impressive and off-putting at the same time. But this has nothing to do with you, personally."

"All right, I'll try to buy that. But, I still have a question. How did he manage to not be there whenever I was with you?"

"I don't know. It's a mystery to me."

"It's weird," Jenn said. "But, we can't think about it now. First, let's survive the next week."

And so, we did. The penultimate week concluded relatively uneventfully, and Monday and Tuesday were much the same. With the big meeting looming on Thursday evening, Wednesday turned subtly and inexplicably strange. I couldn't explain it at the time. It was very calm. Everyone I met at the church seemed to be tip-toeing and whispering. Conversations hushed as I came near. Detractors would excuse themselves and walk away. Supporters would shake my hand and make an inane compliment. It was as if we were surrounded by nitro glycerin and no one wanted to be the one to set it off.

I finally asked Janice, "What is going on? There is a very odd vibe around here."

"Yes, there is," she answered, "I think there is a lot of communication out there, what the Homeland Security people call *chatter*. But it is like no one wants to be caught talking."

"Everybody?" I asked.

"Yeah, pretty much everybody."

"Tomorrow night can't come soon enough," I said.

The day finally came. This meeting actually had the potential for action. The district superintendent and the Staff Parish Relations Committee could set in motion my being cleared or charged or moved. Jenn and I sat down to an early supper and tried to prepare.

"Who all is on the SPRC?" Jenn asked.

"There are more than what usually show up, but you can bet your lunch money that every one of them will be there for this. That is, you could if you weren't a United Methodist."

"Could what?" Jenn asked, looking mildly miffed.

"Bet your lunch money. United Methodists aren't allowed to gamble."

"Proceed, funny guy."

"As you know, Daisy Watkins has been the Chair ever since we got here."

"Aren't there supposed to be term limits?"

"Yeah, but things were going so smoothly that I didn't make a change. Anyway, she is reasonable and will try to be fair and professional."

"And, the others?"

"Hard to say. There's Vern Snively. Quiet fellow. Not prone to emotionalism. Kevin Cloverton, Condi's husband. Smart. Considers things carefully. With him, it could be touchy. He's technically not supposed to be on the committee."

"Why not?" Jenn asked.

"Because his wife is an employee of the church. Staff/Parish deals with employee matters, so relatives are ineligible. But, Kevin is Director of Human Resources at the bank. He's too good to pass up, so I put him on with the proviso that he recuse himself on all matters involving Condi. It has worked fine so far, but now it probably depends on how upset Condi is."

"Is she upset?"

"I'm not sure. She is certainly in an emotional spot. Who knows where she stands. Patty Ellis is on the committee. She's serious. Almost somber. She very much likes order, so she can't be too thrilled with the state of the church. Then, there's Virgy Lou."

"That can't be good," Jenn stated the obvious.

"No help there, that's for sure. Jane Petra is too flaky to predict. Jeb Whitman works for the William's hardware, but he hasn't attended a meeting in over a year."

"That'll be Big Bob's inside contact, for sure," Jenn said. "It sounds like you've got some maybes and some enemies. Anyone you can count on?"

"Yeah. Lenora Brown thinks I'm special. She e-mailed a couple times to offer support."

"Who's this woman who thinks you're special?" Jenn asked with a smirk.

"Well, she is eighty-three or eighty-four, but she's still kinda hot."

"If you're talking that way in front of anyone else, we might as well start packing."

"Nah, we're safe. Anyway, other than Mark Wilder, who has never once shown his face at a meeting, that's it. Nine in all."

"And that's it? You, the DS and those nine are the only ones who can get in?"

"That's right. Staff Parish deals with me and all of the employees of the church. We have fourteen. So, the *Book of Discipline and* Equal Employment Opportunity laws require private meetings. You can't deal with employee information in a public forum."

"But, you stated publicly that you are not an employee."

"I know. But, sometimes I am. That's the system."

"So, I just stay home and sit here wondering and going crazy?"

"You could pray. That would be nice."

"Okay, I'll wonder and go crazy and pray. Williams won't be there?"

"Nope."

"If he is there, you text me. If he gets to be there, then so do I."

"I will . . . but he won't. I love you. I wish you could be with me. I love you."

"Hush up. I'm not blaming you. Go wash up. It's almost time."

I got myself cleaned up and ready to go. I took my time. I planned on making a late entrance, at seven o'clock on the nose. Everyone there, even the district superintendent, would be nervous about how to speak with me. It would be best to get right into the meeting. At 6:45 I pocketed my wallet and my keys and a pair of reading glasses.

"Pray with me before I go, Jenn," I said.

She began, "Dear Heavenly Father, Nathan is a man who is both good and dedicated to serving you. You have called him to speak on your behalf. And, he really, really tries. Give him the words to say this evening, that your message will be heard. Thank you for giving me such a husband. I admire his work and I try to make my work supportive of his. Let us not be too wound up about our own lives and our own future. Help Nate to do what he must do and say what he must say. We can live through whatever comes next. And please take care of everyone involved in this messy situation. We pray that everyone is moved closer to you, no matter where they start. Even Bob Williams. Amen."

I was appreciative of the Bob Williams crack at the end, as it helped me to stop crying.

"Good bye, my love," I said, as I kissed Jenn on the forehead. "I will be back with you as soon as I can."

A Dragon in the Church   237

The drive to the church was only a mile, but I took the five-mile route. I needed to dry my eyes and get focused. This experience could be short and sweet, or long and traumatic.

"Help me God," I said as I pulled into the church lot. "Be clear with me," I added.

It took but an instant for my focus to disappear completely. At the front entrance to the church, which is actually on the side of the building, stood two crowds. Perhaps *mobs* is a better description. On my left gathered easily a hundred and fifty people, chanting and jumping up and down. I stopped half way up the drive. It took a minute to break through my emotional chaos and register in my brain that they were chanting: *It's our church!! It's our church!!* Many of them held signs high in the air. *It's our church! We pay the bills! Is this still America! Why can't we choose our own pastor!?! Locked out of our own church!! Church our way! Why the secret meeting!?! If this is Methodism, let's be something else!* I felt as if I had been slugged in the gut when I spotted one that read: *Pastor Martin has got to go!!*

On the other side of the entryway, not twenty feet from Mob One, stood Mob Two. There were more of them, maybe two hundred in all, but they were less volatile. In fact, they were silent, staring across the way at the boisterousness of Mob One. Still, their intent was made clear by similar signs. *It's our church, too! Life-long Methodist! We stand with Pastor Nathan! Let the system work! Does Williams have to own everything!?!* A particularly clever one read simply: *We should be ashamed of ourselves!* Another read: *This must make God happy!*

How did I not find out about this? I noted in the back of my head that the battle over me had generated, perhaps revealed, anger and dissatisfaction with United Methodist Church practices. I must have been about the only one who didn't know about this protest rally. *This had to take a lot of planning,* I thought. *Is it possible for a pastor to be a cuckold in his own church?*

As I started to search out a parking space, the *anti*-crowd let out a roar. A TV reporter and camera-person were making their way up the sidewalk, between the mobs, panning the crowd. The volume of the chanting doubled. Signs bobbed up and down. The camera paused on a man who stood front and center, moving in for a close-up. Good ole Bob Williams. He stepped forward and appeared about to speak, when the reporter and camera moved on to more yelling and hollering and jumping and bobbing. Reaching the church door, and the end of the *anti*-line, the news-team swept around and panned the *pro*-crowd. Silence. Indecision. Massive discomfort. I looked about and saw that there were two television news shows represented: WEFM from East Fork, and WGRM from Grand Rapids. Next to Bob stood *this reporter* from the East Fork Chronicle. She was writing furiously.

My mind flurried. *Did I have to go in? Could I just drive away? Was the district superintendent inside? What was said before I got here? How many Book of Discipline rules were being broken by all these people? Based on this, what must the world think of the Church?* At that moment I felt a strong nudge; *All you have to do is go inside.*

"Okay," I said out loud, "I could do that."

I got out of my car and started walking. One foot in front of the other. One step at a time. I kept my head up and looked into the crowd. Members. People I knew well. Some, not as well. People I had prayed with and buried their loved ones and baptized their children. People with whom I had shared the Good News. Lots of them . . . on both sides.

Half way down, I had an inclination. I took a business card out of my wallet. It contained my cell number, church number and two email addresses. I held it out to *this reporter* and said, "Hello, Ms. Skiba. Contact me anytime, day or night. I'll be happy to comment."

"Thank you," I heard her say, as I moved on.

Just a few steps further, Frank and Sylvie stepped out from the other side.

"We love you," said Sylvie.

Frank rushed up and gave me a manly bear hug.

"I still know some guys," he whispered in my ear.

He laughed uproariously, and so did I.

I started inside, when I heard a shout, "Pastor! Pastor! Care to make a comment!?!"

I turned around to a microphone in my face and a camera not too far behind.

"First, love God," I said. "Second, just as important, love each other. We are all in this together."

I turned and proceeded into the building. As the door closed automatically behind me, I thought, *That was pretty good! I wish I had thought of it.*

Chapter 33

Inside, it was an entirely different scene. I saw no one and heard nothing except the murmur from outside. I knew exactly where the conference room was, of course, but I took the long way down the hall and through the sanctuary. I was trying to get my focus back. I never made it to the conference room. As I walked past the Fellowship Hall, I looked in and there they were, arranged in a carefully non-hierarchical circle. DS Reverend Judy Halliday, Daisy Watkins, Kevin Cloverton, Vern Snively, Patty Ellis, Jeb Whitman, Virgy Lou, Jane Petra, Lenora Brown and Mark Wilder were all in place. The seat between the DS and Chairperson Daisy was empty.

"Hi, Judy," I said while approaching the DS.

She offered her hand. "Good to see you," she said. "Albeit under testy circumstances."

"Ah, we'll be fine," I replied. "Just doing the business of the church."

I decided to greet each member of the committee individually, and see if I could get a read on the situation.

"Hi, Daisy," I said.

"Hello, Pastor Nate," she said. "I'm glad to see you."

Possible *yes*.

"Good evening, Kevin," I continued.

"Evening, Reverend Martin," Kevin replied while standing to shake my hand.

Another possible *yes*.

"Vern, good to see you."

"Pastor," was all he said. He moved not at all and did not look at me.

Definite *no*.

"Hi Patty," I said to Patty Ellis, "Good to see you."
"Hello, Reverend," she said, "Here to do my job."
No way to tell.
"Hi, Virgy Lou, so good to see you," I said.
"I'd prefer you to refer to me as Mrs. Dekker."
Ouch! I was falling behind.
"Hello, Jane, how have you been?"
"I've been real busy. Busy all the time. How about you?"
No telling with Jane.
"Evening, Jeb."
"Could we just get on with this?" he replied.
A firm *no*.
"Lenora! How are you!" I asked.
"I am fine Reverend Martin. I hope we can clear up this unpleasantness in a jiff."
A dependable *yes*.
"Mark Wilder. How have you been?"
"Fine."
No clue there.
"Well, thank you all for coming," I went on, as I took my seat. "This can be tough work, and most people in the church don't even know that someone has to do it."

My poll was only informal, but it stood at three *for*, three *against* and three *undecided*.

"Okay," Reverend Halliday jumped in, reclaiming control of the meeting. "Now that we are settled in, let's get on with the business of this meeting. I'll pray us in, and then you can call the meeting to order, Daisy. Who is the recording secretary?"

"I am," Patty answered.

"Good. Patty . . . it is Patty, isn't it?" Reverend Halliday asked, stumbling a bit.

"Yes. Patty."

"Good. At this type of meeting, it is essential to have very complete notes, so please ask us to stop if you need to catch up. Okay?"

"Okay."

"Good. Let us pray."

After a nondescript opening prayer, Reverend Halliday spoke.

"I have been made aware of what has been going on here at East Fork. I will admit to you right up front I have not dealt with anything quite like this in my three years as District Superintendent. I am not sure how we can possibly make sense of all of the various and random elements, unless we narrow the discussion quite a bit. Then, Daisy, you can let me know how you want to progress. Our polity, the way we do things, gives a lot of power to the clergy, but also a lot of power to the lay leadership of the church. This committee has certain choices it can make."

"Yes, that would be good," Daisy said. "This is all so overwhelming."

"It is," Reverend Halliday said, "so let me give you some choices and see if that helps. Is that all right with everybody?"

Most only nodded, but Jeb spoke, asking, "Do we get to tell what's wrong around here?"

"Yes, all that needs to be said will be said. Okay," the DS continued, "let's go from least severe to most severe. First, this committee can choose to do nothing at all . . ."

"Hey, we didn't come here to do nothin'!" Jeb interrupted, "We . . ."

"Be quiet and give it a minute, Jeb," Vern said abruptly. "Let the woman finish explaining before you get all wound up. We'll be here all night."

"Okay, as I started to say," the DS said, "you can do nothing. The Staff Parish Relations Committee does not have to do anything unless it decides to. You could decide that none of these complaints are worth disciplining a pastor for and just go home. Others would simply have to accept your decision and the church would move on as normal."

Jeb harrumphed.

"Next, this committee could decide, by a simple majority vote, to request another pastor. You just fill out a form called an *Advisory* and turn it in by the end of the year. There does not have to be a particular or proven set of reasons for the Advisory. You can do that if you wish."

"Excuse me," Kevin broke in. "Please elaborate on that. I can't believe we just sign a paper and get a new pastor."

"No, not quite. And, thank you for asking me to clarify. First, while you don't need anything in particular to file the Advisory, if it doesn't come with good, proper, well thought out rationale, it probably won't get much attention from the bishop."

"That's who decides? One person? Some bishop?" Virgy Lou spat out. "Sounds about like the Methodists."

Virgy Lou has been a Methodist since she was born, I thought. *Why is she talking like they are the enemy?*

"Technically, that is correct," Reverend Halliday responded. "All of the district superintendents make up a body called the *cabinet*. We advise the bishop on pastoral appointments, but the bishop can make whatever decision he or she wants to make. Anyway, you could turn in an Advisory, work up a good, persuasive set of reasons your church would benefit from a change of pastors, and see what the bishop decides to do. He does not have to honor an Advisory. In the church, only the SPRC committee or the pastor can file an Advisory."

"For the record," the DS said, turning to me, "are you considering turning in an Advisory this year, Reverend Martin? These things are often granted if both sides make the request."

"No, I am not."

"Very well, then. Just checking for accuracy's sake," she said.

"I understand," I commented. "I prefer to continue my ministry here."

"Good," said Lenora. "We've never had a finer pastor. I cannot begin to understand what all the commotion is about."

"Somebody gonna shush her?" Jeb asked.

"Let's move on," the DS said, "and finish this list. The other choices involve the bringing of formal charges. This is quite different. It is much more like a legal matter. This committee could ask that Reverend Martin be charged with a violation of what we refer to as church law. This has to be much more specific. You pretty much have to quote the paragraphs of the *United Methodist Book of Discipline* that you believe have been violated, and be prepared to bring evidence. This can be given to me or to the bishop. After that, there are several technical steps that we won't try to cover now, but it is very much like assigning a prosecutor and a defense attorney to argue the merits of the case, just like civil court. Who is hearing the case depends on what kind of charges are brought. Charges of incompetency or ineptitude are handled differently than charges of a moral or legal nature. These trials don't happen often, and we try to settle things without going that far, but it does happen occasionally."

"What if we don't bring charges?" Daisy asked. "Is that it, or can someone else do it?"

"Excellent question. Actually, anyone can bring charges and, if there is an actual violation and some good evidence, it will be pursued."

"Let me try to narrow this down," Kevin said. "If enough of us are upset with preaching style, preaching topics, music choices, whether he visits old people enough or not, about all we can do is one of these Advisories. If we want to do a trial, it has to be a more serious breach of some specific rule or another. Is that correct?"

"There are all kinds of technicalities that could be involved," Reverend Halliday answered, "but for discussion purposes, yes, that is pretty accurate."

"Okay," Daisy said, "Then I think it is time to see where we are. Reverend Halliday, if it is all right with you, I would like to take the temperature of the committee members, so to speak."

"Yes, Daisy, please do."

A Dragon in the Church 245

"Thank you. Starting at my left and working around the circle, I am giving each of you two minutes to summarize what you are thinking and feeling right now. Hopefully, we will all be open to changing opinions as we receive more information, but this will be a start."

Daisy is morphing into a real leader, I thought.

"Two rules," Daisy continued. "I will cut you off, no bones about it, at two minutes. And, no one speaks a word during someone else's turn. Not a peep. I don't want to sound mean, but I don't want the debates to flare up until everyone has had their chance. Does everyone agree to start this way?"

No one objected.

"Very well, then. I will go last, and then I will give Reverend Martin five minutes to respond. Before anybody complains that he gets extra minutes, I probably ought to be giving him eighteen. He has to respond to all of us. So, five it is. After that, I have no idea, so I will turn to Reverend Halliday for guidance. Any questions?"

No questions were asked, but the body language in the room changed noticeably. Some leaned forward. Some leaned back. Some crossed their arms, forming a protective barrier. It was clear is that things were about to get serious, and perhaps ugly.

"Kevin," Daisy said, "You are first. Say whatever you wish, in two minutes."

"Thank you, Daisy. I don't feel like I have enough information to make authoritative remarks, but these are my first impressions. While my wife and I have not always been happy with decisions that Pastor Nathan has made, or directions that he has taken the church regarding worship and music and certain things, I don't think any of it has been out of the ordinary. I understand that pastors are being encouraged to modernize and update things, as the United Methodist Church has been shrinking for years. And, much of what he has been blamed for is actually correct according to United Methodist rules. So, I'm not sure a person should be punished for that. Also, I believe it is important to note that he is quite skilled and unusually capable at many of the areas of ministry. The claims against his wife are unfair. She does not belong to us. I might, and might not, support an Advisory, given the turmoil the church is in. But I will not support charges. And, I might add, we probably ought to be talking about how to discipline Bob Williams. He is at the core of most of the discord."

"Hey!" Jeb Whitman broke in. "We're not talking about Bob, here. Stick to the point."

"Don't say another word," Daisy commanded. "Kevin can say what he wants, and we'll discuss later whether the actions of others need to be considered. Anything else, Kevin?"

"No. I have said what I need to say at this point."

"Thank you," Daisy responded. "And, right at two minutes. Thank you. Vern?"

Vern launched in right away. "I am not in cahoots with anybody. I don't take sides and I don't much care what anybody else thinks. Mostly I think this is a ridiculous mess. We sit in here and discuss things all nice and proper, and pretend there's not three-four hundred people outside fighting for the TV cameras and the newspapers. It's crazy and it makes me ashamed to be a part of it. I am not entirely sure who to blame, but it doesn't much matter. When a ball team falls apart, and things get so bad you can't even figure it out anymore, you fire the manager. What else can you do? Fire the whole team? Fire the fans? I say, and I truly mean you no harm or disrespect, Pastor, the only way to regroup and fix this mess is make a big move, calm everybody down, get the reporters to go home, start fresh and see if we can pull this thing back together. The whole church is more important than the one pastor, and he can probably go somewhere else and start fresh, too. I don't see any other way to go. I'm done."

"Thank you, Vern," Daisy said. "Right to the point."

"Excuse me," DS Halliday interrupted. "I want to check and see if this is all getting in the minutes."

"We're good," Patty answered.

"Thank you, Patty," Daisy said, taking her meeting back. "It's your turn. Can you speak and make notes at the same time?"

"Yes. I don't have a lot to say. I am not as up on all this as some of you are. My present feeling is something has to be done soon. I kind of agree with what Vern is saying about the mess and the chaos. I really, really want to be fair to everyone. Right now that means especially you, Pastor Nathan. But, I can't help but wonder how we fix this. Even if we find that nothing has happened that *should* get anyone punished, how does that make all this conflict and side-taking go away? Our church is in serious jeopardy, and if we don't find a way out of this we aren't going to be half the church we used to be. People will leave, pure and simple. Still, I want to hear more before I vote. That's it."

Jeb's turn, I thought. *Now we get a look at what the organized opposition is up to.*

"Thank you, Patty. Jeb, you're up." Daisy's voice had a slight catch on *you're up.*

Jeb opened his notebook and withdrew a stack of papers.

"At this time, I would like to present to each member of the Staff/Parish Relations Committee a copy of a petition, signed by one hundred and seventy-two members and constituents of the East Fork First United Methodist Church."

Jeb's voice was flat, monotone and halting, as if he was reading something that he did not quite understand. Because he was. A closer look revealed that Jeb was reading from a script fastened inside the notebook.

"As I pass these out, please take time to consider . . ."

"Put those away!"

I had never seen such fire and fury in Daisy's eyes.

"Now! You are a member of this committee and those other people are not. You have to speak for yourself! This passing stuff out trick is not going to happen here!"

"I am speaking for myself!" Jeb spat back. "This is what I think is the problem, a hundred and seventy-two people who are pissed off and want changes around here! Why can everyone else have their say, and me you shut up! Huh? Why is that?"

"Please! Let's control ourselves," DS Halliday interjected. "Let's clean up the language and calm down. Now, Jeb—Mr. Whitman, right?—in a procedure like this, you can get your information and opinions wherever you like, but you have to express them as your own thoughts. Just say *I think,* instead of *we* and you can proceed. Please."

Jeb seethed, showing no sign of moving on. I knew him well enough to know that he was angry, but also did not know what to do next. He was used to operating under orders.

"How about this?" I asked. "A petition starts out with a statement telling what it is about or what it is asking for. How about Jeb reads that, without passing out the names? That will help us know what we're dealing with, without bringing personalities into it."

Of course, I really, really want to see the names on the list, I thought.

Daisy looked to Reverend Halliday, who responded, "Yes. I think that would work."

Jeb scowled and grunted a couple of times. Then, evidently deciding that he had better accomplish part of his mission, he read, *We the undersigned believe that, number one) the people of our congregation should have the right to decide when we are in need of a new pastor, regardless of the presumptions, assumptions and traditions of the United Methodist Church hierarchy—our church, our say-so—and, number two) we find the performance of our employee, The Reverend Nathan Martin, to be unsatisfactory and not up to expected standards, particularly in the areas of worship, music, leadership, ethics and moral leadership. Therefore, we the undersigned demand that Reverend Martin be removed immediately from our church, and a new pastor be provided ASAP, by the bishop of our annual conference, and subject to the approval of the Church Council of the East Fork First United Methodist Church.* Jeb finished and showed no sign of adding anything.

"Anything else, Jeb?" Daisy asked.

"Just that a hundred and seventy-two people have signed it already and we haven't even asked everyone yet."

"All right. Thank you," Daisy went on. "I think that opened up a whole bunch of questions . . . but let's go ahead and finish this process first. Mrs. Dekker?"

"*You* may call me Virgy Lou, Daisy. I, and many like me, have been serving East Fork First for decades. Pastors come and go, but the women's leagues and societies, and the men, too, all the volunteers and unpaid soldiers in God's army, stay the course. I was here well before *this* pastor arrived, and I shall remain here long after he is gone, which, in my estimation, should begin very soon. East Fork First is a particular kind of church. We have a proud and proper and decent history here, filled with good people living good lives. Worshipping our God in right ways and as proud Americans and good citizens, with reverence and sacred music and appropriate traditions. There may be room for other types of churches for other types of people. I'll allow that there might even be a need for such churches. But not here. Not at East Fork First United Methodist Church! *This* pastor has no respect for people like me. *This* pastor has no respect for our church. Therefore, I have no respect for him. He's got to go. Move on."

"Jane?" Daisy said. "Your turn."

"Well, I have to admit that I am pretty much flabbergasted. How long has this been going on? Forgive me for asking this right in front of you, Pastor Nate, but what in heaven's name did he do? I knew people were fussing about new music and there's been some complaining about his wife not being around, but, holy cow, what did I miss?"

"Okay," Daisy started. "Right this minute is not the time for a rundown of accusations and such. However, I am quite sure we will be doing some of that in a few minutes. So, if it is acceptable to you, Jane, let's call it good for now, and pick it up later."

"Fine by me. I'm lost anyway."

"Okay. Lenora? What do you have to add?"

"Honestly, I feel like I am starring in an episode of *The Twilight Zone*. Have I been attending an entirely different church than the rest of you? Reverend Martin, he prefers Pastor Nate, is a good man and a fine pastor. He is intelligent and well-educated and more articulate than any pastor we have ever had. He teaches wonderful Bible studies, he digs into the Scriptures so deeply and yet makes it so easy to understand. When I was in the hospital, he visited me and was so comforting. Why, until all this nonsense came up, he had even cut down on some of the petty conflict and gossip around here. And, if you would take the time to get to know his wife, you would love her, too. But, you can only hurt a person's feelings so many times before they are going to want to be someplace else. And what is all the hoop-la about some modern music in a separate service that you don't even have to go to if you don't feel like it!? Grow up. If we don't bring in some young people, the church will die. We have all gotten older. I hope that doesn't mean we've turned stupid. And another thing that I think you ought to think about, real hard . . ."

"I hate to say it," Daisy said, "But that's two minutes."

"She can have one of mine," Mark offered.

"Thank you, young man. As I was saying, I want you to think real hard about how come Pastor Nate was so successful in other churches. We are a big, rich, important, arrogant church. We demand the best and that is what they send us. So here is Pastor Nate with all kinds of awards and credentials and positions of power and respect, until he gets here. Maybe it's us! I think we ought to be ashamed of ourselves and beg for a second chance. That's what I think."

I had no idea that Lenora was so intelligent and insightful! I thought.

"Thank you, Lenora. We're up to you, Mark."

"Thank you. I choose to not say anything at this time."

Daisy was taken by surprise. "Oh . . . very well. Then, it is my turn. I will use my two minutes in a different manner. I believe we are doing a good job of getting the various sides out on the table, so let me say this about our task. The Staff Parish Relations Committee stands in a funny position in the scheme of things. On the one hand, we are supposed to support and help the pastor to be as effective as possible, and be a liaison between the pastor and the congregation. On the other hand, we are to supervise the pastor and keep an eye on things, to make sure that the congregation is protected from a wayward pastor. And on the third hand—I told you it is a funny position—we are also a liaison between the local church and the rest of the church; the district superintendent and the bishop and the Annual Conference and such. And part of that is we *are* a United Methodist Church, and there are rules that we have to follow."

"Or what?" Jeb chimed in as rudely as he could muster.

"Let me," DS Halliday offered. "I guess the easiest way to answer that is to say that, while there is plenty of leeway for the local church to act, there are some rules that can't be broken without choosing to not be a United Methodist Church anymore."

"That would be fine by me, and a lot of other people, too!" Jeb was getting carried away.

"We all have choices, of course. Anyone can leave at any time. However, it is only proper to make clear that this church, The East Fork First United Methodist Church, was built by Methodists who gave time, effort and money to the United Methodist Church. Therefore, it will stay a United Methodist

Church, no matter how many people choose to leave. The building, the property and all the assets will stay United Methodist."

Jeb looked as if he was about to explode and implode at the same time. Red in the face, chin quivering with rage, sputtering as he tried to get words out, Jeb stood so violently that his chair flew into the wall behind him.

"What the he . . .!"

"Jeb! Sit down and shut up. Now!" *I never saw that coming,* I thought. *Who'd of thought it would be Kevin to the rescue?*

"I'll say whatever I want!" Jeb retorted.

But he sat down.

"First, Jeb," Kevin continued, "Everyone else is showing respect for each other and for due process. You will, too. Second, you are about to make a fool of yourself by making a lot of noise about something you don't understand. I've studied this. She's right. End of story."

"Okay," Daisy said. "I guess this makes clear how complicated and touchy all this can get. I admit that I cannot follow it all. I am not sure how we are going to make sense of it."

Once again, the best impulses of the Church stymied by Agendor, I thought.

"But," Daisy continued, "this committee is going to try. If anyone is going to find a fair and workable solution for everyone involved, it pretty much has to be us. If we fail, someone else will step in and do it for us, and that might result in something that none of us likes."

"Pastor," Daisy said, "respond however you wish. Five minutes, please."

"Let's start with a moment of silence," I said. "I really need to think a little."

We sat for a full minute. I was glad that I had practiced the art of waiting. As for the others, the experience appeared to be various degrees of painful. I had my eyes firmly closed, but I could hear a lot of fidgeting and throat-clearing and even overly-rapid breathing. Waiting is not something that we Americans do well. I was specifically hoping for some sort of direction. There was so much being said, most of it personal attacks or defenses of me, that I was, frankly, overwhelmed. Anger? Counter-attacks? Tears? Submission? Apologies? Explanations? What should it be? Then, I just started to talk.

"Thank you, all of you, sincerely. There are all kinds of people saying all kinds of things today. Who knows what is being said outside right now. Yet, you are the ones who have to speak on the record, carefully consider difficult information and make even more difficult decisions. Thank you.

"At this moment, I feel like a man without a place to stand. My life, at least my professional life as a United Methodist pastor, seems to be vaporizing around me. On the one hand, I am being openly criticized and blamed for many things. Some of the accusations are true, and represent my short-comings. Although, as closely as I am capable of examining my own performance, they are just the kinds of short-comings that comes with each and every pastor. Some of the accusations are driven solely by the anger, privilege, personal preferences and misconceptions of others. It is not particularly fair or constructive—there are many who are in drastic need of self-examination—but there it is. The result has grown and morphed and developed into chaos, complete with side-taking and mud-slinging and political strategizing, all intended to win a great battle that has not, as yet, even been defined. Our church has become a public mess, perhaps a microcosm of the mess that the greater church is in. And, we are spending most of our time attempting to allocate the blame.

"Thankfully, my faith in God and my personal life have never been stronger. My desire to serve and obey God is at an all time high. Which leads to the other half of my quandary. I have always benefited from the United Methodist way of doing things. We codify and systematize and institutionalize every aspect of the church in a very human attempt to control everything that happens or might happen. Heaven forbid that God or Human should try to act outside of the system, or without the latest edition of the *Book of Discipline* at hand. And, I have been a master at working within that system. I have jumped through the hoops and made the right moves and been elevated and credentialed and advanced and rewarded, because I know how this stuff works. Reverend Halliday, I am sorry if I disappoint you in any way, but I find it less and less palatable that we quash dissent, whether it be legitimate or stupid, with a flurry of rules and procedures that make sure no one really stands a chance. If, in the end, the institution has been preserved, we declare victory and on we go.

"I may not fit in anymore. However, so far, I think I am to continue to be in this place, a place that clearly needs to hear from God. So, I will not voluntarily leave. Nor, will I fall back into line to fix this. I will say and do whatever I believe God wants said and done, and live with the consequences. That's my bottom line."

Chapter 34

The suggestion was made that, for clarification purposes, the business before the Staff Parish Relations Committee be divided into two major areas of consideration. The first task would be to decide what action should or should not be taken regarding me and my position at East Fork First United Methodist Church. Should there be an Advisory requesting a change in pastor? Should the SPRC bring charges? Or, should the committee just leave it alone?

The second task, which may or may not be tied to the first, would be to decide what, if any, action to take regarding the unrest in the church. The protests and the media reports were causing quite a stir, and it would get worse. Reverend Halliday pointed out this would not stay local, or even regional, for long. Hundreds of church members standing divided and protesting at the door of their own church is not something that happens every day. Neither was a pastor attempting to settle an argument by slugging a congregant. What might seem only a local tempest in a teapot would soon transform into a great national story.

Daisy began by saying, "So, how shall we begin?" There erupted an hour of highly emotional back and forth. I sat in the middle of it and soaked up a myriad of versions of the same complaints and the same defenses as had become common place.

Finally, I interrupted. "Excuse me! Excuse me! May I speak?" It took a minute, but quiet came and all attention was on me. "I would like to request a vote, based on the following question: Assuming satisfactory rationale was written explaining our reasons for requesting a change in pastors, would you vote that the SPRC of the East Fork First UMC should turn in such an Advisory? *Yes* for Advisory. *No* against Advisory. Could we do that, please?" I asked.

Daisy looked to the DS, who said, "Somebody just has to put it in the form of a motion."

"So moved!" said Kevin.

"Second!" said at least four others.

"Patty, do you have the motion written down?" Daisy asked.

"Maybe. How's this? *It is moved that the East Fork First United Methodist Staff Parish Relations Committee shall prepare and send an Advisory letter to the bishop of the Lower Michigan Annual Conference, requesting that Reverend Nathan Martin be replaced as pastor of our church. This motion is contingent upon the committee's agreement on proper rationale language.* How's that?"

"Pointing out that an actual Advisory would require a whole new motion, this is adequate to find out what the committee wishes," said DS Halliday.

"Okay," Daisy said. "Kevin, do you make that motion?"

"So moved."

"Who's going to second?"

"I will."

"Thank you. Seconded by Jane," Daisy continued. "I am about to ask for discussion. May I remind you the whole purpose of this motion is to stop the discussing long enough to see where we are. Is there any discussion?"

"Yes, sort of. Not discussion. Just a question."

"Sure, go ahead, Mark."

"What does this vote do, exactly?"

Once again, Daisy looked to the district superintendent.

Reverend Halliday began, "A *no* vote means we are done considering an Advisory. A *yes* vote means we *might* do an Advisory, if we can agree on the language."

"Thank you," Daisy said. "Anything else? There being no further discussion, let's vote. For this particular vote, I am going to poll the committee. I think that is the only way we accomplish the goal of finding out where we are. So, Kevin?"

"*No*."

"Vern?"

"Sorry Pastor, *yes*."

"Patty?"

"*No*."

"Jeb?"

"One hundred percent *yes*!"

"Virgy Lou?"

"*Yes*."

"Jane?"

"I think . . . *no*."

"Lenora?"

"One Thousand percent *no*!"

I swear, right after her resounding *no*, dear, sweet, elderly Lenora glared at Jeb and stuck her tongue out.

"Okay, okay. Enough," Daisy said.

She looked at Mark Wilder, and hesitated. A *no* from Mark and the vote would be decided. A *yes*, and a tie would fall on Daisy to break.

"Mark?"

"*No*."

"There's going to be a lot of ticked off people!"

Daisy flared. "Please, for once Jeb! Just once . . . be quiet! For the record, my vote is *no*. Now, take a ten-minute break and we will reconvene to decide on bringing charges."

"I move," Kevin Cloverton broke in, "That we do not bring formal charges of any sort against Reverend Martin."

"Second!" cried Lenora with much glee.

"Very well, if the committee feels so moved. Any discussion?"

"No need," Jeb answered. "You people aren't going to listen to anything, anyways. You already knew what you were gonna do. Discuss all you want. The charges are coming, anyhow. Punch anybody out, lately . . . *Reverend Pastor?!*"

"Nope," I said as quickly as I could. The rest of the group was about done listening to Jeb. "Only the one time, which I will always regret. It was a bad moment for me."

Jeb did, for once, shut up.

"Further discussion?" Daisy asked. "Hearing none, those in favor say *aye.*"

Eight *ayes.*

"Those opposed, say *no.*"

A single *no.*

"Motion carried," Daisy announced. "No charges. Now, take that break. Then we'll decide if there is anything we can do about the turmoil in the church. We are going to have to get the membership to accept our decisions and start working together, and it won't be easy."

Most stood up, stretched and started to mosey toward the restrooms. Jeb gathered his petitions, jumped up and shot straight down the hallway and out the nearest exit. *From SPRC member to protester in 30 seconds flat,* I thought.

The district superintendent, Reverend Judy Halliday, tapped me on the shoulder and whispered, "Let's find a place to talk."

We made our way to my office, and sat.

"Nathan," she said, "tell me what you're thinking. The decisions just made mean that the official church body is not going to ask for a change or bring charges. Obviously, someone else might."

"Sounds like a given," I said. "If they are smart enough to bring only the *physical violence against a member* complaint, I'm a goner. I won't lie about it. It happened."

"Yeah, it did. Perhaps the fact that this Williams fellow took the blame publicly would help. You might get some sort of a remedial sentence: anger management, a promise to never do it again. That sort of thing."

"Yeah," I mumbled, ". . . that might work."

The DS paused, then said, "You won't promise to not do it again, will you?"

"Mostly, I will. Unless I'm asked if there is a situation in which it could happen again."

"You mean to protect yourself or someone else?"

"Or if some guy talks about my wife like that again."

"Okay," Nathan, "let me get clear, here. The bishop is more than a little concerned about this whole situation. And, please be aware, I work for the bishop."

"I know. I understand and appreciate your situation."

"Thank you. My recommendation to the bishop allows for giving you a lot of rope. I admire your zeal. So does the bishop. The fact that the SPRC chooses not to ask for action only complicates things. Now any immediate action has to come at the bishop's own volition. The level of controversy and bad press already had concerns high, and then we get here and see an outright protest going on. Nathan, the polity of the whole United Methodist denomination is about to be debated in the public square!"

"Maybe it's about time it was." I said.

"Really! Really! Are you sure that's what you want to say to me right now? You said you wanted to speak for God. Okay, fine. Are you telling me that mob out there speaks for God? Are you telling me that a bunch of angry, self-centered people who understand absolutely nothing about how the UMC works—and don't really care except to get their own way—is suddenly the best and highest forum to discuss how well the United Methodist Church is serving God! Really?! Is this your grand plan, Nathan? Because if it is, I do not know if I can save you from yourself. What do you expect me to do with this mess?"

I felt both calm and embarrassed.

"I'm sorry, Judy. I realize that I have put you and the bishop in an unfamiliar and difficult position. But, not by myself. Up until recently, I was not doing one thing that the system did not train me to do. Running the church. Even growing the church. Trying to slowly and diplomatically move the church into new territory, without upsetting the apple cart. I was just what you asked for. And, I was good at it."

"Yes, Nathan, you were."

"Then a self-centered, self-important and powerful member of the church decided he was going to make over the venerable East Fork First United Methodist Church in his own image. And he went to work. If I was the way I used to be, I would have chosen to play with the devil. I would have tried to shape and bend and influence his plans to turn out looking like something we could live with. I would have tried to keep the pews full, fill the coffers and declare partial victory. And you and the bishop would have patted me on the back, told others to be more like me, and left me here for a few more productive years. Am I wrong yet?"

"Probably not."

"I'm sorry," I said. "I really am. I shouldn't have insinuated the denomination has it coming. That was stupid. To be clear, I think we are in a huge mess. But I realize having people fighting and screaming about things they know nothing about is not helpful."

Judy Halliday smiled. "You have turned into an atypical pastor. So, Nathan, Mr. forthright and honest, I ask again. What the heck do we do?"

"District superintendents are supposed to advise. How do you advise me?"

"The bishop wants to avoid formal charges. Church trials are horrible for everyone involved. But, if formal charges are brought, the bishop, the Board of Ordained Ministry and others will have to respond. You already know what the bishop can do most easily to stop this."

"Move me."

"Yes. We let the protestors know the bishop will move you out, if they promise not to bring charges. They promise. The bishop decides which church to play switch-pastors with. The moving company makes a few bucks. Done."

"Are you announcing the decision has already been made?"

"Surprisingly, no. I've been told to try everything to have you stay and finish the job."

"No joke? Why?"

"Bishop Clayton Burns does not like to be pushed into a corner. Bishop Burns says that a United Methodist pastor who is listening to God and making waves ought not to be brushed aside by, and I quote, a 'small-town punk Napoleon.' In short, the bishop is ticked off."

"Well, I must admit that I am pleasantly surprised," I said. "I have been under the impression my wife and I are in this alone."

"You are decidedly not alone. However, this grows more and more complicated. I sure wish you hadn't hit that guy."

"Yeah, I know."

"Still, the bishop wants you and me to find a way to get back on track. What has happened with the SPRC here tonight is a good start, at least officially. But the unofficial stuff might be out of control. Let's get back to the meeting; they must be waiting on us."

"There's nothing the SPRC can do to stop the open protest," I said. "A statement of support will help, but I am not sure what it will take to slow the protestors down. We could be looking at a major split. Half the congregation could walk."

"Maybe," the DS replied. If it does, let's make sure we keep the right half. You ready?"

"Yeah, I sure am."

"Can your wife take what's coming?"

"Yes. The woman is a wonder."

"Okay. Let's give it a try."

It didn't take long for the Staff Parish Relations Committee to finish its work, at least for the time being. Building upon decisions already made, a statement was drafted. It read: *The Staff Parish Relations Committee of the East Fork First United Methodist Church, being the sole local church body responsible for matters of performance and competence of the appointed pastor, has carefully reviewed all recent concerns and allegations made against the Reverend Nathan Martin. We find no matters warranting the bringing of formal charges, nor do we believe that the East Fork First UMC need request a pastoral change at this time. We believe that Reverend Martin has been effective during his time as our pastor, and we are confident that he will continue to be effective in the future. The SPRC encourages all members and constituents of the church to reunite and be open to new beginnings and an exciting future, serving God and the greater East Fork community.*

The statement was quickly typed up and copied. It was agreed—not happily or readily by all—this would be the only statement released by the SPRC to the press or the church body. With that, we adjourned with a prayer for harmony, and prepared to exit the building.

Jane Petra ran ahead and peeked out a front window. She came back and breathlessly said, "The crowd's still out there. They look quiet, but it doesn't look like anyone has left."

"All right," I said, "everybody listen up. They are after me, not you. Go on out. Hand out a copy of the official statement to anyone who asks questions. Then say, *The pastor will be out to make a statement in just a minute.* Then keep moving. Go on home and try to relax. And thank you. All of you. You did your work just as you should. Good night."

Vern asked, "What about Madam District Superintendent? I think we ought to make sure she gets safely out of here."

"I can handle myself," DS Halliday began.

"Yes," I interrupted. "Please, Judy, go with the others. You'll be gone before they know what happened. You're doing your job, but this does not need to get all over you. Go."

"Okay," she replied, "But, what are you going to say out there?"

"I'm not sure, yet, but at least it will be only me saying it."

The DS and the committee easily ran the gauntlet. As I watched their cars leaving the parking lot, both the crowd and the press pushed closer to the doors, straining to be the first to get at me. I said a quick *Holy Spirit, help me now* prayer and stepped out.

People started yelling and waving signs. A few pathetic attempts were made to restart chants and cheers. Three camera crews—I couldn't tell where the third team came from—aggressively rushed me. In an instant, I had three microphones in my face, amid dozens of shouted questions. I stood perfectly still and said absolutely nothing. The noise grew louder. The shouts came faster. The jostling became more pronounced. I stood perfectly still and said absolutely nothing. For fully five minutes, the hubbub went on.

Some shouted at me to start talking. Then they started to yell to each other. *What's the matter with him!? When is he going to say something?! Should we call an ambulance? Maybe he's had a stroke!*

I stood perfectly still and said absolutely nothing. *Zen-Master Nathan,* I thought. *Thank you, Pastor Carl.* At the ten-minute mark, the tide finally turned. The noise level dropped. The shouting and the questions slowed down. Confusion set in. A nice, calm confusion. Finally, silence ruled, with the promise of some sort of order.

"First, I would like to make a statement," I said. "Then, and only then, will I answer your questions. The Staff Parish Relations Committee of the East Fork First United Methodist Church has done its work, openly, fairly and completely. I commend them on taking a difficult, nuanced and emotional matter under consideration, and arriving at a carefully examined position. I believe that you have copies of their statement. In short, the committee has recommended that no change be made, and that we return to serving God and neighbor as best we can. I agree with this line of thinking. I do not think that we have yet accomplished all that can and will be accomplished. In short, neither the East Fork First UMC, nor I, will be seeking any changes in pastoral appointment."

"Yeah, but it wasn't unanimous, was it!" Jeb shouted from the crowd.

He stood not two feet from Bob Williams. Surprisingly, the hush held.

"Why no, Jeb!" I said. "You know that. You were there! Don't you remember?" There were a few snickers. "The vote was six to three. So, here we are, still working together."

With that the dam broke and the questions flew. I held up a hand and order returned.

"How about I answer a few questions from our visitors," I said, indicating the news-people right in front of me. "Then we can all go home and get some rest. Those of us from the church will have plenty of time to talk later. Okay? One at a time, in rotation."

The first question came from an unfamiliar TV reporter.

"Reverend," he shouted, "how are our viewers supposed to take a respectable, well-established church like yours, settling differences in such a confrontational manner?"

I tried to think through a comprehensive, yet diplomatic, answer, but the next thing I knew, my mouth was talking.

"I would expect most of them to laugh at us. I know I would. Maybe some will feel sorry for us. A few will empathize, especially other church leaders. But, mostly, I think they'll mock us. Next question."

Another reporter said, "I had a good question ready to go, but, I have to ask you, how do you feel about what you just said?"

"Embarrassed. Humiliated. Ashamed. Yeah, I feel those things. I feel them for my own role in all of this, and for the behavior of others. The Church is supposed to represent God on earth, and here we are, fighting over power and turf and personal preferences. It's sad. Now, when you report this, don't forget to include how generous and loving and devout and faithful these same people can be. Check the records. The good that comes out of this place is astounding. But, we are human, and sometimes we get rolling down the wrong road. This time, we are way far gone, and it is embarrassing as all get out."

The final TV reporter jumped in. "What have you got to say about the local church's desire to decide for themselves who should be their pastor? Is the United Methodist denomination operating some kind of dictatorship here?"

I recognized this guy. Chad Bushnell. His idea of news was *all America, all the time.*

"I think that God's position on our recent behavior would be what it always is. Love. Is God disappointed in us? I assume he has to be. This is not how God wants his Church to act. God has gone to great effort, sending us the holy Word in both the Bible and personified in Jesus Christ, to make sure we know how we are supposed to act. Love God. Love our neighbors, near and far. Try to behave more and more like Jesus behaved. Instead, we get all caught up in personal preferences and power trips. And then, we try to solve it with tons of rules and regulations and hierarchical guidelines. Thankfully, God's love and patience are boundless. God will be watching and encouraging us to take the mess we have created, and work something good out of it. I sincerely hope that we can."

"You did not answer the question that I asked," Bushnell whined.

"I know. I answered the question that you should have asked."

"That's cute," Bushnell continued, "but what people want to know is what you did to make so many of your own people this angry? And, why can't the good folks of this church, right here in East Fork, U.S. of A., decide whether they want you to stay on as their pastor, or not? It's their church. They pay the bills. They sit in the pews. The people want to know, *What are the United Methodists doing?* And, I promise you, this reporter, Chad Bushnell from the WEFM *In Search of the Truth* News-Team, will not rest until our viewers have answers!"

"Good for you!" I said, my mouth still working a bit ahead of my brain. "I am glad that someone has pledged, right here in front of hundreds of people, to get all the information before commenting. That is what I heard you say, right? Good," I continued. "Next Tuesday night, I will be personally conducting a class on how the United Methodist Church, the second-largest denomination of Protestants in the U.S. of A., actually functions. This will be great! It will be a four-hour affair. It will take at least that. Don't worry, because we are Methodists, there will be sandwiches and red punch at the break. I will present three hours on the history of the United Methodist Church, and its basic doctrines and practices. Then, there will be one hour for Q and A. I want to thank Chad Bushnell of WEFM news for being so dedicated to gathering good, accurate information. I know I can count on him to attend. All the rest of you reporters are invited, too. And, I would love to see many members of our own church there as well. Clearly, we are all in need of solid information."

I started moving.

"This is fantastic! Who would have dared to think that such a hunger for understanding could rise up from all of this acrimony!"

I paused momentarily and played to the crowd on my right, and then on my left.

"I have got to get started! I have so much excellent material to choose from!"

I kept moving. The crowd turned around to look at me, and the back became the front.

"My whole career, I have been hoping and begging to have a whole room full of people who were *really* excited to actually know what they are talking about! Thank you Chad Bushnell! Thank you everyone!"

I sidestepped and kept right on talking—yelling, really.

"I look forward to seeing many of you next week. That's Tuesday evening starting at six o'clock sharp! Good night!"

I ran the last forty feet to my car, jumped in, started it up and drove over the curb and onto the street. Four minutes later, I was in my living room, hugging my wife in the dark.

"Do we really have to stand here with the lights out?" Jenn asked.

"I suppose we could lie down instead."

"Okay, smart boy. Why does it have to be dark?"

"The press is sure to be after us."

"Surely, you're kidding," she said.

"I am not kidding . . . and don't call me Shirley."

"So funny," Jenn said. "Just like the first five hundred times. The press?"

"Yeah, three TV stations and a bunch of reporters. This thing has gone viral. I'm sure it's all over the web by now. It's crazy. I just want to be unavailable for a while."

"Fine. We can sit in the dark. But nothing else happens until I hear the whole story . . . every word."

It took me an hour, sitting in the dark guzzling Diet Cokes. I summarized the entire meeting and so-called press conference, being careful to include the contributions of every character in the drama. When I finally finished, Jenn still had her questions.

"So, no one official is asking for a move, and the bishop wants you to *finish the job*, whatever that is?"

"Correct," I answered.

"Does that actually mean that we are not moving?"

"Yes, but as we Methodists all know, that could change at any time. But right now it seems the story plays out here."

"All right, let's assume that is what God wants," Jenn said. "How might this go? What do we do? Those reporters and news people, not to mention The Bob Williams Army, aren't going to accept a committee vote and go home."

"No, they won't," I agreed. "For some of them, this is just the beginning."

"What can they do now?"

"Charges will be brought. Williams will act like he still forgives me for hitting him. He has to, now. Being the bigger man, and all that. But his followers will bring charges. It continues the pressure on me, and it slaps back at the United Methodist system. The DS and the bishop and the Board of Ordained Ministry will all be forced to act, quite possibly resulting in a church trial. And, the whole hierarchy hates church trials."

"Will Bishop Burns suffer through a church trial to see this battle through?"

"A great question. That's an unknown we can't predict. What the press does, we can't predict. How many people just stop coming to church we can't predict."

"Do you expect a lot of that?"

"Yes. It almost has to happen. We pastors like to think that all of the people attending church are dedicated, motivated Christians, seeking God and God's Word. But that's not so."

"I know," Jenn said, shaking her head sadly. "In my years with you, I've sure seen it. Some are here out of habit. Some for comfort. Some for the music. Some of them—especially some of the older ones—are here because it's what good people are supposed to do. Some come to be in charge of something. Some come to have someone who cares about them. Some come to be better than the people who don't come. Some come due to pressure from someone else. And, of course, some are dedicated, motivated Christians, seeking God and God's Word."

"Exactly. You've got this down better than I do," I said, chuckling.

"I pay attention."

"Yes, you sure do. So, how do you suppose those people will decide this Sunday and next Sunday and all the Sundays to come, whether or not to bother with attending church?"

"I guess, any number of ways."

"Exactly. Some who are against us will leave because they will now feel like they lost. Some who are against us will stay and keep fighting. Some who are with us will leave because they are disappointed in us. I've lost control. I hit a guy. You called a fat lady . . . fat."

"Yeah, I did."

"Some who are with us will stay, because we're still here and still trying. Until Williams started this whole mess, most people in the church would have said things were going well. A lot of them want to stay and reclaim that."

"That's a lot of *somes*," Jenn said. "But none of the things you have said so far are the real problem, are they?" Jenn said, more than asking.

"No."

"Most of the ones who leave will stop coming because . . . what? How do you say it?" Jenn implored, stuck for the right description.

"Because, for them, it simply is not a big decision at all."

"Go to church. Don't go to church. No big deal?" she asked.

"Yep. Church made me happy, so I went. Now church is full of hassle, so I'll stay home. Either way. Whatever."

"How many of them are like that?"

"We have about nine hundred who attend. Five or six hundred a week. About four hundred come almost every week. The others rotate."

"How many of the nine hundred don't care enough to fight through the adversity?"

"About half."

"Wow," Jenn responded. "That's a lot of people."

"It's also a lot of money. The rotators don't give a lot. Losing them will cost us numbers, but not too much financially. But losing regulars will cost the church a lot of income. The loss of Williams and ten or twenty like him will be where the finances take the biggest hit."

"So, you think Williams is gone?" Jenn asked, her eyes lighting up.

"Oh no, he's not gone. But his money is."

We sat in silence for a few minutes.

Finally, I asked Jenn, "Are you up for this, my love?

"Yes. Absolutely. What's the plan?"

"The plan is simple. We do church. You attend church. We respond honestly and forthrightly to all situations, comments and questions. We say and do whatever we believe God wants. We do not factor in politics, or job security, or consensus building. We do not quote the *Book of Discipline* or wonder what Bob Williams or the bishop might think."

"No more Agendor," Jenn added.

"Exactly," I responded. "We just *do* Christianity. We just *be* Christians."

"Sounds good. I'm ready."

"Even if everything changes real fast?"

"Yep. It's kind of exciting," Jenn said. "Not to change the subject, but are you really going to hold that big meeting on Tuesday?"

"Of course. Although, I don't know how big it is going to be. It will be very interesting to see who shows."

"What about ole Chad Bushnell, protector of the people and American patriot extraordinaire? Do you think he'll appear?"

"Yes, I think he will. The gauntlet has been thrown down and he has to pick it up. The real question is, what will he do when he gets there? I'm also very interested in when *this reporter,* Alicia Skiba, will resurface."

Before Tuesday, came Sunday. And, before Sunday came Friday morning. At 7:15 I checked my phone. I was still leaving it off overnight. I had dozens of missed calls and messages, some from names I had programmed into my phone, some from local numbers and a growing percentage from area codes I did not recognize. One name jumped out at me, a name I had only recently added to my contact list—Skiba. It had come in at 6:45 a.m. I dialed up my voicemail and waded through several less-interesting messages, saved a couple for later and deleted the rest.

When I finally got to newshound Alicia Skiba's message, it was short and to the point.

"I am told you have office hours today, beginning at ten o'clock," she said. "I will be in your office at ten o'clock. I hope I will see you then. Thank you. Oh, this is Alicia Skiba."

I answered a couple of texts, had some breakfast, waited for Jenn to finish getting ready for her day, saw here off with kisses and good words, showered, shaved and got dressed. Still only 8:45. I was anxious to see Skiba, but wasn't sure why. I know part of me wanted to respond to her first story, but there was something more than that. I busied myself, picked up around the house and at 9:30 gave up and went in. There were news trucks in the church parking lot. Two of them. And, there were at least twenty people waiting outside my office. I drove away. Once at a safe distance, I called the office. It took four tries, but I finally got Janice.

"Hey there, Janice! I'll bet you never expected a job as a church secretary to be so glamorous as this," I said.

"Very funny," she said. "What am I supposed to do with all these people? They're pretty orderly so far. They started to push and shove a bit, so I handed out numbers like at the deli counter. I sent them down to the kitchen to make their own coffee, but only half of them went. You coming in?"

"I don't know," I admitted. "What happens if I do? What happens if I don't?"

"If you do, you had better pack a lunch. These people want something to report. If you don't, I guess they will eventually go away. But, then what do they report? It's going to be something, you can bet on that."

"Tell them I will do a press conference, in the Fellowship Hall, at noon. Also, when the reporter Alicia Skiba comes in, tell her . . ."

I completed my instructions and kept driving. I worked my way back to Carl's church and parked behind the building. As expected, the place was deserted. I entered through the back and sat in a pew. I waited. I prayed. Then, I kind of forgot to wait and only prayed. It felt great. I gradually became aware that there was another human being in the room.

"Hello, Miss Skiba," I said. "Thank you for coming here. This is not my first plan, but you saw what it's like back there."

"Hi, Reverend Martin," she said. "Thank you for going to the effort to see me. I don't think I've ever noticed this place. What is it? I mean, it's a church, but why are you here?"

"It's closed right now. I have been helping a friend to restore it, so he can start it back up. I'd appreciate if you didn't write about that, at least until it's time."

"Sure. That's okay," she said. She hesitated, then sat down. "I am not sure how to get started," she said. "When I did the first story, I was just jumping on something exciting that I got a hold of. It seemed like a story I could sell, and I did."

Having not been asked anything, I waited.

"Now," she went on, "it has turned into a whole other kind of thing. It's gotten huge! I'm confused. Is this just some juicy soap opera action, or is there something more important going on? What is the actual story?"

"Good question, Alicia. It is petty, and it is cosmic. It is about people who want their own way, and our relationship with God. It is about human fragility, and God's eternal plan. It is about worldly things versus Godly things. It is about our inability to handle all that very well."

"Wow," she said. "How do I get a handle on that in a five-hundred word story?"

"You don't."

"So, what do I do then?"

"Maybe you do what I do when I am looking at scripture, verses and verses filled with lessons great and small, with the idea of creating just one twenty-minute sermon."

"How do you do it?"

"I look for something that matters. One thing that really strikes me as worth knowing more about. Something that, if I do a good job of telling people that one thing, they might be just a little bit closer to God . . . a little more in love with Jesus . . . a little more willing to let the Holy Spirit mold their lives, instead of depending on the untrustworthy ways of this world. All the other great stuff will wait for another sermon to come along."

"Wow," she said again. "I never thought anything like that about, you know, church.

"Maybe we just don't tell it well enough."

She thought momentarily and then shook her shoulders, sat up straight, and asked, "So, what is your take on how all of this church controversy got started?"

"I think I already answered that, Alicia. Power, turf, our need to be right and win and get what we want. The details don't matter a bit. Once this is over, the same story will play out again with new details. A different place. Different people. Different battles, but the same stories. People ignoring God and running their own show to their own advantage."

"Okay," she said, "but what about right now?"

"Right now doesn't matter very much. Maybe that's the point."

"But what about your church, and your job, and Mr. Williams and his friends, and you and your wife, and all this stuff about the United Methodist Church? I had no idea what a big, complicated organization that is. What about all that? What's going to happen?"

"I have no idea."

"But, aren't you worried about it. Scared? Mad? Whatever?"

"Oh, I have been all those things and many more, Alicia, but you know what?"

"What?"

"Less and less."

"This is not the interview I expected," she said. "I don't know what kind of a story to make of all of this."

"Look for something that matters, and go with that. I think it is time for you to go."

Alicia looked startled—hurt, even.

"I am not mad at you. I just think we've said all that we should right now. I hope to see you again one day. Soon. Maybe talk some more. I'm going to pray for you in a minute."

"Really?" she paused and then seemed to gather herself again. "What about the article?"

"Write whatever you decide. Thank you for caring. Bye."

She left. I prayed. It was good.

Chapter 35

The conflict between a faction of the East Fork First United Methodist Church congregation and the Reverend Nathan Martin—little ole me—exploded exponentially. Events and communications ramped up to a level that I could not even keep track of, much less control.

By the time I returned to the church for the hastily announced noon press conference, nearly a hundred people had flocked in. Instead of putting them off, my giving them a two-hour warning had obviously given them time to organize. There were four camera crews, at least ten print reporters, and dozens of Williams supporters. Surprisingly, the group did not include Chad Bushnell. Of course, right in the front row, sat the magnificent Mr. Williams. There were a few who I could count on for some level of positivity and support. Frank and Sylvie . . . God bless them. Daisy Watkins was there, as were Kevin and Condi Cloverton. *Was the music program going to come up again?* I also saw young Jeremy Clark, his I-Pad in hand.

As I took the podium, the yelling and fighting for position started. I had often seen these crazy press conferences on TV, with rabid reporters and shameless camera crews, caring about nothing but the one shot or the one sound bite that would make it on air, in print, or, the holy grail of news-making, go viral. Seen from the point of view of the object of their mania, it is actually pretty scary.

Once again, I said nothing. Once again they continued to shout for a while. Once again they eventually shut up. Once again they got their turns and wasted them with repetitive, accusatory, hollow questions intended to get me to say something self-damning. I non sequitured them to death. No matter their question, I answered with the Good News of Jesus Christ. Asked about what came next, I praised God for providing us lives filled with opportunities and possibilities. Asked about my failures, I rhapsodized about a God of forgiveness and second, third, and hundredth chances. Asked about my feeling for Bob Williams and others who opposed me, I labeled them all "beloved children of God." Mostly, I even meant it. Asked if I thought I would be the pastor at East Fork First much longer, I pledged my continued fidelity to God, serving wherever I was called.

One of the TV reporters angrily called out, "Are you going to answer the questions that have been asked, or are you going to keep philosophizing about whatever you please?"

This one, I decided to answer.

"Firstly, I am not philosophizing. I am theologizing. There is a huge difference. Philosophizing comes from the person—the thinker. You can philosophize anything you please. But theologizing is about what God thinks. I do not seek to create, or write, or think up any new *truth*. I seek only to discover what God thinks, report it as clearly and as persuasively as I can, and to do my best to live my own life according to that understanding. So, sir, your question should be, am I going to answer your questions, or am I going to keep *theologizing?* Now, that would be a useful question. It has two answers. Part two: yes, I am going to keep theologizing. Part one: I will answer your questions when you ask something besides silly, sensational, regurgitations of old complaints and accusations. Those I have already answered. Again, I do not know or care what will happen next or who will win what battles and who, in the end, will be able to declare victory. Quote that, if you must."

"What *do* you care about, Pastor!?"

I looked to the source, and there stood Sylvie, ready to take on the world.

A Dragon in the Church 277

"I care about you and Frank. I love you and everyone else in this room. Of course, I have to love all of you. It's a rule."
There was a least a smattering of laughter and relief.
"Difference is, Frank and Sylvie and some others in this room, I also like."
Better laughter this time.
"I also care that God so loved the world that he gave his only Son, that whoever believes in him shall not perish, but have eternal life. That's Bible verse John 3:16 for those of you who are looking for a good quote today. And, I care that God asked us to base all of our behavior on loving God and loving each other. Ask me some questions about that, and I'll answer all day."
Say whatever else you want about Bob Williams, but the man can read a room. Just as things got quiet and maybe even thoughtful, Bob spoke up.
"All of us at East Fork First United Methodist Church agree, Pastor. We have agreed with that long before you got here, and we will agree with that long after you are gone. We have lived out that philos . . . theology, for many years. Check the records. No church in East Fork has done nearly as much for others as we have. The question that you have so smoothly avoided, Reverend Martin, is not whether our church listens to God, but whether you can lead this church to its best advantage, or whether, on your watch, this place has become a mess!" Bob stepped away from the crowd, so the cameras could better crowd around him.
He went on, "And, as someone who has loved and supported this church for decades, I must say that this place is a mess! The town is laughing at us! The state is laughing at us! Increasingly, people around the country and the world have discovered something new to laugh at. Us! Have you checked the internet lately! Try Googling *fighting church* or *What's wrong with the United Methodists?* or *pastor slugs parishioner*. We have become a laughing stock! And I do not care what our bishop thinks. I do not care what the United Methodist Book of

Rules says. This is our church. And I want this mess to stop! We want our church back!"

Bob quieted. He had offered several dandy sound-bites, all wrapped up in one short tirade. Skilled manipulator that he is, he waited to see if I would say something to bury myself. The cameras turned back toward me awaiting my retort.

I said, "It seems that we have two positions so divergent as to make one wonder if we are talking about the same things. I have said my piece. The duly elected Staff Parish Relations Committee of our church has met, voted and agreed to continue on together. Bishop Clayton Burns, the only person who decides who will or won't be the pastor of the East Fork First UMC, has so far elected to leave me here. I have not felt God moving me to make a change. I am prepared to do my very best to be an effective pastor here, each and every day. That is all."

"What do you hope, or expect, us to report about this?!" shouted one of the reporters.

"I suggest you find out what is true, and report that. You will have to decide who and what you believe. God bless you all, friends, enemies and undecideds. Good bye."

I left amid shouts and pleas for more. Jenn was home much earlier than I expected.

"Hi, honey," I said, "I thought you were going to be gone most of the day."

"I was. But the conference was boring and at lunch people starting asking me questions. There's all kinds of tweeting and facebooking and such going on, and they were sticking smart phones and tablets and such in my face. Every Tom, Dick and Jane, most of whom I barely know, seem to think if they just sidle up to me real slow and say, *So, what is the real scoop on all this buzz at the church?* that I will suddenly get the urge to divulge untold secrets for them to pass along as quickly as they can find someone to tell. I just left."

"Sorry, sweetheart. I love you."

"Yeah yeah, love love, hug hug. They are right about one thing, though, it is all over the net, especially those pastor groups on Facebook. Holy moly, *Preachers Gone Berserk!*"

I had been avoiding this very thing. I was (no longer!) a part of three different clergy groups on Facebook. *United Methodist Clergy Talk, United Methodist Clergy Conferencing* (it is a verb in United Methodism to "conference") and *Pastor Talk* (a multi-denominational group) were all dedicated to the *idea* of clergy persons from around the country discussing topics of common interest. In reality, they were generally dominated by a few contributors who were forever supporting their favorite causes and discrediting those who dared disagree. I participated only rarely, and often went days without bothering to check in.

"I guess it is inevitable," I said, "What's it look like?"

"Well," Jenn began, "there is good news and bad news, although after awhile it is really hard to differentiate. *Clergy Talk* has, in the last two days, over three hundred comments. A spot check seems to indicate that most of the information being debated is wrong, and that about forty percent of the posts think you are an example of bravery and prophetic leadership, and another forty percent think you are a violent, out of control embarrassment."

"What about the other twenty percent?" I felt compelled to ask.

"Not sure. They seem to be talking about completely unrelated things. One asks if any of the other pastors have yet found a good, gluten-free communion bread that does not crumble."

"It's good to know that the Church goes on."

"*Clergy Conferencing* started out about you, but within ten moves, they found a way to make it about LGBTQ inclusion and wrote another hundred and fifty comments on that."

"Bigger fish to fry," I said. "Praise God for small favors."

"And *Pastor Talk* is dominated by questions of why the church doesn't just fire you and get a new pastor. One wrote that he would like to be contacted right away, if this results in an opening. The rest of it is United Methodist clergy trying to explain and justify our methods, and the others expressing their disbelief that a church could operate in such a strange way."

"Most of it is empty fire and fury," I replied, "except when taken as a whole. The UMC bishops are aware of what the online buzz is. Bishop Burns will hear from his colleagues."

"Is that bad?" Jenn asked.

"*Yes, no,* and *maybe.* They will be mixed, too. But mostly they respond to anything that upsets the applecart. They don't like trouble. Let's just stay focused on God . It's getting so there is nothing else we can do, anyway. It's out of control."

Supper was uneventful. Afterwards, we took a ride out to see if we could catch Carl, but he wasn't working. On Saturday I resolved to hide out and write a good sermon. The recent extremes of emotion made it difficult to focus on preaching. I settled in, my concentration returned, and the Holy Spirit nudged me toward some excellent stuff that would speak into our upheaval and uncertainty. I love the process of creating the sermon. Preaching is perhaps the most important thing I do, and provides the best opportunity to speak on God's behalf. Anyway, it seems that I was unnecessarily concerned about privacy. Eerily, there were no urgent calls or e-mails or texts. It is too cliché to say *the calm before the storm,* but it cannot be overstated that in the calm of Saturday, I could have never predicted the events of Sunday.

The Sunday traditional service started out without incident. In fact, I was pleasantly surprised at the excellent attendance. Bob Williams was there, as were many of his most visible supporters. Not a few of those who were sticking with me were in-house, as well. I noticed that there were even some who usually attended only the earlier, praise band service. While it first appeared that battle lines had been drawn, the worship service went off without a hitch. The choir was in excellent form. There were more than the usual number of children (especially considering that it was the *traditional* service) who participated in the Children's Moment. My sermon was well-received (this is humble pastor-talk for *it was a good one).* There was no out-of-place excitement or controversy at all.

As I always do, I stood at the middle exit from the sanctuary, either shaking hands or hugging people (one has to learn quickly who is a hugger and who is a shaker). The most common comment is *nice sermon, Pastor.* This means nothing. It is what is said so as to gracefully escape the pastor, exit the church, and get home before the pot roast dries out. On a good Sunday, the preacher might hear things like: *that one spoke to me,* or *it was like you were preaching right to me,* or *that one gives us all something to think about.* For me, it was a good Sunday. For a couple of minutes.

There was a longer line than usual leaving through the north exit. It took until the lines thinned out a bit before I could see what was going on over there. Certain people, at least a hundred of them, were filing past Bob Williams. He had a heavy leather strap around his neck, resting on his right shoulder. The ends of the strap were attached to what appeared to be a stainless steel attaché case, which rested on Bob's opposite hip. As those certain people passed by, they shoved envelopes into a slot in the attaché. I was naturally beyond curious as to what was going on now. I dispensed with my line as fast as I could. By the time I was finally free, I could only see Bob's back as he disappeared into the parking lot.

"Pastor!" I heard behind me, "Can I speak with you one moment?"

It was Lenora Brown, my biggest fan. I had no choice but to let Bob go.

"Yes, Lenora, I always have time for you," I said, doing my best to beam. "What is it?"

As I walked Lenora to coffee and cookie time in the Fellowship Hall, she told me that the service had been lovely, and she was glad "all that nonsense has blown over."

I stayed until Jenn and the last of the parishioners had left. I went to my office, as I always do, to drop some things off. There sat Bob, without his secret carrying case.

"Hi, Bob," I said, hoping not to look shocked. "Fancy meeting you here."

"Morning, Pastor. Nice sermon."

"Thank you, Bob. What brings you in today? Feeling the need for reconciliation?"

"You may need reconciliation, Pastor. I have nothing to reconcile."

"We all do, Bob. We all do."

"Maybe so. Not today. I stopped to encourage you to take special notice of your offering today. I know that pastors pretend they aren't keeping track of the money, but you all do."

"Sure we do. It is one way of seeing how the church is doing, and how well we are obeying God's instructions to give. No secret there."

"Well, today the people were very generous in their giving," Bob said. "Very generous."

"Excellent," I replied.

"Yeah . . . excellent. I don't know what your offering looks like, but my offering was real healthy. A quick count looks like something north of twelve thousand dollars. I sure hope that doesn't hurt your offering too much."

"Bob, just what are you talking about, *your* offering? You can't take an offering!"

"The hell you say. It seems as if I can . . . and I did."

"That's not legal. You are going to cause yourself no end of legal trouble."

"It's legal if you're a church!" Bob said with so much glee that he nearly squealed.

"What have you done, Bob?"

"Not just me. Several other folks who care about our church got together and formed the Church of Christian Concern. Fully incorporated. Officially non-profit, with 501c3 in hand. We meet weekly. My sister-in-law Rebecca is our pastor. She actually does a pretty good job. There's twelve of us. We meet in the back of one of my stores."

"I've never heard of the Church of Christian Concern!" I said, more angrily than intended.

"Just because you haven't heard of something doesn't mean it doesn't exist, Pastor. So far we have kept it quiet and just big enough to be legal."

"What qualifications does this Rebecca have to pastor a church?"

"She meets all the legal requirements . . . which is none. Isn't that something, Reverend? You need a license to cut hair, but it turns out there are no legal criteria of any kind to be clergy, except a church to call you to the pulpit. We have a church and we called her to the pulpit. Your precious United Methodist rules—do—not—apply!"

"It takes a long time to get a 501c3," I said, "How could you possibly . . .?"

"You're playing with the big boys, now. You've always had other people do the hard work for you, so you don't think ahead like I do. Do you think that I would have given you my original demands, if I hadn't already prepared to win the war? Grow up. Give up."

"But, you cannot stand in one church and collect for another!"

"Let me sum it up for you. My lawyers assure me that all church donations are voluntary, some people give and some do not. You can't make them. You've always had people who come to church and use church services, without giving a penny. Right?"

"Yes. That is true," I said warily.

"Now you have more of those. Me, for instance. And several of my friends and associates, those with money. I now control at least forty percent of the money. I am confident that there will be more than that, as confirmed by the enthusiastic response that I got to our first offering. That money now belongs to the Church of Christian Concern. As will nearly half of what used to be your offering, every week, from now on."

"But, Bob, you can't stand in this church and collect for the Church of Christian Concern."

"You may be right about that. According to my lawyers, I would be in a more defensible position if I stood outside on the sidewalk. I'll be happy to do that, if you wish."

"Bob, you say you love this church. You can't just . . ."

"I can do whatever I want!" Bob exploded. "You had better get used to it. The bishop better get used to it! The United Methodist Church better get used to it! It is because I love it that I have to save it! Take your dog and pony show somewhere else, and leave East Fork alone!"

Bob looked as if his reddened face was about to pop through his eyes. I realized that I had reacted exactly as I shouldn't have, immediately trying to work out my own solutions. Again. I tried to let go of my *self*. Bob tried to breathe. Gradually, he returned to his normal color, breaths coming more slowly. I went empty, grateful for the pause.

Eventually, I spoke. "I understand, Bob. What is it that you think will happen now?"

"I'm sorry I got angry," he said, "I tried not to do that."

"I believe you," I said.

"At what, for now, is still your church, Pastor, you have been operating on about nine hundred thousand dollars a year, with nearly that much in expenses. You will now be receiving approximately four hundred and fifty thousand dollars a year, with no reduction in costs. The Church of Christian Concern will now be receiving about four hundred and fifty thousand dollars a year. Our expenses are, and will remain, zero."

A Dragon in the Church 285

"What will you do with the money?"

"Bank it. The balance will be held in escrow. If you are moved out in a timely manner and replaced by a United Methodist pastor who understands our needs and agrees to fulfill them, the money will be donated back to East Fork First United Methodist Church. Financial difficulties will be immediately relieved, and we will get back to normal."

"And if the bishop doesn't do as you wish?"

"We can be patient. Our bank balance will grow quickly, while East Fork First UMC will soon be bankrupt. Pretty soon, we will have so much money we could buy a church building left behind by a bankrupt church, and invite the former Methodist congregation to join us in a new day in an old place. Or any number of other exciting options, all under our own control. Although I do not know exactly how it is going to turn out, it is a foolproof plan."

"Bob, a lot of people are going to get hurt."

"Says you. Many people still want the church, but would be happy for it to be different. The United Methodist institution might suffer, but our people will be just fine."

"Bob, is there anything that can be said that will get you to not do this?"

"Only what I already told you . . . a new pastor. It's not personal. But it needs to happen."

"Okay, then," I said, "Thanks for stopping by."

"Okay? Thanks for stopping by? Is that all you're going to say?"

"Yeah, I'm already late getting home. Jenn will be waiting dinner on me."

"That's it? What are you going to do?"

"After dinner? I don't know yet."

"Not after dinner! What are you going to do about what I just told you?"

"Right now? Nothing."

"Nothing!"

"Bob, at this moment, Staff Parish says I'm staying. The bishop says I'm staying. I intend to stay, my wife wants me to stay, and God has not given me instructions otherwise. What you are doing changes none of that. You see yourself as in charge. You are not."

While lecturing Bob, I stood up, put on my jacket and pocketed my essential junk.

I continued, "I am going home to have a nice dinner with Jenn. Please make sure the doors are locked when you leave."

As I exited my office and started down the hallway, Bob shouted, "You can pretend all you want! This isn't over!" The last thing I heard from a very angry Bob Williams was, "The bishop will get a report on how much money we have, every Monday!!"

I hurried toward home. My loving wife and a slow-cooker pot roast were waiting.

Chapter 36

Jenn saw me pulling in and was already filling our plates by the time I made it inside. We carried them into the living room and sat down at our designated TV trays (I know, we are horrible people). We left the set off and ate and talked.

"The service went well, I thought," Jenn said. "Sorry I left so quickly, but I wasn't sure how much explaining I wanted to do."

"That's okay," I answered. "You did miss some excitement, though."

"I was just going to say that I have something exciting to show you," she said. "You want to go first, or shall I?"

"Go ahead," I said, "but let's finish our dinner first."

We sat quietly and finished our meal. I carried the plates to the kitchen, and when I returned Jenn handed me a copy of the Sunday paper.

"There is another article by *this reporter*, Alicia Skiba. I think you will want to read it. Go ahead, out loud."

I read: *This reporter was the first to bring to you the story of the uproar going on at the East Fork First United Methodist Church. The pastor there, the Reverend Nathan Martin, has come under fire by part of the congregation. He has been accused of poor leadership, bringing unwanted music, sermon topics and worship styles into the church, allowing a teenager to serve in voting positions in the church, and having a wife who does not show enough interest in the church. A key argument seems to be whether the pastor of the church is, or is not, a church employee, subject to the requirements of the church* leadership. At one point, the arguing got so ugly that prominent church member Bob Williams, of the various Williams family enterprises, disrespected the pastor's wife, Jennifer Martin, calling her a vile name. Reverend Martin struck Mr. Williams. Although an arrest was made, charges were dropped, and Mr. Williams took responsibility for the incident.

The arguing and the power struggles have grown worse. Now official United Methodist policy, by which the entire denomination of over thirty thousand U.S. churches operates, is being called into question. It will be a long while before this all gets sorted out.

Information on how that happens will have to come from someone besides me. I wrote the first article on this growing story, but this will be my last. In the first article, I made it sound like Reverend Martin had repeatedly and consciously refused to be interviewed. That's technically true, but not practically true. I contacted him in ways that I was confident he would not see. Recently, I did sit down with Reverend Martin. It was a strange interview. I still do not know what to make of it, except to say whatever I thought I knew . . . I do not know. Reverend Martin refused to defend himself or influence the story in any way. Faced with my prying questions, he simply spoke of God and God's love. Most notably, he seemed perfectly willing to trust God for whatever might happen next. Reverend Martin could lose his position, his home, even his career, yet he showed concern for me, respect for his adversaries and a patience I have rarely seen. As a child, I did my time in church. Since then, I have not been a religious person. Today, I am still not, I don't think. I am confused about much. One important thing I do know, is that there is something more going on here than what all the noise, accusations and anger is about. I prefer not to trivialize whatever that is. I'll be writing more soon, but not about this. Thank you, Alicia Skiba."

"Wow," I said. "Never saw that coming."

"Nope, I didn't either," Jenn said. "But it does show if we keep plugging down the right road, God can create the unexpected."

"Speaking of the unexpected . . ." I said.

I recounted the whole exchange *offering plate incident* with Bob Williams, as close to verbatim as possible.

"Can he actually do that?" Jenn asked incredulously. "It seems so wrong, like it has to be illegal or something."

"It's unethical as all get out, but I don't know about illegal. With the separation of church and state, law-makers have long accepted an unusual status for churches. Once people give money to a church, it's gone. The courts have ruled that, even if the church doesn't use it for promised purposes, money donated to the church belongs to the church. No charge is made for services. People can use what the church has to offer, and not a pay a dime. People voluntarily give money to the church. No contracts, no promises. Not legally anyway. Usually, it just works out. Bob and his cronies have decided to change the way the game is played."

"The church can't survive this, can it?" she asked. "It will be bankrupt in a few weeks."

"Probably. Others could step up and make up the difference, but we're talking an awful lot of money. We could cut staff and use up reserve funds and last a while. But, what's the point? The end of the money will still come at some point, and Bob will have more and more."

"What's the bishop going to think about this?" Jenn asked.

"He'll be terrified. Bob is evil, but he is not stupid. There are plenty of churches out there who would be happy to leave the United Methodist denomination, if they could keep their church building and their assets, but they can't."

"The ole reserve clause," Jenn said, nodding her head. "You keep what's yours, as long as you are still a United

Methodist Church, but if you try to leave, all your stuff and your money goes to the denomination."

"That's one way to put it," I said. "Another is what people donated to the United Methodist Church, stays with the United Methodist Church."

"Tomayto, Tomahto," she said.

"Yeah. Anyway, the upper, upper powers are going to panic if it looks like Williams has come up with a way to break the system."

"Okay then" Jenn said, "whatever happens, happens. Isn't that what we said?"

"Why yes, I believe we did. What shall we think about instead?"

"You're off the rest of the day and tomorrow. Let's pack a bag and head up to the Apple Tree. It's off-season in Petoskey. We'll get a room and hide under the covers for a day!"

I was already halfway to the basement to fetch the good suitcase. The drive up was a great time, especially with our cell phones turned off. A nice supper out, alone time, midnight snacks, alone time in the morning, and I almost felt like a real person again. I admit, as I admired the wife God gave me, that retirement crossed my mind. I would have to make a living doing something, because benefits were at least five years off, but it would work somehow. Just before we had to check out, I popped the TV on. After a few minutes of a bunch of women who used to be celebrities talking about what is *in* this year, a news blurb came on. I didn't pay much attention until the anchorwoman said, "And there is breaking news on the East Fork United Methodist uprising. Rebel leader Bob Williams has said, quote, *victory is near."*

Jenn ran over and sat down with me.

"Mr. Williams says, *Soon the local leadership of our church will control everything and own everything and the national leadership of the United Methodist Church will be forced to go home and leave us alone!*

"Tune in to the WTCC News at 5:00 and 11:00, for the full story."

"I told you to leave the TV alone," Jenn whispered.

"That's not an East Fork or Grand Rapids station," I said.

"Nope, it's Traverse City. Looks like everybody's talking."

We managed to shrug it off, after a few prayers, and went home. There is a certain peace that comes with letting go of the details and waiting for God to move. In between moments of excitement, anger and panic, it felt as if we were more observers than participants.

Once back at the parsonage, we snuck in the back way and kept a low profile. We couldn't help turning on the evening news, even though we could not get the Traverse City station that had promised *more from Bob Williams!* Instead, we got *Stay tuned! After the break, a special report from our own Chad Bushnell: THE UNITED METHODIST CHURCH ON TRIAL?*

"Oh man," Jenn said, "have all these people gone mad?"

"It's too late for some of them to *go* mad," I replied. "Where's he going with this?"

It didn't take long to find out. After an unusually long bundle of commercials, the station came back to a giant close up of the Magnificent Bushnell, himself, all puffed up, his makeup fighting a losing battle to cover the red puffiness creeping up his neck from underneath his askew tie and shirt collar that was too tight to button. Beneath his huge, bulbous face scrolled *Editorial Content... Editorial Content... Editorial Content.*

Good evening, good citizens of East Fork and surrounding areas! This is Chad Bushnell of the WEFM In Search of the Truth News-Team, with this editorial commentary. Many of you have been following the ever-expanding saga of conflict at the East Fork First United Methodist Church. There are many facets to this complicated story, but, for this reporter, the key concern is a battle between oppression by and from a far-away power, and the freedom of local citizens to set their own course and make their own decisions. A large segment of the church congregation wants to remove their present pastor—the Reverend Nathan Martin, by all accounts a decent man—and hire a new one of their own choosing. As an American, I stand on the side of freedom. Does this battle not remind us of a similar story over two hundred years ago? Is not the congregation much like those brave, honorable first Americans, who wanted to govern themselves and make their own decisions about the land where they did all the work, paid all the bills, and even sent tax money back to England? And did not evil King George respond by saying NO! No! No! You keep working and paying and paying, and I will decide what happens to you. And did not our brave forefathers rebel in any way they knew how! Did they not fight! These United Methodists, right here in the middle of our beloved country, do all of the work at East Fork First UMC. They pay all the bills, with money donated locally. And, they even pay taxes! I have learned that all United Methodist churches are forced to pay upwards of fourteen percent of their gross income to the higher power—the hierarchy of powerful fat cats of the denomination. They call this apportionments, but it's just another name for taxes. And for all of this, they still cannot decide who their own pastor will be. Someone else, someone far away and powerful, called a bishop, will decide that for them. And there is . . . no . . . way . . . out. At least, like ole King George of England, that's what the bishop thinks. But, these good American citizens of East Fork are fighting back. They are marshaling all of their power, and especially their money, to bring the United Methodist denomination to its knees. Just like King George, the bishop will not like this. Just like King George, the bishop will try to exercise even more power to make it stop. Which brings up another startling and disturbing fact that I have discovered while doing research on your behalf. In 1776, at the very borning of our great land, the founder and head of early Methodism, a man named John Wesley, sided not with our brave forefathers . . . but sided with the King of England!! But the patriots won anyway, and the people, the people of East Fork First United Methodist Church, will win as well. As freedom, eventually, always will. This may be only one man's opinion, but, it is the RIGHT opinion. Good night, fellow Americans. This is Chad Bushnell.

An anchorwoman immediately followed and said. "For those who wish to get greater detail on the operations of the United Methodist Church, there will be a seminar, open to the public, from 6:00 p.m. until 10:00 p.m. tomorrow at the East Fork United Methodist Church. The Reverend Nathan Martin, himself, will be teaching for three hours and then answering questions for another hour. Methodist sandwiches and red punch will be served."

"Angela," a co-anchor chimed in, "what is a Methodist sandwich?"

"No idea, Keith, but we're going to find out. The cameras of WEFM will be there."

"Red punch and Methodist sandwiches!" Keith shouted. "Who would want to miss that!? This has been the *In Search of the Truth News Team!* Goodnight!"

We sat and stared for quite some time. I was at a loss for words or complete thoughts. I stole a look at Jenn, who sat as dumbstruck as I.

Finally, she said, "I'll be Alice."

I responded, "I'm the White Rabbit."

We laughed until we couldn't breathe.

Chapter 37

"Let's go see if Carl is at his church," I said out of the blue.

We had laughed ourselves into exhaustion and were now just lying around.

"You think?" Jenn asked, "I haven't had any luck with that, so far."

"I think we ought to try. Come on, what's one more disappointment?"

"Okay, I'm game."

We pulled ourselves together and drove out to the four corners. The lights were on, and as we pulled around to the far side, Carl's truck came into view.

"How about that. He's here," I announced.

"Now I'm nervous," Jenn said. "Too much build up."

"It'll be fine."

We went in the front and there stood Carl, in the middle of packing up tools, construction scraps and general trash.

"Hello!" he said with great enthusiasm. "How fortuitous that you have come by, and both of you, too!"

"Pastor Carl," I began, "I would like you to meet my wife, Jenn."

"Jennifer! At last we meet. I have been anxious to meet you in the flesh. This one here is so in love with you that he has described you to me in great detail, but he either under-promised, or you over-deliver."

"Wow," Jennifer said, "meeting you is something I could do every day!"

"Pastor Carl," I said, "I am sorry I have not been here in quite a while. Things have been a little crazy."

"So I hear. And read. And see on TV. It has become quite a story, hasn't it."

"Yes, it sure has."

"And you needn't worry about this place," Carl went on. "This phase is officially finished!"

"Congratulations," I said. "You pulled off a good and wonderful thing."

"It's not only beautiful, but it carries some sort of power," my Jennifer chimed in. "I felt it before, and I feel it now. And—I hope I am not being too forward—it flows. There is a movement to it."

Carl thought a moment and said, "This church building is ready for use only because God wanted it done. That's where the power comes from. It is truly sacred space. Not everyone will feel it. One has to be tuned in and willing to take it in. I'm glad the two of you get that."

"What now?" I asked. "Surely, there is a next step."

"Yes!" Carl beamed. "I am happy to say that in the last couple of days, God has been quite clear with me. I am to start up a congregation here, a group of Christian men, women and children who are especially in tune with God, and especially willing to ride the wave of God's Word and God's Way. Highly committed, very spiritual people who are ready to obey whatever calling comes to them. It will not be a large congregation, but I know that God wants it to be a powerful one. I am so honored and scared and humbled that God has shown me how to do this."

"I am not at all surprised, good friend Carl," I said. "I think God has been building toward this all along. I can't wait to see where this goes."

"Come, both of you," Carl said.

He led us to the front of the sanctuary, directly beneath the rugged cross.

"Close your eyes," he said. "Most holy, gracious and generous God, you have brought the three of us though many trials and triumphs, along different roads and different experiences, but, for this moment, to this place. We will diverge again. You have clarified my next quest, while your servants Nathan and Jennifer are still awaiting your next, immediate plans for them. They stand ready, more ready than they have ever been, to live into whatever you have in store, for you, in you, and to your glory. You, Holy God, are ours, and we are yours."

My eyes shut tightly against rising tears, I heard a tiny noise—not a moan or a sigh, but something like that—come from Jennifer. I sneaked a peak. Pastor Carl was anointing her forehead with oil, marking her with the sign of the cross.

He said, "Jennifer, with oil consecrated in the name of Jesus Christ, I anoint you as one of God's servants, called to special purposes. May the Holy Spirit guide you, enlighten you, protect and strengthen you to whatever task it is that you are called. May your realization you belong to God, Father, Son and Holy Spirit, and to God only, be your focus, and your comfort. We pray this in Jesus name. Amen."

He moved to me. I felt myself trembling, and didn't try to hide it.

He said, "Nathan, with oil consecrated in the name of Jesus Christ, I anoint you as one of God's servants, called to special purposes. May the Holy Spirit guide you, enlighten you, protect and strengthen you to whatever task it is . . ."

I lost track of his words as his touch, light but sure, and the feel of a drop of oil running toward the bridge of my nose overwhelmed my other senses. It was not a bolt of electricity that shot through me, but a warmth, the feeling of a great hug that spread over me slowly and fully. It took my breath away. I had been anointed before. This was nothing like that.

Drawn back to what was going on around me, I heard Carl say, "Would you please?"

I opened my eyes, expecting to receive the vial of blessed oil from Carl, so that I could anoint him. But, he was approaching Jennifer.

"Oh my," she said.

"Please," he said.

She tentatively took the vial from his hand, and covered the open mouth with her thumb. She tipped the vial. As the oil began to wet the tip of her thumb, her face changed. Radiance? Connectedness? Inspiration? Ecstasy? I don't know. I didn't have the words then, or now.

She started to trace the sign of the cross on Carl's forehead, but stopped in the middle, while she said, "Carl, with oil consecrated in the name of Jesus Christ, I anoint you a servant of God, called to obedience, devotion and a level of service expected from few. May the Holy Spirit guide you and keep you strong as you carry out your work, in this sacred place and anywhere else God chooses to send you. You belong to God, Father, Son and Holy Spirit, and to God only. We pray this in Jesus' name. Amen."

She finished Carl's cross.

"Thank you both for coming this evening," Carl said. "I cannot begin to tell you how much this has meant to me. Go now. You are soon to find out what God wants of you. We are not finished with each other, either. Goodbye, Jennifer. Goodbye, Nathan. God bless."

We said our short goodbyes and went out to the car.

"Now I understand why you kept coming out here," Jennifer said. "That was not something that happens in the church every day."

"No, it does not. And is that not an incredible shame."

"That was the exact opposite of Agendor. No battles. No politics. No bureaucracy. Just relationship between God and God's people. I hope we can find a lot more of that."

"That's for sure," I replied. "We will. The tricky part is we have been called to help others discover the same thing."

We were pretty quiet the rest of the night. In the morning, we still held onto some of the contentment and certainty from the night before.

"I don't know how you are going to face this circus tonight, Sweetheart," Jennifer said as we finished our breakfast.

"I am not sure, either. Part of me wants to just be cloistered for a while, but another part wants to straighten out some of the nonsense that is being said. That Bushnell spew was so incomplete and stupid and misleading about what the United Methodist Church is all about. I love being a Methodist! We get an awful lot right, and when we're wrong at least we usually err on the side of grace. And I truly believe our system of placing clergy is the best way there is. It does a lot of good! And, Wesley was an Englishman, for crying out loud! It is hard to stand by and listen to some buffoon with zero understanding pontificating on a subject he doesn't begin to comprehend!"

"Well," Jennifer said, "At least your adversary can be clearly seen. You're stepping into the very mouth of Agendor. Between Williams and Bushnell and all the destructive nonsense on that end of the spectrum, and district superintendents, bishops, the *Book of Discipline* and all the general boards and agencies trying to self-preserve, I don't know how you're going to make any sense of it."

"I really don't have to," I replied. "It gives a whole new meaning to *let go and let God*."

"Sure does. I hope today goes well, my love. I will be praying for you. It's like they say," Jennifer added with a smirk, "The church would be a great place, except for the people."

"Yeah, that will always be hard. But, wherever we go, there are going to be people there. They may have different names, but they will act pretty much the same."

"And we need to love them and care for them, no matter what," Jennifer said. "Nate, I apologize. I don't think I have ever realized until right now how hard that is on clergy. I have been able to dismiss those who bothered me, walk right away from them, but you can't. I'm sorry I didn't know that."

"Thank you, dear. I appreciate hearing that."

"Now go to the church and get ready. If you can, come home for an early supper and I'll go to the seminar with you."

"Are you sure?"

"You bet. I gotta git me some of them Methodist sammiches!"

I got to the church at about 10:00 a.m. and found the doors locked. That was odd, as Janice's car was in her spot. I let myself in. Instinctively, I locked the door behind me.

"Good morning, Pastor. I am telling everyone that set-up for the big meeting starts at 3:00 p.m. and until then the doors are locked. The phone is ringing off the hook, and I've already had camera crews in here, trying to get the best spot. These people are nuts."

"Good thinking, Janice. You're the best. Whatever you say, goes."

"I know," she said with a grin, "but, I wanted you to feel like you had a choice."

"Understood," I replied, with a slight bow. "So, what's the game plan?"

"I don't think anybody can control this, but here is what I am shooting for. I've quit answering the phone. I will check messages every few minutes and respond to any that matter. At 2 o'clock, I am sneaking some of the kitchen ladies in the back door. They will be preparing red punch and Methodist sandwi...!"

She broke into laughter before she could get it all out.

"There's a story behind that," I said.

"Yeah, I bet," Janice said. "Sherry Vandenberg said she is going to stir up a batch of *Extra Methodist Sauce*, on account of *the people from the TV* are coming."

"Are they really making sandwiches?" I asked.

"Yep. Company's coming, so we're making food."

"What is the mood, Janice? What are you hearing?"

"A little of everything. It's like we've been hit by a tornado and everyone is walking around in shock. People aren't fighting with each other, too much, though. I guess that's good."

"They're all waiting for the next shoe to drop," I said.

"Yes, they are," Janice replied. "And, they want to know what you're going to do next."

"If I knew, I would tell them," I said. "When I know, I'll let you know. Okay?"

"Fair enough. I've been holding the line the best I can. You know that, right?"

"I do know, Janice. I know I haven't acknowledged that enough, but it's because when you go into battle, you don't worry about your best guys. You worry about the shaky ones. You're one of my best guys, if you don't mind the clumsy, sexist analogy."

"I don't mind a bit. I'll gladly take a good *best guy*, any day. Now get in your office and get ready for tonight. Have you actually got a whole lesson to give?"

"I'll have to cut it down to three hours! It might not seem like it lately, but I love this Methodist stuff."

I got to work. I had no idea what was really going to happen, but in case anyone was actually interested, I was going to be ready with a great presentation. I called home and let Jennifer know that I would rustle up some lunch at the church and work through until about 4:00. Then, I would come home for final preparations before we went to the meeting.

As I worked, I was reminded why I chose the United Methodist Church to live out my call to the pulpit. While the contemporary church had gotten off track here and there, the life and teachings of our founder John Wesley throughout most of the eighteenth century were awe-inspiring. As I had many times in the past, I wondered about what an authentic, Godly denomination we would have if we had just stuck closer to what Wesley taught. I absolutely cherish Wesley. As I gathered historical material together, I was also forced to accept, but only to myself, that Wesley was a bureaucratic control freak, prone to write a rule for everything and demand that others follow each one. The birth of *Agendor!?!* The presentation was shaping up nicely, when Janice burst in to my office.

"There is a message from Jenn . . . came in about ten minutes ago. Sorry. She says don't call, don't talk to anyone and come home right away. Bishop Burns is at the parsonage!"

For some reason, I looked at the clock. It was 2:12 p.m. I scurried out to the car, my mind racing. There were dozens of people lined up at the door waiting for the three o'clock opening. I just kept going, ignoring their shouts of recognition. I drove in the opposite direction of the house, took several sharp turns and approached the parsonage from the back side. Thankfully, there was only one car in the drive. *Has to belong to Burns,* I thought. I parked in the garage and ran into the house through the kitchen. Bishop Clayton Burns and my darling wife sat together in the living room, both sipping from cans of Diet Coke.

The bishop stood and offered his hand. "Hello, Nathan. Good to see you again, even under complex circumstances."

"Thank you, Bishop Burns. Thank you for coming."

"You've always called me Clay, Nathan. Don't stop now. In fact, I think we might get through this better if we lean on friendship as much as we can."

"Fine . . . Clay," I said.

I kissed Jennifer on the cheek and took a chair next to her. The two of us sat, facing the man who had the power to change our lives.

"Let me start by saying that I admire a lot of what you have both been trying to do here. We encourage pastors to take bold steps to bring about needed change, and you have done just that. Judy Halliday has kept me well informed."

I felt like responding to his every point, but resisted the urge.

"However," Bishop Burns went on, "I have never seen anything quite like what has happened here. I have been in communication with several other bishops, and no one can compare this to any precedent."

Bishop Burns paused, looking for a reaction from me. I did not give him one.

"Okay, what I am saying is that we are struggling to find an easy or obvious way to manage this situation. This is highly unusual. Do you agree, Nathan?"

"Yes."

"Okay. Well then, I guess I had better lay this out. I am aware of the phantom church created to siphon money away from our church. Our lawyer says we have arguments to make, but that we may or may not prevail in court. And, it would take years to litigate. Meanwhile, the church suffers. The conflict in the church will almost necessarily lead to a major split in the congregation. That, we have seen before. Then, there are the news media and the social networks and all of that. Every day I hope there will be less buzz out there, and every day there is more. Several bishops have expressed great concern over what seems to have turned into a public referendum on United Methodist polity and praxis. If this were a calm, balanced and fair discussion, we would welcome the opportunity for this unusual level of interest. However, there seems to be a determined effort to keep this more in the mud-slinging and slander territory."

The bishop paused and looked at the two of us. He flushed and sniffed and coughed.

Finally, he asked, "Aren't you going to say anything?"

"You have not asked me a question," I said.

"Come on, Nathan! Don't play games with me!"

"I'm not."

"Fine, do you agree with my assessment of the situation?"

"So far, yes. Yes, I do."

"What do you mean by *so far*?"

A Dragon in the Church 303

"Only that there are other issues. A lay person has laid claim to a United Methodist Church as his own kingdom. His motives are not Godly in any way. Many, many false claims have been made. Threats have been made. Something at least close to blackmail and/or extortion has been initiated, right in front of us all. Those things are true, too."

"Yes . . . Nathan . . . I know that. I really do. How would you like me to respond to that?"

"Respond any way you wish. I only wanted to be sure you had all the information."

"Oh. Okay. Then let me finish this line of reasoning. There is another factor that might at first seem like an additional problem, but might be our saving grace. That is the matter of the assault on a Mr. Bob Williams. Our information is you struck him, punched him in the face. Is that accurate?"

"Yes."

"So I hear it from you, is there a mitigating circumstance?"

"Mr. Bob Williams called me a skank in front of my husband. He learned not to do that again. Sorry to interrupt."

"No, Jennifer," the bishop replied. "Thank you. However, there has been a formal complaint filed with my office, a complaint signed by nearly a hundred members of East Fork UMC. They want you tried . . . unless certain actions are taken."

"Let's pray," Jennifer said, and then immediately started. "Dear Heavenly Father, we are grateful for all of the many gifts you have given us, especially the gift of salvation through the Son, and the ministrations of the Holy Spirit. In uncertain times, we are especially dependent on your love and your call upon us. Whatever you have in store for us, whatever you might call us to next, we are excited and ready to say *yes, yes* again and again. We love you, God, and accept you as our only authority. In Jesus name we pray. Amen."

"Thank you, Jennifer," the bishop stammered. "We should have done that earlier."

"You were saying that the formal charges against my husband might be our saving grace. How is that?"

"What I hope to do is to extricate the two of you from this turmoil, which I am sure would be a relief. And, I want to try to salvage what has been for decades an excellent and productive church here in East Fork, and give someone else a chance to start with a clean slate. However, there is the broader concern regarding the public outcry about United Methodist practices and the perception that a rebellious lay-person has somehow defeated the church."

"And?" I asked.

"The plan is that we announce, concerning everything else, you have the full support of the denomination, me, the district superintendent, and East Fork's own SPRC. You have done a great job, and we are sure that everything would work out in a positive manner. However, we will say, despite all of the positives, we are a church with no tolerance for violence. Therefore, you will be placed on a year or two of probation—we can make that painless—and, to ensure peace going forward, you will be immediately reappointed to another charge, and a new pastor for East Fork UMC will be named shortly. The complaint against you will be dropped. No trial. The offering money will be returned to its rightful place in the East Fork UMC account. We report to the media that peace has been restored and United Methodist policies have successfully worked things out. Then, we wait for the furor to die down. Which it will. All local parties have agreed to deal with future issues quietly and not stoke the fires of discontent."

"And according to this plan, when and how do we get from point A to point B?" Jennifer asked, almost whispering.

Bishop Burns cleared his throat, sat up straighter, and said, "It happens tonight. As of this moment, Nathan, you are no longer appointed to East Fork. You will simply stay home this

A Dragon in the Church 305

evening. Judy Halliday and I will address the media and the public at tonight's meeting. We will announce everything I just described to you. Given the entire circumstance, it is best that you are done right now. I'll have the secretary box up your things. You can live here for the next sixty days, if necessary. You will receive full salary. A week or two from now, I will announce that you are now appointed as pastor to the United Methodist Church in Petoskey. I think you'll both like it there. When she thinks the time is right, Judy Halliday will arrange for you to come back here for a going away party. No one will interfere, and you have a great many people here who love you and will want to see you off. There's more detail, but that's the gist of it."

"Okay," both Jennifer and I said.

"Okay? That's it? I expected some pushback, some negotiation, or something. Believe me, I know this is not easy."

"Sure it is," I said. "This is what is now. Soon we will know what is next."

"What do you mean by that? Next is Petoskey."

"Only if God says so," Jennifer replied. "And, I feel confident announcing right now that all of what you just said is going to happen, except the Petoskey part."

I looked over at Jennifer. She smiled at me and nodded.

"Very well," I said, "my terms are simple. Go do all that you are going to do. I'll quietly retire. You'll make sure that my standing is good so that benefits are available when I'm old enough. Within sixty days we will out of here. You won't have to deal with us anymore, at all."

"Are you sure? You'll be giving up an awful lot. Maybe you should sleep on it."

"No, thank you," I said.

Jennifer and I stood.

I said, "I'm sorry that you have to deal with all this, Clay. I know this kind of stuff wears bishops right out. We'll pray for you and for Judy and especially for the church. I sure hope this settles down and God can squeeze his way back in. You have done an excellent job, Bishop, and I mean it. Now, if you don't mind getting on to your duties, my wife needs time to get dolled up. I'm taking her out somewhere real nice, tonight. Somewhere not too close to here."

Chapter 38

Most of the days of our lives are rather mundane. We get up in the morning, eat breakfast, get cleaned up, and go out to do whatever it is that we do. We work and we shop and we raise our families. Then we come home and finish what needs doing, and crash in front of the TV or the computer screen. Then we go to bed, and start all over. But, once in a great while a day comes along that completely changes the course of our lives. This was such a day.

The bishop left, we got dressed and drove away from East Fork. We giggled. We laughed at our own mind-blowing uncertainty. Were we doing the right thing? What, in heaven's name, would happen now? I laughed even more when Jennifer attempted to apologize/explain how she came to announce, all on her own, *we* would not be accepting reappointment in Petoskey. *I just opened my mouth and words came out,* she said. And, most of all, we laughed at having a crushing load of conflict, gossip, decision-making, hurt, anger, politics and general chaos suddenly removed from our lives. Whatever was going on back at the East Fork First United Methodist Church—and there had to be an incredible level of turmoil and angst—now had nothing to do with us. It was a time for dinner and dancing (and I hate dancing). It was also a time for mourning, introspection, prayer and discernment. But, that would have to wait.

The next morning we woke up slowly and started to move about casually, as if we had nowhere to go . . . because we had nowhere to go. The night before, we'd dined and talked. We thought about dancing, but Jennifer overruled that idea (thank you, God!). We might have just gone home, but we were concerned that there might be people staking out the house. We went to a late movie, but couldn't concentrate enough to follow the plot. Upon our return, all was quiet at home—if we could still call it home. We went to bed and, soon, to sleep.

E-mails, texts and voice messages were rolling in. Most expressed shock and condolences from those who supported us. A few tried to describe what happened the night before, blow by blow accounts of the big meeting. We erased those. We would eventually answer correspondence and make an open statement to those who would miss us. Indeed, someday we might even have that going away party Bishop Burns mentioned. But for today, we were consciously separated and freed from all that was old.

"As scary as it is to be so unattached and so uncertain," Jennifer said, "we have never been as available to God as we are at this moment."

In the largest font my computer could print, I made a sign that read, *Until things settle down and become more clear, we are required to remain out of contact with the people of the East Fork First UMC. We cannot talk today, but will soon. We still love you all. God bless, Pastor Nathan and Jennifer.* I printed three copies and hung them on all the entrances to the house. Today, we would just stay cocooned, the three of us, me, Jennifer and God. At one point I asked Jennifer what she might like to see happen next.

"Let's not even get started down that road!" she said, abruptly. "The less we speculate or allow our personal preferences into the mix, the better!"

Great, I thought. *She has always been more devout than me, and now she is wiser, too.*

What I actually said was, "You're right Honey."

We wiled away the day, flipping TV channels, starting projects but not finishing them, trying to fill the time. It was so unlike previous weeks that I felt something akin to whiplash.

A Dragon in the Church 309

The inactivity and lack of focus did not last long. After eating supper, Jennifer announced that she was going to sneak out to the box and bring in the evening paper. As she sat in her chair, reading, I searched in vain for a TV show that could hold my interest. She turned a page and rustled the paper under control.

"Oh, my God!" she rasped. "Oh, my God! Nathan! Oh, my God!"

"What is it, Honey? Did someone die?"

"Oh, my God! No. No one is dead. Well, I'm sure someone is dead, but nobody that we know. Oh, my God!"

"Jennifer! Spill it!"

"Okay," she said, forcing herself to relax. "Okay. Listen. There is an ad in the paper . . . part article, part ad." She read aloud, *We are pleased to announce that the former Grant Center Township Congregational Church—closed for over 20 years—will be reopened as an independent church. Worship services begin this coming Sunday morning, at 10:30.*

"Hey!" I said, "Carl is on the move. We'll have somewhere to go to church!"

"Hush up, husband. You need to hear the rest of this." She continued, *Pastor Carl Rider, who has completely renovated the building, explained, "This will not be a typical church. There won't be much for social events or pot-lucks or clubs or committees or any of that. It will be for truly dedicated Christian people, who find themselves unable to resist God's call to a deeper, more active, more obedient and more dedicated faith. Those newly seeking Christ would be better off to try a different church." The name of the church reflects Reverend Rider's description, albeit in a way that has to be studied a bit. The church will be called WWW.God Christian Church. "It sounds like an internet thing," Rider admitted. "But what it stands for is: God's Word . . . God's Way . . . God's Will. It will be a church of high expectations, not a church for dabblers or the faint of heart. It will never be a large church, but I expect that it will be a powerful place."* Reverend Rider went on to explain more about the mission of the church. For details, please see the attached paid advertisement.

"Wow," I interrupted again. "You can't accuse Pastor Carl of being a coward, that's for sure. Most pastors trying to plant a church would not be so bold as to tell anyone to stay away. Sounds just like him, though. I don't know why you are so shocked. We're the only ones besides Carl who knew this was coming."

"Okay, Mr. Calm, let's see how this hits you. The ad says: *Sincere, practicing Christians of any background are invited to the inaugural worship service at the new, nondenominational WWW.God Christian Church. The church will seek to live out God's Word . . . God's Way . . . and God's Will. The service time will be 10:30 Sunday morning, beginning immediately. The newly renovated church is located at the crossing of Compton and Williams roads, ten miles west of East Fork. If you are ready to turn your entire life over to God, please attend.*

Jennifer's voice grew louder and began to quaver noticeably, as she continued reading the advertisement. *The new church will be led by the husband and wife clergy team of the Reverends Nathan Lee Martin and Jennifer Pool Martin. Pastor Nathan is a former United Methodist pastor of considerable experience. He is a Prophet of God, and will be the main teacher and preacher at WWW.God. Pastor Jennifer is by all accounts even more devout than Pastor Nathan (by his own admission) and will serve as Minister of Spiritual Growth and Formation. Let us take up our crosses, and follow Jesus.*

"Get in the car!" I spewed out. "Get in the car!"

Jennifer started, "But, what do you think is . . ."

"Get in the car! I love you, my dearest, but get in the car! We can talk on the way!"

A Dragon in the Church 311

On the road, Jennifer dared speak again. "What is going on?" she asked. "Obviously, Carl did this, but how could he . . . I mean . . ."

"I don't know," I said, beginning to breathe easier. "I just feel like we have to get to the church."

Amazing how quickly "the church" changed from the East Fork UMC to the WWW.God.

"Is this real?" Jennifer asked.

"I think so," I replied, smiling. "Carl said that God would soon tell us what was next! Maybe this is it!"

"Almost like getting *the call* from a bishop," Jennifer said, and started laughing. "But, didn't Carl say that God told him to start up a congregation?"

"Yes. But he also said that God told him how to do it. Evidently, this is the way!"

"Holy cow!" she said.

"That's for sure," I replied. "But, Honey, one thing…"

"What?"

"Now that you are a pastor, you can't be worshipping cows."

"Fine, smart butt," she said as I drove faster and she laughed louder. "By the way, how can I be listed as a Reverend? That's not right."

"Well, Reverend Martin, that is not necessarily so. If a bona fide church calls you to be clergy, you are. As the famous scholar Robert Williams once said, *United Methodist rules do . . . not . . . apply!* He's right."

"But, what church? There is no church. Not yet."

"That," I said, "is one of about a thousand things I want to find out from Carl."

We got to the church in record time. The first thing that caught our attention was a brand new sign next to the road:

WWW.GOD CHRISTIAN CHURCH

God's **W**ord—God's **W**ay—God's **W**ill

Sunday Worship: 10:30 a.m.

Pastors Nathan Lee Martin and Jennifer Pool Martin

Breathlessly, Jennifer said, "Never once did I ever think I'd see my name like that."

I nodded and said, "This is getting more real by the minute, isn't it?"

"Yeah . . . wow."

Carl's truck was nowhere to be seen. We went inside, both of us lost to our own thoughts. The sanctuary looked exactly as it had when we had last seen it. I stood inside, staring at the new sign, through the little window-cross in the door. A car approached the corner and paused. The occupants seemed to be looking at the sign. After a moment, it pulled slowly away.

"I wonder where Carl is?" I asked absently.

"We won't find him tonight," Jennifer said. "We're not meant to. Look at this."

I joined her at the old altar-table, beneath the weighty, rugged cross. On it was a lock box, the kind used to store files. Leaning against the front of it was a single sheet of paper. Jennifer picked it up and handed it to me. I read out loud:

Dear Nathan and Jennifer;

What joy it has been that God has allowed me to share a bit of my life with yours. God has been clear. Your next assignment, your next calling, is right here. This place has been prepared as sacred space. A home base. A launching pad for whatever God wills next. Nathan, God has called you to be his Prophet, to speak his Word without hesitation. Your preparation is complete. Your time is now. Jennifer, you have been gifted with great discernment, a special relationship with Jesus and a connection with the Holy Spirit that is rare and precious. You will help others to know as you know, feel as you feel and understand as you understand. The gifts that both of you bring to this place are not to stay imprisoned here. This shall be a center of a great outward expansion of God's Kingdom.

Rightfully, you will have practical questions. Thanks to a very old woman named Edwina Fine, this building has never ceased to be a legal church (she said she always knew that God would bring revival). The incorporation papers have been regularly updated, meetings held, contributions given, all that is required. The file box includes the incorporation papers (you will need to form a new board very quickly, Edwina is running out of living members to keep things going) and the still-valid 501c3. The deed is included. Paperwork to change the name, as well. You'll work out the rest. The point is, this is a church in every sense of the word, except for not yet having a congregation. That is now in the hands of the Holy Spirit.

Your personal concerns will soon be addressed. I have only the assurance of God on that, but I know it to be true. That's it. The rest will unfold. My thoughts, my prayers and my love will be with you always. Who knows, perhaps one day we will be brought together again.

In Christ's great love;
Brother Carl Rider
P.S. The building is never to be locked.
P.P.S. Edwina Fine lives in a nursing home in Cedar Springs. Wouldn't it be sweet if you could somehow get her to the first service?

"Wow," Jennifer said again. "This is really happening, isn't it?"

"It is as real as anything could be. We asked God to take over, and he did just that."

"What happens to Carl?" Jennifer asked. "Are we going to hear from him?"

"No, at least not for a long time. He did exactly what God needed him to do. I suspect he'll being doing more of the same, in another time and place."

"What do we do now?" Jennifer whispered.

"We have gas in the car, a place to live for fifty-nine more days and the refrigerator isn't empty yet. I suggest that we pray awhile . . . and then get ready for church."

Epilogue

I find it almost impossible to explain how wrapping up the East Fork First UMC phase of our life, and entering into the WWW.God phase has changed our lives. That first Sunday service, and the preparations that led up to it, will always remain the most incredible four-day transition I have ever lived through or witnessed. We quickly became laser-focused on the opening of the new church. All of the people, and the conflict and the rules and the tensions and the worry about a thousand different things (Agendor!) that were tied to the old experience, gave way to a freshness and a simplicity and a power that was actually new territory for us. It was freeing. And, it was terrifying.

Pastor Jennifer and I (I love saying that!) prayed and discussed and prayed. How would God have us do this new service? We discerned that it need not be a completed whole to get started and over time would take many shapes, never tied to or held back by the previous model.

It seemed that we should worship God in all the ways we could think up, like newlyweds desperate to convey their love to each other. It seemed that we must pray in as many manners as there are, with only one guiding principle—all prayers should be fifty percent talking or thinking, and fifty percent listening. It seemed that we should sing in any manner that would develop meaning or emotion or love. And it seemed that God's Holy Scripture was to be read and taught and lived out. Diluting nothing. Holding nothing back.

So, I agonized for hours and nights about my first scripture, my first sermon. I racked my brain and tortured my soul. Then on Saturday evening, I finally asked God, *Where do you want me to start?* I went to bed thinking that maybe I would have to recycle one of my hundreds of old sermons. I woke up at 3:00 a.m., and went to my desk. I immediately wrote, *Title: First Things First* and *Scripture: 2 Corinthians 6:16*, which reads: *... For we are the temple of the living God. As God has said, "I will live with them and walk among them, and I will be their God, and they will be my people."*

The message came as fast as I could type. I returned to bed for a couple hours of restful sleep, knowing that God had something to say . . . and I would say it.

We knew we could worship and we knew we could pray. Music presented another challenge. I can't sing a lick. Jennifer can sing some, but her piano lessons got her just a notch or two past *Mary Had a Little Lamb.* Still, being as brave as she is, my pastor wife went right out and borrowed an electronic keyboard and commenced to mastering *How Great thou Art* and *Blessed Assurance,* figuring we could at least start there. As I prepared to print copies of the lyrics, I asked Jennifer how many she thought we would need. We looked at each other and giggled hysterically (something we had become much more prone to do).

"Well, there is you and me," she said, "That's two for sure!"

I said, "Edwina Fine's grandson is bringing her for the big day. That's four."

"How many can we seat?" Jennifer asked.

"Around a hundred, packed in tight."

"Okay then," she said, "make between four and a hundred. Problem solved."

I decided to make fifty, then made eighty. I'm like that. Truth is, I had zero idea what the initial response would be. The ad only ran once. It was worded to *dis-invite* most people, even casual church-goers. There was no reason to expect anybody. On the other hand, God had engineered the whole project . . . so who knew?

As I continued to work the numbers in my head, Jennifer piped up and said, "I imagine there will be exactly as many people there as God wants there to be."

I resisted the urge to start a scholarly debate about *God's Sovereignty vs. Free Will,* and said, "I think you're right."

Sunday came as early as Christmas morning in a house filled with little kids. We arrived at the crossroads of Compton and Williams roads at 9:15. Only an hour and fifteen minutes to go. We prayed together . . . 9:30. Jennifer played her entire two-song repertoire, twice . . . 9:45. Together we went to the little cross in the door and looked outside. Nobody . . . 9:46. I practiced in the pulpit, moving around, turning pages, getting the feel. There was no sound system, so I worked on my projection. I felt like I was bellowing, so I quit . . . 10:05.

"Maybe we should pray some more," I said.

A car door slammed. We both ran to the door.

"Our first customer," Jennifer said, breathlessly.

As he came around to the front and approached the three steps, we jumped back so as not to be seen staring out the window like anxious children.

"It's Jeremy Clark!" I said. "Our first person is a sixteen year old boy carrying his electronic Bible!"

Barely breathing, Jennifer whispered, "Sweet."

As Jeremy reached for the doorknob, I heard another door slam and then another. Soon, they were streaming in like a constant . . . trickle. After Jeremy, we welcomed a couple we had never seen, Art and Leta. Francine Cook, another stranger, arrived. I admit that I had done some wondering about whether any members of East Fork First UMC might be in. As I reminded myself to quit thinking too far ahead, in walked Frank and Sylvie.

"Guess we'll be gettin' married here!" Frank boomed, while Sylvie beamed.

They hugged Jennifer almost as much as they did me.

Another couple arrived. After greetings and such, they moved past us and I heard the husband say to his wife, "Choose careful, once you take a spot you gotta live with it."

Up the steps came Kevin and Condi Cloverton. *What will East Fork do for music?* popped into my head.

"Kevin, Condi," I said. "Welcome."

Kevin stepped back, and Condi spilled out what she had to say. "I will do as little or as much as you ask, Reverend Martin. I will play any music you ask for, or do the dishes and mop the floor. You hit my nail right on the head and for a while I hated you for it. I want to get it right this time."

As I was crafting a proper, pastoral response to her shockingly honest revelation, Jennifer came up from behind me and said, "Condi, my husband will say something wise and wonderful a little later. For now, may I show you our lovely new keyboard?"

Condi smiled broadly and looked to Kevin, "Do you mind?"

"Of course not, my love. There's no good in putting your light under a bushel. Go on, you've only got a few minutes to get ready."

Jennifer and Condi scurried off in glee. Kevin took a spot from where he could admire his wife. I was approached by a man, who looked to be about thirty-five or forty.

"I am Clete Fine, Edwina Fine's grandson," he said, shaking my hand.

"Wonderful!" I interrupted. "I am looking forward to welcoming her and . . ."

"Excuse me, Reverend," he stopped me. "She sent me in here to tell you that she is not to be introduced or acknowledged in any way. Otherwise, she won't come in. She just wants to witness her church coming back into God's use, as she puts it. Can we do that?"

A Dragon in the Church   319

"Of course. Bring her in and tell her I'll be good."

"Thank you, Reverend. She sure is happy. Says she can go ahead and die now. If you knew her, you'd know that is a really good thing for her to say."

He went out to retrieve a Great Lady of God's Church.

A few more strangers came in. Also, there was Jane Petra, from the East Fork SPRC, and Janice.

"I'm done over there," Janice said. "I'll be helping out here."

With that, she sat down.

Edwina made her way in, somehow having negotiated the steps with a walker. I made a mental note, *Build a ramp*!

Two things happened with Edwina's entrance. A few steps in, she paused to observe. A tiny, old-lady gasp escaped her throat. She smiled and she started to cry, but being a proper church lady of a certain age, she quickly choked back the tears. Secondly, she started toward the third pew from the back, on the left side of the aisle. It was obviously *her pew*. In it, she found Jeremy Clark, firing up his I-Pad and getting ready for church.

She paused a moment and said, "Young man, for decades I sat in that exact spot every Sunday, would you mind . . ."

"Oh, I'm sorry, I'll move . . ."

"Young man, what I wished to ask you was, may I sit with you and share your spot?"

"Yes Ma'am! That would be great."

And so they shared.

At 10:25—forty-three people all sitting in their places—I was getting ready to start the service, growing more and more excited in anticipation of wonderful, undefined things to come. My focus was shattered once again as Berta Lou and Virgy Lou walked through the front door.

"May we see you and your wife for sixty seconds, please?" Berta Lou asked.

"Yes," I said, "Jennifer, would you join us please?"

We made the short walk to the back room.

"Time is very short, we know," said Virgy Lou. "While we remain unhappy with certain aspects of your stay at East Fork First, it is clear that you have been treated unfairly."

Berta Lou picked up the thread, "At first Mr. Williams seemed to be protecting our church, and we supported that. Eventually, he did things beyond what we find proper."

"We think he's nuts," Virgy Lou piped up.

Jennifer snorted just a bit.

"Anyway," Berta Lou retook control, "In this envelope you will find enough to tide you over for a few months, and some extra for a down payment on a house. Please see to that as quickly as you can. We have a church that needs a lot of fixing, and we need to get a new pastor in place."

"Mr. Williams has embarrassed us," said Virgy Lou. "He'll have to answer for that."

"Ladies," I began, "I can't tell you how generous, overly generous, this is. Are you sure you can comfortably . . ."

"We must go now," declared Berta Lou. "You have a new church to begin, and we have one to fix. And, yes, we can afford it. Between the two of us, we can buy and sell the Williams family several times over. Maybe we will."

"We never told anyone we had money before—didn't see the need. But it's time," explained Virgy Lou.

"We believe all things to be even now," Berta Lou announced. "Good luck with your new endeavor."

The two Lous left the building. We Two Reverends shook our heads in wonder and laughed. It was 10:29.

Jennifer took my head in her hands. I responded by taking hers.

She said, "Dear Heavenly Father, bless what is about to happen in this place."

I added, "We shall be your people, and you shall be our God. Amen."

We walked, hand in hand, into God's sanctuary.

About the Author

Michael Riegler resides in Edmore, Michigan, where he is blessed to be the pastor of the Faith United Methodist Church. He can be contacted by email at pastormikeriegler@gmail.com or by phone (voice/text) at (231) 631-4712.